Greenwich Council
Library & Information Service

IN HOUSE
QUALITY
SYSTEMS

Mobile and Home Service at Plumstead Library
Plumstead High Street, SE18 1JL
020 8319 5875

Please return by the last date shown		
2/09 NE OCT. 09 Aug 13 - - DEC 2013 Malton - - APR 2018 =-- FEB 2019	 *Thank You!*	
To renew, please contact any Greenwich library		

Issue: 02	Issue Date: 06.06.00	Ref: RM.RBL.LIS

Maeve Haran shot to fame with her first bestselling novel. Since then she has written a number of other successful novels. A former journalist and producer she is now a full-time writer and lives in north London with her partner and their three children.

SOFT TOUCH

Pretty, well-balanced Rachel used to be every mother's dream. Now she's every mother's nightmare. The reason? Sexy, sultry Marko, Mr Darcy with a nose stud. As Marko lures Rachel off to save a woodland and lose her virginity, her nice liberal mum, Catherine, wishes she could lock her in the bedroom, while Rachel's disapproving granny, Lavinia, decides on some far more dramatic action. In this war between the generations, all three women find their values — and their love lives — changed forever.

Books by Maeve Haran
Published by The House of Ulverscroft:

BABY COME BACK

MAEVE HARAN

◆

SOFT TOUCH

Complete and Unabridged

ULVERSCROFT
Leicester

First published in Great Britain in 1999 by
Little, Brown and Company
London

First Large Print Edition
published 2002
by arrangement with
Little, Brown and Company (UK)
London

The moral right of the author has been asserted

British Library CIP Data

Haran, Maeve
    Soft touch.—Large print ed.—
    Ulverscroft large print series: general fiction
    1. Intergenerational relations—Fiction
    2. Mothers and daughters—Fiction 3. Middle class
    women—Fiction 4. Domestic fiction 5. Large type books
    I. Title
    823.9'14 [F]

    ISBN 0–7089–4610–0

Published by
F. A. Thorpe (Publishing)
Anstey, Leicestershire

Set by Words & Graphics Ltd.
Anstey, Leicestershire
Printed and bound in Great Britain by
T. J. International Ltd., Padstow, Cornwall

This book is printed on acid-free paper

For my much loved sister
and for my daughters,
Georgia and Holly,
who are never, ever, going
to be rebellious teenagers

Acknowledgements

I would like to thank the following for their witty and perceptive advice on living with a teenager and on other aspects of this story:

Yvonne Roberts, Barbara Toner, Angela Neustatter, Lindsey Bareham, Claire L'Enfant, Tony Cohen, Rusty Haran, Pat Boyer, Nigel Thomas, and John Vidal of the *Guardian* for his invaluable background on road rebels.

And of course my agent and friend, Carole Blake, and my editor and friend, Imogen Taylor.

1

Catherine Hope, thirty-nine, sane, and usually too responsible for her own good, lurked in the dense bushes outside Wolsey School for Girls and waited. The school, though in a tough area of north-east London, harked back to more glorious days and was in several acres of parkland which, fortunately for Catherine, offered her plenty of cover.

This must be what it felt like to be a paparazzi, or, to be pedantic (another of Catherine's faults, her husband said), a paparazzo. And certainly a paparazzo wouldn't have felt disappointed at the range of burgeoning female adolescence streaming out of Wolsey's gates.

It may have been the middle of winter, with Christmas only weeks away, but the Wolsey Look consisted of a tiny microskirt barely visible beneath a brown school blazer (surely they ought to be wearing winter coats, but what mother these days, grateful that they wore uniform at all, would push her luck on this one), an oversized cardigan, thick brown tights and thumping great shoes.

The only sign of the academic potential that had parents moving here from miles

1

around just in the hope of getting their daughters into the school, was the briefcase each girl carried, bulging with two hours of homework, fodder for several bitter parental arguments about whether it should be tackled before *EastEnders*.

Catherine knew she shouldn't be here — she *certainly* oughtn't to be in the bushes — but safely back marking worksheets at the school where she taught, only two miles away geographically but several continents in terms of privilege. Her daughter Rachel would kill her if she found out she was here. But really it was Rachel's fault. Six months before A levels, with a university place in the bag provided she got the grades, Rachel had turned into the Daughter from Hell, refusing to do her homework, disappearing without trace at the first opportunity, and dressing in clothes that frankly made the Spice Girls look subtle. Worst of all was the way she treated her mother — with the kind of contempt normally reserved for traffic wardens and paedophiles.

Catherine had had enough. Confrontation had failed. Reason had been laughed at. All that remained was low cunning.

The pavement was crowded now, mostly with wellheeled mothers who clearly didn't need to work and the occasional keen father.

2

As usual, the air was thick with parental paranoia that someone else's child might be scrabbling up life's ladder faster than their own.

'Miranda's been offered a place at Jesus, Oxford,' boasted one mother.

'Eleanor turned them down,' countered the other. 'Manchester's the only place they teach archaeology properly, she says. Where's Miranda going for her gap year?'

Before Catherine discovered the answer to this burning question she made the mistake of leaning forward, thereby impaling herself on the intruder-repelling barbed wire hidden in the ivy. She yelped in pain and stumbled out of the bushes, into the astonished gaze of parents, pupils and, worst of all, Rachel's best friend Stephanie.

'Ah, Mrs Hope,' Rachel's form teacher bore down upon her out of the gloaming, apparently oblivious to the unorthodox method of Catherine's arrival, 'just the person I wanted to speak to. How are Rachel's teeth?'

'Her teeth?' As far as Catherine knew, Rachel's teeth were one of the few aspects of Rachel that weren't worrying. Her little brother Ricky was the one with the problem. Rachel's teeth were pearly and perfect as a toothpaste ad.

'Yes,' the woman pressed on. 'She left early for her orthodontistry appointment.'

Catherine swore under her breath. Ricky had an orthodontist's appointment this afternoon, certainly not Rachel. The little beast.

'As a matter of fact,' continued her teacher, 'I'm a trifle worried about Rachel. Such a clever girl but I fear her mind isn't on her work. No problems at home, are there?' She leaned towards Catherine with all the enthusiasm of a sex therapist who suspects premature ejaculation.

'No, none,' Catherine said hastily, pushing from her mind the fight over the Bran Flakes that morning and the growing tension between herself and her husband Christopher. Tension entirely caused by Rachel. Someone ought to print badges. Teenagers Are Bad for Your Marriage. They'd be a sellout.

'Good.' The teacher smiled encouragingly. 'Not long now. Mocks next month. Awful system, I know. Only tests the ones who're good at exams, I always say. Still, Rachel's always shone then, hasn't she?'

With a furtive pat of her leaf-tangled hair Catherine smiled at the other assembled parents. Maybe they hadn't noticed that she'd been hiding in the bushes after all.

'Excuse me, Mrs Hope.' It was Stephanie, her daughter's best friend. The girl's tone was pious and helpful but her eyes glowed with the anticipation of recounting every glorious detail to Rachel as soon as it was humanly possible. 'But did you know you had a big hole in the back of your skirt?'

★ ★ ★

'Hi, Mum!' Ricky rushed up the garden path to meet her, looking delighted with himself. He was almost eleven with floppy brown hair she loved to stroke even though he wouldn't let her if anyone else was looking, a toothy grin and wire-rimmed specs.

'Hello, darling. Where's Gran?' Catherine's posh mother-in-law, Lavinia, had taken him to the orthodontist as a favour. Sometimes asking Lavinia for a favour wasn't worth the price tag. 'Did you get your brace fitted?'

'She's gone home. You said you'd be back hours ago. She was going to miss her bridge.' Ricky opened his mouth to reveal a mouthful of wire known as train tracks.

'Good God, Ricky! Why on earth are they red and white?'

Ricky grinned. 'Arsenal colours, der. I said I wouldn't wear them otherwise.'

'And what did Gran say to that?' She could

5

imagine her mother-in-law's expression all too easily. 'She said she supposed it was better than having the awful sticking-out teeth I've got at the moment.'

That was pure Lavinia. Don't bother reassuring when you can get in a dig instead. Catherine tried to remind herself that Lavinia's generation were simply different. They believed in knocking children down in case they got a big head, not building them up as her generation did.

Lavinia clearly found her daughter-in-law's policy of telling her children at every opportunity that they were wonderful eccentric bordering on the harmful. 'What happens when they grow up and the world doesn't agree with you?' Lavinia often asked.

But by then, Catherine hoped, her children would have the confidence not to care what people thought anyway. The only trouble was that Rachel seemed to have rather too much confidence already. But then maybe Wallis Simpson's famous saying applied to this area as well. You couldn't be too thin, or too rich — or too confident, either.

Behind her the front door banged and Catherine felt her stomach knit up. Why was it she could manage a class of tough ten-year-olds, including the ones who slipped in a few 'Fuck-Off-Mis-sis-Hopes' among the

6

more usual 'Good Mornings', but not her own daughter? The trouble was that dealing with Rachel you needed the skills of a UN negotiator. Catherine would love to lock Yasser Arafat and Gerry Adams in a room with Rachel and see if *they* could get her to do her revision any better than Catherine could.

'Hello, Rach, is that you?' she called.

She knew it was Rachel. No one else banged the door so hard the windows rattled. Ricky and she listened to the thump of Rachel's clumpy boots on the polished boards of the hall from the cosy safety of the basement kitchen. She sounded to Catherine like the Tyrannosaurus rex in Ricky's CD of dinosaur effects. In fact Rachel had quite a lot in common with a teenage T-rex. No doubt they both ranged around looking for food, working their way through an entire week's store of salt-and-vinegar crisps, Quavers, mini-cheddars and any other high-cholesterol, low-nutrition snack they could find, then complained to their mothers that there was never anything nice to eat in the house.

Finally Rachel appeared at the door, hair fanned out behind her from running, cheeks flushed, eyes glittering with righteous fury. Although Rachel hated to be reminded of it, she and her mother were startlingly similar. They both shared the same luxuriant long wavy hair, the colour of a polished conker, and deep brown eyes. 'Mum . . . ' she paused dramatically, 'how *could* you? How could you humiliate me in front of the entire school like that? Everyone's laughing at me.' She dropped her face into her hands in an epic gesture of tragedy.

'Now look here, young lady.' (Had she really said that? It sounded pure Lavinia.) 'You're the one who has the explaining to do. Telling your school you were at the orthodontist. Your teacher's worried about you. We're worried about you. Your work's slipping. You're not concentrating.'

'Is it surprising when I have a mother who treats me as if I were ten, checking up on me all the time, always wanting to know where I'm going.' She pulled herself up to her full height, which for several years now had been three inches taller than the already-tall Catherine, making it doubly hard for Catherine to squeeze out the smallest drop of respect. 'Steph's allowed to go wherever she wants. Her parents don't lurk in bushes or hang round outside parties as if she were a child.'

Catherine seethed. Nothing would give her more pleasure than being allowed to stay at home, curled up in bed or on the sofa, instead of stuck in a freezing car hanging on endlessly for Rachel to appear from some gruesome gathering the other side of London. Rachel's friends always seemed to live in places at the other end of the A-Z. It even meant Catherine had to limit herself to a single glass of wine, forgoing one of the few consolations of the parent whose child's social life has long ago overtaken its own.

'You do realize it's only five months till your whole future's settled?'

'Six actually. Anyway who cares about bloody A levels? They aren't a real test of anything. Wolsey's just a sausage factory that produces exam results, not interesting people.'

Catherine, having heard this one before, had the good sense to keep her mouth shut.

'A levels!' Rachel shouted, getting into her stride. 'That's all you ever think about. You don't care about ME, just my exam results! You wouldn't care if I committed suicide under the pressure as long as I got my grades! Anyway I can catch up at the weekend.'

'No you can't.' Catherine waited for the nuclear explosion. 'We're going to your gran's, remember?'

'Oh my God, that's all I need. A boring weekend at Gran's with nothing to do except listen to her bang on about bridge and the vicar, with an odd disapproving remark about young people's manners just for variety. Great.'

Actually, her mother rather agreed, but Christopher had promised Lavinia they'd go and, as Catherine was frequently reminding them all, they had to sometimes do things as a family.

'So that we all have a terrible time, you mean,' Rachel was prone to comment at times like these, 'instead of just one of us.'

Catherine reminded herself of what the books on how to handle your teenager insisted: Remember Who's The Adult Here.

She was about to suggest in a quiet and adult way that Rachel could bloody well go to her bedroom if she was going to be so sodding difficult when Rachel picked up her school bag and stalked out.

'I'm going to my room,' she announced haughtily, thereby removing even that small sanction from her mother's dwindling armoury.

'Round one to Rach, I'd say, Mum,' piped up Ricky.

'You can watch it or you'll be the next one to go to your bedroom.'

'But, Mum,' he pointed out helpfully, 'I'm the one you're always stopping from going to his bedroom because I get obsessed with the Internet, remember?'

Catherine sank down at the seventies pine kitchen table and wondered if it was too early for a drink. How had children managed to change — in mere decades — from being seen and not heard to completely ruling the roost? It seemed so very unfair. Like the rest of her generation she'd grown up intimidated by the look in her parents' eyes and now, at nearly forty, she was intimidated by the look in her children's. When was it their turn to have the power?

She went back to preparing family supper — another institution Catherine tried to cling to so that at least they all spent five minutes a day together. Of course it never worked because the phone always went for Rachel, and if they told the caller to ring back after supper she sat in sullen silence refusing a single mouthful, carefully working the conversation round to anorexia and how it was clever girls with pushy parents who usually got it.

By the time Christopher's key turned in the lock the lasagne was almost ready and Catherine was on to her second glass of white wine. Wine, she mused, was her contemporaries' solution to the problem of bolshy children. After several glasses you stopped noticing.

Christopher kissed her and eyed the bottle. 'Two glasses? Does that mean it was a good day at school or a bad day at school?'

Catherine almost confessed her débâcle in the bushes but decided not to. Christopher would probably be livid, take Rachel's side, and Catherine's pathetic shadow of authority would be at an even lower ebb. You were supposed to put on a united front and support each other in front of the children, as Ricky often reminded them, but Catherine and Christopher rarely managed this level of sainthood. Largely, she supposed, because they had such different attitudes about parenting. Catherine believed some limits had to be maintained — a minimal level of politeness instead of mere grunts, some visible floorspace in their bedrooms and an occasional attempt at personal hygiene. Christopher thought this overprotective and irrelevant; children ought to decide for themselves where the boundaries lay or how would they achieve independence? The result was that ever since Rachel had become a teenager Catherine quite often wanted to kill him.

'I had a wonderful day.' Catherine banged down her drink. 'Year Seven have nits, the school was evacuated for a police stake-out, someone pinched the worksheets I spent all last night preparing. Oh — and Rachel bunked off school, telling them she was going to the orthodontist.'

'Fairly average, then?' Christopher reached out a hand to her strained face. 'Where is she?'

'Upstairs in her bedroom.'

'I'll go up.'

Their comfortably scruffy, three-storey terraced house had been fine when the children were little, but in recent years with one almost-eighteen-year-old and another energetic ten-year-old, it was almost bursting at the seams. The rooms, especially on the top floor, were what an estate agent would have described as compact. Even so, Rachel had made the most of hers. Along with the posters of boy bands and kittens, she had constructed a tent made of voile over her bed, giving it a harem-like quality unique in suburban north-east London. Rachel had toured thrift shops collecting old fabric and cheap bedspreads and cushions in jewel-like colours. The effect made her father think of stepping inside a kaleidoscope. He felt the usual burst of pride at Rachel's talents. She was clever and artistic. But he also acknowledged, because he shared the same qualities, that she could be mulish and stubborn. When she dug her heels in Rachel could be a one-girl Resistance movement. Her mother, rational and reasonable herself, expected Rachel to respond to logic. But logic didn't matter to Rachel. Rachel wanted passion and excitement, to start living and to hell with exams if they got in the way of Life: Christopher, although he had a sneaking sympathy, knew he must never admit this to his challenging daughter. The party line was clear. Exams were important. Life could come later.

'Hello, noodle,' he only used this pet name when they were alone together. 'How's things?'

She looked up from her revision and smiled. 'Fine. Except that Mum keeps nagging me about my work all the time. If I don't get A grades I'll feel like a criminal.'

Christopher sat down on the harem bed. 'She just thinks education will give you more choices, that's all.'

Rachel snapped shut her copy of Virginia Woolf's *To the Lighthouse*. 'I know. I've heard the story a hundred times. How her dad died and she couldn't go to university even though she was clever enough, and how I shouldn't waste my chances. I know all that, I really do. But I just wish she would get off my case. I'm nearly eighteen. Lots of girls are married with babies at my age. I just wish she'd stop treating me like a child.'

Rachel, now out of her school uniform in favour of fake leopardskin shorts, thick black tights and a vast black jumper, certainly didn't look like a child. It sometimes touched Christopher to the core how physically alike the two women in his life were. Ironic given the difference in their personalities, and perhaps hard for both of them for Rachel to be compared with her mother and for Catherine to see a youthful, glowing incarnation of herself, imbued with passion instead of caution.

'So why, if everything's fine, did you bunk off school?'

Rachel tossed her long hair, neatly side-stepping the question. 'I bet she didn't tell you what *she* did today? She hid in the bushes outside the school like a Peeping Tom. The school-keeper said if she'd been a bloke he would have called the police.'

'Rachel, don't be ridiculous.'

'I'm not. Go and ask her. And, Dad,' Rachel decided to press home her advantage while her father was still suffering from shock, 'can I go to Steph's house when I've finished my revision?' She was eager to hear more evidence of her mother's war crime.

'Fine.' He realized too late that Catherine

15

might not approve of this weekday concession.

Downstairs Catherine was trying to prise Ricky away from *Viz* to come to the supper table.

'Cath,' Christopher demanded, 'is it true?'

'Is what true?' Catherine busied herself with serving.

'That you were lurking in the bushes outside her school, for God's sake.'

'She keeps disappearing without saying where she's going. She refuses to tell me anything. She's skipping school. How else can I find out?'

'You could try trusting her for a change.'

'Bye, Mum, bye, Dad,' Rachel breezed through the hall on her way out. 'I've finished my homework.'

'Who said you could go out? We haven't even had supper yet.' Catherine hated the hectoring tone that crept into her voice. But what could she do? If she left it to Christopher, Rachel would be out every night expressing her individuality till three a.m.

'I'm not hungry. I had a sandwich.'

Catherine let this go. She didn't feel strong enough for another battle. 'Be back by ten, then.'

'I will.'

After supper Catherine hesitated between

16

the unattractive choice of marking Year Six's maths and tackling the ironing basket, and, marginally, marking won. She felt exhausted but determined to wait up till Rachel got back. Not to check up on her. Or rather not just to check up on her, but because she wanted to have a chat.

By five to ten the marking and ironing were both done and Catherine longed for bed. Christopher had just gone up. She could tell from his stiff back and refusal to look at her that he was still angry.

At three minutes past ten Rachel appeared, smiling sweetly. 'Fancy a cup of tea, Mum?'

Catherine leaped at the idea. An offer like this was about as common as Rachel tidying her bedroom or volunteering a description of her day.

Rachel clinked peacefully around the kitchen, filling the kettle and taking cups down from the crowded dresser. 'Are there any biscuits?'

Catherine pointed at the tin. 'I bought three packs of Kit-Kats the day before yesterday.' How naïve of her to think they'd last. Only the wrappers remained, abandoned in the tin like foil shrouds.

'Look, Rach, I'm sorry about today. If you'd only tell me where you're going I

17

wouldn't need to worry. Where were you anyway?'

'Please, Mum, let's have a cup of tea, not the Spanish Inquisition.'

Catherine bit back a sharp retort. In Rachel's eyes having to leave a phone number when she went out was a breach of the Geneva Convention.

Halfway up the stairs Rachel stopped and hugged her. It lasted only a nanosecond, but was infinitely reassuring.

'I'm only tough for your sake, you know,' Catherine told her softly. 'One day you'll thank me for it.'

'Like the Czechs thanked Hitler for invading their country?'

Catherine flinched, wondering if Rachel had any idea how contemptuous she sounded.

It's only a stage, Catherine repeated to herself like a mantra, I'm sure it's only a stage.

Christopher was already asleep on his side of the bed, his back towards her. Usually she would cuddle up to him, either out of comfort or lust or even if things had been difficult at school. Whatever her motivation, it usually worked. Curled up together, two against the world, his presence gave her strength. But tonight her anger still burned brightly. It was a cold night with a high, almost perfect moon illuminating their bedroom with its liquid white light. For a moment she thought of waking him up and showing him. Once, when they were just married, they had danced round their bedroom by moonlight, and found the old lady across the road watching them, smiling. Instead she slipped into the cold bed and shivered. She loved electric blankets but Christopher, brought up under Lavinia's tough regime, couldn't bear them.

The words of a Paul Simon song drifted into her mind. It was about two lovers. One wanted to sleep with the window open, the other liked it closed. So they decided to call it quits and part.

Usually the absurdity of the song made her laugh. But tonight it seemed ominous.

2

'Where's Rachel got to?'

Christopher had packed the wine and the box of chocolates, dutiful offerings for his mother, into the car already. Lavinia always claimed to have no money for such luxuries although she lived in an enviably beautiful cottage, had an open-topped Rover and Mrs Wright in to clean twice a week, and since Christopher had been one of the executors of his father's will, he knew perfectly well she wasn't short of a few quid. So they all took Lavinia's economies — melting down candle ends, re-using paper napkins, making one teabag last for three cups — in a spirit of indulgent toleration which infuriated her.

'Rachel promised she was ready ten minutes ago,' Catherine pointed out. 'This is a delaying tactic because she doesn't want to go.'

Before Catherine could get out of the car and shout for her daughter, Rachel tripped down the front steps wearing black velvet loon pants, platform trainers and a white crop top with the word SEMTEX across the chest.

'Rachel,' squeaked her mother, 'you can't

go like that. Gran will have a fit. At least change your top.'

'It's supposed to be a joke, Mum.'

Catherine caught her husband's eye and found that he was laughing at her. In spite of herself, she smiled back. 'OK, OK,' she conceded, 'spare me the structural analysis. Humour is about the collision of the expected and the unexpected. Tastelessness can be funny. I just hope she doesn't bump into any Peace People.'

'In Maxted?' Rachel demanded, getting into the back. 'They'd probably be shot on sight.'

★   ★   ★

In her pretty cottage just outside the small market town of Maxted, Lavinia was getting ready to receive her son and his family. The garden, Lavinia's great love in life, was sparse at this time of year but she had still managed an arrangement of Christmas roses, lichen-covered twigs and ivy which wouldn't disgrace the 'artistic' section of the Maxted flower show. In fact, it was so successful that she made a second, larger version for the church. She was on the flower rota this week and the time going up to Christmas was always tricky. Some of the other arrangers

21

succumbed to sticking red glass balls on fir branches or even angel-shaped candles — hopelessly impractical in Lavinia's view since, apart from their tastelessness, lighting them would probably burn the church down. Worst of all, to Lavinia's exacting standards, were those who resorted to using silk chrysanthemums, a vulgar plant even when it was genuine and beyond the pale when fake. Lavinia smiled in anticipation of the praise her arrangement would receive from the more discerning members of the congregation.

Everything was under control. The lunch keeping warm in the Hostess trolley (kept discreetly in the kitchen since Lavinia suspected that it, like the silk chrysanthemums, was a little on the non-U side), dry sherry out, flowers done. Lavinia surveyed the room with satisfaction. She loved this place. She had spent her whole married life here. Despite the depredations of the twentieth century Maxted had kept much of its charm. Colour-washed cottages in ochre, green, pale pink and yellow climbed precariously up its hillsides, cheek by jowl with pale grey half-timbered houses, their upper storeys oversailing the narrow street below. Neat almshouses lined one street, with a guildhall used for trade by the wealthy wool merchants in medieval times. There was even a small mill on the outskirts, giving way to watermeadows and the rolling farmland that John Constable had painted so often. 'I love every stile and stump and lane,' he'd said three hundred years ago. 'These are the scenes that made me a painter.' Lavinia's heart swelled with the same pride and love, but her drawing skills had sadly proved to be rather less evident than Constable's. Determination and perseverance she certainly had in plenty, but her attempts at charming watercolours brought sniggers rather than appreciation. Flower-arranging was a little easier.

'Are they here yet?' her next-door neighbour Eunice called over the mellow brick wall that divided their gardens. Lavinia clucked with irritation. Eunice was hanging out her washing. It wasn't that Lavinia disapproved of washing on lines, in fact she'd often been heard to remark at the weekly village coffee-morning that washing on a line was part of the country scene. She couldn't abide tumble-dried sheets next to her skin, with that horrid smell of synthetic gardenias. But there were rules, unspoken perhaps, but still rules, that decreed washing had to be hung out only on weekdays. Of course Eunice, having moved here from a town a mere six years ago, was still learning and would no doubt welcome a little rural wisdom from someone so much more experienced, like herself.

But before she had time to impart this advice, her son's ancient estate car drew up in the lane opposite.

'Hi, Gran!' Ricky, who had put on wellingtons over his staggeringly expensive designer tracksuit as a generous concession to country life, bounded over the road, hugged Lavinia and disappeared to look for her cat. Ricky and the cat had a long-standing relationship, based on mutual distrust and deep underlying affection. The cat let Ricky get away with liberties provided Ricky put up with the occasional claws-out bat on the nose and slipped it Kitty Treats.

Rachel, next out of the car in her Semtex top and bare midriff, achieved the unprecedented effect of silencing her grandmother completely. 'Hello, Gran, you're looking lovely.'

Lavinia, who took care to always co-ordinate her tweed skirts and lambswool (cashmere was too flashy) jerseys in flattering heathery tones, finally recovered her voice. 'I wish I could say the same for you. Aren't you absolutely freezing?'

A brief image of her other son Martin's children flitted into Lavinia's mind. Lucy and

Robin were always so well turned out.

'Hello, Lavinia,' Catherine kissed her mother-in-law on her powdered cheek catching the faint tones of Chanel No. 5, a surprising frippery in the otherwise steadfastly practical Lavinia. 'How are you? The garden's looking marvellous.'

Lavinia eyed her beadily. The garden wasn't looking marvellous at all so this had to be an attempt at flattery. Lavinia disliked insincere flattery intensely. 'Do you think so?' she responded in tones that implied that Catherine must be mad or her judgement affected by living in a scrubby corner of London where no sane person would, in Lavinia's opinion, ever choose to inhabit. 'How's school?'

Catherine knew Lavinia wasn't really interested in hearing about the hopes and dreams of a lot of snotty-nosed children from London council estates. 'Fine.'

Christopher struggled in with the overnight bags. 'Cath,' he demanded in that plaintive age-old male cry. 'Did we *have* to bring so much stuff for one night. Hello, Ma. How are you?'

'Sparkling, thank you.' Lavinia had the disconcerting habit of always being in the pink of health and had very little sympathy for lesser mortals who succumbed to coughs, flu or terminal diseases. 'Now,' Lavinia's voice sank to a whisper as if her son were a heroin dealer instead of a respectable tea importer, 'did you manage to get me any of that lovely Lapsang Souchong you promised?'

Christopher patted the carrier bag of goodies. 'In here. Now when's lunch? I'm starving.'

'In ten minutes. Oh my God, we haven't got any redcurrant jelly for the lamb.' Lavinia's anguished tones conveyed just how life-threatening a matter this was. 'If that stupid Eunice hadn't hung out her washing . . . '

Christopher and Catherine exchanged glances, both knowing Lavinia well enough not to suggest that an absence of redcurrant jelly could be overlooked in the great scheme of things.

'Hang on, Gran, I'll go to the shop,' Rachel offered diplomatically.

Lavinia was clearly on the horns of one of life's dilemmas. If she refused the meal would, in her eyes, be ruined. On the other hand if she let Rachel go to the shop the entire street would witness the sight of her grand-daughter in that ridiculous top, navel exposed to the elements, the ghastly nose-stud her mother should never have agreed to glinting in the winter sun.

Catherine, sensing her mother-in-law's difficulty, came up with a compromise. 'Take my coat, Rach, or you'll freeze. It's twice as cold here as it is in London.'

Lavinia ignored this slight on her beloved Maxted and shooed Rachel out of the door. 'They shut in ten minutes, so get a move on.'

'On a Saturday?' Rachel was used to a world of shopping malls, credit card booking and all-night Safeways.

The shop, always known as the 'village shop' even though it was technically part of Maxted, was only a few hundred yards away. In order to survive it doubled as a Post Office, card shop, newsagent and minimart. Its current owners, a couple who had recently arrived from Purley, had spent all the husband's redundancy money taking out the plate-glass shop window and installing diamond-paned latticework, erecting country pine shelving, putting white lace doilies all along it to achieve a dresser-effect and generally turning it into the kind of Beatrix Potter wonderland that no real country person could spend more than five minutes in.

Rachel speeded up her step, which was tricky given the height of her platform trainers. Outside the shop she was met by the unexpected sight of a young woman holding a dog on a piece of string. Neither was of the variety usually spotted in Maxted. The girl had straggly blond hair, cut short at the back and caught at the front in dreadlocks plaited with cloth. She was pretty in a victimish kind of way. The dog wasn't pretty but made up for it in friendliness. Rachel tried to puzzle out its parentage. Bearded collie, with a touch of whippet, and a sliver of standard poodle perhaps. Rachel stroked him, then hurried into the shop. The girl said nothing.

There were only two people inside. One, a local man, but from the socially uncharted areas of Maxted known as The Leas, sniggeringly referred to by more upmarket residents as The Fleas, where the few working-class people of the area lived. He was busy bewailing the latest lottery winner's declaration that they weren't going to let it change their lives.

'I'd bloody let it change my life,' he confided to the new owner. 'You wouldn't see me for dust. I'd show those snobs up the road a thing or two, I can tell you.'

The remaining customer was at the far end of the shop filling a wire basket with what looked like a lifetime supply of Jaffa cakes. The only other thing she noticed was a curtain of dark shining hair, not unlike her own in length, but straight while hers was curly. It was unclear if the owner was male or female.

She busied herself looking for the redcurrant jelly. They had only a gourmet version at an extortionate price, but Rachel knew better than to return to her grandmother's empty-handed, so she took it to the counter.

The purchaser of the Jaffa cakes was already there ahead of her. There was no doubt about his gender from this angle. He gestured for her to go before him and Rachel's heart lurched.

She was a tall girl and he was only a fraction taller, dressed in black, from a huge black greatcoat to tight black trousers tucked into motorcycle boots. But it was his face that held her gaze like a startled rabbit. Dark scowly brows, almost joined together in the middle, giving way to surprisingly blue eyes, which at this moment fixed Rachel with a knowing intensity. Then he smiled. 'After you.'

'Just this, thanks.' She was grateful to have a reason to look away, in case he could see in her eyes the shocking truth, that he was the first man she'd seen in her life whom she truly wanted to go to bed with.

Once the redcurrant jelly, stowed inside a dinky paper carrier bag, was handed back to her, it was his turn. To Rachel, awestruck by his dark attraction, even his shopping list held fascination.

'This lot, two pints of milk and a packet of Rizlas, thanks.'

'I'm sorry,' the owner banged the till shut. 'I'm afraid we're closed.'

Rachel gasped and waited for the young man to protest or argue. Instead he laughed a warm, good-humoured laugh that held neither surprise nor resentment. The silver eyebrow stud that adorned his black brows tinkled gently as he did so. 'Pity,' he remarked calmly, ignoring the man's shuttered face, 'I could have murdered a Jaffa cake.'

Furious on his behalf, Rachel scrabbled in her purse and handed over Lavinia's change. 'Here, I'll buy some.'

'Thanks.' He calmly opened the packet and offered it to her. 'Go on, have one. I don't think our friend here's feeling hungry.'

Rachel, who had never liked Jaffa cakes, took one anyway.

'My name's Marko, by the way. That's my dog outside.' Now the smile was faintly embarrassed 'I'm afraid he's called Polo.'

'Polo?'

'You know, as in Marco Polo.'

Now it was Rachel's turn to laugh. Then she remembered the lunch that awaited, redcurrant jellyless, until she returned. By now the lamb might be less than the demanding shade of pink her grandmother required. For one mad moment she thought of inviting Marko and Polo and even the girl to join them, but could imagine Lavinia's reaction all too clearly.

They were by the door now, with the owner hovering inches behind them. 'Look,' Marko insisted to the man, anger finally bubbling up, 'I don't sign on, I am not a burden to you or the state and I haven't nicked anything. OK? Sorry about that,' he said to Rachel once they were on the pavement.

'You're sorry . . . ' Rachel exploded. 'That man behaved outrageously. I'll tell my grandmother never to shop there again.'

The smile was back. It made Rachel's backbone feel like the redcurrant jelly she was clutching to her chest. 'You get used to it. We're the enemy, you see. The good people of Maxted want a bypass in order to preserve their historic heritage, and who could blame them? It's just that it means driving a six-lane highway through Gosse's Wood, which just happens to be even older than Maxted. So we're doing our best to stop them.'

'How are you doing that?'

'Climbing trees, digging tunnels, a little bit of harmless sabotage.'

'I can see that would make you unpopular round here.'

'Ah, but then we don't mind being unpopular, do we, Zo?' He ignored the blond girl's dagger glance. 'You should come to our little camp and see.'

Rachel hesitated, eager to seem more sophisticated than she felt.

'Why not drop in next week?'

'That'd be a bit tricky. We're just visiting my grandmother. I live in London. I'm studying for my A levels.'

'Whenever you're down then. Where does your grandmother live?'

'The cottage down there at the end of the village.'

'Leave it, Marko,' said the girl, a shade too quickly. 'She doesn't want to come. She's a nice middle-class girl. Why should she be interested in having to shit in the woods when she's probably got a nice en suite bathroom at home?'

Rachel wanted to protest that far from having an ensuite bathroom they had a horrible turd-coloured one that they all had to crowd into.

Marko smiled regretfully, his blue eyes opening up vistas of possibility blighted by the fifty miles that would come between them. 'Another time then. Come on, boy,' he snapped at Polo, 'back to the fun.'

Rachel watched them go. Curtains twitched all down the street as they passed.

They were almost out of sight when Zoe spoke. 'A schoolgirl, eh? That'd be a first. Even for you.'

'An intelligent schoolgirl,' he tapped his forehead. 'We need intelligence if we're going to win in the end.'

'For some reason,' Zoe drawled, safely out of Rachel's earshot, 'I'm not convinced it's her brains you're interested in.'

★ ★ ★

'Where has that wretched child got to?' Lavinia was hopping up and down like an agitated budgie. The meat was carved, the wine poured, the vegetables steamed and still no sign of the redcurrant jelly. It really was too much.

They were all about to sit down when Rachel flew in, her eyes shining, and flung her coat down on Lavinia's dainty sofa. It was amazing how pretty she managed to look even in those awful clothes. 'So sorry, Gran. Here's the redcurrant jelly. You're going to have to boycott that shop by the way, the man who runs it is way out of order.'

'Mr Benson? He and his wife are perfectly

charming. They work all the hours God gives and they've greatly improved the range of foods. With the last people all you could get was Mother's Pride, baked beans and Dairylea cheese, and do you know what I found last week?' Lavinia waited for them to lean forward in their seats. 'Bath Oliver biscuits.'

'You didn't!' Ricky repeated in hushed tones. His mother kicked him under the table.

'Anyway,' Rachel ignored her younger brother, 'he was incredibly rude to these people. He refused to even serve them.'

'Were they Londoners?' Lavinia's tone implied that, if so, his behaviour was totally understandable.

'Actually they're camping in the woods.'

'Scouts, you mean, or Brownies? I can't see Mr Benson being beastly to a Brownie.'

'Not exactly. They said they were opposing some road scheme.'

'*Road protesters?*' yelped Lavinia. 'Lay-abouts, you mean. Benefit scroungers. I'm right behind Mr Benson there. They're the scum of the earth.'

'Gran! How could you. You sound worse than he did. We do live in a democracy, you know. Not a fascist regime.' Rachel threw down her fork and stalked out.

34

'How dare she?' demanded Lavinia. 'I know a lot more about fascist regimes than she does. I lived through the last war, remember.'

Christopher wisely failed to remind his mother that she had spent the entire war in the Home Counties where the nearest thing to a fascist regime was the admissions committee of the local golf club. But Lavinia was in full flood. 'Really, Christopher, you let that child get away with murder. Ever since she was born you've run around after her. You've let her think she's the centre of the universe and this is the result. The trouble with your generation is that you have the authority of a damp dishrag!'

Yes, Catherine wanted to shout, because the lot before did such a bloody bad job on us. We didn't want to put the fear of God into our children. We wanted them to like us and talk to us and come out to dinner in Italian restaurants with us.

The trouble was, though she'd die rather than admit it to her mother-in-law, somewhere along the line her sympathetic, understanding generation had lost control of their offspring altogether.

★　★　★

35

After the tension of the weekend, Monday morning seemed positively alluring. Catherine walked in to Rosemount Primary via the side entrance, across the asphalt playground. A gaggle of little ones rushed up. 'Good mor-ning, Miss-is Hope,' chanted Dorene, a sunny West Indian child who always made Catherine want to pick her up and cuddle her. 'You look very nice today, Miss-is Hope.'

Catherine laughed. As a matter of fact this morning had been such a rush that she hadn't got round to looking in the mirror yet. 'Thank you, Dorene, it's very nice of you to say so.'

'Morning, Miss Hope,' shouted Wesley, a cheeky ten-year-old. 'We've got you for PE today. Miss Wilson's sick.' Unprompted he put his arm round her waist as she walked along.

'That'll be fun. You can show me how to do star-jumps. I can never get those right.'

'No problem.' He winked reassuringly and dashed off to join his friends. Catherine felt her usual surge of pride at what they'd achieved at Rosemount. Friends who taught at better-resourced schools often asked how she stuck it out somewhere so tough. What they didn't understand was that to kids like these school was everything. They were like little sponges, so eager to learn it touched your heart.

The staff room was its usual fug of fan heater, cigarette smoke and gossip. There had been various politically correct attempts to ban smoking from the staff room but they'd always been defeated. A quick fag, Catherine's friend Anita maintained, was often all that came between your average teacher and a nervous breakdown. Today the fug was so thick that the plate-glass window at the end of the room was clouded with condensation. The window overlooked the playground and staff were supposed to keep an eye on the pupils playing there. What actually happened was that the pupils kept an eye on the staff, eager to catch someone out with a Silk Cut and dob to their mum and dad, who'd come steaming in to complain about Setting a Bad Example even if they had a sixty-a-day habit themselves.

The staff room, the one haven of privacy and peace in the school, wallowed in its customary mess. It was hard to believe it was cleaned every night. By nine a.m. it was always knee-deep in takeaway coffee cups, old copies of the *Times Educational Supplement*, particularly well thumbed in the Jobs Section, discarded Pot Noodle cartons and uncomfortable shoes.

'Who's doing the Tesco run today?' demanded Anita. The school food was so indescribably bad that the staff organized a daily mercy dash to the supermarket. 'I'll have a chicken pitta, no mayonnaise, and with the calories I've saved on the mayo you can get me a Crunchie.'

The temporary supply teacher, whose go it turned out to be, paled at the complexity of the orders. Only one person never participated but brought his own neatly packed plastic container. The same person who kept his personal stash of ground coffee in the fridge. 'Have you ever seen those ads in magazines for single-cup cafetières and wondered what kind of sad bastard would buy one?' Anita often demanded when he was out of the room. 'Brian Wickes, that's who. He probably puts a mark on the milk bottle too.'

Catherine had been at Rosemount for eight years, Brian Wickes for seven, and in all that time he had never ceased to resent her seniority and her friendship with Simon Marshall, the head teacher. His way of compensating was to be as authoritarian as possible.

There was a timid knock at the door and half the staff covered up their cigarettes with anything they could find. In one case a copy of the *Guardian* Education Supplement, which promptly caught fire and had to be doused with Brian's fresh-ground coffee.

'Yes, what is it?' barked Brian, who disapproved of pupils being allowed anywhere near this inner sanctum.

A dumpy figure in an unflattering lilac shell suit appeared, eased itself into the room, gazing nervously through lenses so thick they looked like an old-fashioned TV screen. 'Excuse me, Mrs Hope, but you said I could take the bell up to assembly.'

'So I did,' Catherine remembered guiltily. 'Here it is, Bonnie. I'll be up in a minute.'

'Her parents must have been blind giving her a name like that,' Brian smirked, as Bonnie lumbered eagerly off with the bell.

'I forgot to tell you,' Catherine confided to Anita, refusing to dignify Brian's remark with a reply. 'Bonnie's going to sit the entrance exam for Wolsey, Rachel's school.'

'She'd better swap her genes then,' Brian remarked. 'I've taught the whole family and changing the TV channel's too much for most of them.'

'As a matter of fact,' Catherine snapped, wanting to pour his remaining coffee over his head, 'Bonnie's a very bright girl. She's got a good chance if she prepares properly.'

'Like hell,' Brian mumbled.

Upstairs, outside the main hall, Bonnie rang the bell to announce the start of assembly. 'Come on,' Anita picked up her bag of marking, 'Simon likes the staff to be first in so at least someone sings 'All Things Bright and Beautiful' in tune. By the way,' she dropped her voice to a whisper so that Catherine had to move her ear nearer, 'I've got some hot news. Something that affects you.'

'What on earth's that?' Catherine had experience of Anita's secrets.

'Can't say now.' She tapped her nose. 'Meet me in the pub at lunchtime.'

Catherine itched all morning to know what Anita had to say. She tried her best to concentrate on the block graphs Year Six was making on the topic of How We Got to School. Five-eighths came on foot, two more by car, the last lot by bus, and Damon, who always liked to be different, was the one per cent who insisted he came by spaceship.

Normally Catherine was far too busy to think of going to the pub unless it was somebody's birthday. Apart from never having time, even less energy, nowadays one glass of wine and she'd sleep through Maths For Fun. It was intriguing, though, trying to guess what Anita had to say.

The morning dragged and by lunchtime

40

Catherine was grateful for the diversion. On the way through the playground she saw a gang of four boys shouting at Bonnie, who was bravely ignoring them and attempting to scale up the climbing frame.

'Yeah, yeah, Bonnie's on it,' yelled one.

'Yuk! Yuk! Soaked in vomit,' chipped in another.

'I'll see you boys later,' Catherine ordered. Bonnie always seemed to attract this kind of thing. 'Be outside my class at five to two on the dot. OK?'

'Yes, Mis-sis Hope.'

The pub was two minutes' walk from school, adjoining the far end of its playground, another reason why the staff rarely used it. It was surprisingly crowded for a weekday. A row of men of varying ages sat at the bar with pints of lager in front of them, gazing up at Sky Sports on large TV screens. But Anita was nowhere to be found.

Eventually Catherine located her in the small paved garden at the back, sitting at a frosty picnic table, blowing on her hands which made her fat row of silver bangles jingle festively.

Catherine watched her friend affection-ately, her sixties haircut, the eccentric clothes. Anita hadn't changed her look since she was twenty-one. 'Age is all in the mind,' was her

41

watchword. There were times when Catherine might not have stuck it out at Rosemount if it hadn't been for Anita. The list-making and the form-filling in teaching had got so bad recently as well as all the criticism and the feeling that sometimes you were being blamed for all the ills of society. Anita had always cheered her up and reminded her what a good teacher she was, how the kids would remember her all their lives.

'Bloody hell, Anita. It's arctic out here. Why aren't you inside?'

'Too smoky and disgusting.'

'But it's smoky and disgusting in the staff room.'

'Yes, but that's female smoke. This is male.'

'I thought maybe you were going to throw in the sponge at school and join some polar expedition.'

'No,' Anita offered her a glass of mulled wine. 'But you might want to when you hear what I've got to say.'

Catherine sat down. It wasn't like Anita to be so mysterious. 'Fire away then.'

'It's about Simon.' Simon was their charismatic head teacher, a human dynamo who seemed to find twenty-five hours in each day. Catherine and Simon had trained together and it had been Simon who'd brought her to Rosemount eight years ago. In

42

those days the school had been so bad no one wanted to come near it. Only the really desperate parents sent their children to Rosemount then. But now the school's reputation had improved dramatically. Only yesterday Catherine had shown round some parents who had attempted subtle bribery to get their child *in* to the school instead of pulling out all the stops to get them out of it. It had been a wonderful moment.

'What about Simon?'

'The rumour is, he's leaving.'

Catherine felt as if she'd been kicked. Not so much because Simon was leaving, heads did leave after the length of time he'd already stayed, but because he hadn't told her. She and Simon were mates. They came from a similar background and shared their ideals. That was how he'd talked her into coming here when in career terms she might have done better for herself. 'Go and teach in a nice middle-class school if you want,' he'd wooed, 'you'll have an easier life. But you won't make so much difference. These are the kids whose lives you'll change.'

She'd believed him and she'd never regretted it — even when friends who taught in private schools boasted of their long holidays and polite, well-behaved pupils. There had been a time, back at college, when

Simon had wanted them to be lovers. 'We're already best friends,' he argued with all his considerable charm, 'why stop there?' She'd been tempted, too. Who wouldn't be? Then, unexpectedly, she'd met Christopher.

'Where is he supposed to be going?' Catherine asked finally.

'To a 'school in crisis' — as if they all aren't. But you haven't heard the worst bit. Who they say is going to be taking over as Acting Head.'

Catherine was only half listening. She was thinking how different Rosemount would be without Simon to share things with. The thought of his departure was even more painful than she'd expected.

'Only Brian Wickes, that's bloody well who,' Anita whispered.

'They wouldn't, would they?'

'The Chair of Governors likes his ideas on discipline apparently. Detentions, exclusions, expulsions. Probably beheading'll be back on the agenda.'

'So what's the status of this rumour, then?'

Anita patted her friend lightly on the cheek. 'Pretty rock solid. Jane Jones saw Brian writing a memo in the computer room and he deleted it when she went in.'

'Oh, really, 'Nita. It could have been anything.'

'Yep. Except the file name was ROSE-MOUNT HEADSHIP.'

If Catherine needed any confirmation she had it when she found Simon standing outside her classroom on her return.

'Have you got a moment?' he asked.

She indicated the boys waiting to see her for teasing Bonnie. 'Come to my office in half an hour,' he instructed. They scuttled off looking nervous and penitent, without even making a smart remark to impress their friends.

Catherine knew at once the rumour was more than gossip. Simon was wearing one of his youthful blue denim shirts, the kind that made him look more like a rugged male model instead of a head teacher, but there was a defensive set to his shoulders. His eyes had the sympathetic look reserved for seeing parents whose child was falling behind.

'It's true then,' Catherine challenged, not waiting to hear his explanation.

'I'm afraid it is. Look, Cath, I argued as strongly as I could for you instead of Brian. You'd be far more effective. But it's Birch 'em Brian they want.'

Catherine turned to the board and furiously began to inscribe a punctuation passage for Year Six's next lesson. Someone had forgotten to put the guinea pig away and

45

it suddenly darted across the floor; Catherine lunged for it, scooped it up and dumped it in Simon's astonished grasp. 'Here's another rodent for you.'

'Is everything OK, Cath, I mean otherwise?'

'Everything's going swimmingly, thank you. Rachel is studying for an A level in teenage rebellion — the only A level she *is* studying for — and treats me with total contempt, that is when she notices me at all. Christopher just indulges her and his mother thinks it's all my fault because I've tried to understand her instead of locking her in her bedroom. And now I'm going to have to answer to Brian bloody Wickes.'

'Poor Cath. You'll cope with Brian. He has his good points, you know. His last school was very sad to lose him. One good thing about my leaving,' he put the guinea pig down and took both of her hands in his, 'we won't be colleagues any longer.'

'And what's so good about that?'

'We might be able to be something more.' He touched her cheek with a gentle finger. 'You don't know how hard it's been to hide how I still feel about you. If only you hadn't met Chris . . . ' his voice trailed off softly.

Catherine could hardly believe what she was hearing. Even if he did still feel something for her, the insensitivity of telling her now, as if it were some consolation prize for her disappointment, was mindblowing. At some other time she might have been both touched and flattered, but to announce it under these circumstances felt like being propositioned at a funeral. And what about Christopher in all this? 'For God's sake, Simon, you can't promote someone over my head and then make a pass at me. Just fuck off, will you!'

With a perfect sense of timing, thirty-two Year Sixes chose this moment to fling open the door and pile into the classroom.

Simon and Catherine sprang apart guiltily.

'I must be off. Those boys you wanted me to see must be waiting.'

Great. Now she'd been passed over and alienated her greatest ally in one wonderful morning.

★　★　★

Sometimes when Catherine got home from school, the house would be dark and quiet. Ricky and Rachel had evolved a whole after-school routine of coming back, consuming some unsuitable snack, then going their separate ways. Ricky's destination was usually the sofa with the remote control and Rachel's her bedroom where, in principle at least, she did her homework before being allowed out or to phone her friends. Tonight, with some sixth sense that all was not well in the family, Ricky had decided to prepare a meal. The whole basement floor was illuminated as he tackled bangers and mash, addressing an imaginary TV audience as he did so, just like the chefs on *Ready Steady Cook*. It was his greatest wish to be invited on to this highly revered programme to share his personal recipe for Ricky's Risqué Ketchup. This consisted of Heinz tomato with a dash of special ingredients Ricky guarded as secretly as the Coca-Cola company did their trillion-dollar formula.

'And now,' Ricky announced with a flourish, 'the really important part . . . '

Catherine dumped her briefcase of marking in the hall. 'Hello, cheffie, where's your sister? Not working, I presume.'

Ricky picked up the telephone extension from the kitchen wall and listened. 'She's not on the phone. I think that's as much as you can expect.'

Catherine hugged him. 'I expect you're right. So, when's supper?'

She was rewarded with a flash of red and white retainer. 'Seven thirty. Dad phoned to say he'd be back at seven.'

Catherine thought about going to check on Rachel and decided against it. She didn't feel strong enough today. What she needed was a calming glass of wine and some nice remote disasters on the TV news. Which was just as well since Rachel was lying on her bed devising all the reasons why her granny, like Little Red Riding Hood's, really ought to be paid a visit very, very soon.

In the end she didn't need an excuse. Five minutes later the phone rang and Catherine, without any suspicion of how this information was about to change her daughter's life, shouted up to Rachel that someone called Marko wanted to speak to her and could she not be too long because it would soon be supper.

Rachel bounded up from the bed faster than the subject of a miracle.

'Marko? Where are you? How on earth did you get my phone number?'

From his perch in a large oak in the middle of Gosse's Wood, Marko pulled his greatcoat a little tighter. 'I'm up a tree, as a matter of fact. Shall I describe the view? It's pitch dark, with a thin little moon shining through the trees like one of those paper cut-out things. The stars are incredibly bright, largely because it's freezing. There's a screech owl, doing what, screeching I guess, and it feels

49

like there's just us left on the face of the earth.'

'You make it sound incredibly romantic.'

'It is. If you get off on total boredom, icy feet and lentil stew, wonderfully romantic.'

Rachel closed her eyes. Her bedroom seemed smaller and more suburban than it had ever looked to her before. She flushed faintly at the thought of Marko finding out she had posters of boy bands and cute kittens still on her walls. 'But why are you up a tree? Are you being chased?'

'Chaste? Yes, god-damnit, chaste as the driven snow and I can't tell you how much I mind now that I've met you.'

Rachel giggled. 'Why are you really up a tree?'

'Because my mobile doesn't work on the ground. Sorry to burst your bubble. But I'll do my best to slay you an evil developer tomorrow, if you like. How's the study going?'

'Fine, thanks,' she replied, eager to impress him with her mind as well as her body. 'I've just been doing the Metaphysicals.'

'Have you? And who are they when they're at home?'

Rachel hesitated. 'Oh, you know, poets like Donne, Herbert.'

'Never heard of them. Preferred John Denver myself.'

Rachel was slightly disconcerted. She couldn't quite tell if this was some postmodern joke. 'Are you really on a mobile? It seems a bit yuppie for a road protester.'

'I know. I always loathed anyone who had one, but they're bloody brilliant for our purposes. We can warn each other when the big bad bailiffs are on their way. So, lovely Rachel, when are you going to be coming down here to put me out of my misery?'

Rachel didn't know how to answer. His question was so loaded that it sent shivers through her. She hardly knew him and yet there was a caressing, teasing tone to his voice that was far more exciting than any poetry. Rachel knew her appearance was in-your-face Londoner and that her mother suspected her of behaving badly, but beneath the Wild Child front she was still surprisingly innocent. This situation was the craziest, most exciting thing that had happened to her. Somehow he'd got hold of her phone number and was phoning her from a tree surrounded by starlight and screech owls. How could she possibly resist?

'This weekend,' she said boldly, which wasn't at all the way she was feeling. 'I'll come down this weekend.'

'Fabulous. I'll kill the fatted lima bean. You

might even see some action. Things are moving at last.'

Rachel's heart drummed with excitement. Trying to stop a road was real. Unlike studying lots of dead male poets. 'Till the weekend then.'

'I'll live for it.'

She remembered as she was about to put down the phone that she had no idea where to find their camp.

'Right in the middle of Gosse's Wood. Just ask the locals. Once they've spat on the ground they might even tell you.'

'Bye. See you at the weekend. Marko . . . '

'Yup?'

'How *did* you get my number.'

'Zoe posed as a nice respectable middle-class girl and asked your grandmother for it.'

Rachel grinned, only slightly disturbed at the touch of tenderness in his voice when he used Zoe's name. She'd better get down there pretty damn quick and stake her claim.

Rachel hugged her secret to her and closed up her books, too excited to do any more English revision. Why did she need Mr Darcy or Sergeant Troy now? She had her own romantic hero. All she had to do was talk her parents into letting her go.

Zoe looked up from stirring their meal and caught Marko's expression of sly delight.

She remembered that look from when it had been her he'd been thinking of. Naturally the relationship had been casual, no strings. Except that strings had a habit of wrapping themselves round you whether you admitted to them or not. Was it just Marko's dark good looks, his jaunty swagger, which even mud and hunger and boredom couldn't quite extinguish, that drew her to him almost against her better judgement?

She pushed away the temptation — it was after all the mantra of the loser — to believe that Marko could change, be less selfish, more able to feel deeply with the help of a good woman.

Marko's sly look broadened into a grin. He was obviously contemplating his next big adventure, and this one had nothing to do with roads. 'That smells great. It's amazing what a way you have with root vegetables, Zo. After this is over you should train as a chef.'

Zoe stirred in some wild thyme. She couldn't imagine life after all this, maybe that was her problem. This way of life had become reality to her.

★ ★ ★

Downstairs in their untidy terraced house, Christopher had just come home. One look at

53

his wife had told him instantly that something was wrong.

'What's happened, Cath?'

'Simon's leaving,' Catherine admitted.

'That's bad. You like him a lot.'

'Worse. Brain Wickes is taking over as Acting Head.'

Christopher put down his briefcase, silently cursing the governors of Catherine's school. He had watched her stoke up her passion for teaching during the tough times. He knew more than anyone how deep her love for the job was. Brian Wickes, from what he'd heard, was an unimaginative teacher of the old school. Why couldn't they see Catherine would be perfect for the job?

'That's disgraceful. You're the far better candidate.'

'They obviously don't think so. And maybe it's all for the best. After all, Rachel needs a lot of attention at the moment. I'd like to be there for her.'

'Own up,' Christopher held out his arms. 'You think they're a bunch of shortsighted, narrow-minded wankers.'

'Do you know what,' Catherine buried herself in his shoulder gratefully. 'I think they're a lot of shortsighted, narrow-minded wankers.'

3

Rachel skipped downstairs to find her parents locked tightly in an embrace. 'Come on, break it up, you two. It's unfair on Ricky and me to be exposed to this kind of thing. Anyway, there's something I need to ask you.'

Her parents jumped apart as if they'd been doing something shameful.

'Dad. I was wondering. Do you think Gran would mind if I went to stay with her this weekend?'

Both of them stared at her.

'But you never want to set foot in Gran's house,' Catherine pointed out. 'I have to drag you there kicking and screaming and bribe you with CDs of Radiohead.'

'Yes, well . . . ' Rachel had the modesty to look embarrassed. 'It's just that I thought Christmas is always pretty hectic and what with my mocks coming up, it might be rather peaceful to do some work there.'

'Good for you,' congratulated her father. 'I'm sure Gran would be delighted to have you. She could show you off to her friends.'

Catherine and Ricky giggled at the improbability of Lavinia parading Rachel proudly round Maxted. One look at Rachel's wardrobe and she'd probably insist on taking her to Laura Ashley.

'You'd better take some sensible clothes then. Gran's a bit conventional when it comes to fashion.'

'Actually, I thought I might do some walking. Could I get some rubber trousers, do you think, and a warmer parka?'

'Gosh, you are taking this seriously,' Catherine murmured reaching for her bag. Still, any plan that involved fresh air and hard work had to be encouraged. She just hoped that, unlike most of Rachel's sudden enthusiasms, it lasted longer than a weekend.

'Well,' Catherine commented to Christopher when Rachel had tripped off with her mother's cash card, 'that's a turn-up for the books. Since when has Rachel been one for the great outdoors?'

'The only rubber trousers Rachel's ever worn,' Ricky pointed out suspiciously, 'are ones with silver studs on them.'

'For pity's sake, you two,' Christopher was always the one to speak up in Rachel's defence, 'just because Rach wants some outdoor clothing you're treating her like she's had a personality transplant. Perhaps she's realized how beautiful the countryside round Maxted is and she just wants to appreciate it.'

'Huh,' commented Ricky, with a cynical lift of his eyebrow. 'Rachel's idea of a good view is the sale rack at Kookaï. Isn't it, Mum?'

Later that night, feeling guilty about her suspicious reaction, Catherine put her head round the door of Rachel's room. Rachel was always the last to go to sleep. Usually her bedroom was so untidy it resembled a WI jumble sale two minutes after the doors had opened, but tonight she must have tidied it. The only things out of place were a neat pile of festering coffee cups, clearly on its way to the kitchen, and a pile of clothes tidily stacked on the bed. Instead of the unseasonal crop tops, Rachel had amassed a pile of sensible jumpers and woolly socks. The only incongruous item was a tiny pair of knickers, thonged at the back with a minuscule patch of lace in the front. Rachel snatched them up and stuffed them into her jeans pocket, blushing furiously.

Catherine pretended not to notice. Was that a prick of jealousy she'd felt then? It was years since she'd worn anything like those herself. She felt the usual difficult complex of emotions when faced with Rachel's emerging sexuality. She'd delivered the expected lectures about Love, Sex, Aids and the Whole Dam' Thing. She'd tried to convey that sex ought to be with someone you cared for. And yet she knew that, deep down, the idea of her own little daughter having sex at all seemed an outrage, a crime against nature. But then who said being a parent wasn't going to be wildly contradictory. You wanted to hang on when you knew you had to let go. You wanted innocence to last when experience was inevitable.

'Rach,' she asked tentatively, 'is everything all right? I mean there's nothing you'd like to talk about?'

Rachel simply gave her mother a hug.

This was such a rare, precious experience that Catherine closed her eyes, breathing in the clean, apple smell of her daughter's hair. It was almost as it used to be after bath-time when Rachel, wrapped in a huge warm bath towel, sat on her mother's knee and permitted herself to be held while the two of them watched *Sesame Street*.

She'd obviously been imagining things. Rachel was fine. She must learn not to be so overprotective.

★   ★   ★

Lavinia sat at the small table she'd placed by the cottage window so that she could admire her garden and thought about her grand-daughter's unexpected visit. She would have to go into Maxted and get some supplies. Teenagers were supposed to have appetites like lions pursuing wildebeest. She'd never actually seen Rachel putting away more than a mouthful but her mother insisted that she could empty fridgeloads providing she was offered the right foods — which seemed to be sugary breakfast cereal and giant-size bars of chocolate. The fact that her mother allowed her to eat such things — and, it seemed, little else — reinforced Lavinia's suspicion that Catherine just gave in to the child at every turn. A weekend wasn't very long to reverse the bad habits of a lifetime but Lavinia had never been one to balk at a challenge. At least she could make a start in Rachel's re-education.

She opened the windows and looked out over the valley. The sun was just beginning to burn off the wraiths of mist still lying over the highest ground to reveal the bare winter landscape beneath. Even in deepest winter, when the fields were hard as metal, and boned bare by the plough, this place had a softness that never failed to lift her spirits. Another fifty miles east and the land became flat and dull but here it was gently contoured, a kind landscape, in Lavinia's view, where man could flourish.

She hung her cosy dressing gown in the

wardrobe and put her slippers away next to the ludicrous present she'd been given last Christmas. It was a furry footwarmer, which reminded Lavinia of a moccasin for a one-legged elephant. The box it had arrived in featured a dozy old dear with blue-rinsed hair, her eyes glued to a TV screen, a tartan rug across her knee, clutching a tray of a supper-for-one. The giver had clearly imagined Lavinia's life to be rather like this. Hah! Lavinia would rather throw herself in the stream at the bottom of her garden than live her life like that old woman. It offended her that people might see her as lonely. And yet, if she wasn't, why was she so absurdly excited about the idea of Rachel arriving on Friday?

Lavinia dispensed with these unhelpful thoughts by leaning precariously out of the window and breathing in the morning air. She'd take Rachel on a good long walk over the tops. Next door she caught sight of Eunice hanging out her washing again, although it was more acceptable this time, being a Wednesday. As tit for tat, telling herself she ought to behave better than this at her age, she draped her eiderdown out of the window. It would, she knew, be bang slap in the middle of Eunice's view of the valley.

Once the house was tidy, she picked up her shopping basket, slipped on her green padded

60

bodywarmer — she didn't approve of full-blown coats until January or February.

Eunice was standing under her thatched porch pretending not to notice Lavinia's duvet. 'You look busy,' she remarked.

'Off to the shops. My grand-daughter's coming to stay this weekend.'

'The one with the bare middle and a nose stud?'

'That's the one.' Typical of Eunice to remember such trifling details. 'But I trust she's at least going to cover up her midriff. If she goes round like that, as I told her mother, she'll end up with a kidney infection.'

'I'm sure your daughter-in-law appreciated the advice, Lavinia.' Lavinia missed her neighbour's wry tone entirely. 'So how are you planning to entertain her?'

Lavinia perked up. 'Her mother lets her run wild so I thought I'd try and be a bit of a stabilizing influence. Early nights, good food, chats by the fire and then perhaps church on Sunday.'

Eunice's eyebrows shot into her carefully coiffed hair at the thought of Rachel enlivening eleven o'clock Communion.

'Then there's the village jumble sale, and it's my week for the church flowers, so she could help me arrange those . . . ' Lavinia lapsed into momentary uncertainty. 'I hope she'll enjoy that. What *do* eighteen-year-olds like doing?'

'Not staying with their grandmothers if mine are anything to go by.'

'Ah but, Eunice,' Lavinia settled her basket in front of her like a battering ram, her confidence returning, 'perhaps that's because you don't have a way with teenagers like I do.'

Lavinia was just approaching the village shop on her way into Maxted when the owner, Mr Benson, popped his head out. 'Mrs Hope, might I have a word?'

Lavinia wondered briefly if she'd forgotten to settle her bill, but just inside the door, right between the Mrs Tiggywinkle's Shortbread Fancies and the Kountry Kitchen home-made jams, Mrs Benson stood brandishing a clipboard. 'We're just collecting signatures to get those louts of road protesters moved out of the wood, Mrs Hope. Would you consider signing?'

'I'd be delighted,' enthused Lavinia. 'The sooner the better in my opinion.'

'We knew you'd see it our way,' simpered Mrs Benson, her gold charm bracelet, which Lavinia couldn't help noticing with a slight shudder consisted of tiny gold thatched cottages, jingled in approval.

Lavinia, satisfied that she had contributed to her citizenly duties, bustled cheerfully into town.

Maxted was looking its loveliest. The High Street with its neat colour-washed cottages, thatch-roofed tea rooms and rows of small shops, shone in the sunshine as if auditioning for a picture postcard of Olde England. Lavinia smiled contentedly as she felt the fruit in Bill the Greengrocer's and declared the pears too hard and the apples too soft. She settled for two pounds of tangerines and some pale green Brussels sprouts, having first ascertained that they were grown in Britain, not Brussels.

She bought a cottage loaf, more because she liked its ludicrous Mae West appearance, nipped in at the waist and ridiculously top-heavy, than for any flavour, then proceeded to the butcher's. Thank heavens Rachel had not, as far as Lavinia could remember, declared herself a vegetarian. All the same, perhaps meat of the red-in-tooth-and-claw variety might be best avoided. The butcher weighed her two nice fat pork chops, which he assured her had been ranging freely, as happy as any pig could be, only days before. She appreciated his consideration but was glad that Rachel wasn't present to share this vision of fulfilled porkers happily sacrificing themselves on the altar of human greed. The young were so squeamish.

On the other side of the road she noticed a

group of people she recognized from the bridge club, Eunice among them, who were gathered round the office of the local paper, and felt miffed that something was going on she hadn't heard about. Eunice must have sprinted to get down here before her. Lavinia stepped into the road to investigate and was almost knocked down by a speeding lorry.

'Really, the traffic here is getting insufferable,' she said aloud to cover her feelings of stupidity at not looking. She bustled up to the crowd outside the paper. 'What on earth's going on?'

'We're picketing,' twittered Eunice. 'Isn't it fun?'

'What's the *Maxted Express* done? Forgotten to advertise the Christmas Bring & Buy Sale?'

'As a matter of fact, Lavinia, the paper's just run a story saying those horrible road protesters might have a case. There's some ludicrous newt they've found that is extinct everywhere else in the country and the paper's saying we should protect it.'

'What absolute nonsense! I expect they brought it themselves and planted it.'

'Goodness, Lavinia, I hadn't thought of that,' marvelled Eunice. 'You're so good at all this. You really ought to get involved.'

In her enthusiasm Eunice failed to notice

her fellow picketers shaking their heads.

Lavinia surveyed the small group. The six or seven elderly ladies, and one token man, would have looked more at home passing round the biscuits for the weekly coffee-morning in the village hall than taking on the might of the press. Perhaps Eunice had a point. Maybe she ought to get involved. Something had to be done to get rid of the traffic. On weekday mornings you almost needed a gas mask to do your shopping. Maxted, once a sleepy picturesque little market town, was hardly visible behind the streams of lorries aiming for the nearby and much bigger centre of Saylworth. A bypass was absolutely essential. 'Have you got a committee?' she demanded. Everything that happened in Maxted happened through a committee.

'Yes,' admitted one of the ladies reluctantly. They knew Lavinia of old. 'There is a committee. Colonel Lawley chairs it.'

'Fine. I'll get myself voted on. You'll second me, won't you, Eunice?'

Eunice nodded enthusiastically.

'Hang on a moment,' pointed out the white-haired old gentleman to Eunice, 'you're not on the committee yourself.'

'I'm sure Lavinia won't let something like that put her off,' pooh-poohed Eunice.

'Lavinia's not one to let technicalities stand in her way.'

'Or anything else, if I know Lavinia Hope,' muttered one of the sweet-looking old ladies darkly.

★ ★ ★

The other Mrs Hope, twenty years younger and at that moment besieged by thirty-three eager ten-year-olds, tried to listen to the machine-gun fire of questions always directed at her when she appeared in her class-room.

'Have you seen my drawing of a nit, Mrs Hope?' Aziz proudly brandished a piece of paper featuring a scorpion-like creature of Spielbergian proportions. 'I made it a bit bigger so it would show up more. Darren's got them, haven't you, Darren?'

A small group descended on the unfortunate Darren with all the enthusiasm of big game hunters.

'I've finished my project on the Black Death, miss. It's really, really gruesome.'

'Good,' Catherine congratulated angelic Ben, who showed an over-keen interest in carbuncles and oozing sores. 'I'll look forward to it.' She finally restored order only to discover that someone had removed the bung from the fish tank and the unfortunate goldfish, who already deserved a Duke of Edinburgh award for survival, was gasping its last.

'For heaven's sake!' she yelled. 'Fill up the jug with water and put that fish in it!'

'Sorry, miss,' Darren apologized sheepishly, 'I was doing an experiment to see how long it could breathe out of water.'

Playtime, when it finally arrived, was a blessed relief. Catherine flopped down in the staff room between Anita and Kevin Tudge, the PE teacher, too exhausted to even make herself some coffee.

'I'll do it,' volunteered Anita. She reached up on the shelf above the kettle and her eyes rested mischievously on Brian Wickes's fresh ground. 'Tell you what, Brian's new status will mean he'll have to move up a coffee notch too. Fresh ground won't be good enough. He'll have to grind his own. So why don't we pinch a bit of this?'

Before Catherine could protest, Anita had filled Brian's cafetière and the aroma of high-roast Colombian suffused the staff room.

Catherine closed her eyes for a moment, allowing the wonderful scent to fill her nostrils. An elbow in the ribs from Kevin brought her down to earth. 'Sorry about the headship. If it's any consolation, the staff would have gone for you like a shot.'

'Thanks, Kev.' Catherine felt genuinely touched. Still, what the staff wanted didn't seem to count. Brian had the job and she had two alternatives. Shut up or ship out.

Just as the bell rang for the end of playtime and a general groan passed through the staff room like a Mexican wave, Brian Wickes opened the door. He took in the situation at a glance.

'Sorry, Brian,' Anita said breezily, 'we were just toasting your appointment.'

'With my coffee?' He accepted it with surprising tolerance. 'Oh, well, I suppose that means I won't need to buy a round after work. Every cloud has a silver lining.'

'You know, Brian,' Anita congratulated, 'that was quite funny. Or should it be Mr Wickes now you're to be our new leader?'

'Brian'll do nicely, thanks.'

They all began to go their separate ways. 'Catherine . . .' Brian put a hand on her arm. They were the last two in the room. 'Look, I'm sure you're disappointed over this head business, but I just wanted to say one thing. I believe in the school too. It's just that my manner's different from yours.'

It was, Catherine saw, Brian's version of an apology. Perhaps life under Brian wouldn't be as gruesome after all.

Later on, when they were both on playground duty during the lunchtime break, Anita sauntered up. It was so cold that they had to stamp their feet and bang their hands together to keep warm. As usual, half the children didn't even have coats on or had abandoned them on the freezing slide. Anita was wearing her famous coloured legwarmers. These might have been discarded several decades ago by the fashion conscious but Anita had cornered the world market in them. Stripey legwarmers with matching hats were her trademark, giving her the look of a rather dated teapot. 'So what was the King of Caning whispering to you, then? Not another one who's got the hots for you, surely. How do you do it, Cath? You look like this overbred, racehorsy kind of gal, though I suppose that long wild hair of yours is a bit of a giveaway, and men come flocking.'

'What do you mean, *another* man who's got the hots for me?' Simon's words of the other day jumped back into her memory, giving her a fright all over again.

'Come on, Cath, we all know Simon fancies you.'

'Oh God, Anita. I'd thought all that finished when we were students and then last week when he told me about Brian he came out with all this stuff about now that we weren't working together, maybe we could have a different kind of relationship.'

'Yep. The horizontal kind.'

'Anita, you don't think that was why I didn't get the job?'

Anita had a nose for sexism the way most people could detect bad kitchen smells.

'Makes you wonder, doesn't it? And there was that business with the student teacher a few years ago, remember? What was her name? Something posh. Edwina? Olivia? No, Georgina. The one who left suddenly without any explanation. If you ask me, saintly Simon's halo slipped that time too, probably along with his trousers. Still, there's one advantage of Brian getting the headship,' she put her arm through her friend's just as a group of infants crowded round them twittering like small birds, 'at least you can't be accused of sleeping your way to the top.'

'Please, miss, Peter Wills pulled my glove off.' A small freezing hand clutched at Catherine's. She restored the child's mitten, sensibly tied on to her coat with elastic.

'Infants' Nativity Play next week,' Anita reminded her. 'I used to love it when my boys had them.' Anita had two huge teenage sons, who'd stayed with her after her divorce and proceeded to consume an alimony's worth of food every day. 'Until Roly bashed the lamb's brains out on stage, that is.'

Catherine sighed. It hardly seemed five minutes ago that Rachel, an angelic five, had been selected to play Mary because of her 'sweet submissiveness'. Not much of that on show now.

As she shooed the infants back towards their classroom at the end of break she thought about Rachel and her extraordinary request to go and stay with Lavinia. There was something about it, no matter what Christopher said, that just didn't add up.

* * *

'Hi, Gran,' Rachel waved as she climbed off the train and ran down the narrow station platform. To Lavinia's relief she was wearing highly suitable country clothes. Lavinia might have preferred a neat little kilt to the thick leggings and huge navy jumper, but, knowing Rachel, the kilt would have been microscopic and teamed with either hobnail boots or ludicrous platform shoes, so perhaps it was better this way. Rachel was even clutching a bunch of wilting tulips, probably wildly overpriced and bought at Liverpool Street Station. Lavinia loathed the florists' fad of producing spring flowers before Christmas; it was quite against nature and spoiled the pleasure of growing things arriving at their appointed time, but she pretended to be thrilled. It always amazed her that people visiting from London brought flowers when the country was full of them.

'Hello, Rachel darling, let me take your bag. Gosh, you have brought a lot of stuff for two days.'

'Revision,' reassured Rachel hoping her grandmother wouldn't detect the bottle of brandy she'd pinched from her parents' ancient cocktail cabinet, or the tin of biscuits she'd thought would come in handy for tree-dwelling protesters.

Lavinia put the bag in the boot of the car.

Her grandmother's car never failed to impress Rachel.

Both her parents drove around in rusting hulks that embarrassed her if they picked her up from school, whereas Lavinia's sporty open-topped Rover was cool to be seen in.

Before buying it Lavinia had toyed with the idea of an ancient Jaguar or a sporty new Honda but had dismissed the first as too unreliable and the second as too flashy and foreign. The secondhand Rover, which was a dashing metallic claret with friendly dents in each wing and a roof that went up and down automatically, represented a perfect marriage between solidity and adventure, rather,

72

Lavinia liked to think, as she did herself.

'Can we put the roof down?' begged Rachel, suddenly sounding five years old. 'Please, Gran.'

'But it's the middle of winter. It's probably below freezing.'

'I thought you liked being braced,' wheedled Rachel.

'All right then. But you'd better put this on,' she chucked her grand-daughter a woolly hat.

She watched as Rachel pulled the knitted cloche snugly over her ears. Lavinia had to admit that when she dressed halfway sensibly, Rachel was an astonishingly pretty girl. She had the kind of angular thinness that always looked faintly undernourished to Lavinia but certainly appealed to Rachel's generation. Her eyes, sparkling in the cold blue morning, were large and luminous. That must come from Catherine's family, Lavinia told herself firmly, cutting out any other thoughts of Rachel's ancestry.

A youth in black leather, leaning on the wall by the ticket office, whistled at them.

Rachel regarded him with disdain, then giggled. 'We've got an admirer.'

'I hardly think it's me he's interested in,' Lavinia pointed out drily. How quickly it happened. One day they were children, all gangly legs and runny noses, the next they were old enough to attract the attention of a young man. Lavinia was glad she was well beyond those years of intensity and heart-break, when every look and word was loaded with meaning and significance, to be decoded like a secret language. And yet, it was sad in a way. Age had some pleasures, but not many surprises — apart of course from the unpleasant ones of pain, loss and reading about your contemporaries only in the obituary columns.

'So,' Lavinia brushed away all this senti-mentality and put her foot down. 'What would you like to do this weekend?' With typical Lavinia-esque sensitivity she failed to wait for an answer. 'I thought a pub lunch today and perhaps a walk.' She eyed Rachel's double-decker trainers. 'That is, if you can walk more than two minutes in those things. And then tomorrow you could revise before church and in the afternoon there's a jumble sale I thought you might enjoy.'

'Actually, Gran,' Rachel stared out fixedly at the passing countryside. 'I've got some friends nearby I'd like to see today, if that's OK with you.'

Lavinia fought back a ludicrous feeling of disappointment. The girl had her life to lead. Besides maybe, if they lived round here, the friends would be nice county types who could counteract all that inner-city liberalism she got at home. All the same, Lavinia thought it was a bit off. Hadn't her parents taught her any sense of good manners?

'I see. Would I know their parents, do you think?'

Rachel thought of Marko and Zoe, and the ex-squaddies and drop-out students whom Marko had said made up their little band. 'Well, actually, Gran, I'm not sure you would.'

Rachel unpacked her things in Lavinia's tiny spare bedroom and sat at the kidney-shaped chintz dressing table, adorned by a delicate vase of Christmas roses, touched by the effort her grandmother had made and more than a little guilty. Then she thought about Marko and forgot everything else. He hadn't mentioned what time she should arrive and it had sounded too bourgeois to ask.

She pulled on her waterproof over-trousers and tucked them into her walking boots, then put on two thin T-shirts, one short-sleeved, the other long, under her jumper with the parka on top. The trickiest thing would be how to get away without arousing her grandmother's suspicions.

She clumped downstairs feeling like The

Michelin Man Goes Hiking.

'Would you like a lift, dear?'

Lavinia's cottage was on a scale where even medium-sized people seemed like giants and Rachel was terrified of knocking over some precious knick-knack. 'No, thanks, Gran. It's such a fabulous day I think I'll walk. I could use some fresh air after London.' She knew this argument would appeal. Lavinia thought anyone who lived in London barmy, and anyone who lived in the run-down corner the Hopes had chosen positively certifiable. 'What time shall I expect you for supper?'

'I think you'd better go ahead without me,' Rachel advised, hoping Lavinia wouldn't mind too much. 'I'm not quite sure how long I'll be.'

Lavinia waved her off. Young people needed some independence and the irony was that although her grand-daughter's genera-tion had been given a disgraceful amount of mental freedom, largely reflected in how rude they were to their elders and betters, they'd been allowed almost no physical freedom at all. In some ways they were the most overprotected generation in history.

Rachel struck confidently out over the hill opposite Lavinia's cottage, and down the valley the other side until she reached the banks of the river Knare. According to the ordnance survey map she'd borrowed from the bookshelf, Gosse's Wood was about three miles to the east. She followed a line of elms and willows dipping down into the river. Even though it was so late in the year, the colours here were green rather than brown, fixed in the minds of everyone who walked this way by Constable's loving portrayals. At one point Rachel stopped on the banks to watch as a man in waders with a hand scythe cut the tall reeds and stored them in a giant willow basket, a distant cousin of the one Lavinia used for shopping. The sense of timelessness was extraordinary. Beyond the river valley she could see the distant tip of a steeple and she began to walk away from it, through several more fields to the beginning of some woodland.

Once inside the wood she consulted the map again. The whole area covered no more than a mile so it should surely be easy enough to find their camp. Nevertheless she, whose usual idea of exercise was three laps around Gap, was about to flop on to the ground when somewhere in the distance she thought she could hear voices. She stopped to get her bearings, breathing in the smell of wood smoke, pungent and atmospheric. And then someone grabbed her from behind and held her tight, her arms behind her.

Rachel knew somehow who it was.

She half expected him to laughingly demand 'And what brings you here, fair maid?' Instead she was roughly spun round, and Marko, with a smile lighting up his dark features, kissed her hard on the lips.

'You came then.' There was the faintest suggestion of triumph in his voice.

Rachel, realizing that modesty or pleading some wild coincidence would hardly be convincing, raised her chin and held his eyes with hers. 'Yes. I came. So, are you going to show me around?'

The camp was several hundred yards into the wood, invisible from any single angle and centred round a clearing to take advantage of its natural surroundings. The central area had been covered with a makeshift flooring consisting of the kind of wooden pallets used in container lorries.

At one end of the clearing there was a cluster of tents, some rounded and new-looking, others made of lengths of plastic sheeting draped with tarpaulin; one boasted a length of canvas with the words SAVE GOSSE FOR POSSTERITY emblazoned on it with more passion than literacy.

Within the circle of the tents was the cooking area, surrounded by old pots and pans and a plastic washing bowl full of dirty crockery, a giant water bottle and a large container of meths. The girl she had met with Marko last time, Zoe, was attempting to light a fire. Even amongst eco warriors, it struck Rachel, the women did the cooking.

The whole of the clearing was deep in mud. The huge tyre marks of caterpillar bulldozers at one end made it seem as if it had recently been visited by dinosaurs. Everything, Rachel couldn't help noticing, from the pallets to the cooking pot, was caked in mud.

'So, what were you expecting from our little camp?' Marko was watching her, his intense blue eyes narrowed in cynical amusement. 'A cross between Woodstock and the Raggle-Taggle Gypsies-O?'

Rachel flushed. He probably wasn't that far from the truth.

'Zoe,' he shouted to the girl at the fire. 'You remember Rachel.'

'Certainly. Got a day-return from suburbia, have you?' Zoe hadn't meant to sound so harsh, but Rachel looked so ludicrously young and blooming, like a hothouse peach to her own dirty, dried-up old orange.

Rachel bit back the retort that she didn't live in suburbia, but thought better of it. Zoe would probably apply that label to anywhere Rachel lived.

'As a matter of fact, I'm staying with my grandmother.'

'Perhaps we should get your gran to join us,' Marko joked. 'A grappling granny on our side would be a real coup.'

'You don't know my grandmother.'

Marko slipped his arm round her. 'No, but I'd like to get to know her grand-daughter. Want to see what it is we're trying to save?' He pulled her away in the direction of the deeper woodland beyond. On the way they came upon a vast, red-haired giant of a man in camouflage fatigues.

'Meet Macduff. He used to be in the army, didn't you, Duff? The toughest nut amongst us. And if you ever get bored — and that's another occupational hazard round here — Duff'll show you two hundred things to do with an inflated condom. And none of them to do with sex.'

'Isn't he an odd character to be involved with you?' Rachel asked as they headed off through the woods, the still-white leaves crunching under their boots like the Frosties Ricky dropped on the kitchen floor. 'He looks more like a policeman or a security guard.'

'Stereotypes, Rachel, stereotypes. We've got to get you to challenge those stereotypes.' He stopped suddenly and brusquely turned her shoulders round to face him. 'For instance, lovely Rachel, what do you think of me? A bit of rough? A romantic rebel? Or are you about to convince me that it's your burning anger with the car culture that's brought you tramping across the fields to our little camp?'

Rachel felt her face burn with a fiery glow of embarrassment. 'If we're talking stereotypes,' she flashed, suddenly furious, 'then yours is the pretty but dumb boy who thinks every girl's lusting after him. There's more to attraction than wanting a quick fuck, you know.'

'Very good, Rachel. So I'm dumb, am I? How do you explain the college place I turned down to fight the good fight?'

'You're conning me.' Too late Rachel realized how insulting her comment sounded.

'No, I'm not. But it was the school who got the results, not me. One of those pansy ones with the knee socks and the year-round shorts.' A shard of bitterness carved through his voice. 'You can imagine how good I looked in those. The bigger boys always wanted me to do their errands. You have heard the word fag, I take it, as it's used in English boarding schools.'

'Of course. I just wouldn't have had you down for a boarding-school boy.'

'Ah. But then it was a school for the poor

81

but clever. After my dad disappeared, my mum turned her middle-class aspirations on to me. Boarding school was the only escape from death by smothering. My brother wasn't so lucky. Still lives at home, poor sod, works in a building society and has three meals cooked for him.'

'But you got away.'

'Never to return.' He twisted a lock of her Pre-Raphaelite hair in his fingers. It almost hurt. 'I had an affair with the headmaster's wife. That sorted the school out. They didn't mind buggery but they drew the line at love.'

Rachel laughed, then stopped herself. There was no mistaking the pain and anger in his voice.

'And how about you, lovely Rachel? What is the story of your life?'

Rachel pulled herself out of his grip and climbed on to a stile. It was beginning to get dark and bone-achingly cold. 'What do you think?' she challenged, throwing her head back and narrowing her eyes provocatively. 'What's your stereotype of me?'

'Do you really want to hear this?' Marko crossed his arms and watched her, half smiling in an infuriating way.

'Why not? You could be as wrong about me as I was about you.'

'Right then. You're eighteen, more or less.

Bright. Overprotected. You've been dropped off and picked up everywhere since you were five in case the bogey man pulled you into the back of his car or ran you over. Your parents love you and they want you to do well. But you're also an investment, all that positive parental input, and they want results. Right now you're starting to terrify them because you're stunning and they think some man might corrupt you and take your mind off your work. They wish you were a little girl again. And they haven't got the faintest fucking idea you're here. Am I right?'

Rachel's shoulders caved in, giving her a temporary impression of defeated vulnerability. 'Am I that obvious?'

'No. I just know the type. Plus I did see the Volvo and imagined the rest.'

'You forgot a few things. They don't agree. Dad wants to give me more freedom than Mum. She's the one who doesn't trust me, and I don't really know why. I'm not dumb or weak or a slut. I haven't got anorexia, I don't drop E, partly because she's always there waiting outside for me. I feel like Cinderella having to leave the rave before I turn into a pumpkin. She tells me she just wants me to be happy but that's a load of bollocks. It's always *their* idea of what should make me happy.'

'Come here.'

Rachel found she was shaking a little. 'Maybe you'd better start deciding for yourself what it is that makes you happy.'

She smiled, feeling stronger, and wrapped herself in his arms. 'Do you know what? I think I already have.'

By the time they got back to the camp the darkness was solid and the ground so cold that Rachel could hardly feel her feet.

'Well, hello,' Zoe greeted them. 'If it isn't the babes in the wood.' She looked at Marko pointedly. 'I hope this fairy story is going to have a happy ending. Most of them don't, you know.'

Marko ignored her. 'Is there any scrumpy left in that flagon?'

He took a swig and offered it to Rachel. 'Some farmer left it for us. It's weird. In public they spit and take our photographs to intimidate us and then they leave us a jar of cider.'

Rachel gulped some of the strong liquid and felt its healing warmth running through her veins. Even sitting by the fire only your front seemed to warm up. A bitter north-east wind had blown up from the valley and stuck its icy fingers into any part of you it could find.

'By the way,' Zoe threw in casually, 'we got

a message from Road Rage. Alexander Bailey's agreed to join us. He's arriving in a few days.' She watched for his reaction, her lips curling slightly. 'So we should get some action soon.'

'Who asked Bailey to stick his nose in here?' Marko threw down the cider flagon petulantly. 'We don't need advice from some superannuated sixty-five-year-old.'

'A superannuated sixty-five-year-old who's stopped three motorways,' Zoe pointed out. 'Actually, I invited him. I think it's time things got moving. We're getting into distractions here.' She eyed Rachel evenly. 'All we're doing is reacting every time they send in the police or security guards. We need to take the initiative with the media. Do something. Think with our brains instead of other parts of our anatomy.'

'As a matter of fact I agree with you,' Marko flashed, his blue eyes narrowing into angry arrow-slits. 'It is time we got the attention of the media. So I've planned a little pixie mission.'

'When?' asked Macduff, suddenly looking enthusiastic.

'Next Friday.'

'Why don't we wait till Alexander gets here?' Zoe asked.

'We don't need Alexander bloody Bailey.

He's too old to go pixying anyway.'

Rachel felt entirely left behind. 'What is pixying?'

Marko patted her hand. 'Just a little gentle sabotage. Nothing too strenuous. You are going to join us, aren't you, Rachel?'

Rachel thought of her parents, her exams, and how bloody cold it was. 'Of course,' she said, realizing that none of those things mattered a shred.

Zoe simply raised an eyebrow and said absolutely nothing.

'I must go now,' Rachel announced, 'or I'll never find my way back.'

'I'll walk you till you get to the easy bit,' insisted Marko.

Macduff watched them go. 'Did they . . . you know . . . *do* anything,' he asked Zoe in a whisper, 'when they went off like that?'

'Nah,' Zoe replied without hesitating, trying to squash down her pain and jealousy and appear unmoved. 'Not yet. Or Marko wouldn't be behaving like Sir Fucking Galahad.'

Marko and Rachel were almost at her grandmother's door when he finally said goodbye. 'Are you sure you're OK for next Friday?'

Rachel nodded. 'I think so. I'll have a bit of

talking to do first. My parents and Gran and that.'

'I'm sure you're up to it. You're going to love it, you know. It'll be the most exciting thing you've ever done, believe me.'

'The pixying, you mean?' Rachel asked provocatively, hardly able to believe her own boldness. 'Or what comes afterwards?'

But Marko had already turned round and was walking swiftly up the hill.

4

'Did you have a nice time with your friends, dear?' Lavinia was standing waiting at her cottage door. 'Goodness me, you're perished. Where did you go, a point to point? I used to love point to points when I was young. But they always were too damn cold.' Luckily for Rachel, Lavinia had a habit of answering her own questions. 'I was beginning to get worried. Who was that with you? Surely you ought to ask them in for a moment? They'll think it's very bad manners, you know. People are more formal in the country.'

Rachel suppressed a smile. The idea of her grandmother proffering a small sherry and polite conversation to Marko on the subject of point to points was too good to be true.

'You're absolutely freezing,' clucked Lavinia, 'sit here by the fire.' She settled Rachel into her own chair next to the inglenook and handed her a small glass of slightly viscous dark red liquid. Rachel sipped it tentatively. It had the fresh taste of summer berries, sharp yet sweet.

'Sloe gin. I made it myself from the sloes down by the river,' Lavinia said proudly.

Marko had told her that they foraged for berries at the camp, and wild mushrooms. It had been a brilliant year for those, he'd said, from the brown woodland variety to huge round puffballs. The thought enchanted Rachel. The nearest she'd ever been to real nature was the organic counter at Sainsbury's. She pictured herself and Marko, up at dawn, hunting for mushrooms in the wood and frying them for breakfast. For some reason Zoe kept superimposing herself on the picture, kicking a fast-asleep Marko and waving her mushrooming bag at him while he turned over and went back to sleep.

Rachel sipped her sloe gin and reeled. God, no wonder old ladies in the country swigged this stuff. Guilt overtook her again at how kind her grandmother was being and the duplicitousness of persuading Lavinia to let her come again next weekend when she fully intended to go pixying with the rest of them. The thought of Marko and what might happen after overcame her better feelings. 'Gran, I was wondering. There's this great point to point next Saturday but my friends want to leave early. Could I come down on Friday night and stay with you again?' She was shocked at herself for her capacity to lie to her grandmother so barefacedly, but surely it was in a good cause?

Lavinia was delighted. Two weekends in a row. This would be one in the eye for Eunice, whose grandchildren only visited under duress. 'Of course. Which point to point is it? The Mitchell Muncaster?'

'I'm not quite sure,' Rachel floundered. 'That sounds familiar. I'm not very well up on horses yet.'

This was an understatement of titanic proportions since Rachel had only been riding once, took one look at all the neat, keen polished horsy little girls and never went again.

They tucked into home-made steak and kidney pudding and apple tart at the little table in front of the window, before Rachel, exhausted after her unaccustomed eight-mile tramp, went up to bed with a hot-water bottle and a dog-eared copy of Georgette Heyer. Marko, it seemed to her, had more than a passing resemblance to the dark, passionate, brooding hero of her particular favourite, *Devil's Cub*. She fell asleep blissfully recalling the moment when the handsome but ruthless Lord Vidal finally has the heroine in his power and announces, in a voice thick with desire, 'And now Miss Mary Challoner . . .'

On this satisfying thought, Rachel Hope, almost eighteen and hungry for dangerous experience, fell asleep dreaming of the sacrifices and deprivations ahead in the name of saving Gosse's Wood, and of one sacrifice in particular, which she had saved far longer than any of her friends, but which she was finally ready to make now that she'd met a worthy recipient.

Lavinia cleared up the things, humming to herself along with Classic FM. She had intended on insisting Rachel helped, she was sure the girl got away with murder at home, but Rachel's eyes were drooping and the elbow supporting her pretty face kept on falling off the table, so she sent her to bed. Away from the influences of London and her mother, the child really wasn't too bad. In fact tomorrow, providing Rachel had brought something halfway decent to wear, she would definitely take her to church and show her off.

To Lavinia's relief Rachel had a black velvet skirt with her and what it lacked in length it at least made up for in quality. With her hair brushed and her baggy jumper hidden under her parka she looked quite acceptable.

The church was already decorated for Christmas. Say what you would against the vicar, he certainly understood the marketing value of the season of goodwill. He wasn't having any of this high church No Finery Till Christmas Eve nonsense, and Rachel, after a rousing version of 'Hark the Herald Angels Sing', had a childish temptation to go and look at the Crib. Unfortunately, she caught the beady eye of Mrs Benson from the village shop, who was studying her thoughtfully.

Lavinia was thrilled to see her arrangement of Christmas roses and ivy had been kept in the star position on the stand at the top of the aisle, where she had modestly placed it, far overshadowing its garish rivals in taste and elegance.

Outside the church Lavinia introduced Rachel to the vicar and anyone else from the village who happened to be passing.

Mrs Benson, thatched cottage charms jingling away, had finally remembered where she'd seen Rachel before. 'Didn't you go off with that scruffy pair of road protesters?' she enquired.

'Oh no,' Rachel clutched her grandmother's arm and hauled her off, 'you must have been thinking of someone else.'

'Really,' Lavinia remarked to Rachel in a perfectly audible voice. 'That woman. Her husband's perfectly nice but she ought to learn the meaning of the word pushy.'

The other parishioners, overhearing this remark, thought to themselves that there would be no one better to teach her.

Lavinia, meanwhile, had spotted Colonel Lawley about to get into his ancient Bentley. 'Hang on a moment, Colonel, I wanted a word. When's your next meeting about the bypass?'

'Tuesday,' the Colonel admitted somewhat unwillingly. He knew Lavinia of old.

'What time?'

'Six p.m. at the Old Lodge.'

'I'll be there.'

'Jolly good.' The Colonel nodded glumly. 'Are you on foot? Want a lift to your cottage?'

'That's very kind of you, Colonel,' Lavinia accepted instantly.

Even though the muscles in the back of her legs still ached from yesterday, the last thing Rachel wanted to do was get into the car with the enemy and have to listen to more sounding off about long-haired yobbos. 'I'll walk, thanks, Gran. Blow the cobwebs away and work up an appetite.'

After lunch Lavinia took Rachel for a stroll by the river, then on to the station. 'Bye, darling, see you next weekend. I'm so pleased you want to visit.'

As the train passed close by Gosse's Wood, Rachel wondered what Marko and Zoe and Macduff were doing. Not having to bother with studying for A levels, that was for sure.

Reminding herself that it was only five more days until she would be seeing Marko again, Rachel took out her revision, but somehow today Georgette Heyer and *Devil's Cub* were far more tempting.

★ ★ ★

'Did you have a good time at Gran's?' Catherine asked when she met her off the train.

'Brilliant, thanks,' Rachel beamed, hugging her.

For about the tenth time in two days, Catherine had to resist pinching herself. What was Lavinia's secret and how could Catherine get hold of it for herself? With her Rachel was rude, elusive, contemptuous and intractable, and yet two days with Lavinia had transformed her into Pollyanna. It was an infuriating mystery.

'Can you hang on a moment while I pop in here?' Catherine indicated the vast station bookshop. She had caught sight of some practice exam papers and wanted to buy them for Bonnie. Rosemount's resources didn't run to that sort of thing and Bonnie would need to put in some hard work between now and the entrance exam to Wolsey in January.

'You really like Bonnie, don't you, Mum?' For once there was no trace of the almost sibling jealousy Rachel had sometimes shown towards Catherine's pupils.

Catherine shrugged. 'I suppose she reminds me of me when I was a child. No one gives a toss about Bonnie, the boys tease her for being fat, her dad discourages her, and she keeps on going despite everything. You have to admire that.'

'Unlike me who's had every advantage, you mean?'

Catherine's heart squeezed up with guilt. That hadn't been what she meant. Or had it?

'Fancy a Big Mac?' They were outside McDonald's, with its disgusting but comforting smell of frying fat.

'Why don't you just get me a Happy Meal? You preferred it when I was eight years old anyway and you could just choose everything for me. You just pretend I'm allowed to make choices.'

'Of course I don't. I encourage you to decide things for yourself. I even let you choose your own Nursery School.'

'Only because it was the one you wanted me to go to anyway.'

How had children got so infuriatingly acute? Catherine wondered, not feeling hungry any more.

'But if I really chose something important for myself — like not wanting to do my A levels — what would you do then?'

Catherine, as she so often did when confronted with an angry Rachel, felt a kind of defeated powerlessness. Where had they gone wrong? They had tried so hard to be understanding, not to lay down arbitrary rules, to make sure she could always talk to them and where had it bloody well got them? To the same war zone they'd had with their own parents. The only difference was that their children were openly rude and contemptuous.

'Rachel,' Catherine replied wearily, feeling cowardly and exhausted in equal measures, 'I don't want to talk about this. Get your exams over with and then make your own decisions. If you don't want to go to university, that's up to you. But at least get the qualifications.'

They drove on without another word. How had beaming, glowing Rachel transformed herself into silent, surly Rachel within seconds of being with her mother?

★ ★ ★

By the next morning Rachel had cheered up a bit, mainly distracted by the school trip that day, which would mean no work, a chance to spend her parents' money, bunk off to the shops and a trip in a coach.

'Rachel!' Catherine yelled up the stairs for the tenth time. 'You should be leaving and you haven't had breakfast yet.' Breakfast with Rachel was always a delicate issue. She never ate the same thing twice, thus outwitting any attempt by her mother at forward planning. Last week she had broken her own rules and had Greek yogurt with honey two days running. The third day Catherine had made the mistake of putting it out. 'Yuk!' Rachel announced. 'I loathe Greek yogurt. Isn't there any muesli?'

'But you loathe muesli!' yelped an exasperated Catherine, all too aware that Rachel ought to be out of the door by now.

'No, I don't,' Rachel persisted.

'Well, there isn't any.'

And then the *coup de grâce*. Rachel wasn't part of the anorexia generation for nothing. 'I won't have any breakfast then.'

'But you've got to have some breakfast!' Catherine's own stomach was by now churning so much with anger and exasperation that she wouldn't eat her own and would have to succumb to a Mars Bar at breaktime.

It was then she noticed that her daughter was still in her dressing gown. 'For God's sake, Rachel, why aren't you up?'

Rachel, infuriatingly casual, reached for the phone. 'I'll just phone Steph and find out what she's wearing.'

'What's wrong with your uniform?' screeched Catherine, watching the seconds slip by. It was her turn for early playground duty.

'We're allowed to wear our own clothes. Sugar! She's not in.'

'She's probably at school by now queuing up for the coach. What's wrong with your tracksuit?'

Rachel laughed witheringly. 'I can't wear that, it's gruesome.'

'Rachel . . . ' You heard plenty about baby battering but surely there must be thousands more cases of parents assaulting their teenagers . . . 'You're only going to the National Gallery.'

'Yes, but it's yards from Covent Garden. I might be spotted by a model agent scout on her lunchbreak. You read about it all the time.'

'RACHEL!! If you don't get dressed in five seconds I'll . . . ' Catherine mentally scrabbled around for an appropriate punishment, 'I'll . . . '

'Stop my pocket money? I am almost eighteen, you know. Besides you pay my allowance through banker's order.' Gauging that she'd probably gone far enough, Rachel skipped upstairs and down again in record-breaking time, tracksuit on and hair brushed.

Catherine was halfway out of the door when Ricky, who was dropped to school by his father, waylaid her. 'I don't suppose this is a good time to talk about my Christmas play costume.' Catherine's heart sank. Drama teachers were out-of-touch sadists who assumed all mothers could whip up a gorilla suit or a pirate's outfit in twenty-four hours flat. 'What is it this time?' Catherine asked wearily. 'No, don't tell me, Melchizedek dressed as a Rasta?' Ricky's school went in for imaginative costume design in their Christmas extravaganzas.

'No, Mum. That was last year,' Ricky replied patiently. 'This year I'm Michael Jackson.'

Even Christopher looked up from his copy of the *Guardian*. 'What does Michael Jackson have to do with Christmas?'

'He's the impresario who stages it all. We're doing the Nativity as if it were a musical and Michael Jackson is directing it.'

'Ah. That figures.' Catherine and Christopher exchanged glances.

'And now,' Catherine bellowed at Rachel, 'will you please get in the car!!!'

'Actually, Mum,' Rachel replied, disdainfully zipping up her parka, 'I'm ready before you are.'

Playground duty was its usual ghastly chaos of girls complaining about the boys footballing across their hopscotch pitch, fights, lost dinner money and snotty noses, but Bonnie's face when Catherine handed her the practice papers almost made up for the hideousness of what went before.

'You mean I can keep them and do them at home?' Bonnie asked, folding them to her chest like some beloved cuddly toy.

'Absolutely. And I'll mark them for you when you've done them.'

'Thanks, Mrs Hope,' the sun glinted on Bonnie's thick smeary specs and there was a tiny break in her voice.

'Come on, don't cry.' She hugged Bonnie to her, remembering her own teacher who, while measuring the pupils' vital statistics for some stupid project, had called out their measurements in front of everyone. Her own had been 32, 32, 32 and Mrs Fry had yelled out, 'Catherine Wasdale. You're positively tubular!' The entire class had collapsed with laughter and Catherine had been called the Tube ever afterwards. Catherine had never understood how a teacher could be so unthinkingly cruel. 'You're going to do brilliantly and get into Wolsey with flying colours.'

'Your daughter goes there, doesn't she, Mrs Hope?' Bonnie asked, not noticing Catherine's change of expression. 'Do you think she'd show me round? That is, if I get an interview.'

'I'm sure she'd be delighted.'

That is, Catherine sighed to herself, if she's still there.

'Can I go and put these in my bag, Mrs Hope?'

'Of course you can, Bonnie,' Catherine replied, remembering she had to rush to the Stock Cupboard before her next lesson.

On the way she bumped into Disappearing Dave, the school keeper, named for the obvious reason that he was never there when you needed him.

'I just wondered if you knew, Mrs Hope,' Dave asked suspiciously, 'that two Year Sixes were listening outside the door. They just ran off sniggering and looking guilty.'

'Thanks, Dave,' Catherine wondered which two of the wide selection of potential eavesdroppers had witnessed her giving Bonnie the papers. She had a damn good idea.

The rest of the day went surprisingly well. All the same, when it was home time

Catherine made a point of following her class into the cloakroom. Everything seemed unusually calm, always a bad sign. 'I'm watching you lot,' she said in a measured, even voice with just a hint of chill in it. 'If there's any suggestion of bullying I want anyone who sees to come and tell me. We've talked about this and you agreed. You have to all watch out for each other because, remember, it could be you next.'

Catherine saw one or two of the smaller ones look at each other shiftily. The trouble with bullying was that you could control it inside school but most of it took place outside.

Bonnie was the last to leave. Catherine saw her eyes mist up under the thick glasses. Poor Bonnie. She was so different from the others. It wasn't just that she was clever, which was often provocation enough in a tough school, but she always looked so different. While they had Nike trainers, Bonnie's would be from a market stall, her tracksuits weren't Adidas, hers came from some sweatshop in the Pacific Rim which always seemed to get the slogan slightly wrong. From May to September Bonnie's jog top had sported 'Save the Wales' in what seemed a doomed and ill-timed reference to the royal marriage, and her winter one said 'Global Warning' when,

Catherine suspected, it was referring to the depletion of the ozone layer.

'Don't let them get to you,' Catherine whispered in a highly un-PC manner, 'they'll end up working in McDonald's when you've got your own computer company.'

'Thanks, Mrs Hope,' mumbled Bonnie. And then, taking a huge breath as if she were setting out up Everest, she ran across the playground, past the toilets where the bully boys sometimes lurked, and out into the street.

She ran most of the way, an incredible feat for one so rotund and unfit, only slowing down to cross the major road, not five minutes from her home. She'd almost done it.

'Here, fatso,' said a voice behind her, 'what have you got in here, then?' Gary Webb grabbed her backpack and turned it out on the pavement, pouncing on the examination papers and waving them triumphantly in the air.

'Please,' begged Bonnie, fear making her short of breath so she seemed even more pathetic than usual, 'don't take those. I'll give you my dinner money tomorrow.'

'All week?'

Bonnie thought of an entire week without dinner and nodded miserably.

'Nah,' said the boy, 'if you want it so much you can walk along that wall for it.' He indicated a nearby wall with glass along the top.

'I couldn't get up there.'

'We'll help yer then.' They descended on her and pushed her upwards on to the wall. 'You ought to go on a diet, Bon. What would you want with dinner money anyway?'

Terrified, Bonnie began to negotiate her way along the high wall, gingerly stepping between the pieces of glass embedded in the top.

Finally she made it to the end and tried to climb down. One of the boys appeared to be going to help. Instead he pulled down her jogging pants, exposing her white behind to the traffic ahead. 'Can I have my papers back?' Bonnie begged miserably, fighting back her tears and trying to pull up her trousers.

'Here you are, then.' He threw them over his head so that the papers fanned out in a perfect arc and landed across all three lanes.

Crying openly now, Bonnie dashed into the road, hardly noticing the aggressive stream of home-going motorists, and gathered them all up.

★ ★ ★

Lavinia listened to the arguments batted backwards and forwards by the group of middle-aged and elderly men and women assembled at Colonel Lawley's house with growing impatience. They sounded, even to Lavinia who was on their side, as fusty and dusty as the faded chintz they were sitting on.

In the end it was too much for her. 'Look here, everyone,' Lavinia put down her china cup of Earl Grey for emphasis, trying to avoid one of the white lace doilies which seemed to cover every surface. There were even lace antimacassars on the chairs, something Lavinia hadn't seen for twenty years. 'If we want to save Maxted High Street from choking itself to death and get that bypass built we're going to have to sharpen up our arguments.' Twenty or so mildly outraged faces turned in Lavinia's direction. 'I've heard these anti-road protesters on the television and they're good. They always sound as if they want to save the planet. Whereas we sound like a bunch of stuffy Not In My Back Yarders whingeing because we can't park outside Boots.'

'Mrs Hope,' reminded the Colonel tetchily, 'you are supposed to direct your comments through the Chairman.'

'Sorry, Chairman,' Lavinia sounded distinctly unapologetic.

'What do you suggest we should be arguing then, Mrs Hope?' enquired Mrs Benson from the shop, the sun glinting through dusty windows on to her enormous brass earrings.

'That I can't answer. But the other side use experts to argue their case. We need facts and figures. We need to sound more authoritative or we end up just sounding selfish.'

'What a wonderful idea,' seconded Eunice, who was passing round the Rich Tea biscuits. The cut-price ones from the Co-op, Lavinia noted.

'If you're so keen, Lavinia,' suggested Colonel Lawley, 'why don't you see what you can dig up? We need to be ready for the press onslaught. These protesters could act any time and we don't want to be caught sitting on our shields, do we?'

'No, Colonel, indeed we don't. A very uncomfortable place to be seated, I'm sure.'

'You are clever, Lavinia,' marvelled Eunice as the meeting broke up.

'Or extremely stupid. I seem to have just landed myself with a lot of work.'

'Go on, Lavinia, you love it.'

After the meeting Eunice and Lavinia briefly lunched at the Copper Kettle, one of Maxted's many tea rooms. Sometimes it seemed to Lavinia that tea rooms were Maxted's only industry. Refreshed by a lively

Welsh Rarebit, Lavinia declared herself, in Colonel Lawley's parlance, ready for the fray.

Maxted Library was at the far end of the High Street. It was small and crowded since, to the locals' outrage, it opened only twice a week due to cutbacks. Today, fortunately for Lavinia and for the council who would have received an excoriating letter of complaint from her had it been closed, it was open.

The Fiction section, Lavinia's natural home, had been squeezed by demand for large-print books for the short-sighted and, to her horror, by an ever-increasing amount of space being devoted to Video and CDs. People wanted things so easy nowadays. They just couldn't make the effort to use their imaginations.

The Reference section was upstairs. It tended to be used by Maxted's few unemployed, to look through the job pages of the newspapers, a few students from the local Tech and the odd child with a school project on the feudal system or Henry VIII's wives. Today it was also occupied by someone she'd never seen before in Maxted. Lavinia stole a glance at him, intrigued.

He was an exceptionally tall man with white hair, slightly too long for Lavinia's taste, he ought to know better at his age, and he seemed to be crammed under the table at a distinctly uncomfortable angle, like an adult forced to sit at a child's desk. In front of him was a box file and a heap of copies of the local paper. Lavinia was about to ring the bell on the receptionist's desk when some instinct told her to glance at him again.

He looked up then and she saw that his white hair stood up at each side like two little horns. The face was thin and bony with a hooked nose and deep grey eyes. He was smiling in wry amusement at something he'd just read, giving him the air of an ascetic saint taking a weekend break in the fleshpots of sin.

As she studied him an icy wind of shock blew through Lavinia. She had to hold on to the desk to steady herself. It couldn't be. Not here. Not after all these years.

He looked briefly in her direction and Lavinia, who prided herself on never fleeing from anything, turned and half-ran down the stairs to the main entrance. She scuttled into the Ladies and sat helplessly down in one of the stalls. She must have made a mistake. What would Alexander Bailey be doing here in Maxted, sitting in the Reference section of her own public library?

But she knew it was him. No one else on earth looked like Alexander Bailey or ever had. Alex Bailey, outrageous charmer and left-wing firebrand, the cleverest man she'd ever met. And, for a few short months when she was twenty years old, the man she thought she was desperately in love with.

5

It had been impossible, of course. Though they were both studying at Oxford University, he at Ruskin College, where trade unionists were sponsored to get a university education, and she at select Lady Margaret Hall, they were still worlds apart. But for a brief moment it had seemed possible when Lavinia, carried along by the beauty of his rhetoric and the passion of his commitment to changing society, found herself deeply in love.

But that was in the fifties, and nice girls didn't marry left-wing firebrands with no money. Not unless they were a lot more unconventional than Lavinia.

She closed her eyes and pictured the summer's day more than forty years ago, when she had last seen Alexander. It was early evening and they had had a glorious afternoon on the river. The sun had shone palely, and the light had a magical opalescent quality about it she had never seen before. Remember this moment, Alexander had murmured, I don't think I could be happier than this. Peace and silence had cocooned them in their private world.

And then she had broken the news. That she was leaving university and getting married to Robert, the sane and steady lawyer who had been quietly courting her all along.

Alexander had been angrier than anyone she had seen in her whole life. He had bellowed that she was wasting her talents, that she would become a suburban housewife and never use a brain cell again, that she owed it to society to put her education to proper use.

Lavinia had listened and had put up no proper arguments. From where she stood there were none. Because the one thing she hadn't told Alexander was that she was pregnant.

In the fifties an unmarried pregnant girl, as Lavinia knew too well, could face a life of disgrace and disapproval or choose a useful life married to someone who could make a home for her and her baby. Someone who would put bread not words, no matter how beautiful, on the table.

Lavinia had chosen safety and Robert, left Oxford after her first year and never seen Alexander since. With her husband's happy collusion she had never admitted to even going there, saw none of her friends from that era, though there were few enough anyway because she had been so wrapped up in Alexander.

Had she done the right thing all those years ago? How different her life would have been with Alexander. Alexander had challenged where Robert conformed. Alexander had wanted to see the world, while Robert had wanted to dig himself in. Robert had been a man of habit, and their life had settled into a comfortable predictability. They had lived in the same house, here in Maxted, all their married life, eaten the same food at the same time each day, and shared the same values. Or had they? Had Lavinia simply adopted Robert's way of thinking for ease's sake and, being Lavinia, lived by it with great efficiency?

Lavinia steeled herself. She couldn't run away. She had to go up there and face her past. After all, they were both old now, what more harm could love or hate do either of them?

She fished in her bag for a hairbrush and tugged it through her wiry grey hair. Lavinia wasn't one for makeup but she dabbed on some powder anyway. There was an ancient lipstick in the depths of her bag, unused for months. Was she that pathetic? Lavinia asked herself, and decided she was. There's no fool like an old fool, she told her reflection and strode upstairs.

Her disappointment when she saw the empty table was almost physical, as if she'd been kicked in the pit of her stomach. She searched behind the stacks, then hunted in the main library, but there was no sign of him. She walked swiftly out into the street, resisting the desire to run. Alexander Bailey had disappeared. It was as if he had vanished from her life as completely as he had forty years ago. Perhaps this was her punishment.

Don't be such a stupid old woman, she told herself. If you had so little in common then, life spent together would probably have made it worse. At least you have your illusions. You don't have to hear that he has a fat wife in Basingstoke or a brood of grey-eyed grandchildren.

Lavinia forced herself back upstairs. She wasn't giving up on her task just because of an emotional upset, no matter how earth-shattering. She resisted the desire to sit in the seat Alexander had just vacated and asked the librarian for anything she could find on the Maxted bypass. 'Cuttings, newspaper articles, public documents, anything you've got.'

'How funny,' smiled the librarian, reaching below the counter, 'that's exactly what the last gentleman asked for.'

Lavinia started. 'Did he say why?'

'No. Just that he was interested in the bypass.'

Lavinia sat down with the box Alexander had just handed back. She started with the dry-as-dust public consultation document. Really, these civil servants ought to be taught plain English. She pored over the maps of proposed routes, sifted through the evidence given by all the interest groups and individuals for and against the proposed route through the wood, and finally reached the newspaper cuttings. At least these were a lot livelier. The last one in the pile seemed to be about a different road scheme altogether, at somewhere called Yelton Common. Here road protesters had built tunnels, climbed trees, fought hand to hand with police and bailiffs and had finally defeated the plan altogether. An irate local businessman was quoted. He blamed the collapse of the road scheme on one man, he said, and one man alone. Alexander Bailey. There was a large picture of Alexander, captioned 'The Guru of the Green Warriors'.

Lavinia's hand crept to her neck. Not only was Alexander famous in this alien world of road protesting. They were on opposite sides of the bitter divide.

By now the library was almost empty and

Lavinia did something she had never done before, and of which she would certainly have disapproved in someone else.

She slipped the article about Alexander into her handbag and snapped it shut. It was, she assured herself, for research purposes only.

Once she was back home she took out the picture and looked at it again.

She was due to go and report on her findings at Wednesday's committee meeting. From the cuttings she'd read, Alexander seemed to have a talent for publicity. He understood the kind of events the media liked to cover. But why should the devil have all the best lines? It seemed to Lavinia that it was high time their side courted a bit of media attention too. And she had to admit, the possibility of bumping into Alexander gave it a wonderful new piquancy.

★   ★   ★

Catherine was deeply grateful that this was the last full week of term. Next week it was the Infants' Nativity Play, the Carol Concert and the Christmas Bazaar so there wasn't a hope of getting any work done. The most challenging thing Year Six were up to by this stage of the term was making their own

Christmas cards and putting an armlock on their parents to dig out gifts for the tombola stall. In her eight years at Rosemount she'd come to recognize some of the tombola gifts as if they were old friends. Catherine could swear she'd seen the silver-plated After Eights trolley and a green plastic foot spa on at least three different Christmases. Sometimes the parents hadn't even removed the tombola ticket attached to it from last time. Catherine was the dummy who was organizing it this year, so the classroom was already filling up with jars of chutney, ancient bottles of Blue Nun, packets of bath salts (who used bath salts any more?) and a three-year-old flagon of Old Spice aftershave. Lucky winners.

She was just sorting it out when Bonnie tore into the classroom and shut the door.

'Everything all right?' Catherine asked. 'You shouldn't really be in here during playtime, Bonnie.'

Bonnie threw her a look of panicky desperation.

'What's the matter? Is someone bullying you?'

Bonnie shook her head vehemently.

'How are the test papers? Anything ready for me to mark yet?'

Bonnie's expression changed. 'Not yet. I'll try and do one tonight.'

'Good girl. Tell you what, why don't you be my tombola monitor? You could make a list of all these lovely prizes here.'

Bonnie looked so touchingly grateful that Catherine wanted to hug her. There was definitely something going on. She would have to keep an eye out and just be grateful there was only another week of term left.

At the end of the day, Bonnie was the last to go, fussing about with the tombola gifts until the cloakroom was almost empty. Catherine was about to go home too, and do her marking and preparation for tomorrow's classes, when Brian Wickes put his head round her door. 'Still here?' he asked, somehow making her presence sound inefficient rather than dedicated.

At the sight of Brian, Bonnie scuttled off. 'She's here late,' Brian remarked.

'I think she's hanging on deliberately because she's frightened of something. I suspect she's being bullied.'

'It wouldn't be surprising, would it? She's fat and she doesn't mix.'

'And that makes it all right to bully her?' Catherine returned. 'Anyway, she's desperate to mix. I've seen her put up with having bags hung round her neck like a coat stand. Once she let the older ones pretend she was their dog and pull her round the playground until

117

her knees were scraped raw. I had to go and stop them, yet Bonnie never breathed a word of complaint. It was heartbreaking.'

'Have you ever considered, Catherine, that you may actually make it worse for her? To be frank, I don't think you've helped that child by making her your teacher's pet. They all know Mrs Hope likes her because she's so clever and they just take it out on her.'

Catherine was cut to the quick. 'Brian, that's not fair. I help her because she's got potential.'

'And they dislike her for the same reasons.'

'So what am I supposed to do? Encourage her to be dumb just so that she'll be accepted?' Catherine felt her temper rising. 'We would really be helping her then, wouldn't we? It's us who're failing *her*, Brian. We've got to root out this bullying.'

'Then perhaps, instead of blaming the school, you should stop singling her out for attention.'

Catherine was still shaking with anger when she got home to find a fresh pot of tea on the kitchen table and a packet of chocolate Hobnobs laid out daintily on a plate. 'Are we expecting company?' Catherine wondered if Rachel had asked a boyfriend round. She would never go to this much trouble for Steph or one of her female mates.

'Actually, it's for you.'

'For *me*?' Catherine asked incredulously. 'What have I done to deserve all this?'

'Just for being you. I know the end of term's exhausting.'

'OK, how much do you want?'

Rachel looked wronged. 'God, you really don't think much of me, do you?'

Catherine swore mentally.

'Actually, there is something . . .'

'OK,' Catherine teased, relieved that she hadn't totally misjudged her daughter.

'I wondered if you'd mind me going to Gran's again this weekend.'

'Good God. What is Gran's magical secret? Does she slip Ecstasy into your Coco Pops or ply you with CDs of Oasis? Don't tell me, she's got a handsome young gardener who quotes poetry and wants to save the planet?'

At this Rachel flushed unexpectedly. 'For God's sake, Mum. I'm not boy mad, you know.'

This was no understatement. Although she struck her mother as entirely gorgeous, Rachel had shown little interest in the opposite sex and ranged round in big gangs of girls. The balance seemed to have swung to the opposite extreme from Catherine's own boy-obsessed youth, when every spotty youth's word or gesture was analysed for hours. Catherine actually felt quite sorry for any boys who dared approach Rachel's friends. Even Christopher was quite scared of them.

'Of course you can go. Do you want me to phone her?'

'It's OK,' Rachel said quickly. 'I'll do it.'

'Give her my love then.' Catherine tucked into a Hobnob. There was no point voicing her astonishment at Rachel's granny-conversion to her husband. He would just accuse her of seeing the cloud behind every silver lining.

Upstairs in the privacy of her room Rachel rang the mobile number Marko had given her. 'It's all right,' she said softly. 'I can come.'

'I'll live for the moment,' he whispered. 'See you on Friday.'

Rachel lay back on the narrow girly bed under her home-made canopy with the Forever Friends teddy bear duvet she'd had since she was thirteen, and closed her eyes. She imagined Marko standing over her, a look of unquenchable desire in his wild blue eyes. A shiver of pure anticipation ran through her. She was glad she had resisted the furtive fumblings of the boys from the local school and those she'd met on holiday. Marko was worth waiting for.

'Not charging your personal calls to the campaign, I hope, Marko?'

Marko jumped. He had thought that in the middle of a wood five miles from civilization you might at least expect some privacy. 'Of course not,' he snapped, furious with Zoe for inviting Alexander to their camp. There were plenty of other camps he could have interfered in.

Zoe stirred the casserole she'd been cooking on the fire in a blackened pot. 'You'll have something to eat, Alexander?'

Alexander smiled. 'I certainly will. It smells wonderful. What have you put in it?'

'Just chicken and vegetables. Macduff wants us to eat rabbit but I won't let him. I've got to know all the animals round here. They're incredibly tame now they've got used to us. Even the badgers don't run away. Eating one of the rabbits would be like tucking into a family member.'

'Come on, Zo,' Marko said, ruffling her short blond hair teasingly. 'You make it sound as though they wear little blue jackets and answer to the name of Peter.'

'You know I don't mean it like that, it's just that, living here, right in the middle of somewhere wild, you start to feel part of it.

121

That's why I'm so passionate about this place, I suppose.' The sharpness in her voice and the way she ducked when Marko stroked her hair intrigued Alexander. Clearly there was or had been something between them. She pulled her coat tighter round her and served the stew. 'That's why I couldn't bear them to chop it all down.'

'But you come from Swindon,' Marko pointed out.

'It doesn't matter where I come from,' Zoe snapped. 'This is my home now.'

'Where do you come from, Marko?' Alexander asked quietly. 'Apart from here, of course.'

There was a long pause. 'Pinner,' Marko admitted finally.

'Pinner!' derided Zoe, almost falling off her upturned log. 'You can't get deeper into suburbia than Pinner! Swindon's cosmopolitan compared to that.'

'Yeah, well, I haven't lived there for a long time. It was all right when I was a kid but now it's full of the bleeding middle class.'

'And you don't like the middle class, do you, Marko?' Alexander said softly. He took a plate of stew from Zoe. 'Zoe here says you're off pixying tomorrow.'

Marko looked daggers at Zoe.

'Where to, exactly?'

'The contractors' compound the other side of Maxted. They've started keeping their bulldozers there.'

'You don't think that's a bit pointless? We don't even know when they're coming here.'

'They won't be able to come at all if their bulldozers are fucked, will they?'

'But what if they've got time to get them mended? And you all end up getting arrested for nothing?'

'We won't be arrested.'

'I think it's a pointless exercise, and too risky. Why don't you wait till we know more about when they're arriving here?'

Marko stood up and kicked a pile of leaves towards the fire. 'It's all set up.'

'He means he's invited his new disciple,' Zoe pointed out rudely. 'And she's gorgeous and sweet eighteen and impressionable.'

Alexander said nothing.

Marko stamped his feet on the icy pallets they used for flooring to keep out the worst of the damp. 'It's going to be bloody cold tonight. I'm going to bed.'

'Don't worry, Marko,' Zoe poured out a cup of tea, 'tomorrow night you'll have your love to keep you warm.'

After he'd disappeared into his tent, the other three sat talking and listening to the sounds of the night. It had taken Alexander a while to get used to real silence when he'd started his campaigns; now he knew every sound. 'What motivates our Marko, do you think?' Alexander asked softly.

'Apart from sex?' Zoe laughed. 'He's genuine enough. He hates the car culture as much as I do. Sometimes I think he's a bit lost. His mum beggared herself sending him to this posh school but he never felt he fitted in. But he doesn't fit in at home either. Or with his family. I think he's happiest here. All this can become a way of life, you know, away from the nasty competitiveness of society and earning a living.'

'He seems to me to have some grudge against the middle class.'

'Marko likes to see himself as a Working-Class Hero.' She giggled. 'Despite coming from Pinner.'

'I hope this girl isn't part of it. She sounds a bit young and vulnerable to me.'

Zoe laughed again. 'I wouldn't be too sure about that. I'm not a bad judge of character and I think this one's got her head screwed on. She knows what she wants from Marko and he's only too happy to give it. She'll be running rings round him in no time. I almost feel sorry for him already.'

'I hope you're right.'

Zoe kicked over the last traces of the fire.

124

They had almost forgotten Macduff was there until he said goodnight.

'You seem to understand a lot, Zoe,' Alexander said quietly. The young woman impressed him. She could only be about twenty-one and yet there was a quiet strength about her; he doubted if anyone else's opinion swayed her much. She was one of those people who operated by instinct and despised intellectual rationalization. She looked to Alexander as if she had come face to face with disappointment and hadn't allowed it to make her bitter. He envied her the quality.

'Do I? I'd never thought of myself like that. Thanks.'

A moment of silence fell between them, like a screen that could be pulled either up or down. 'Are you planning to stay here tonight?' Zoe asked opaquely, trying to disguise the attraction she was beginning to feel for him even though they'd only just met and he was so much older. She had heard so much about him by reputation, of course, and it was all true. Alexander Bailey was an impressive character.

'No, Zoe, I'm not.' Alexander touched her face with a gentle finger. 'I'm renting a cottage a mile over the hill. Besides,' he added, returning her smile, 'there's probably forty years between us. Thank you for the offer, though, if that's what it was. I'm very flattered.'

She watched as he pulled himself a little stiffly to his feet. For a man of sixty-five he had extraordinary presence. Forty years ago he must have been irresistible.

'Isn't that rather a conventional view?' she challenged, surprised at her own persistence. 'I thought you were the master of the unconventional.'

'Perhaps you're right. But I always find old men with lovely young women rather a sad sight. Goodnight, Zoe, and good luck with the pixying.'

She waved, a small touching figure with her aggressively blond hair and her row of earrings and her spiky manner. After he'd gone she sat in the cold night listening to the silence she loved so much, thinking about Alexander and about how it took a special kind of man to turn you down without making you feel bad.

★   ★   ★

Bonnie Miles sat up in bed and nearly cried out. She'd had the dream again. The one where Gary and the others chased her, but this time they caught her, and instead of just stealing her papers or pulling down her trousers, they started kicking her. At first some of the smaller ones didn't want to join in but Gary made them. By the end they were all doing it. And the most terrifying thing was that a look of pure pleasure lit up their faces.

Bonnie wept into the pillow. She had cried so much lately that the foam of her pillow had started to bunch up into lumps, and both sides were continually damp. At least her dad couldn't hear her. He was on the floor above. She wondered for a miserable moment where her mum had got to. Her dad didn't even like talking about it and every time she raised the subject he disappeared downstairs into the shop. She'd thought of asking her older brother or sister but she rarely saw them these days. The only person who seemed to care about her was Mrs Hope, but even she couldn't stop the bullying.

She sat up in bed and reached for her precious pack of exam papers. Going to Wolsey would get her away from Gary and the others. But it wouldn't be for another six months. Could she stand it that long? She wondered whether it was worth telling her dad, but he never got involved at school. He didn't even go to parents' evenings because he said he couldn't afford to pay someone to mind the shop now that Mum was gone. He wasn't the kind of dad who would go and sort out Gary's dad or storm into school like something out of a film. He'd probably tell her to toughen up and forget about it, that people like them always got bullied.

In the cold light of the early morning, Bonnie longed for the feel of her mother's arms. It had been her mum who always said that the Almighty might not have given her beauty, but he'd given her brains, and by God she should use them to get away from here. But it also had been her mother who had gone away and left her to fend for herself.

For the first time Bonnie felt her nerve melting away. Maybe she should just give in and drop the idea of going to Wolsey. Her dad didn't really want her to and maybe Gary and the rest would lay off her then. She had almost come to her decision when she pictured the kind, encouraging face of Mrs Hope. Mrs Hope was the one person who did believe in her. How could she tell her she'd changed her mind?

Bonnie curled herself into a ball of loneliness, clutching her sodden pillow to her plump chest. Maybe, the thought splintered terrifyingly into the darkest corners of her mind, Gary and the rest were right, she would be better off dead. Then she wouldn't be letting anyone down.

*   *   *

'Ladies and gentlemen.' Colonel Lawley and the rest of the Pro-Bypass Committee had hardly settled themselves with their minuscule glasses of dry sherry before Lavinia had jumped to her feet. 'I have a proposal to put to you. I'm sure, like me, you are fed up with seeing the anti-road lobby get all the attention. They're the ones who get interviewed on television and in the proper papers, and our case never gets heard. And there's one good reason. We're too nice. We have our committee meetings and our tea and scones and we all agree amongst ourselves that we've got to save Maxted, and then we go home and watch these grungies and so-called eco-warriors on the television again saying we're selfish and narrow-minded.'

Looking round the audience, it struck Lavinia that the eco-warriors might have a point. The tea and scones and the glasses of sherry were probably the real reason half of them turned up anyway. But surely that was because so little was expected of them. Demand something more, a bit of Dunkirk spirit, and they might rival the other side in radicalism.

'So,' she continued, 'my proposal is this. It's our turn to grab the limelight. We need to

129

show the world just how congested it is in Maxted. You have to have drama for the media and that's exactly what we'll give them. Next Saturday afternoon, when it's nice and busy with Christmas traffic, we'll stage a sit-in on the zebra crossing outside Boots. It'll all be very genteel, just some sane and sensible citizens making their point. What do you think?'

Colonel Lawley and his wife looked at Lavinia as if she'd just suggested they parade naked at the village fête.

'I think it's a terrific idea,' piped up Eunice.

'So do I,' added Mrs Winton-Jones, the retired doctor's wife. 'Why should those louts always hog the limelight?'

'I've never been on television,' Eunice confided.

'But how could you be sure we would be on television?' enquired the Misses Smith, who'd lived in the almshouses for sixty years and seen their street change from a quiet lane to a noisy thoroughfare.

'Exactly,' reiterated Colonel Lawley, not liking the way the mood of the meeting was leaning.

'I can be pretty persistent.' Several of Lavinia's bridge companions nodded at this. 'I think if I try hard enough I can get the cameras to come down, don't you worry. Shall we take a vote on it, Colonel?'

Just over half the hands were raised in approval of Lavinia's scheme.

'Damn crazy idea if you ask me,' the Colonel muttered to his wife.

'Oh, no, Colonel,' Eunice breathed. 'It'll be terribly exciting. Like being on the oldies section of *Blind Date*.'

★ ★ ★

It should all work out fine, Rachel told herself. It was risky telling her parents that she would be at Gran's from Friday night and telling Lavinia herself that she wouldn't be arriving till Saturday morning, but unless Gran happened to ring them, or her parents suddenly decided to call her there, it should be OK. As a matter of fact, Rachel told herself, she didn't really care. What could they do anyway? She would be with Marko in Gosse's Wood and they'd have absolutely no idea of their whereabouts. A slight murmur of guilt disturbed her confidence. What if they thought she'd been kidnapped or gone missing and called the police? If they did get into a real panic, she could tell her best friend Steph she was allowed to admit the truth about where Rachel really was. Sod it, no.

She was nearly eighteen and it was time they trusted her. Even if she didn't deserve it.

'Aren't you scared?' Steph whispered during the double European History period they all loathed so much on Friday afternoons.

'A bit,' Rachel conceded. 'But the thought of seeing Marko makes it worth it.'

'But isn't he part of the scary bit? I mean if you really are going to, you know . . . '

Steph was still amazed not so much that her friend had so determinedly chosen the moment of her defloration, but that she hadn't done it before. Nearly everyone else in their class had been at it since sixteen. 'I know,' Steph had once suggested as a joke during break, 'why don't we do a graph on the average age everyone in the class lost their virginity? That would make Personal Health and Hygiene worth turning up for.'

Rachel shushed her. Knowing Steph, she probably meant it.

'Tell you what,' Rachel promised, 'I'll give you an update on Monday.'

'Can't wait that long. I want blow job by blow job coverage a lot sooner than that.'

'Fine,' Rachel said drily. 'I'll call you from Marko's mobile as soon as he climbs off, shall I?'

Stephanie giggled. 'Just don't do it up a

tree. You might fall out and get traumatized for life.'

'I'll try to remember that.'

It was nearly seven before she finally got out of the house. 'Bye, darling,' she allowed her mother to kiss her goodbye for once. 'You look well wrapped up.'

'Yes,' Rachel hopped from one booted foot to the other, 'you know me. I'd feel cold in Jamaica. And Maxted can be pretty arctic.'

'Love to Gran, and ask her what she wants for Christmas, will you?'

'Sure. And don't phone tonight if you can help it. Gran said something about an early night. She's got some big do on tomorrow.'

Half of this was true, Rachel told herself. The other half might be a lie, but what were you supposed to do when parents always wanted to stop you from starting out on life and having a few adventures of your own?

★ ★ ★

'Is Alexander coming with us?' Marko asked Zoe as they sat round the blazing camp fire. For once he had been out and gathered a great pile of wood and kindling. It had to be in honour of Rachel, Zoe concluded, since he usually let someone else do the work. He had even bought a bottle of cheap cider and mulled it.

'No. He doesn't approve.'

'Zo.' Marko stirred the fire with a stick and the sudden leap of flame threw dark hollows on to his handsome face. 'You don't mind, do you?'

'About what?' She knew perfectly well but wasn't going to make it easy for him.

'You know, Rachel coming along.'

Zoe took the stick from him and poked harder at the fire. She had been about to make some smart remark about making sure Rachel was over age, but Marko actually seemed rather nervous.

'Are you worried about getting arrested?'

'No, not that . . . it's just that . . . Rachel's so young and pretty . . . and I don't think she's ever . . . '

'Shit, Marko,' Zoe laughed, but there was affection in her voice, 'you've got a conscience. Who would have thought it?'

Marko laughed too, reminding Zoe why, apart from his Brontë-esque good looks, she'd liked him in the first place. Underneath all his defences he was quite scared.

'If it's any consolation, I think Miss Rachel Hope knows exactly what she's doing. She probably sees sleeping with you rather like passing her exams. And I'm sure she'll want to get an A in it. Lucky you.'

'Hang on,' Marko looked even more nervous, 'I'm not sure I like the sound of this.'

'Don't worry. I'm sure she'll be gentle with you.'

They were interrupted by the arrival of Macduff jubilantly brandishing a set of wire cutters. 'I borrowed them from Road Rage. They want them back tomorrow.'

'Have some cider,' Marko offered. 'You've certainly entered into the spirit of things.' Macduff always wore camouflage fatigues but tonight he'd actually smeared his face with grease and disguised his thatch of red hair under a woollen hat. Yet, somehow, instead of looking threatening, he reminded Marko of a blacked-up Big Ears.

It was almost nine and so cold even Marko, normally casually dismissive about the temperature, had resorted to wearing shooting socks inside his boots by the time Rachel finally found her way to the camp.

'Rachel!' Marko's voice was all tender concern. 'I thought you were going to call me from the station. I'd have come and got you in Macduff's van.'

'It's OK. I needed to get used to the cold. I don't want to let you all down by crying wimp, do I?'

Rachel looked appropriately wrapped up in her parka, with a scarf tied round her neck and her long red hair tucked inside a woollen cloche hat. Even so her nose and cheeks were red with cold and a small drip of liquid hung from the end of her nose.

'Very Julia Roberts,' commented Marko, wiping it away for her.

Rachel wrinkled her nose. 'Too girly. I'd rather be someone tougher. Demi Moore maybe.'

'You're much better looking.'

'OK,' Zoe announced, muffling herself up in a Yasser Arafat shawl, 'if you two lovebirds could postpone the compliments till later, then a-pixying we should go.'

They drove down a farm track in Macduff's ancient van, which rattled terminally every time they went over another bump. Macduff, always the silent type, concentrated on driving without lights. Suddenly he swerved, almost throwing them all off the front seat.

'Rabbit,' he explained.

'For God's sake, Macduff,' Marko pointed out, 'you're supposed to be the tough para type.'

'You wouldn't hurt a fly, would you, Macduff?' Zoe asked.

'Only if it wanted to build a road through this wood.'

The last couple of miles were on foot, tramping across ploughed fields, which reminded Rachel of the carol about the deep midwinter when the ground was hard as iron. They'd probably be singing that in assembly next week. The thought of the two dissonant images, schoolgirl and saboteur, gave her a jolt of pleasure which almost, but not quite, took her mind off how cold her feet were. A freezing mist lay on the land which seemed to penetrate even where there were no gaps in her clothing. It was physically painful, like having a stitch in your chest.

'This is nothing,' teased Macduff, reading her thoughts. 'At two or three in the morning it really gets nippy.'

'He should know,' Marko poked him affectionately, 'the mad bastard doesn't even use a sleeping bag.'

Rachel listened in awe, unable to comprehend how anyone could choose to be that uncomfortable.

'Duffo would have made a good hermit. Like the one who spent the winter on top of a pole.'

'It gets addictive,' Zoe explained. 'You push yourself. See how far you can go. How much of bourgeois consumerism you can do without. We want society to cut down on cars, but why stop there? We've got ourselves used to having too much. People don't even know what it is to feel cold any more. We've gone soft. Mind you,' she grinned at Rachel, not unkindly, 'I still haven't given up my hot-water bottle yet.'

They arrived at a large compound protected by an eight-foot fence. A sign announced that it was patrolled by Securitec. A fearsome illustration of a drooling Alsatian underlined the point.

'Any sign of a guard?' asked Marko.

They all stopped and listened. Rachel wondered if they could hear her heart, its pounding almost drowning out the sound of Marko's voice.

'Nah,' Macduff got out the wire cutters, 'it's all show. There's no one for miles.' He started to snip, snip, snip, each break of the wire distinct and oddly threatening in the thin night air. The hole widened from six inches to a foot and then two. Finally he stood back and let them climb through to where a line of bulldozers stood neatly parked, waiting.

Macduff climbed under the first one to disable it while Marko held the torch. 'I'm glad Duffo's army training wasn't a complete waste of taxpayers' money,' remarked Marko.

'Hold the torch steady for Christ's sake,'

shouted Macduff, 'I can't see a bloody thing.'

'It's just that my hands are so frigging cold,' Marko apologized.

'Here, let me.' Zoe reached for the torch.

'Scared?' Marko squeezed Rachel's hand.

'A bit.' The truth was, she was terrified. Thoughts of her parents, her grandmother and a brace of burly security guards were making her teeth rattle more than the bone-chilling cold.

'It'll be fine.'

Five minutes later they had finished. Macduff produced a bottle of cheap red wine from one of his many pockets and handed it round cheerfully.

'Couldn't you at least mull it?' laughed Marko.

The relief in the air made it feel like a party.

'To another successful pixie mission.'

Behind them a twig cracked and Macduff swung round.

'Don't be so paranoid.' Marko took another swig of the wine. 'It's probably only a badger.'

'In a blue uniform?' Zoe asked drily.

Rachel's heart froze as five uniformed officers stepped out of the darkness and surrounded them.

6

'Right, sir,' said the policeman in front, 'if you want to take trucks apart I suggest you buy a Meccano set. That way you won't be arrested for criminal damage.'

'I never liked Meccano sets,' Marko drawled insolently. 'I always preferred playing with dolls.'

'All right. I think it's time we continued this party somewhere more official,' the policeman gestured in the direction of the woods. 'If you would like to follow me to your transport.'

'I think you'll find, officer,' Zoe pointed out politely, 'that you'll have to let us off with a caution. None of us has been arrested for criminal damage before.'

'Zoe's our legal expert,' whispered Marko. 'You wait.'

'We'll see about that down at the station,' said the officer, getting more tetchy by the moment.

Even though the others seemed to be treating it as a huge joke, Rachel was so frightened she could hardly speak. Torn between terror and a desire not to appear uncool, she simply followed silently, imagining her parents' faces when they were asked to come and collect her. How had she let herself get into this mess?

'Would you like to call the duty solicitor?' the desk sergeant asked when they arrived at the warm and brightly lit police station. 'They can explain your rights to you.'

'I don't think that'll be necessary,' Marko grinned. Rachel wished to God he'd be a little more humble. He was clearly annoying the hell out of the officer who'd arrested them. 'We already have our legal adviser with us.' He indicated Zoe. 'I think you'll find she knows the laws associated with trespass and criminal damage pretty well. If she says this time it's just a caution then I'd be inclined to believe her.'

'And just who are you, Sonny Jim, the Lord Chancellor?' The policeman's genial manner was fading fast. 'Let's have your names and addresses. And third tree on the right, Gosse's Wood, will not be acceptable.'

Writing down her phone number was the worst moment for Rachel. She was counting the moments till they used it to ring her parents.

'What's this, a mobile number?' demanded the officer when Marko jotted down his.

'They all have them now,' the desk sergeant

explained. 'We may not be able to afford them but they can. Bloody middle-class protesters.'

'Sorry, what was that you called us?' Marko asked, hugely enjoying himself. 'The reception from the trees is excellent. Though not so good in the tunnels.'

Having taken their statements and details the desk sergeant disappeared and they sat in the bare office, waiting. Marko squeezed Rachel's hand. She tried not to cry as she imagined a night in the cells, her parents arriving to get her, their anguished faces as they told her she would have a criminal record, and then never being allowed out of their sight for months.

'Would you like to make your phone call?' the policeman asked.

Rachel wondered if she should ring her parents herself, before the police did, or perhaps Lavinia. But Lavinia would be even more horrified than her parents.

Macduff had no one to ring anyway. Marko affected not to want to. Only Zoe accepted. Marko looked at her in surprise, but Zoe gave nothing away.

The desk sergeant returned, looking weary. 'She's right, I'm afraid, Michael. You'll have to caution them and let them go.'

The policeman's geniality peeled away into

furious bitterness. 'For Christ's sake, Derek, why do we do this job?'

'Beats me,' the sergeant said. 'Why don't you go home to your mummies and daddies instead of clogging up the woods and the courts.'

'Because we believe in what we're doing,' flashed Zoe, as angry as they were. 'We're not doing this for fun any more than you are.'

The desk sergeant was called back to the front and they were left alone with the policeman who'd arrested them. 'It'll still happen, you know. They'll build the road whatever you do. In six months that wood will be a nice six-lane highway and Derek and I will drive up and down it laughing.'

'You're scum,' Zoe accused.

'Hang on, isn't that supposed to be our line?'

'Just leave us alone, will you?'

After twenty minutes the policeman put his head round the door. 'Someone here for you. Time to go home, boys and girls.'

In the brightly lit reception area Alexander Bailey stood talking to the desk sergeant.

'This gentleman has kindly offered to drive you back to your residence.' He grinned. 'Just so that the neighbours don't worry when they see a police car.'

Marko flashed a look of fury at Zoe.

143

'Congratulations.' Alexander opened the door of his ancient Land Rover for them. 'I gather you got off.'

'Yes,' Rachel said in a small voice, 'thanks to Zoe. She was brilliant.'

Marko continued to sulk.

'Actually,' Alexander added thoughtfully, 'I think you might have a bit of a convert in that desk sergeant. He told me he used to go camping in Gosse's Wood when he was a boy scout.'

'O lucky us,' Marko sneered.

'Don't underestimate local people. They can be the best friends we have. By the way, I heard an interesting rumour from a TV chap I know. The other side have finally got up off their chintz sofas and done something. They're organising a demo in Maxted High Street tomorrow and the cameras will be there to cover it.'

'Sounds like fun. Maybe we'd better go along.'

Marko took Rachel's hand in his. It was freezing and he blew on it, trying to warm it up.

She smiled, relief and elation beginning to take hold of her. They had done it. They had been pixying and almost got arrested, disaster had stared them in the face, but it had all been all right in the end.

'Here you are,' Alexander stopped the Land Rover to let them off. Marko helped Rachel out and almost carried her across the glistening frosty duck boards to his tent.

Macduff took his usual post up the tree.

Zoe looked at Alexander. 'I bet your cottage is lovely and warm. I don't suppose you want to share it democratically?'

Alexander just smiled. 'See you tomorrow. Wrap up warm.'

'Hah!' said Zoe. 'You must be joking. Though I expect some people will find a way.'

She watched as Alexander's headlights swept round in a circle, catching several rabbits in the light for a brief second before they scampered away.

Zoe headed for her own tent, grateful that it was about ten feet away from Marko's, and climbed into her sleeping bag.

'It's lovely in here,' Rachel breathed when Marko put her down in his tent and started to light a candle, 'I didn't realize you'd actually decorated it.' She knew she was gabbling but couldn't stop herself. She was suddenly terrified.

'Hardly decorated. Just a couple of Indian bedspreads and my trusty goatskin. Hang on, I'll light another candle. Now, come over here, lovely Rachel.'

It was too cold for any foreplay and

somehow that made it easier. They just tore off their clothes and leaped, giggling, into Marko's sleeping bag. 'It's a double one!' Rachel teased. 'I didn't know you could get double ones.'

'You didn't think arctic explorers or mountaineers up Everest did any screwing, then?' He put his hand on her breast. She jumped because it was so cold. 'There's only one way they keep warm in the arctic,' he sat astride her, his penis so hard despite the cold that her eyes widened. 'Why do you think they call it the North Pole?' he leered, laughing. And then without more debate he slipped on a condom and eased himself into her.

Rachel winced at the shock, then tried to relax, as Marko rocked backwards and forwards, still astride her, until he came.

'Is that it?' she asked when it was over.

'Is what it?'

'That. There must be more to it. You've forgotten something.'

'What were you expecting?' His tone was angry and hurt. 'A bloody certificate or something?'

'I just can't see what all the fuss is about, that's all.' He realized with relief that she was teasing.

'All right then,' he leaned down and began

to very gently lick her nipple until it stiffened, and not just with cold this time, then worked his way with agonizing slowness down her belly. 'I'll see what I can do.'

★ ★ ★

The sun was climbing in a china blue sky, every sign of the frost of the night before dissipated by the time Alexander arrived at the camp next morning. No one seemed to have stirred yet, so he built up the fire within its socially responsible circle of stones, designed to prevent any chance of it spreading to the wood.

It was, he realized, as he deftly snapped twigs from larger branches for kindling, a long time since he'd actually made a fire himself. He looked round at the cooking pots, the bowl of washing-up which had frozen over, the tarpaulin stretched out to catch rainwater, and thought of his warm cottage. The deprivations these kids put up with amazed him, especially since most of them had left comfortable homes behind. He'd always been, he knew, more of a theoretician than a front-line fighter.

Sometimes he felt a little sorry for their parents, probably nice liberals who thought their children wouldn't need to rebel, what would they rebel *against*, after all, when they'd been brought up so reasonably? They hadn't understood that children had to rebel anyway, had to prove themselves as adults, to reject their parents' values, via whatever route they found possible. In a funny way it was nothing personal. If only parents could see that and realize that their revolting children would be perfectly nice in the end, everything would be fine. He wondered if Rachel was choosing Marko as her means of rebellion. He had a feeling her parents weren't going to like Marko. Still, it wasn't his problem. He had never believed in telling people what to do with their lives.

One of the tent flaps parted and Rachel emerged. With her waves of red hair freed from her woollen hat, he took in again how exceptionally pretty she was, delicate yet with a touch of elemental strength. She made Alexander think of one of those pioneer women who held off the Indians in a poke bonnet. In some strange way she also reminded him of someone. Alexander found himself unexpectedly stirred, not in a sexual way, but by tenderness and the desire to protect her.

'Isn't this wonderful?' She smiled, stretching her arms as if she wanted to reach out to the bare trees. She broke suddenly into a chorus of 'Who Will Buy This Beautiful Morning?' complete with dance movements.

Alexander watched, taken aback.

'Sorry,' laughed Rachel, 'it's from *Oliver*. We did it at school last term. I didn't get a part. As usual.'

The sudden reference to school disconcerted him, given the way she had clearly spent the night. Perhaps he wasn't as liberated as he thought. 'What year are you in?' He hoped to God she didn't say Year Ten.

'The final one. A levels in May. Mocks next month. My mother never lets me forget.'

'Ah. If only parents knew how to handle their children, eh?'

'She's a teacher, which makes it worse. Sometimes I don't think she gives a damn about me. Only my results.' There was something about Alexander's almost Zen calm that made her trust him and want to open up.

'Of course, irritating though they may be, parents are right. Qualifications do give you more choices in life. It's the people who don't have them who get stuck.'

'You aren't a deprogrammer hired by my mother, by any chance?'

Alexander laughed. 'I've always thought A levels and GCSEs were at precisely the wrong time in a young person's life. Just when the

149

hormones are raging most fiercely.' Rachel blushed vermilion. 'Anyway, how did you get involved in all this, or was it just the lure of our leftie Lothario?'

Alexander realized this was rather a low blow. He had, after all, been something of a leftie Lothario himself once.

'Actually, I'm here because my grand-mother lives a couple of miles away and I played in this wood as a child. I used to pretend one of these oaks was The Magic Faraway Tree like in Enid Blyton. I couldn't bear to see them chopped down for a motorway.' She stopped, feeling suddenly foolish, but he was smiling. 'Of course I'm interested in the political issues too.' She grinned engagingly, and again that sense of somehow knowing her hit Alexander. 'At least I would be if I knew them.'

Alexander found himself warming to her. She had spirit. 'Would you like me to lay them out, as it were, in a nutshell?' He proceeded to do so with great wit and clarity.

Rachel listened, fascinated. 'You should have been a teacher.'

'I was once, sort of.'

'Where?'

'Ruskin College in Oxford, the trade union college. But I left after a few years. There was nothing for me there. So I became a writer, did a little painting. And lately a campaigner to save what little we have left of England's green and pleasant land. How about you? Are you planning to be a student?'

'Actually, I've got a place at university already, reading English, providing I get my grades.'

Behind them a tent flap rustled and Marko appeared. Even though it was still so cold their breaths spiralled together as they talked, Marko was stripped naked to the waist. He stretched like a young animal, his taut body still golden from some Cretan beach, and shook out his black hair.

Alexander had to admit that he mightn't think much of Marko's moral depth, but that physical beauty was a powerful thing.

Marko sat down next to them and nuzzled Rachel's neck with such a proprietorial air that Alexander felt a sudden and overwhelming temptation to hit him.

What the hell's the matter with me? Alexander asked himself. God knew, he ought to be used to student behaviour by now.

'What do you think we should do about this demo this afternoon, Alexander?' Zoe had come out of her tent and was watching them. With the delicate sensitivity that belied her wild image, she had seen that the situation needed rescuing in some way.

Alexander smiled gratefully. 'I think we should go and see what's happening.'

'And I think,' Marko interjected, 'we should get down there before them and steal their thunder.'

'Provided there's no violence. The last thing we need is to look as if we're a bunch of thugs breaking up the pensioners' tea party.'

'Come on, Rach,' Marko stood up and pulled her with him, 'you can come and help me get dressed.' He smiled lasciviously.

Rachel simply laughed. 'I would have thought you were old enough to get dressed on your own.' But she followed him all the same.

Alexander announced he was going to get the Land Rover and disappeared into the wood.

'What's going on between Alexander and Marko, then?' Macduff asked Zoe, jumping down from his perch in the tree.

'The usual stuff. The old lion and the new. Personally I'd back the old one.'

'With the girl, you mean?'

'No. I don't think this is about Rachel, at least not in an overtly sexual way. There's something complicated going on here and I'm not sure I understand it. Anyway, not for the likes of you and me to reason why. Let's go and do something easy like sit down on a zebra crossing. If we're lucky we might even get arrested in front of the cameras.'

'Oh my God, I forgot. My grandmother!' Rachel rolled out of the sleeping bag she'd climbed back into with Marko and looked at her watch. It was nine thirty. Her grandmother was supposed to be picking her up from the station at ten twenty.

'Have you got your phone?'

The irony struck her that Marko the apparently penniless road protester had a cellphone while she didn't. Fortunately he'd charged it up in Alexander's car and she got through to Lavinia.

'Gran, thank heavens! Look, don't bother to meet me at the station. I've got a bit sidetracked.' Marko bit her ear to endorse this. 'Owww! No, it's fine. I just banged my foot. Is your key still under the bird table in the garden? I'll just let myself in then. See you later. Lots of love.'

Rachel breathed with relief. Her grandmother hadn't noticed anything untoward.

In fact Lavinia was delighted. She'd forgotten about the extra complication of picking her grand-daughter up from the station and wanted to use the Rover as a taxi service to ferry supporters into town for the demonstration. What was worrying her most of all was that she'd had no answer from the

TV people about whether or not they were coming. The sit-in was scheduled for midday and she was going to look bloody silly if they didn't turn up.

On her way out Lavinia glanced in the mirror. It had been hard to know what was appropriate apparel for a protest. The nearest she'd ever got to this before was signing a petition against changing the Book of Common Prayer into that frightful whiny New Liturgy. She'd hit upon tweed trousers, an old dusty pink sweater and her trusty Barbour for good measure. Glancing out of the window, she wished Eunice had followed her example.

'We're not actually going to, you know, *sit down*, are we?' Eunice asked. 'I've got my best cream slacks on for the television.'

'Of course we're going to sit down. It's a sit-in. What else do you suggest? A cocktail party with canapés in the middle of the zebra crossing?'

'Will there be something to sit on?'

'No, there will not. This isn't Ascot, Eunice, it's a serious demonstration.'

'Perhaps I shouldn't bring my Thermos then. What do you think?'

★　★　★

If Lavinia had only known it, she could have relaxed. The local TV reporter, his cameraman and soundman were already in Maxted High Street, eating their bacon sandwiches and sizing up their shot.

'So where are the wrinklies planning to sit down?' asked the soundman, waving his furry microphone and starting to test for level.

'On the zebra crossing outside Boots.'

'OK,' instructed the reporter, who saw himself more a director *manqué*, 'I want a nice pan across those cottages, church spire, bit of fields in the background, leave out the thatched hamburger place if you can. Old England under threat. Ending up on that juggernaut.' He pointed to the lone lorry present in the street. 'Can someone pay the man to rev it up a bit?'

When Lavinia and her troops emerged from the church hall where they'd been assembling, the reporter thought he must have died and gone to heaven. They were classic. It was too good to be true.

'Quick,' he ordered the cameraman, 'we've got to get that shot. Just look at them! Not one under sixty and some of them in flowery hats with picnic baskets!'

'Makes a nice change from those nasty eco-warriors,' breathed the soundman. 'They shout peace and kick you in the . . . '

'Don't be too sure,' chipped in the cameraman at a brisk trot in the wake of the reporter, 'this lot might be even more lethal.'

'Look, Lavinia!' shouted Eunice, thrilled. 'Here come the TV people, just like you said.'

Alexander's Land Rover drew up just as the TV crew chased off in the direction of the church hall, leaving the zebra crossing temptingly free.

'Come on,' grinned Marko, his black hair blowing across his face in the sharp breeze that had started up, 'let's get in first.'

Zoe and Macduff plonked themselves in the middle, next to Marko. Alexander noticed that Rachel was holding back. 'Do you want to stay in the Land Rover? There's no obligation, you know.'

With a small shake of her head Rachel sat down next to Marko. Why was she here, after all? Just because of Marko, as Alexander had suggested, or because she believed as passionately as they did in the cause of saving Gosse's Wood from the bulldozers?

Eunice was the first to notice what was happening. 'I say, Lavinia, look. Someone else is invading our crossing!'

Thirty outraged pensioners hallooed and made a mad dash for the crossing just as an unmarked grey van of police arrived. Policemen tumbled out of the van and headed for the crossing, attempting to halt the flood of pensioners before it contested the occupation. But they were too late for Lavinia. Boadicea-like, she was leading from the front and flopped down at the head of her troop, only inches away from the enemy.

Rachel, who had been asking Alexander what was likely to happen next, turned to find herself almost face to face with her warring grandmother.

'Gran!' she yelped, shocked and disbelieving.

'Rachel!' countered Lavinia. 'But you're supposed to be stuck in London!'

Seated between both of them, Alexander Bailey stared in disbelief.

'Lavinia?' The word sounded as if it had been painfully chipped letter by letter out of his heart. 'It can't be you. Not after all these years.'

'Hello, Alexander,' Lavinia was enjoying herself hugely. 'Still making trouble, I see.'

'Can someone tell me,' gasped the TV reporter, out of breath from trying to catch up with them, 'what the bloody hell is going on here?'

7

The look on Alexander's face had almost been worth the forty years' wait. His hawklike grey gaze was fixed on her as if she were a dream that had taken solid form.

Lavinia made the most of it. After all, it hadn't been often that she'd managed to silence Alexander.

She offered him her hand in a friendly shake. 'So, Alexander, how are you?'

'Do you two know each other?' Marko asked irritably. Alexander always seemed to know someone. High-ranking officials, important civil servants, even the occasional policeman. The old-boy network, Marko assumed. Privilege again. For someone who claimed to have rejected the values of the power elite, Alexander had a habit of knowing an awful lot of them.

'As a matter of fact we do.' Alexander held on to Lavinia's hand stubbornly. 'Though we haven't seen each other for forty years.'

'Forty years and five months,' corrected Lavinia. 'It was July.'

'Indeed it was.' Alexander's voice held a tenderness none of them had heard before.

'How wonderful to see you being irresponsible at last, Lavinia.'

'Irresponsible?' Lavinia exploded. 'Do you call it being irresponsible to try to stop juggernauts destroying this six-hundred-year-old street, choking us with their fumes, probably running down some harmless shopper . . . '

'Excuse *me*,' interrupted the TV reporter, surveying the extraordinary scene of blue-rinsed ladies carrying shopping baskets sharing the crossing with long-haired hippie-types in greatcoats, 'but could someone explain what you're all demonstrating about here?'

'Demonstrating?' snorted Marko. 'Having the Mad Hatter's Tea Party more like.'

Lavinia ignored him. 'This is our show, young man. We arranged it to publicize just how congested Maxted has become and why a bypass is so essential.'

'And we came,' interrupted Marko, 'to point out that their precious bypass will involve the destruction of woodland that is older than Maxted itself.'

Everyone's attention was momentarily distracted by the arrival of a second police bus. About forty policemen were now ranged along the pavements.

'Gosh, this is exciting,' Eunice whispered.

159

'What do we do now, Lavinia?'

Lavinia, who hadn't thought beyond simply getting here, was temporarily at a loss.

'I think it's customary,' Alexander said softly, leaning over in her direction, 'to do some chanting at this point.'

'But what should we chant?' whispered Lavinia.

'Simple is best. How about 'Save Maxted. Juggernauts Out.' Something like that.'

'Save Maxted,' Lavinia attempted. 'Juggernauts out.'

'Come on, Lavinia,' teased Alexander, 'you can do better than that.'

'Save Maxted!' Lavinia shouted. 'Juggernauts Out!'

'Save Maxted!' echoed Eunice and the others. 'Juggernauts Out!'

'Whose side are you on?' Marko hissed to Alexander as the cameraman finally leaped into action.

The police took this as their signal that something was required of them and began to march in a somewhat ragged line towards the zebra crossing, which was by now, thanks more to the presence of TV cameras than the demonstration itself, beginning to attract a crowd of shoppers, the publican from the White Hart and a gaggle of small boys who wanted to see themselves on telly.

'Save Maxted!' the chanting continued. 'Juggernauts Out!'

'Sorry to disappoint you, Lavinia,' confided Alexander. 'The only lorry for miles has just departed. But perhaps you could ascribe that to your chanting.'

Rachel giggled just as the posse of police arrived at the crossing. Her nerve wavered a little when she recognized the sergeant and the unpleasant constable from the night before.

'All right, who's in charge here?' the sergeant asked tetchily.

Eunice pointed gaily to Lavinia.

'Right. You good people have made your point now. You've got yourselves on the box. Now I suggest you get back to your whist and your bingo.'

Some of the demonstrators started to get up, clearly relieved to be off the hook so easily, but Lavinia was made of sterner stuff. 'Hang on, everyone. We have a right to demonstrate peacefully. We are the generation who fought the war, officer, and we're not leaving until we've finished making our point.'

The constable raised his eyes to heaven. 'If you're peacefully demonstrating you can do it on the pavement, not here where you are causing an obstruction.' As if to emphasize this a young man in a Mini tooted angrily. 'Why not move up there next to the Salvation Army? They've got some nice carols on.'

'Sorry, officer,' Lavinia insisted. 'I'm not going anywhere.'

Eunice eyed her dubiously. 'Are you sure, Lavinia?'

'Neither am I,' Rachel chipped in. She glinted angrily at Marko and the others. 'What's the point in being here if we don't make our point too? Stop the Bypass!' she set up a rival chant. 'Save the woodland!'

'Well, well,' pointed out the constable, 'if it isn't our friends from the woods again. You're busier than the little elves, you lot. Now move along, please.'

Rachel put her arms stubbornly round her legs and sat tight.

'Look, young lady, we had enough trouble with you lot last night. You were bloody lucky to get off.'

'Last night?' Lavinia objected. 'But you were in London last night.'

'That's what she told you, was it?' the constable asked nastily. 'So she forgot to mention breaking into the Securitec compound and sabotaging three of their bulldozers?'

'Rachel? Is this true?'

Rachel stared ahead stubbornly.

Lavinia looked to Alexander for a denial.

162

'I'm afraid it is. I tried to stop them.' He ignored the look of disgust on Marko's face.

'I expect it slipped her mind,' the constable commented. 'Let's all just go home, shall we? Before things turn nasty.'

'Tell you what, officer,' Marko challenged, 'why don't you arrest us? Or are those TV cameras making you nervous?'

The sneer in Marko's tone was too much for the constable. He hated people like this. People who'd been given all the advantages and used them to make trouble. Even the OAPs seemed to be at it now. No respect for authority. He was screwed if he was going to be talked to like that by long-haired scum who'd probably had a decent education and were too lazy to use it.

'Right, sunshine. I might do exactly that.'

'I'm afraid he means it, Lavinia,' Alexander counselled.

Lavinia seemed to come to her senses. It was one thing for her to get arrested, she only had herself to think of, but Rachel was a different matter. Rachel was at the beginning of her life when her whole future might be affected. Besides there was the responsibility Lavinia had to Rachel's mother and father, who presumably had no idea their precious daughter was here. 'Come on, Rachel, I think we've made our point for the moment.'

Rachel ignored her and sat tight. She had heard the loathing and disapproval in the policeman's voice and it had made her burn with fury. Who was he to dismiss them like that, to call them elves, and treat them as if they were playing some childish game when this issue was deadly serious? 'Sorry, Gran, but I'm not moving.'

'Rachel,' Lavinia pleaded, 'just think about your parents . . . '

She realized too late that this was probably the worst possible argument she could have used. Rachel's face hardened.

'Rachel,' Alexander endorsed, 'Lavinia's right. You've made your point. If you're going to make a stand, let's choose the issue carefully.'

'Stop telling me what to do, all of you! I'm not some kid in kindergarten. I'm old enough to decide for myself what I want to make a stand over.'

Lavinia watched helplessly as the rest of her supporters dribbled away, leaving Rachel in sole possession of the crossing. By now the queue of angry motorists was lengthening and most of them were hitting their horns. Rachel calmly ignored them and stared ahead.

'Come on, young lady,' the sergeant urged, more kindly than his colleague. He had a grand-daughter who was nagging her parents for a nose stud and he felt he understood her generation. 'You really must move along.'

'Don't patronize me!' Rachel flashed.

It was all too much for the other policeman. His own children either ignored him or treated him with contempt and he was damned if he was going to take it from this brattish girl. He leaned down and put a hand on her shoulder.

Rachel wrenched it away.

He grabbed her arm, more roughly than he intended, and pulled it behind her back, trying to lever her into an upright position. Rachel pulled it back again with surprising strength, almost causing the man to fall forwards.

'Right,' he hissed, 'that's enough from you, young lady.' He quickly pushed his arms under hers, grabbing her around the waist and attempted to pull her bodily from the crossing. Rachel dived for the central bollard and hung on. He prised away her hands and stood on one. Rachel screamed.

The man simply watched in satisfaction. 'You shouldn't have been such a stupid little girl then, should you?' he demanded, taking advantage of the moment to grab her bodily again. This time Rachel was in too much agony to resist.

The sight of her grand-daughter in pain goaded Lavinia beyond the limits of her tolerance. All her life she'd respected and upheld the law and now she saw that its official guardians could be as petty and unpleasant as anyone else. 'Leave her alone! Can't you see she's hurt?'

The constable ignored her and continued to pull Rachel off the crossing.

'For the second time,' demanded Lavinia angrily, 'will you please leave my grand-daughter alone? I'm sure she'll walk now without being dragged.'

'Why don't you just stick to bingo and stop setting a bad example,' the constable advised. 'You ought to know better at your age. I'm arresting this young lady for obstructing the highway, and if you're not careful I'll arrest you too.'

Lavinia answered with a sharp kick in his shins. 'Go on, then, arrest me.'

With a dramatic flourish she looked to see where the TV crew had got to. They were a few feet away, having a field day. Lavinia turned to face the camera. 'Sixty-three years old and not even a parking ticket. And today I am being arrested for defending what I believe to be right.'

The cameraman moved in for a close-up.

By now the constable was beginning to

wish he'd never started this, but he could hardly give up now. 'People believe in a lot of things,' he stated sanctimoniously, 'but they don't go round breaking the law all the time. This will need sorting out at the station.' This time it was Lavinia's arm that was held in a vice-like grip.

'Take Rachel home,' Lavinia shouted to Alexander as the constable led her off. 'Phone her parents. And then you'd better come and see what's happened to me.'

They watched silently as Lavinia was ushered, very politely now, into the grey van. Eunice and the straggle of supporters still remaining cheered and waved their picnic baskets.

'What a triumph,' Zoe remarked drily to no one in particular. 'We've just given them a Maxted Martyr.'

Rachel looked as if she might cry. Her hand hurt like hell and her principled protest had been a disaster. Marko put his arm round her and hugged her in an ineffectual kind of way.

Alexander watched the van departing and thought how extraordinary it was that after forty years of absence, within one brief half-hour his life seemed once more to be bound up with Lavinia's.

★ ★ ★

167

'Hang on,' Alexander said as he parked the ancient Land Rover opposite Lavinia's cottage. Its welcoming wreath on the front door seemed ironic under the circumstances. 'We haven't got a key.'

'She hardly ever locks it,' Rachel explained. 'She still believes people round here are trustworthy.'

'At least she did until today,' Alexander said wryly. 'Poor Lavinia. I think some of her illusions are in the process of being shattered. The world isn't quite as straightforward a place as she thought it was.'

For once the door was locked. Rachel went to look for the keys under the bird table. It was in the shade of a fir tree and the wood was still frosted in a layer of thick clear white. Rachel scrabbled about for the keys, longing for the cosy comforting familiarity of Lavinia's fireside. Finally she found them but her hands were too cold and painful to open the door.

'I'll do it,' offered Alexander and pushed open the thick four-hundred-year-old door. Unlike the usual cottage colours of white or magnolia, the walls were painted a surprising dark red, lit by glowing wall lights and red table lamps. It felt to Alexander like walking inside a jewel, especially after the sparse bareness of his own rented home. Somehow he'd expected chintz and convention from Lavinia. Instead the whole place made him think of a rather Bohemian doll's house. But then Lavinia was turning out to be full of surprises.

'I'll light the fire,' offered Rachel. 'So we can warm it up ready for Gran when they let her go.' Suddenly she looked guilty and uncertain, like a child that knows it has done something and is about to be found out. 'They will let her go, won't they? I mean they won't really charge her.'

'Of course they won't. I imagine they're as annoyed as she is that it's got this far. It'll probably be all over the news.' He smiled to himself at the thought. 'Lavinia seems to have a natural flair for the dramatic.'

'God,' said Rachel. 'This is all my fault. I don't know what came over me, except that man's patronizing tone. I just felt I had to *do* something or the whole thing would be a farce and a waste of time. Everyone seemed to be forgetting what we were there for.'

'How's that hand of yours?' Alexander asked gently. 'Can I have a look?' It was badly bruised and the knuckle joints were swollen to double their normal size. 'Marko, go and see if there are any frozen peas or ice cubes in the kitchen.'

Marko looked mutinous, but at the sight of

Rachel's small pale face, streaked with the tears she was trying to wipe away with her good hand, he shut up. He came back with a packet of frozen petit pois.

'Excellent, you can have a gourmet ice-pack. Now, what are we going to do about your parents? Do you want me to ring them, as Lavinia suggested?'

The fire began to crackle and jump comfortingly in the huge fireplace. It seemed a long way away from London and home. 'No, I will if you don't mind. I promise I won't do a whitewash.'

Alexander patted her good hand. 'Look, I'm not your parents and obviously they're going to be shocked if they thought you were staying with Lavinia all along, but they sound like understanding people.'

'Understanding! All my mother cares about is university. She wouldn't see how saving a wood could matter an iota compared with getting a degree.'

'Have you ever tried to explain to them how you feel about Gosse's Wood? Why it matters to you so much?'

'It wouldn't be worth it.'

'Your parents might be touched that you'd trusted them.'

'Hah! You haven't met my mother.'

'People aren't always as predictable as you

think. Even parents. Look at your grand-mother. Who would ever have expected Lavinia to kick a policeman.'

Rachel smiled a little at the memory. 'And did you see the expression on that awful Colonel whatsisname's face?' She took a deep breath and stared into the fire for a moment. 'I suppose I'd better make that call.'

'And I ought to get down to the police station and make sure Lavinia hasn't kicked any more policemen. Will you stay with Rachel, Marko?'

Marko nodded. 'I'll come with you,' Zoe offered. 'I can tell you whether they're trying to pull a fast one.'

'I do know a thing or two about the law myself, you know. And I suspect Lavinia might prefer a respectable solicitor to either you or me.'

'The trouble with a respectable solicitor,' Zoe grinned, 'especially in a half-timbered town like Maxted, is that they'll know fuck all about trespass, obstruction and kicking one of Her Majesty's police officers in the goolies.'

'Be fair now, Zoe,' Alexander replied, the twinkle returning to his eye, 'unless my anatomy's all to pot, she only touched him strictly below the knee.'

171

'Then I'll have to give her some lessons in how to aim more accurately.'

★ ★ ★

Rachel took a deep breath, closed her eyes, then dialled the number. With luck they would all be out.

'Hello,' Ricky said in his slightly distant, I'm-on-a-Cyber-Planet voice.

'Ricky? Are Mum and Dad out? Can you give them a message?'

'Oh, hi, Rach. Actually Mum's just got back from the supermarket. Do you want to speak to her?'

Rachel's heart lurched. 'I suppose so. Yes.'

'Hello, darling,' her mother's voice sounded busy and happy, 'how's country life? Don't tell me, Gran's driving you mad, and you want to come home?'

'No, actually. It's fine here, well, no actually it isn't . . . ' she trailed off.

'Rachel, what's the matter?'

'It's Gran. She's been arrested.'

'*Arrested?*' Catherine's voice squeaked up several semi-tones. 'Whatever for?' Catherine raked through the possibilities of wrongdoing her mother-in-law might be capable of, from absconding with the bridge stakes to overdoing the sherry, but none seemed in character.

'She kicked a policeman.'

This time all Catherine could produce was stunned silence. 'Lavinia's been arrested for kicking a policeman. Why would she do that?'

Rachel hesitated. 'It's a long story. I think I'd better explain when you get here. Alexander's gone to the police station to try and get her out.'

'Who's Alexander?'

'Alexander Bailey. He's quite famous actually. He's a writer and lecturer who specializes in stopping motorways. The developers practically give up and go home when they hear he's around. And the amazing thing is, Gran knows him but they hadn't seen each other for forty years.'

But Catherine wasn't really listening. She was still trying to make sense of the picture Rachel had just painted of her strait-laced mother-in-law, who always argued in favour of the forces of authority and discipline, getting herself arrested for kicking a policeman.

'I'll get Dad. We'll come at once. Which police station is she at?'

'The one in Maxted.'

'Rachel . . . ' The concern in her mother's voice made her squirm, it wouldn't last long when she found out the truth. 'Are you all right there?'

'I'm fine,' Rachel said humbly, 'don't worry about me.'

'We'll get Gran and bring her to the cottage. Just stay by a phone.'

'Yes, Mum. I love you.'

Rachel put down the phone to find Marko grinning at her. 'Not so principled now. You left out one little detail in that story.'

'I know. I just couldn't get up the nerve to tell her. I'll do it as soon as I see her.'

'Is she so scary, this mother of yours?'

'It's just that she disapproves of anything that gets in the way of my precious education.'

'And Gosse's Wood is a pretty big obstruction?' He pulled the curtains, leaving them enclosed and private within the ruby warmth of Lavinia's sitting room. 'Come here,' he ordered, patting the rug in front of the fire, 'the forces of authority are all either at the police station or on their way there. That leaves us at least an hour of anarchy.'

Rachel sat down beside him shyly, suddenly forgetting the pain in her hand, and Marko began to pull off her jumper. 'Besides,' he added, dipping his lips to the pale firmness of her breast, 'you seemed to be getting the hang of things pretty quickly last time we did this.'

He saw a spark of anger light up her eyes and pushed her back, laughing. 'You're too easy to wind up, lovely Rachel. If you're going to be a seasoned campaigner you have to learn to keep your temper.'

'Like you do, you mean?' she teased, before he came up with a diversionary tactic that prevented further argument.

* * *

'There has to be some simple explanation,' Christopher insisted again as they parked in Maxted police station car park. They had discussed possible scenarios endlessly on the way down and all of them seemed ludicrous.

The crime rate in Maxted was so low that the police station turned out to be based in a PortaCabin in the library car park. It consisted of a small front office where the desk sergeant alternated with a part-time secretary in taking details of lost wallets, acts of minor vandalism and the odd exciting burglary. Making an actual arrest was so rare that the place had an air of having surprised itself.

The sight that awaited Christopher and Catherine was of a tall, distinguished-looking man with white hair and piercing grey eyes, dressed in an ancient grey corduroy jacket, in friendly conversation with a uniformed police sergeant, who appeared to be showing him a photograph of some kind of dog. There was no sign of Lavinia.

Christopher spoke first. 'We've come about my mother, Mrs Lavinia Hope. We can't actually believe this, but our daughter tells us she's been arrested.'

The sergeant had the grace to look embarrassed and was clearly grateful when the older man took the initiative.

'You must be Lavinia's son and daughter-in-law. My name is Alexander Bailey.'

Christopher shook his hand. 'Rachel mentioned that you know my mother already.'

'Yes. Extraordinary, isn't it? We were at Oxford together forty years ago.'

'But my mother never went to Oxford.' Christopher felt as if he'd wandered into an Alice-like fantasy, which was growing odder by the moment.

Why on earth, Alexander wondered, had Lavinia suppressed her time at university? 'She was at Lady Margaret Hall, as a matter of fact. She was doing brilliantly, a star student, until she disappeared at the end of the first summer term. Presumably to marry your father. And I hadn't seen her since. Until today.'

Christopher shook his head at Catherine in amazement.

'Are you sure about this? She's never once mentioned Oxford and neither did my father.'

'Perhaps there was something she wanted to forget.' Alexander's voice dropped slightly.

'Where is my mother? Not in the cells, surely?'

'She's in the back office, having a cup of tea with our WPC. We've decided not to press charges this time, so she's free to go.'

'I should bloody well hope so,' muttered Christopher, as he and Catherine were led through to the back office. Lavinia was sitting on a straight-backed chair drinking out of a mug that said You're Nicked.

'Christopher! Catherine! How lovely to see you!'

'Look, Ma, what the hell is going on?'

'Haven't Rachel or Alexander explained?' She looked at Alexander disapprovingly. 'It's perfectly straightforward. I organized a sit-in on the zebra crossing to show the TV people how bad the traffic is in Maxted and how much we need a bypass and Alexander and his friends, who're on the other side, gatecrashed our little protest. Then this policeman, not the nice one out there, the other one, tried to arrest Rachel and was really hurting her, so I kicked him and he

177

arrested me instead. You should be grateful.'

'*Rachel?*' Catherine and Christopher chorused together. 'Ma, you didn't drag Rachel into all this?'

Lavinia laughed hollowly. 'It's that young lady who dragged me into it. She told you she was staying with me when all the time she'd gone to join Marko and his friends in the wood.'

'Marko? Who the hell is Marko?' In fact the name rang a faint bell with Catherine. Hadn't someone with a curious name like that rung Rachel a few weeks ago?

'Marko is one of the anti-road protesters who's living in Gosse's Wood. Rachel bumped into him that day you came to lunch with me. It seems she's kept in touch with him ever since.'

'So that's why she's been so keen on coming to stay with you all of a sudden.'

'Exactly. Though Marko's obviously the real attraction.'

'And who is he, this Marko character?' Christopher demanded.

'If you mean who are his parents,' Lavinia snapped, tired and wanting to go home, 'and what are his intentions towards your daughter, I don't think road protesters go in for that sort of thing.'

'His name is Mark Williams,' announced

Alexander, 'and he comes from Pinner, although he would chain himself to a bulldozer rather than admit it. Marko likes to see himself as the James Dean of road protesting. He's reasonably intelligent, turned down university, and — I'm sorry to have to tell you this — is extremely attractive, especially to spirited middle-class girls.'

'Now I wonder who that reminds me of?' Lavinia asked, looking directly at Alexander.

'Excuse me,' chipped in the desk sergeant, 'but there's someone out here to see Mrs Hope. And perhaps the rest of you good people might go home now so that we can get on with our work?'

Colonel Lawley was waiting for them in the outer office, wrapped up in an ageing shooting jacket, a scarf wound round half of his face giving him the look of a bandit with grog blossoms. 'About time too,' Lavinia scolded. 'I wondered when someone from the committee would offer some support. It's all right, Colonel, I haven't been charged. The police came to their senses in time.'

Lavinia flung her own scarf round her neck à la Isadora Duncan and swept out with the others in her wake.

'Look!' pointed out a man in the car park. 'It's that woman who was on the news!'

'Was I?' Lavinia danced like a schoolgirl round the car park. 'Was I really on the news, Colonel? At last our side of the story is getting some coverage. I was right, wasn't I, about taking some action?'

'Well, actually, Lavinia, I'm very glad you haven't been charged but I, that is, we on the committee, don't feel this kind of publicity is at all desirable.' He had the grace to colour up until his cheeks rivalled the plum of his extraordinary nose. 'The thing is, Lavinia, I'm afraid we feel it would be better if you stood down. We've had to issue a statement to the press disassociating ourselves from your action in assaulting that officer. It simply isn't the kind of thing we want to do.'

Lavinia listened wrathfully, unable to believe what she was hearing. These were her neighbours whom she'd known all her married life, people she'd played bridge with, regulars at the village coffee-morning and they were abandoning her, turning against her when she needed them most.

'Do you know what you can tell your committee. That they're a bunch of pompous farts!'

'Poor Lavinia,' the tenderness in Alexander Bailey's voice took Catherine and Christopher aback, 'you didn't see that coming, did

180

you? People like that never do anything to rock the boat, even if it happens to be the *Titanic*. They probably only have meetings to get themselves out of the house. Actually taking action terrifies the life out of them. If it's any consolation, I'm sure some of them are behind you but just wouldn't dare show it.'

'But, Alexander,' Lavinia suddenly looked vulnerable, like a fierce animal with nothing left to protect, 'those people are my neighbours, my friends.'

'Maybe you need some new friends then. Come on, Lavinia. You go with your son and daughter-in-law, they've come to look after you. You've had an unpleasant shock.'

'But where are you going, Alexander?' Catherine detected a hint of panic in her indomitable mother-in-law's manner.

'To your cottage to pick up Marko. I expect you'd like some time to yourselves as a family.'

At this moment the Hopes looked as if that was the last thing they wanted. 'Come on, Cath,' Christopher held open the door of the car. 'I think it's time we went and met this Marko.'

★ ★ ★

181

Darkness had descended firmly over the thatched roofs of Maxted when Rachel opened the curtains again. Over the road Eunice, who was in the act of closing hers, like any decent person would, noticed this and wondered what on earth Rachel was doing. She was about to nip over the road and ask for news of Lavinia when Alexander's Land Rover followed by an estate car drew up outside. As if that weren't enough activity the phone started ringing and Colonel Lawley was on the line asking Eunice if he could have a quick word.

Rachel opened the front door before Lavinia had a chance to reach for her key and threw herself into her grandmother's arms. 'Gran! Thank God, they've let you out. I'm so sorry. It was all my fault.'

'All right, darling,' Lavinia was an imposing woman but her grand-daughter was even taller than she was. 'I think it's your parents you should be apologizing to.'

Rachel stiffened at the sight of her mother and father and darted back into the house.

'May I offer a word of advice?' Alexander said softly to Catherine and Christopher. He liked these people, just as he liked their daughter, but he could sense the dangers ahead. 'At the risk of sounding like something out of *West Side Story*, tread carefully. If you push her she'll join him, exams or no exams. I've seen it happen often enough. It's the bright and spirited ones who're the most tempted to rebel. It may not sound reassuring, but it's often when they love you most they need to kick the hardest.'

'Hello, Mum. Hello, Dad.' Rachel held herself straight, all hint of apology banished, as her parents filed into the small room. 'I expect you've heard the delinquent daughter story by now.'

'Does anyone feel like a cup of tea?' All eyes swivelled towards the young man standing in the small adjoining kitchen. 'It does wonders at times of family crisis, so I'm told.'

'Mum and Dad,' Rachel announced, with a hint of challenge in her voice, 'meet my friend Marko.'

The young man standing in the doorway possessed a stylishness that even living rough in the woods couldn't quite diminish. He was tall with long black hair and black brows that met in the middle, over eyes of a pale dazzling blue that seemed to be mocking them all for their petty suburban concerns.

Alexander was right, Catherine thought with a sinking heart and an awful omen of things to come, Marko was indeed your average parent's nightmare.

8

'For heaven's sake, Rachel,' her father sat down on the small sofa, 'there's only one thing I mind in all this. Why didn't you tell us where you were going? We're not Victorian parents who're going to lock you in the cellar for having your own opinions.' Christopher was conscious of a certain dishonesty here. At this precise moment he would have bloody well loved to lock her in the cellar for all the worry she'd caused them. 'Couldn't you just have trusted us?'

'And what would you have said if I'd trusted you? 'Dear Mum and Dad, I want to go and join my lover,' ' her parents flinched at the word, just as she'd intended them to, ' 'and live in the woods for a bit and sod my A levels'.'

'We could have at least discussed it,' Catherine said, struggling to keep her temper. Making them angry was clearly Rachel's goal. Then she'd be the one on the moral high ground.

'Bollocks to that. You always say you want me to think for myself, but you mean you want me to agree with you. You say you want me to be happy. But what you really mean is you want me to be a good girl and get into university like you want me to. You just want me to be like you all the way. But I don't want to be like you! You're sad and pathetic. You never do anything except see the same boring friends, who all think exactly like you do, drink too much wine and go to bed at ten o'clock. Why should I want to be like you?'

Catherine, with all her training in how to deal with tricky situations at school, felt an overwhelming temptation to get up and hit her daughter. The contempt in Rachel's words stung her to the quick.

'But we've never stopped you having relationships,' Christopher pointed out quietly. 'You've never really been that interested.'

'Look, Dad,' Rachel flashed, as if addressing some small, rather slow child, 'this isn't about relationships. Marko may be part of it but he isn't the main part. I believe in Gosse's Wood. It's a magical place. I played there every time I stayed with Gran. Why should it be bulldozed so that people like you can get wherever you're going ten minutes quicker?'

'We're the bad guys now, are we, worshippers of the car culture?' Even Christopher was losing his temper. 'That's why we have a nine-year-old Volvo and waste our time schlepping to the bottle bank, is it, because we're greedy consumers who want to chop down the rainforest and slaughter the whales?'

Alexander had told himself he was going to keep out of this, but it was a play he'd seen before, could almost recite the lines to. Rachel was breaking away, trying to reject all that her parents stood for. To them she was just being unfair, hurtful and naïve. 'I know it's none of my business,' he chipped in gently, 'and you can all just tell me to get lost, but isn't there some compromise possible? It's Christmas and even security guards and policemen take time off at Christmas, so everything will be dead here anyway. Then Rachel's got her mocks. Why don't you let her join us for some weekends after that?'

Catherine's first reaction was to tell this man, whom none of them knew anyway, to stay out of it, but surprisingly it was Christopher who shushed her and insisted they hear him out.

'She could feel part of things if she did that. This fight will go on for months, Rachel, you'll still be involved in it.' He almost added that their fight needed clever people with qualifications, but decided he would start sounding like her parents.

'You could all use my cottage as a base if you liked,' Lavinia offered unexpectedly. 'For

186

baths and meals and the odd bit of washing.'

Marko raised his black brows in astonishment. 'But you're the enemy. You want the road to be built.'

'That doesn't mean I can't help out my grand-daughter from time to time.'

'You wouldn't be very popular with your neighbours,' Alexander pointed out.

'Yes, well. Right at this moment my neighbours aren't very popular with me.'

'Tsk tsk, Lavinia,' Alexander chided, 'using kindness as revenge? I'm not sure what Christian theologians would make of that.'

'Christian theologians can go and dance on the head of a pin as far as I'm concerned,' Lavinia snapped. 'Besides it wouldn't entirely be for revenge. I'd enjoy it.'

'That's settled then,' winked Marko.

'Hang on a minute,' Rachel jumped up, making Marko spill his tea and scald himself, 'I'll decide what I want to do for myself, thank you. Maybe I'll go and join another camp in the woods. Yours isn't the only one, you know.'

Watching Marko's anguished expression, though whether at Rachel's lashing speech or the effect of boiling water on the groin, Alexander couldn't tell, he felt a passing sympathy for Marko. Rachel wasn't the malleable little schoolgirl Marko had taken her for.

Alexander's eyes rested for a moment on Lavinia. She had been just as spirited and spiky once, arguing with him through the night about the rights of man, the value of surplus labour and the virtues of taking over the means of production. But Lavinia had repressed that side of herself and channelled her relentless energy into home, children and the rights not of man but of Maxted. She had even, according to her son, denied that she'd ever been to Oxford. Alexander smarted keenly at being so effectively airbrushed out of her history. Yet watching her earlier today, Alexander wondered whether the spirit of that young girl had entirely vanished after all.

'We need to get back for Ricky,' Catherine reminded, struggling to keep her temper under control. 'Are you coming with us, Rachel?'

'I'll come tomorrow. I'd like to spend another night at the camp and say goodbye to the others.' She didn't need to add, *and to spend the night with Marko*. But to underline its clear implication, Marko put his arm around her possessively. 'We'll set off, then. Could you give us a lift, Alexander?' Rachel pleaded.

'Couldn't we?' offered Christopher. 'I'd

like to see the camp for myself.'

Rachel shrugged. 'All right then, but you'll probably get stuck in the mud. There isn't a car park like at the Forte Crest, you know.'

Lavinia and Alexander waved them good-bye.

Christopher struggled with the desire to grab Rachel and bundle her into the car. It would be highly satisfying. Instead he acknowledged the wisdom of Alexander's advice and drove silently down the road as far as he could, glancing occasionally at his wife, then down a single-track lane, and stopped where Marko indicated. The last five minutes were on foot.

The camp was much smaller than they'd expected, just three tents covered in tarpaulins, a cooking and washing-up area, a campfire, the whole thing sitting on wooden pallets. Marko opened up each tent for them. The first, Zoe's, was exotic and pretty inside; Zoe had hung up bright chenille bedspreads and draped a folding chair with hangings. Touchingly, there was a photograph of what must be the girl's very normal-looking parents, plus younger sister and family dog on an orange box next to her camp bed. Catherine felt a lump in her throat. Did these parents know she thought about them and kept their photograph near, or did they feel, as she was beginning to, despised and abandoned, the embodiment of everything sad and pathetic?

Next to the photograph was a row of contact lens cleaning equipment. How amazing in all this mud and grime that this girl clearly cleaned her lenses night and day.

The next tent was even more surprising. Everything in it was neat and folded and orderly, almost like a cubicle in a hospital or a Buddhist monk's cell. If there had been slippers they would have been ranged in an absolutely straight line at a right angle to the bed. 'That's Macduff for you. He used to be in the army. Old habits die hard. He even polishes his trainers.'

'The bed doesn't even looked slept in.'

'That's because he sleeps in the trees most of the time.' Marko was enjoying their amazement. 'He says if squirrels can, why can't he?'

'He doesn't even use a sleeping bag,' Rachel confided with pride. 'Macduff says sleeping bags are for wimps.'

'But it's two or three below at the moment!' marvelled Christopher. 'What about the last tent?' Christopher knew the question was pure masochism. What was he expecting to see? Used condoms spelling out the words 'Rachel Was Here'? Marko pulled back the flap to reveal an untidy sleeping bag with Rachel's bag on top. Christopher's heart shrivelled. It was her old backpack, the one she used to take to Brownie camp.

'Where do you get water to wash?' Catherine was fascinated in spite of herself.

'Washing isn't that much of a priority, to be frank, Mrs Hope,' said Marko.

'And that,' pointed out Rachel, 'is my fire. I gathered the wood and kindling and cooked the breakfast on it.'

The pride in her voice tore at Christopher. This was his daughter who until now had had about as much interest in domesticity as Madonna.

'And just like home,' Catherine lamely attempted a joke, 'you left the washing-up for someone else.'

'For Marko actually,' Rachel said sternly.

'I expected there to be more of you. How can you stop a motorway with four people?'

'There are dozens of small camps all over the woods. And when the action hots up people descend from all over.'

'So what do you actually *do* to stop the road?' Christopher found himself asking.

'All kinds of things. Dig tunnels, climb trees, build walkways between them, have camps up there, fifty, sixty feet above the ground.'

Catherine shuddered. 'Isn't it incredibly dangerous?'

'Only when the sodding bailiffs try and get us down. They sent in steeplejacks and window cleaners last time. They'd have enlisted Red Indians, sorry, Native Americans, if they could have found any.'

'Why?' asked Christopher, bemused.

'Because they have this incredible head for heights. Then on the ground we do tunnelling, chain ourselves to bulldozers, that sort of thing. Anything to slow them down or embarrass them or get our mugs on telly, basically.'

'Are you sure you won't freeze tonight? The temperature's really dropping.' Catherine's maternal instincts broke through her irritation as they finally said goodbye.

'Sure,' shrugged Rachel. 'If not I'll find a way of keeping warm.'

Catherine looked away. This suggestiveness was too much for her. 'See you tomorrow then.'

'Bye, Dad, hope you can find the car.'

They walked back through the leaf-strewn woods. The darkness was fast enveloping the whole landscape. Beyond the line of trees a thin moon was just discernible low in the sky. The silence was deeper than Christopher could ever remember. 'I must admit, it's beautiful enough here. I can see their point in wanting to protect it.'

'For God's sake, Christopher,' Catherine's anxiety over Rachel and whether she really would come home tomorrow, and what the hell they would do if she didn't, made her tone sharper than she'd intended. 'Don't you bloody well start! You were ineffectual enough with her as it is.'

'*I* was ineffectual?' Christopher countered. 'What did you expect me to do, drag her back by her hair? And perhaps this is our fault too. We've taught her to think for herself and overprotected her at the same time. Ever since she was three she's been dropped off and picked up. She's gone to a privileged school. When has she ever had any real freedom, except now when she's grabbed it?'

'At the cost of her education.'

'I'm with Rachel on this one. You harp on too much about her bloody education. She's a bright girl. Maybe she'll learn something about life from this that school can't teach her.'

'Like playing Marie Antoinette Goes Demonstrating, you mean? And How To Get Laid By a Long-Haired Lout.'

'Do you know, Cath.' They'd reached the car by now and Christopher undid his door and left her to cope with her own. 'I used to think that out of the two of us you were the one who had the passion and I was a bit of a dry stick, but it's you who's sounding narrow-minded and prejudiced now.'

Catherine got in and slammed the door, too furious to answer him, and they drove silently back to London, as if a plate of glass had been lowered between them.

★ ★ ★

Rachel put down her backpack in the hall of her parents' warm, comfortable house and hung her parka on the pegs instead of throwing it down as she usually did.

'Hi, little brother. How's trickies, Ricky?'

Ricky squinted up at his sister from his post at the PlayStation to make sure it was indeed her and not some alien visitor who had assumed sisterly form. Mostly she ignored him or treated him as if he were the lowest form of earth life, far beneath her attention. Today she was actually friendly.

Ricky messed up his shot, wondering what had happened to bring about this transformation. It was a pity, he mused, that the same miracle hadn't affected his parents, who seemed to be not only avoiding each other but doing so as noisily as possible. It was all very disorientating.

'Where are Mum and Dad?'

'In the kitchen not speaking to each other.'

Rachel felt a flash of guilt. You didn't have to be a rocket scientist to work out why this might be. 'How bad is it?'

'Not even asking for the marmalade.'

'That *is* bad.'

She tiptoed gingerly down the stairs to the basement kitchen. Only her mother was in the room, sitting at one end of the pine kitchen table, hiding behind the *Guardian* Education Supplement. Normally her mother cleared the table and Dad stacked the dishwasher, but today the table and worktop both looked like Bosnia.

'Mum . . . ' Rachel offered tentatively.

The newspaper dropped an inch or two.

'I just wanted to say thank you about Marko and the wood. I know it must be hard for you to accept and I really appreciate that you're not grounding me and stopping me seeing him. I do promise to work hard and get good results. I know how much they matter to you. I'm quite sensible really, you know.'

The *Guardian* crumpled and slipped to the floor. 'C'm here, you.' She jumped up and grabbed her daughter in a tight embrace. 'You're bright and you're beautiful and you could do whatever you want in life, you know.'

195

'I know. And it's thanks to you I feel that. You've just got to leave me to find out what that is and accept it may not be what you're expecting.'

Catherine felt chastened. She knew Rachel's words were deeply heartfelt — but if only she could have waited another six months. On the other hand, as that strange man Alexander had pointed out, if they weren't careful they might push her into doing something desperate. From now on she would trust Rachel to make her own decisions. Really.

Well, she would try anyway.

'Off you go or you'll be late for school.'

'There you go again, Mum.' But this time the words were spoken with affection. 'Besides we're going to a museum today and I've just got time to call Steph and find out what she's wearing.'

Catherine was about to protest that if she did she would miss the bus. But for once she kept her mouth shut and went to sort out her briefcase.

★ ★ ★

'Only two more days on the old school bench,' Anita pointed out to Catherine as they did gate duty together, 'then it's the

196

Christmas holidays, thank God. Where are you going? Barbados this year? Or have you plumped for the Seychelles?'

They both sighed at the thought.

'Christopher's brother's in Oxshott, actually.'

'At least you won't have to cook the dinner.'

'No, but staying with Martin and Jennifer is about as relaxing as three days with the Gestapo. The trains not only run on time but the house is immaculate, the children never have a hair out of place and they don't watch television during the week.'

'My God, that's seriously weird. My two couldn't get through the week without ten hours of solid soap opera.'

'Rachel and her cousin Lucy are the same age but they've got about as much in common as Kim Basinger and the Singing Nun. Lucy behaves so well all the other mothers deprogramme her. They're desperate to know why she does what she's told and what her parents' secret is.'

'And what *is* her parents' secret? Not that it'd be any use in our house unless it's a thermonuclear weapon.'

'Fear.'

'Ah, fear. I remember it well from my childhood. Whatever happened to fear, Catherine?'

'Our generation abolished it in favour of honesty and discussing things as a family, remember.'

'How foolish of us. Is that when children started to get the upper hand?'

'Very probably. Then we just gave in and put our entire lives at their disposal.'

'And are they grateful?'

'No!' Catherine and Anita chorused together.

A posse of little ones from the Reception class engulfed them. 'Are you coming to our play, miss? I'm one of the Free Kings.'

'Darlene was asked to be Mary, miss.'

Catherine smiled at the prospect of a lovely West Indian madonna. 'So are you going to wear a blue dress and carry baby Jesus?'

Darlene shook her head, 'No, miss, I turned it down. Mary ain't got enough to say.'

'That's the mother of God written out of history,' whispered Anita. 'How's Rachel, by the way? She was a lovely Virgin Mary. I still remember her.'

'She wouldn't get the part any longer,' Catherine replied gloomily. 'She hasn't got the qualifications. Not since last Friday night.'

'Go on! If she was still a virgin till last Friday in this day and age she deserves canonizing! The average in north London is fifteen and a half, so my niece tells me. Anyway how on earth do you know?'

'Guesswork. And that she's always thought the boys pretty pathetic.' She sighed. 'Until she met this Marko.'

'And what's so special about this Marko?'

'He's sex incarnate. Heathcliff with a nose stud. And being a road protester he's got plenty of time to polish his skills. Unfortunately it's on my daughter.'

'How did she get mixed up with road protesters?'

'They're trying to save the woods near my mother-in-law's in Essex. Rachel met him there and seems to have fallen for him hook, line and bulldozer. And bloody Christopher's only agreed to let her go down there again if she does well in her mocks.'

'Whereas you'd like to ban her from seeing him altogether. You know what'll happen if you do, of course.'

'What?' The bell was going and it was time to go in for Assembly.

'She'll fancy him twice as much because he'll be forbidden fruit.'

'And if I don't, I have to watch her failing her exams in everything except sex and saving the woodland.'

'Oh dear . . . ' Anita trailed off dreamily.

'What?'

'I was just thinking how much more fun that sounded than Applied Maths or European History.'

* * *

Back in her classroom Catherine set about creating order out of chaos, and began the Geography lesson.

At the far table in the corner Gary Webb, two sizes taller than anyone else, was holding court, with his hangers-on Tommy Mates and Kelly Hanlon, both of whom were about a foot shorter. Did Gary deliberately choose friends he could dominate? she wondered. Silly question.

'Right, Gary,' she enquired, 'what city is the capital of the USA?'

Gary fell silent as a church on a Monday afternoon.

'Why is it, Gary, that the only time you're ever quiet is when I actually want you to say something?'

She glanced round for Bonnie. Normally Bonnie would be clamouring to reply. But Bonnie sat in the far corner of the room, her arms by her side, staring ahead. It was almost as if she weren't physically present at all.

'New York, miss,' offered one pupil.

'Miami, miss,' offered another to general derision.

'Come on, some of you must know. What about you, Bonnie?'

'Sorry, Mrs Hope,' Bonnie seemed like a tyre with a slow puncture, as if all her liveliness and knowledge were slowly and invisibly seeping out of her.

Catherine's heart creased up for her. This wasn't the Bonnie she knew. She was going to have to look into this.

She turned to the board and wrote 'The capital of the United States of America is Washington DC'. So she didn't notice Gary Webb flick a ball of paper dampened with glue at the back of Bonnie's neck, or hear the smothered giggle when Bonnie registered the attack only by the smallest twitch of her shoulders.

'Bonnie,' she called quietly at the end of the period while the others jostled out into the corridor on their way to RE. 'Is everything all right? You seemed a bit quiet today.'

Bonnie avoided her eyes. 'I'm fine, Mrs Hope. Thank you.'

Catherine had some marking to do after school had finished for the day. There was so much to get organized, with the plays, concerts and Christmas bazaar to be sorted out, that finding time to do any marking or lesson preparation was almost impossible. She'd just worked her way through a good solid pile when there was a knock on the classroom door. She jumped up, worried that it was Bonnie and that Gary Webb had been lying in wait for her, but it was someone entirely different.

Simon had slipped into the back of the classroom and was leaning against the door. She noticed for the first time the few grey hairs that had begun to streak his head, just above the temple. It seemed impossible that Simon, with his boyish charm and his fizzling energy, could ever get middle-aged. Remembering his last words to her and their obvious invitation, she found herself colouring.

'Hello, Simon.' Catherine busied herself putting the books into her briefcase. She hated this habit of hers, which made playing it cool and sophisticated almost impossible. She might aim for Lauren Bacall but what came out was Julie Andrews.

'I wondered if you felt like a drink to celebrate the onset of the winter solstice?'

'I didn't think that was till next week.'

'Let's celebrate it early then. I can't stand celebrating Christmas. Give me the pagan festivals any time.'

Catherine hesitated, reminding herself that

she ought to be furious with him.

'Come on, Cath,' he prompted. 'Look, we're old friends. I can see something's bothering you. Why don't you come and talk about it?'

It was true, there was something bothering her: more than just the threat to Rachel's A levels, it was the thought of Marko and her daughter going to bed together. Why did it bother her quite so much? Was she horrified by her daughter's emerging sexuality, or worse still, jealous of it? Did she feel consigned to the scrapheap of womanhood by Rachel's beauty and thirst for adventure? It was true that she felt invisible sometimes, both to her children and to her husband. A fixture and fitting so familiar that they sometimes seemed to walk through her. Simon, on the other hand, seemed aware of other qualities in her.

'Well?' he noticed the chink in her defences and pushed harder. 'Catherine, I'm asking you for a drink, not to tie you to a bed and do unmentionable things to you.' He smiled at her expression. 'Although I'm more than happy to if only you'd let me. But let's start with a straightforward glass of wine, eh?'

If she hadn't been so angry with Christopher for being soft on Rachel, she would probably never have gone.

But the fact was, she was still furious. Why should she always have to be the tough one because Christopher refused to set sensible limits?

So she agreed.

And since she was breaking one rule by going for a drink with him when she knew his intentions perfectly well, she might as well break another. So, instead of drinking one glass of Californian Chardonnay, or even two, she ordered a bottle.

After the first couple of drinks she forgot about being angry over the job or over Rachel's behaviour. Simon was dazzling company. Interesting, witty and always asking her opinion on everything. Catherine felt herself blossom in the warmth of his obvious admiration. She wasn't old quite yet. Besides, they had so much in common, whereas hers and Christopher's world rarely coincided. Maybe if she'd got involved with Simon, instead of settling down with Christopher all those years ago, they would have been far better suited.

She was having such a good time that she failed to notice how often Simon was filling her glass without emptying his own. It was a shock to see that by now there was only one other couple in the whole place.

'Let me give you a lift home,' he offered as even they got up to leave.

Catherine wobbled. To her immense annoyance Simon seemed as sober as when they'd gone in there.

'Come on, I'll drop you back. Don't worry,' he read her concern, 'I won't take you to your door. You can walk the last block on your own and appear entirely innocent.'

His car was parked in the darkest corner of the wine bar's car park. She climbed in, about to protest that she *was* entirely innocent when he leaned over and kissed her hard on the mouth. Catherine was shocked by her own reaction. She had already anticipated this and how she would push him off humorously yet firmly. Instead she found herself returning his kiss with an answering hunger. She actually cried out when she felt his hand slip inside her jacket and caress her breast through the silk shirt under her sensible blazer. Shockwaves of sensation flooded downwards into a pinprick of desire as his other hand moved steadily up from knee to thigh and found its way to the soft flesh concealed there.

Fifty denier of opaque tight might have proved a barrier to another man. But not to Simon. The sound of ripping Lycra echoed through the car. Forgetting everything from where she was to who she was with, and even whether she should be there at all, Catherine's back arched in shameless longing.

9

Behind them a car switched on the engine and its headlights flooded the car park with a sudden dazzling glare.

Catherine sat up, her sanity snapping back into place, and opened her eyes. Like a missed heartbeat in a dream that gives the terrifying sensation of falling, she woke up to the impact of what she'd been about to do and the intense relief that she hadn't yet done it.

'Simon . . . ' She pushed his hand away as if it were burning her. 'I can't. Believe me, I'd like to . . . '

She caught sight of his face, illuminated in the car's headlights. It wasn't the pleasant and witty Simon of earlier.

'I know, I know,' the bitterness in his voice shocked her, 'you like the fantasy of an affair, but you just can't cope with the reality.'

Catherine felt as if she'd been hit. Simon was her friend and yet this man sitting next to her seemed almost to hate her, as if refusing him were some kind of weakness.

'Don't tell me,' he drawled, his voice dripping with sarcasm. 'This is nothing to do with me. It's between you and your husband.'

Through the brutality, the unintended truth of his words struck home. It *was* between her and Christopher. She was angry with her husband and she'd let the anger lie like some sea of acid between them.

'Yes, you're absolutely right,' she agreed quietly.

'Spare me the Relate counselling. If you don't want this to happen that's fine by me.'

Catherine buttoned up her coat, feeling dirty and used. How often before had Simon been in this situation? She knew he didn't have a long-time partner and there were rumours of affairs with colleagues, but she'd never paid much attention to them. Staff rooms were bitchier than auditions for the chorus line. But there were men who got involved with married women because it meant there was no risk of real commitment and maybe Simon was one of them.

'I think I'd better go.'

'Yes.'

Catherine climbed out of the car, feeling both stupid and furious. She had gone into this with her eyes wide open. Simon's intentions couldn't have been clearer if he'd written them down and handed them to her. Thank God at least she didn't have to work with him for much longer.

Simon was staring ahead when she turned and walked away from the car park and back in the direction of her home.

Round the corner she hid in an alley and pulled off her torn tights. Moments ago having them ripped had seemed exciting, now it was a grubby reminder of her mistake. She stuffed them into a black bag of rubbish by the roadside.

By the time she got home it was almost eleven. Christopher would be in bed, his angry back reproaching her as usual. He wouldn't even ask her where she'd been.

Instead the whole house was lit up as though there were a party. Catherine stood staring at it. Christopher always made a point of switching off the lights when he left each room. She turned her key in the door and listened. The television was off and no noisy pop music blared from the children's bedrooms.

She expected to find him in the basement kitchen, but it was scrupulously tidy, except for one of Ricky's Capri-Sun orange juice packs. Without thinking she opened the bin to throw it in.

Staring at her from the top of the pile of rubbish was a Marks & Spencer Peking Duck dinner for two, their favourite treat, too expensive to have except on birthdays and celebrations. It was cooked but untouched. Next to it was an empty bottle of their best red wine. Catherine lifted the packaging for the duck. Underneath was a small posy of bright jewel-like anemones, her favourite flowers.

A sick feeling of shame and regret flooded through her. Christopher must have planned all this as a surprise.

She searched through every room, including Rachel and Ricky's. They were sleeping peacefully, Ricky still clutching the joystick of his computer game, Rachel asleep on her Forever Friends pillow. Their own bed was empty. She grabbed a pair of tights from her drawer and searched the sitting room.

Panic gripped Catherine. Why would he have left all the lights on and gone out? Next to her the hot-water pipes rattled, reminding her that she ought to have called a plumber to check them. But why were they noisy at this time of night? She ran upstairs two at a time, forgetting she still had her coat on.

Christopher was lying back in the bath, a large glass of red wine in his hand, fast asleep. Catherine dipped her hand in the water. It was almost cold. She gently removed the glass from his hand and sat back on her heels watching him. In sleep he looked younger, almost as he had when they'd met. His dark eyelashes curled over his cheeks and his hair, not yet streaked with grey, looked as if it could do with a trim. She had seen their difficulties with Rachel entirely from her own perspective. She had been angry with him for being soft and yet he had different ideas from her about how to handle Rachel. And who knew whether his ideas mightn't be more effective? After all, they couldn't seriously have locked her up. Rachel was a strong-minded young woman who could think for herself.

Gently she reached out and stroked his face.

Christopher opened his eyes. Before surprise clouded over into hostility she leaned forward and kissed him.

'Mind out. You'll get wet.'

'Too bad. I wanted to say sorry for being so shitty lately. The dinner looked delicious.'

'How did you know about the dinner?'

'I saw it in the bin. You should have told me.'

'The essence of surprise is not to tell. Where the hell were you?'

She thought of lying, but decided against it.

'Having a drink with Simon.'

'Till this time?'

'One bottle led to another, you know how it is.'

He looked her firmly in the eyes until she glanced away, hoping he hadn't guessed.

'And you say teachers' salaries aren't enough to keep a budgie in seed.'

'It was very cheap wine.'

'You know what they say about alcohol?'

'What do they say about alcohol?'

'That it lowers the defences. Come here.' He stepped dripping from the bath and pushed her quite roughly on to the carpeted floor of the bathroom.

'Hey, I'm getting soaked.'

'Too bad.'

'Rachel might come in.'

'Time she learned she isn't the only one allowed to make love around here.'

Catherine laughed and began to undo her skirt. Catching them at it might be the one thing that put Rachel off.

★ ★ ★

'You look happy with life,' Anita remarked the next morning in the staff room before anyone else had arrived. 'Nothing to do with you and Simon being spotted together in Wells Wine Bar last night, I trust? You want to watch it, my girl, or you'll be accused of extracurricular activity.'

'My God,' Catherine laughed hollowly. 'The jungle drums beat fast round here. And no, my mood has nothing to do with Simon. That was a bit of a disaster actually. I'll be lucky if Simon gives me the time of day after last night.'

'Don't tell me you turned him down?'

'How did you even know he asked?'

'Oh, come on, Cath, don't be so naïve. Why else would he ask you out after what he said to you? To discuss inner-city education? Anyway, what happened? Half the staff room would give up their Christmas break for a proposition from charismatic, compassionate yet sexy Simon.'

'Well, I'm not one of them. Though I have to admit that for ten minutes I might have given him slightly the wrong impression.'

'Catherine Hope, you prick-tease you.'

Catherine looked guilty. 'Simon said much the same thing.'

'There's a surprise. So what happened, then?'

'I went home of course.'

'How tragic. So you're being gossiped about without even having done the deed.'

Catherine smiled a small secret smile. 'Actually I did do the deed, but not with Simon. Thanks to Simon, Christopher and

I are talking again.'

'And not just talking by the sound of things,' said Anita.

'Anyway, I don't think I'm Simon's favourite person any more.'

'Surely he must have realized you had an awful lot at stake.'

'One thing I found out about Simon is that though he may seem incredibly caring and sensitive, he doesn't actually think about anyone much but Simon.'

They were interrupted by a knock on the door. Bonnie leaned against the wall opposite. 'Sorry to disturb you, Mrs Hope, but I knew you often came in early.'

Bonnie seemed to have lost weight, and with it the vitality and enthusiasm for life that had always characterized her. Her hair, Bonnie's one asset, needed a wash, and her tracksuit, one of three she alternated, had a hole in one knee. Catherine wanted to scoop her up and give her a cuddle. Had Bonnie's mother thought through the effect it would have on this sensitive child to run off and leave her?

'Yes, Bonnie,' Catherine asked kindly, 'what is it?'

Bonnie avoided looking her in the eye. 'I just wanted to tell you that I've decided against doing the exam to Wolsey. I'm sorry when you've been to so much trouble for me, but I think it's for the best.'

'Oh, Bonnie.' Disappointment gripped Catherine as if Bonnie were her own child. 'Are you sure?'

'Yes, I've really thought about it a lot.'

One of the other teachers arrived and Bonnie used it as an excuse to make her escape.

The pleasure seeped from Catherine's day at Bonnie's news.

'It's that little shit Gary Webb,' Anita asserted. 'He's been getting at her, I'll bet. Can't bear to have anyone do well.'

'Oh, Anita, what can I do? I've tried to get Brian Wickes to do something, but he doesn't want to know.'

'Have you approached her father?'

'He's not the type to get involved. I don't think he can cope now the mother's left. In fact, I had thought of asking Simon to weigh in.'

'And you don't think that's on the agenda now you've left him with a lump in his trousers where his vanity used to be? Look, Cath, you've done so much for that kid. You can hardly be expected to give her twenty-four-hour protection from thugs like Gary.'

Catherine gathered up her things for the next lesson. She had to do something about

Bonnie, but at the moment she hadn't the slightest idea what.

The day passed in what seemed only minutes to Catherine. But days were like that as the year wound down. The last week of the Christmas term might be hellishly busy but it had always been Catherine's favourite time. The amount of hard work generated by the plays, bazaars and by thinking of original and creative holiday projects, as well as getting all the marking over with, was backbreaking, but there was always such a festive atmosphere that it was worth it. And on top of that today was Friday.

'Hey, Bonnie,' the child had been so quiet all day that Catherine had almost forgotten her presence. 'You haven't forgotten you're helping me with the tombola tomorrow? I'm relying on you, you know.'

*　*　*

The Christmas fair was always a mad scramble so Catherine decided to go in a little earlier than usual and make a stunning display to try to disguise the bath salts, boxes of ageing crystallized fruits and the famous After Eights holder so that they didn't look quite so familiar to all the parents. She'd bought a few metres of cheap tartan cloth and ferreted out some red and green satin bows from her box of Christmas decorations at home, and set about draping the trestle table with it.

Anita arrived and started pricing the jumble on the stall next door to hers. 'Cor, that's not bad!' Anita held out an outrageous lycra mini-dress, which looked as if it would fit a skinny eight-year-old, against her solid ten-stone frame. 'I'll have that one.'

She put fifty pence in the change box.

'Anita, you'll never fit in that. Besides, aren't you supposed to be selling the stuff to the parents?'

'Organizers' perks. Even the helpers at the church jumble sales know that. God rewards his helpers, you know.'

Catherine had almost finished her display before she glanced at her watch. It was one thirty and the bazaar would be starting in an hour. The rest of the assembly hall was now a flurry of activity. She realized there had been no sign of Bonnie.

'Hold the fort for me, would you, Anita?' she shouted. 'I'm all ready. Back in ten minutes.' At least she hoped she would be. She ran down the street towards the block of shops where Bonnie's dad had his video shop. Maybe she'd been made to help there.

But Bonnie's father hadn't seen her. 'She

said she was going to school to help you,' he snapped, attending to a queue of customers renting horror films for a cosy Saturday afternoon in.

Catherine struggled to keep calm. There were plenty of places Bonnie could have gone. 'She didn't turn up. Could she be with a friend?'

His snort of laughter made Catherine wince. Poor little Bonnie obviously didn't have any friends.

'Where does she like going to?'

'You could try the library. Failing that, Woolworths or the park. I'll kill her, scaring us all like this.'

Catherine started with the library. The librarian in the reference section knew Bonnie well but hadn't seen her this morning. Woolworth's, two doors down from the video shop, was teeming with Christmas shoppers who'd clearly forgotten it was the season of goodwill and were mowing each other down in their eagerness to get to the till. A small dumpy figure stood staring longingly at the Pick 'n' Mix. 'Bonnie!' shouted Catherine, relief making her voice louder than she'd meant. The child turned suddenly. It wasn't Bonnie.

The bazaar opened in twenty minutes and there was always a mad rush to get in, as if it were sale time at Harrods instead of some old tat at the school fair.

Catherine ran as fast as she could to the park, but it was empty. An old man with a little dog sat on a bench at the far end, oblivious to the four-letter words that adorned the colourful playground equipment. Catherine slumped on to the next bench up. It was no good. She'd have to get back to school.

The small sound was so quiet she almost missed it. Then the man's comical little dog came and nuzzled her leg and she bent down to stroke it. There it was again. This time it was unmistakable as a sob.

Catherine rushed over to the children's playhouse. There, huddled in one corner, weeping quietly, was Bonnie. Catherine said nothing. She simply climbed into the tiny house and held Bonnie in her arms.

'Have they gone?' Bonnie whispered, her eyes red and puffy and very frightened.

Catherine didn't need to ask who. 'Yes. There's no one out there. I'm taking you home now, Bonnie.'

The shop was mercifully quiet when they got there. 'Look, Mr Miles, you must know Bonnie's being bullied. She probably won't tell you herself but Gary Webb's the ringleader. I've tried to get the school to act, but they feel they can't as a lot of it's outside school premises. I think maybe you should talk to his parents. I'm sure that's why she's changed her mind about the exam.'

Mr Miles was small and overweight, with sloping shoulders as if a permanent chip had worn them down. He looked as if he'd been picked on too, by his school mates and maybe also his wife. He didn't speak. He didn't need to. His whole stance proclaimed that for people like him and Bonnie, natural losers, bullying was a fact of life.

Catherine took a chance. 'Look, Mr Miles, maybe you were bullied too, maybe you know what she's going through. But she has a way out. She's really bright. She could get the kind of education that will make her a winner. But she needs your help. Mr Miles, she needs *you*.'

Bonnie's father hesitated and for a moment Catherine thought he might look at her. Instead he shuffled the videos on the counter.

Eventually, still without meeting her eye, he spoke. 'Gary Webb's father is one of my best customers.'

Catherine turned round and walked out. Bonnie had already run upstairs. She could imagine what kind of videos Gary Webb's dad watched.

The bazaar had well and truly started by the time she got to school.

Anita's jumble had almost sold. Most of the stalls had clearly been doing riproaring business and everyone looked delighted. She rushed to the tombola to find Brian Wickes, stony-faced, manning the stall for her. 'They couldn't find anyone else,' he carped angrily.

'Sorry,' mouthed Anita.

Catherine was tempted to shout out the truth of what had happened at the top of her voice, except that she wasn't sure it would help Bonnie. 'I need to talk to you, Brian. This bullying business with Bonnie Miles is getting out of hand. I just found her hiding from Gary Webb's gang in the playhouse at the park and she's decided against sitting the entrance exam for Wolsey.'

'We don't have gangs in this school, Catherine,' Brian said tetchily. 'It's against school policy. And this question of getting into Wolsey. Are you sure it's not you, rather than her, who really minds the most?'

Catherine was still furious by the time she got home. Christopher sat her down and made her a soothing cup of tea.

'Thank God I married a tea importer,' Catherine pointed out, grabbing his hand and holding it against her cheek. 'Think, if you'd been a wine shipper I would probably have been permanently pissed.'

'Mum,' Rachel decided to approach her mother while she was drinking the first cup. As the child of a tea expert, she knew that by the second cup the taste of the tannin intruded and the moment of total bliss was over. 'I just wondered whether it might be possible for me to stay at Gran's for Christmas. I'm not sure I'm up to spending it with the Perfect Hopes.'

Catherine's eyes snapped open. 'Of course you can't stay with Gran. Gran will be coming to the PHs' as well. And you're *certainly* not allowed there on your own. Your cousins may be, er . . . ' She caught Christopher's eye, wondering how insulting she could be about his brother Martin and her sister-in-law Jennifer.

' . . . completely ghastly,' supplied Christopher amiably.

'Completely ghastly,' Catherine grinned, 'but they *are* family. And you've always got your cousin Lucy. It'll be fun to have someone your own age.'

'God, Mum. Lucy's idea of doing something daring is getting out a new library book.'

'I expect she'll be a very good influence.'

'And Robin just wants to play chess all the time,' protested Ricky. 'He thinks PlayStation's infantile.'

'He has my sympathy there,' conceded Christopher. 'Anyway, it's only two days. You'll survive.'

★ ★ ★

Fifty miles away, but several millennia in terms of peace and beauty, Lavinia and Alexander strolled down a path between high elm trees. The day had started cold and grey and they had wrapped themselves up in layer after layer against the penetrating mist that often hung over the fields until well into the day.

'I don't know why you insisted on walking on a day like this,' Lavinia complained. 'I'd much rather be by my warm fireside.'

'That's the trouble with you, Lavinia,' Alexander chided. 'You live in the middle of this glorious landscape and you don't really use your eyes. If you did you wouldn't have considered supporting that ghastly road for an instant.'

'Ah, ha. I might have known a gentle stroll with you would have an agenda. So far it's very nice but it looks pretty ordinary to me, much like any other bit of English countryside.'

'That's because we haven't got there yet.'

They walked on in silence for a few hundred yards.

'Right, you can stop here. Cover your eyes.'

'Really, Alexander, this isn't some children's party game.' Her feet were beginning to freeze and Alexander's enthusiasm, which she'd found so charming at twenty, was wearing a little thin four decades later. He really ought to grow up.

'All right,' he turned her round bodily, 'you can open them now.'

Lavinia did so and she found herself looking at the end of the path, where the two lines of elms opened into rolling farmland. Straight ahead, through a wooden gate, was a cornfield, bare now, and by the side of the path a small stream burbled gently. In the distance elms and oaks dotted the horizon and a square church tower was just visible to the right. It was quintessentially English, pretty but otherwise, in Lavinia's view, unremarkable.

'Now, look at this.'

Alexander produced a postcard of a painting from his pocket.

Lavinia studied it. It was the same view. The cornfield with its gate, the church, the elms, even the stream. 'My God, it's here! Absolutely identical. How extraordinary.'

'Notice the little boy drinking in the left-hand corner.' Alexander dropped down on to the stream bank and dipped his face into the water. 'You can still do it.'

'Alexander, for God's sake! There's probably a dead sheep round the corner, or at least poisonous chemicals in it.'

Alexander laughed. 'Do you know who painted that? And when?'

Lavinia suddenly realized what this revelation was all about, why he'd brought her here. 'Not Constable, surely?'

'*The Cornfield*. John Constable, 1776–1837, probably the greatest English landscape painter of all time. And the amazing thing is, it's exactly the same!'

He produced another piece of paper from his pocket. 'Now look at that.'

'What is it?'

'The plans for the proposed Maxted bypass. Six lanes of motorway. Check the grid reference if you like.'

'Not . . . ?' But Lavinia didn't need to elaborate. She could tell from the look of triumph on Alexander's face.

'Do you think they realize?'

'Conspiracy or cock-up, you mean? Life has taught me it's cock-up nearly every time. And I doubt if they would have deliberately designed a road right through the middle of one of England's most famous paintings. They're going to look a little bit foolish if it comes out, aren't they?'

They had come to the stile leading to the cornfield. Lavinia leaned against it. 'Alexander, there's something I've been wanting to ask you.'

'Well? Come on, Lavinia, I don't see you as the shy, silent type.'

'I was just wondering what you'd done with your life after Oxford.' She hesitated, colouring slightly and looking away. 'I mean did you get married or anything?'

Alexander laughed. 'Not even 'or anything' as it happens. A wife would have always been interrupting demonstrations to talk about shopping lists or something.'

'Shopping lists are part of life, Alexander.'

'Not my life. I've spent sixty-five years surviving without them.'

'And have you been content with your list-free life?'

'Perfectly.'

'And you never ran out of sugar once?'

'You're laughing at me, Lavinia.' He smiled back all the same. 'You should come and join us, you know. It would be excellent publicity value.'

'Same old Alexander. Always an eye on the main chance.'

'Is that why you left, because you thought I was on the make? That I'd advance my future by saddling up with a nice middle-class girl?'

She could still hear the pain splintering through the years of hard-won indifference. 'How could you abandon your degree, just like that? You had such a bright future . . . And me, Lavinia . . . '

'There were reasons . . . '

Lavinia felt all the certainty and composure she'd struggled for draining out of her. Even after all this time she couldn't bring herself to tell him the truth. 'I just don't think it would have worked out between us. You're mercurial and I'm down-to-earth. We would never have been happy.'

'And were you happy with the man you chose?'

'He was a good husband.'

'That usually means he was a boring man.'

'Not everyone can be as exciting as you.'

'Why did you really go, and why didn't you tell me?'

The brightness of the sun made a halo around Alexander's white hair, giving him the look of a fiery god.

Did she owe it to him to tell the truth, that he had been the real love of her life but she had never allowed herself to admit it?

It was no use. She still wasn't brave enough.

'Thank you for the offer of joining you. I'm not sure my grand-daughter would appreciate me as a convert, stealing the glory of her rebellion. Anyway, you know perfectly well I'm in favour of the road. Right isn't all on your and Constable's side, you know. The road is necessary to save the town.'

'Ah, Lavinia, you don't honestly believe that.'

'Look, Alexander Bailey, I'm not some impressionable eighteen-year-old whom you can, pardon the expression, bulldoze into submission.'

'Do you know, that speech reminded me so much of Rachel it was uncanny?'

'She is my grand-daughter, after all, though she'd be horrified to know she reminded you of me. Alexander, there's one other small thing . . . ' She hesitated, as if she couldn't quite work up the nerve.

Alexander stopped, intrigued. 'Yes, Lavinia, what was this small thing that you wanted to ask me?'

'I just wondered,' Lavinia looked him squarely in the eye, 'what you were doing for Christmas Day and whether you would like to spend it with me.'

'Aren't you going to spend Christmas with your family? In my mind's eye you are firmly the matriarch.'

'Perhaps I feel I've been the matriarch for long enough. Besides I can always see them on Boxing Day. You haven't answered my question.'

'Nothing as a matter of fact. I usually spend it with the World Service. If you're serious, then I accept. I can't think of a more delightful way of spending Christmas. Even better than being chained to a bulldozer.'

'I'm very grateful,' Lavinia thanked him faintly, 'though I can't help feeling your standards are rather low.'

'That's settled then. I come to you for Christmas and scandalize the entire village. What tremendous fun.'

10

'Are these all real Tudor houses?' Ricky's head swivelled along the row of grotesque mini-mansions, each with its own neatly nipped grass and immaculate Jag or Audi in the driveway.

'Absolutely,' Rachel confirmed. 'The Tudors really went in for double garages and en suite bathrooms.'

'In Uncle Martin's house,' Catherine giggled, 'even the en suite bathroom has an en suite bathroom.'

'Now, now,' chided their father, 'just because your uncle Martin has more money than taste there's no need to mock.'

'Mock as in mock-Tudor, you mean?' teased Catherine.

Martin and Jennifer's house distinguished itself by the fairy lights adorning the cherry tree on the front lawn, the fairy lights lining the imitation arch over the front door and the fairy lights running along the top of the garage. Other people had fairy lights too, just not as many as Martin and Jennifer.

'Come on, everyone,' reminded Catherine, 'it's the season of goodwill. Peace and love.

It's only two days after all.'

'Two days too long,' grumbled Rachel. She couldn't wait to get to a phone so that she could try Marko on his mobile. She kept being haunted by images of him shivering in his greatcoat in the middle of Gosse's Wood. These were, it had to be admitted, followed by images of him in suburban Pinner being stuffed like a turkey by his doting mum, or worse, still back in the wood with Zoe holding a cracker and a piece of tinsel, climbing into his sleeping bag to keep him warm.

'Hello, Jennifer, hello, Martin.' Christopher shook his brother's hand enthusiastically. He had once tried to give Martin a brotherly hug but Martin had reacted like Prince Charles when some pleb invaded his private space, with ill-concealed horror.

Watching them greet each other, Catherine wasn't surprised they saw each other only at Christmas. Christopher was tactile, warm, and possessed of a natural enthusiasm for life and people, sometimes bordering on the naïve. Martin, apart from being four inches shorter than his brother, had the kind of cautious nature that assessed the risks before getting out of bed in the morning. Martin might be the younger brother but he seemed to have come out of the womb with a pipe and slippers. And whereas Christopher's hair was still dark and crinkly and plentiful, Martin's had given up the fight and receded gently backwards till his forehead shone pink and green and blue from the reflected fairy lights.

If she were honest, there was another reason Catherine resented Martin and Jennifer. Their children, Lucy and Robin, had excelled at school, were outstanding musicians who actually *practised* without complaining, and they had, as far as Catherine knew, never given their parents the slightest trouble. Nose studs, trainers that cost the national budget of Brazil, computer addiction, these were not things that had kept Martin and Jennifer awake at night. 'We just say no,' Jennifer explained, as if dealing with your children were as simple as that. Catherine occasionally wished Lucy would do something just slightly aberrant, like become a teenage prostitute, or discover Ecstasy. It seemed on the face of it unlikely.

And on top of this, she knew Lavinia preferred them to her own children.

'Come in, come in,' Martin ushered. 'How was your journey?'

The journey, as it happened, had been diabolical. Though a mere thirty miles separated their homes, this being Christmas

Eve it had taken over four hours. Martin proceeded to give them a detailed run-down on all the shortcuts they should have taken to reduce their journey time by half.

Jennifer, in pale pink leisure wear, reminded Catherine of a sugared almond stripped for aerobics. How on earth could she have cooked for Christmas in that colour? On Catherine it would have been streaked in cranberry sauce hours ago. Instead, Jennifer, untarnished by gravy, was offering glasses of blush wine around.

Rachel rushed upstairs with Lucy, as wholesome as her mother, no doubt to instruct her cousin in the joys of sex with a road rebel.

Oh, God.

Jennifer seated them all in the sitting room, fresh from the pages of *Ideal Home*. Upstairs, Catherine knew, the beds would be immaculately made with a neat pile of matching towels, embroidered with a satin flower, on each and your own small guest soap.

On the sofa opposite, Robin and Ricky sat like a pair of bookends that didn't match.

'How's the world of tea importing?' Martin asked. He never enquired about Catherine's job. The idea of teaching in the state sector so appalled him he didn't trust himself.

'Fine. People are still drinking it.'

'We prefer coffee ourselves,' Jennifer added, as if to dismiss the half of the world that disagreed.

The conversation, which hadn't really ever started, temporarily lapsed. 'So,' Christopher asked brightly, 'when's Ma arriving?'

Martin and Jennifer exchanged glances. 'Well, Chris, the most extraordinary development, you see, the thing is . . . she isn't.'

Christopher thought he must have misheard. 'Not coming? Ma? But that's ludicrous. We always spend Christmas Day together.'

'Not this year. She's arriving on Boxing Day. And even more bizarre, she didn't even say why. She rang Jenny a couple of days ago and announced that she felt like a change this year and she'd see us the day after.'

'She must have said *something*,' Christopher was staggered. 'Ma's keener on Christmas than the Queen. She usually starts getting ready in August, for God's sake. You're sure she's all right? This wasn't a cry for help or anything?'

'To tell you the truth,' Jennifer added, 'she did sound rather odd. But not depressed. Sort of . . . well . . . happy really. There was a kind of smile in her voice.'

Jennifer sipped her blush wine, exhausted by this descriptive *tour de force*.

'Well, Cath,' Christopher asked her as they

unpacked their rather tatty suitcase and hung their clothes on the peach-scented satin hangers Jennifer had put out for them, 'what do you make of that?'

Catherine sniffed her hanger and grimaced. It smelled pungent and artificial, reminiscent of ladies' toilets in expensive department stores. 'It seems to me that your mother has found someone else she'd rather spend Christmas with.'

'Not that pea-brained neighbour of hers? You'd want to strangle her with her own tinsel before you'd even got through *Carols from Kings.*'

'Not Eunice, no.'

'You mean her frightful bridge-playing cronies? Colonel whatsisname who came to the police station?'

'No,' Catherine smiled slowly. 'I'm thinking of someone who came to the police station, but not the Colonel.'

Suddenly, the seas parted in Christopher's mind. 'You don't mean him, Alexander Bailey? She hasn't seen him for years. Ma wouldn't spend Christmas with Alexander Bailey. Besides, he's the enemy, isn't he? It'd be like Romeo and Juliet kept apart not by Montagues and Capulets but six lanes of brand-new motorway.'

'I think it's rather touching. Maybe they're

old and wise enough to keep politics and friendship apart.'

'You're serious, aren't you? My God, that'll start some fluttering in the dovecots of Maxted.'

'Yes,' agreed Catherine, 'I think it probably will.'

★   ★   ★

Christmas Day at the Perfect Hopes' followed a well-oiled pattern to which the Hopes were expected to conform absolutely. Jennifer was up at seven thirty to light the oven and consult the running order she'd Blu-tacked to her kitchen units. Eight thirty was breakfast, bacon and eggs.

'But I don't want bacon and eggs,' whispered Christopher, 'we're about to stuff ourselves as well as the turkey.'

'Shut up and eat,' advised his wife. Catherine, exhausted by the end-of-term rush, was relieved it wasn't her turn to produce three dozen mince pies, a cake, Christmas pudding no one would eat anyway once they'd savaged it to find the charms buried within, plus three entire meals for eight. The only trouble was, Jennifer didn't like anyone else even mucking in and peeling the occasional sprout, so you were left there, eager to demonstrate your Christmas spirit but sentenced to watch *Songs of Praise* instead.

After breakfast it was a desperate battle to dig Rachel out of bed, clothe her suitably and persuade her that it didn't matter whether she *wanted* to come, going to church was part of the Christmas ritual.

Catherine held out her black velvet skirt and deafened her ears to the usual accusation of 'You're so hypocritical'.

This was the constant refrain every time Catherine counselled her daughter to be punctual, not to drink too much, or spend hours on the phone to people she'd just seen five minutes earlier. 'You're so hypocritical,' Rachel would sneer, 'you're late for everything, drink like a fish, and ring up your friends to moan about Dad all the time.'

Catherine refrained from answering. One day when Rachel had children of her own, she would learn that hypocrisy was a natural condition of parenthood.

After church they had a cup of coffee, jiggled the perfect roast potatoes (how *did* Jennifer manage to get them brown and crispy on gas mark 2?) and Jennifer basted the turkey.

'By the way,' Jennifer asked casually, 'did we tell you how well Lucy did in her mocks?

They have them early at her school to leave plenty of time for revision.'

Catherine's heart sank. You could bet your chestnut stuffing Jennifer wouldn't be asking this unless Lucy had done brilliantly.

'She got an A star in all three subjects,' glowed Jennifer. 'And the teachers said her cello and gymnastics demonstrated what an all-round pupil she is. She's such a reader, too, and she's just started voluntary work in her spare time. Does Rachel do any voluntary work?'

Catherine tried to think up an answer. No work Rachel ever did was voluntary. She had to be held at gunpoint to even open her textbooks unless she got something in return, like being allowed to go to the wretched wood. Unless, of course, you counted being a road rebel as voluntary work. Catherine had a feeling Jennifer wouldn't see it that way.

'Too busy with her studies,' lied Catherine, swiftly changing the subject. 'I say, what fabulous roast potatoes. How do you get them like that?'

For the next ten minutes Catherine was able to switch off while her sister-in-law Delia'd on about parboiling and half sunflower to half unsalted butter.

The last hour before lunch was spent in the

time-honoured ritual of swapping Boots vouchers for Our Price tokens, with the occasional lapse into silence as the wrapping paper fell away revealing something too ghastly to comment on.

'Oh, thanks, Dad,' enthused Lucy in apparent sincerity as she undid a CD of Beethoven sonatas.

'Oh, cool, Dad,' Rachel hugged Christopher, 'you managed to get me the Puff Daddy!'

Finally it was time for the feast. The table was laid to perfection with a white table cloth, caught up at intervals in swags and adorned with tartan bows, individual flower arrangements of gold pine cones and plastic holly berries, paper napkins with Christmas bells on them and enough cutlery to start a kitchen shop.

Jennifer carried the turkey in as if it were some Eastern potentate posing on a platter, while Martin and the children clapped. Any minute now, Catherine thought meanly, they'll get down and worship it.

Martin was halfway through the carving when there was a ring at the doorbell.

'Who on earth,' Jennifer demanded, 'would be crass enough to visit someone at one fifteen on Christmas Day?'

'Ma?' suggested Christopher.

'Yes,' conceded Jennifer, flinging down her paper napkin, 'she would be crass enough.'

The doorbell rang again, more insistent this time.

'I'll go,' Martin offered grudgingly. 'You go on carving.'

'I'm coming, I'm coming,' he insisted crossly, pulling back the heavy curtain that kept out the draughts in winter.

On the doorstep a young man with long black hair, a shabby greatcoat, and a week's stubble held out a bottle of Bailey's Irish Cream as if it were gold, frankincense or myrrh. 'Happy Christmas, Mr Hope. Rachel invited me. She said she couldn't bear the idea of me spending it up a tree.'

Martin's face was a picture. 'Do I know you?' he asked faintly, wondering if they were about to be robbed at gunpoint.

Christopher appeared behind him. 'Er, hello, Marko,' he took the bottle, wincing slightly when he caught sight of the label, and ushered him in, 'I'm afraid I don't know your other name.'

'Williams,' announced Marko jovially. 'I hope this isn't too unexpected, only I was supposed to be going home to Pinner and to be frank I couldn't face it. Even the stockbroker belt's better than bloody Pinner.'

240

Christopher led the little party back to the dining room.

'Rachel, I think you'd better lay an extra place. A friend of yours has arrived for Christmas dinner.'

11

'How *could* you let her go out with a lout like that, Catherine?' Jennifer's voice almost squeaked with outrage. 'He isn't even clean. Where on earth did she find him? My God, he's not *homeless*, is he?'

Jennifer somehow made homelessness sound like leprosy, making Catherine, who had disliked Marko on sight, feel she had to jump to his defence. 'Not exactly. He's involved in this road protest near Lavinia's. It's probably quite hard to keep clean when you're camping in a wood.'

'Well, I hope he doesn't think he's staying here.'

The thought of Marko climbing under any of Jennifer's crisp white duvet covers did stretch the imagination, Catherine had to admit. 'Perhaps you could just offer him a bath after lunch and point out that he can't possibly stay the night.'

'Nothing would give me more pleasure,' Jennifer agreed. 'I still don't see why you don't just tell her she can't see him.'

'Because that isn't the way we've brought her up,' Christopher explained wearily. 'We brought her up to think and make choices.'

'And she's chosen this lout. You must be proud.'

'The thing that pisses me off,' Catherine murmured as Jennifer disappeared to offer Marko a satin embroidered guest towel, 'is that *their* children would do what they were told.'

'Yes,' hissed Christopher, 'but look at their children. Dull as ditchwater, just like Martin. Would you rather have their children than ours?'

Catherine glanced across at Lucy and Robin, immaculate in neatly pressed jumpers, next to her own children. Rachel wore an outsize grey pullover that looked as if Oxfam had rejected it, and Ricky's mouth glinted with red and white Arsenal colours. She paused. This was a tricky one.

Christopher, following her train of thought, said, 'You wouldn't really. No surprises.'

Catherine tried to smile back. Sometimes she felt there were too many surprises in their liberated theory of childcare.

Jennifer bustled back into the room, reminding Catherine of a rather officious hedgehog. 'So,' she whispered in a tone most people would call a normal speaking voice, 'what's the story about Lavinia? Martin never questions anything, but there has to be more to all this than she's letting on.'

Catherine opened her mouth to put forward her own theory, that Lavinia was spending it with Alexander, then, remembering Jennifer's face at the sight of Marko, decided to leave things as they stood. She couldn't be absolutely sure Alexander Bailey had anything to do with it.

One road rebel was probably enough for today.

★   ★   ★

Lavinia hummed along with her tape of the *Four Seasons* as she got everything ready for Alexander's arrival. She stopped for a moment and breathed in the aroma that filled the house. Pungent pine from the small tree — each year she told herself it was too much trouble to get a real one and each year she caved in and got one — competed with her Christmas pot-pourri liberally doused in spicy oils: cinnamon, lemon and orange, musk. The fire flickered in its grate, illuminating the jewel red of the walls.

Yes, thought Lavinia with a small smile of pride, this was a good place to be on Christmas Day. At the back of her mind guilt tried to wave its warning flag, telling her she should phone her children and wish them

Happy Christmas, but Lavinia ignored it. Today belonged to her. All her married life she had either cooked or eaten Christmas dinner with her family. She was shocked at herself and elated too.

Last night she had been to midnight service in the small parish church. The path from the village street to the church had been lit by nightlights in milk bottles, welcoming in the worshippers. For once the handshake of friendship during the service, usually an empty ritual in her eyes, had felt genuine. As she walked home the sky was clear and wildly starry and she could hear bells ringing not just from their own church, but answering churches for miles around. The Christmas miracle had seemed possible.

She laid the table by the window and added, for good measure, a red candle. The knock on the door, when it came, made her jump. She was angry to find herself nervous as a girl.

Straightening her hair in the tiny mirror held by two angels, she opened the front door.

'Lavinia,' chirruped Eunice, 'why on earth aren't you with your family? I saw the light on and thought you might like company.' Her eyes fixed on the table set for two by the window. 'Oh,' disappointment dripped from her tones, 'I see you're already expecting some.'

It was at this moment that Alexander chose to open the garden gate.

'Eunice,' Lavinia gave in to inevitability, 'may I introduce my old friend from Oxford days, Alexander Bailey?'

'But you were the man on the zebra crossing,' Eunice pointed out incredulously, looking as if she were making the acquaintance of the devil himself.

'Indeed I was. Lavinia and I are destined to be on opposite sides of this argument, but we have decided, haven't we, Lavinia, that friendship ought to be able to survive a little opposition.'

Lavinia knew she ought to ask Eunice, who was obviously alone, if she wanted to stay, but she had to squeeze out the very last drops of human kindness to utter the invitation. 'Would you care to join us, Eunice? We can easily lay another place.'

Eunice's eyes fixed on the table as if it were a bed with black satin sheets instead of a harmless place-setting for two. She held her handbag in front of her like a breast-plate in the fight against sin and depravity. 'No, no, I couldn't possibly intrude . . .'

'If you're sure,' Lavinia breathed out again.

Eunice excused herself and dashed next

door without looking back, clearly convinced that if she did some terrible sight of moral corruption might assault her.

'Good God,' Alexander commented, 'what was all that about?'

'Don't be so liberal, Alexander. If you want to be effective as a campaigner you have to understand what narrow-minded people think. Eunice is shocked.'

'Surely she doesn't think we need a chaperone at our age? Why don't I just explain that we'll be keeping one foot on the floor at all times?'

Lavinia laughed. That had indeed been the rule at her Oxford college whenever a young man visited your room. The regulation, intended to protect the young lady's virtue, had led to great mirth and had challenged the imagination of scores of students who tried to work out which unsuitable acts could still be performed with one foot on the floor.

Silence fell between them, but it was the comfortable silence of friends.

'I hope you aren't expecting turkey and all the trimmings,' Lavinia challenged.

'Cheese and biscuits, eaten in your company, would be a delightful treat.'

'You never were a good liar. It's smoked salmon and scrambled eggs with a nice bottle of Moët as a matter of fact. Maxted Wines didn't run to Vintage Krug.'

'That's a relief. It always struck me as decadent to pay that much for one bottle when you could get three for the same outlay.'

'Is that what they call champagne socialism?'

Alexander laughed out loud. His clear grey eyes, which had once reminded her of a winter sky, rested briefly on hers. Age had not dimmed them, nor any other aspect of him. The years had simply honed and simplified him, leaving the essential nature of the man untouched.

'Doesn't your family see all this scrambled eggs and smoked salmon as a derogation of duty? There must be a grandmaternal niche somewhere without a grandmother in it, surely.'

'Has it ever struck you, Alexander, that duty is a four-letter word too? I think my family can survive the day without me. Besides I feel as if the tramlines of my life have gone too deep and straight. They are taking me on a straight road towards eternity and I felt like a little detour.'

'I'm honoured you've invited me along for the trip.'

They ate their scrambled eggs to the sound of Vivaldi and toasted each other with red-stemmed glasses that caught the firelight and reflected it back to the deeper lacquer of the walls. It was amazing, Lavinia thought, how comfortable they seemed with each other even though their lives had taken such different paths. Maybe it was only when you were old, and had genuine premonitions of the end being in sight, that you could truly let go of what didn't count, perhaps never had counted.

'I have a little present,' Lavinia almost apologized. Maybe she hadn't quite reached that state of nirvana, she reflected, where embarrassment was no longer a factor. Alexander opened the gold parcel to find an immaculate first edition of *Lady Chatterley's Lover*.

'How extraordinary!' he opened the pages carefully. 'It feels brand new.' He looked up to find Lavinia smiling at him.

'They had it in the antiquarian bookshop in Maxted. Even they were impressed that no one had looked for the racy bits.'

'I always was the Mellors to your Constance.'

Lavinia's face changed. 'I didn't intend any parallels. You always thought me posher than I really was.'

Alexander's eyes held hers. 'And yet you must have thought I wasn't good enough or you wouldn't have run off and married Robert.'

The anger and pain in his voice rang out across the years, raw and anguished as if he still stood on the river bank where they had last seen each other that summer's afternoon.

Lavinia struggled with her conscience. Had she earned the right, after all these years of taking her life in a different direction, to speak out? 'Alexander, I — '

The ring of the telephone cut through the room, shrill and shocking. Lavinia reached for it on the third ring.

'Ma, it's Martin. Just ringing to say Happy Christmas.'

Lavinia clutched the phone as if it were an omen from above. Martin sounded so exactly like his father. Kind, solid, reliable, dull. An image of her husband, dead now for five years, etched itself into her mind. It had been her idea, when they'd got married, to pretend that Oxford had never existed for her. It had seemed the most painless way of forgetting Alexander and all that he stood for, and Robert had agreed instantly. He had taken it as a sign of commitment to their marriage, an endorsement that she had embraced domesticity wholeheartedly. Robert, she had seen at once, didn't really want a clever wife.

'Happy Christmas, darling,' Lavinia replied.

She thought of Martin and Jennifer's neat and well-behaved children and their safe and settled life, so like the one she had built for herself. 'Is Christopher there too?'

Martin felt a kick of disappointment as he handed the phone to his elder brother. He, Martin, was the one who always did the right thing and yet so often he got the feeling that it was Christopher his mother loved the most.

'Hello, Mother,' Christopher smiled. 'Kicked any coppers lately?'

In spite of herself, Lavinia trilled with laughter.

'Have a lovely Christmas,' she said hastily, 'and love to all your brood. Goodbye, darling.'

Christopher found himself staring down the dead instrument. 'I must admit,' he commented to Martin, 'Ma is behaving a bit strangely. She didn't even ask to speak to the kids.'

Lavinia kept her hand on the telephone for a moment, staring out of the window to compose herself. When she turned, Alexander was on his feet. She thought for a brief panicky moment that he might be leaving, but his teasing, affectionate smile reassured her. 'Just need something from the car.'

He came back carrying a large canvas which only just fitted under his arm, swathed in yards of bubble wrap and sporting a huge red bow. 'For you,' he announced, a wicked smile lighting up his lean, ascetic features.

Lavinia opened it suspiciously. She gasped. It was a masterly oil painting of John Constable's *The Cornfield*. The same line of towering elms drew the eye past a stream and a flock of sheep to the open field of golden corn beyond. But in this version instead of the famous shepherd boy leaning over in the foreground to drink from the pure stream water, a six-lane highway slashed its way obscenely through the foreground.

'My God, Alexander,' the power of the image was extraordinary. 'Where on earth did you get it?'

'I painted it myself. The idea came to me the other day when we were walking. I've been working on it ever since.'

'Alexander,' Lavinia shook her head. 'You are extraordinary. I didn't even know you could paint.'

'I taught myself. I make quite a good living from it actually. That's how I support my campaigning. Not a lot of money in road protests. Though I was offered ten thousand by one developer just to go away.'

'And did you take it?'

'Of course.'

'And did you go away?'

'Of course not. I used the money to stop the road. He gave up in the end and built it somewhere else.'

'You're an old rogue, Alexander. That's obtaining money by deception.'

'All's fair in love and road protesting.'

Lavinia studied her Christmas present again, wondering where on earth to put it.

'So,' Alexander grinned wickedly, reading her thoughts. 'Where do you reckon? Somewhere your friends can't see it obviously. The upstairs lavatory?'

'Too big. I'll put it in my bedroom. It'll be food for thought.'

Darkness was beginning to fall and Alexander got to his feet again. 'I shall cherish the thought. And now I think I'd better leave before your reputation is completely destroyed.'

'Really, Alexander. I think my reputation ought to be safe by my age.'

'And you're the one lecturing me about people in the country being narrow-minded. Thank you for my delicious lunch.'

She waved him goodbye at the gate, irritated at him for being so silly. She was beyond gossip at her age and now he would be going back to a rented cottage to spend the evening alone just for the sake of convention. Damn convention. She had respected it too much in her life already.

At the last minute Alexander turned. 'By the way, can you give a message to Rachel from me? Tell her things are going to hot up at the wood soon and that she needs to be careful. Her grandmother won't always be around to kick a policeman for her.'

'Alexander, don't. Rachel's more than capable of kicking a policeman for herself.'

'I know that. I'll do my best to try to keep an eye on her.'

For just a fraction of a second his hand touched hers and Lavinia felt a jolt run through her. But what of? She was too old for attraction. Excitement perhaps? Alexander had always been able to generate that wherever he went.

Next door a curtain fluttered as if a window had been opened. Lavinia raised her hand in greeting but there was no one there.

* * *

'Rach — ellll!'

'Steph — ie!!!'

The yelps of delighted friends united on the first day of a new term with a whole holidayful of rebellion and parent-scaring to report was always a joyous occasion, even with the spectre of mocks peering over their shoulders.

'Did you do *any* work, then?' Steph demanded.

'Nah,' exaggerated Rachel, who had in fact impressed her mother and irritated Marko by suddenly shutting herself away during the last week of the holidays and studying.

Catherine smiled at the girls, then took herself off to the School Secretary's office to hand over her hard-earned cash for Rachel's fees, trying to regard it as an investment in Rachel's future rather than the sacrifice of nice clothes and foreign holidays it actually represented.

The secretary took her cheque absent-mindedly. 'Sorry, Mrs Hope. I'm up to my ears. Some genius gave today as the deadline for the new entry applications and every child in the county seems to have applied.'

Catherine leaned over the sheaf of papers casually. 'Have you had Bonnie Miles's application yet?'

The secretary consulted her alphabetical files. 'Not so far. Could be second post.'

The voice of the headmistress, a terrifying personage, summoned the secretary to her office. 'Excuse me,' apologized the secretary and dashed off. On her desk Catherine could see a pile of blank application forms.

Knowing it would be absolutely wrong for her to fill in one for Bonnie, she did so all the same. What harm could it do? It only kept an option open. She slipped the form in the file marked M for Miles just as the secretary bustled back in.

'Was there something else?' the secretary asked, surprised to find Catherine still there.

'Plimsolls,' Catherine announced, unable to think of anything else.

'Plimsolls?'

'I just wanted you to tell the gym mistress we can't get any big enough for Rachel. Girls have such huge feet these days.'

The secretary looked relieved. This was familiar ground. Fussy, overprotective mothers were thick on the ground at Wolsey. 'They do, don't they? I'll pass on the message.'

Rachel was still yakking to her friend. 'Where did you get to?' she asked her mother suspiciously.

'Just putting in Bonnie's application form,' Catherine bluffed. 'Her father asked me to.'

'You really care about that kid, don't you?' Catherine was touched to hear the tumble of emotions in her daughter's voice, a combination of envy and grudging respect.

'Don't send her here then,' Stephanie counselled and she and Rachel fell about laughing.

★ ★ ★

The post-Christmas atmosphere at Rosemount Primary was less festive. The children
seemed happy enough but the staff had
clearly returned to the brave new world under
Brian Wickes half-heartedly.

'Look on the bright side,' advised Anita. 'At
least he won't be in the staff room any
longer.'

Even this guarded optimism fell away
during the morning as news of Brian's
changes to the timetable spread their way
through the school. Sport, drama, singing and
orchestra practice had been nipped in favour
of improving the school's results in the league
tables. Once, the parents would have
objected, but they were becoming equally
obsessed with grades. Rather like she was
with Rachel. Catherine tried not to think
about the irony of this.

'But what about the kids who don't have a
cat's chance in hell of getting good academic
results?' railed Catherine. 'At least they could
shine in other things.'

'Not any more,' muttered Anita.

Catherine's class was sluggish and unen-
thusiastic. They looked as if they'd all been
up late watching videos. It was so difficult to
get them going that she resorted to setting

257

them a quiz and sat back to watch them complete it. Gary Webb stared out of the window, with the occasional provocative glance in her direction. She'd separated him from his second in command, Tommy Mates, who was sitting staring at the paper as if it were in Swahili. Of their gang only little Kelly was actually attempting to answer the questions.

The only sign of enthusiasm in the whole double period was when the bell rang for playtime and thirty-four children tumbled out whooping into the cold January air. Bonnie was always one of the last and Catherine stopped her, unsure whether to confess about Wolsey and the application form she'd just filled in.

'How were the holidays?' she asked gently. 'Get any of those papers I gave you done?'

'What would be the point? I'm not applying.'

There was a pathetic droop to her shoulders and Bonnie looked even more pale and lumpen than usual. 'You could if you wanted to. It's your big chance, Bonnie. To get away from the Gary Webbs of this world. You can do it.'

Bonnie shook her head dejectedly. 'It's too late now.'

'No it's not. I was in the school secretary's

office this morning and I filled in a form for you. You can still do it if you want to.'

Bonnie's small eyes lit up as if a light had been suddenly switched on inside her. 'Can I? Can I really?'

'Yes. The exam's next Wednesday.' She paused, knowing she was probably overstepping the mark, but what the hell, no one else seemed bothered about Bonnie. 'I'll take you if you like.'

'I'll be all right,' the child insisted. Perhaps for once her father would exert himself.

If she'd needed any reassurance that her interference was justified, Bonnie handed it to her in spades. The child seemed like a flower in the desert who'd been given a long cool drink.

The next week passed in a flash. Bonnie completed some practice papers and surreptitiously handed them to Catherine to mark. The results were excellent. The only cloud on Catherine's horizon was the feeling that Gary Webb was watching them.

★   ★   ★

It was bright, crisp and clear, with a sky the blue of a child's painting on the day of Bonnie's entrance exam. Catherine wished Bonnie had let her drive her to Wolsey, but convinced herself that Bonnie's father had probably done so instead.

Fifteen peaceful minutes passed with none of the usual tussles for playground power. The bell for Assembly had already started ringing before Catherine realized quite why it was this peaceful. Gary, Tommy and Kelly were all missing. There could only be one possible reason today of all days. Catherine's stomach lurched painfully. She was teaching all morning and there was no way she could get away. She would have to somehow phone Bonnie's father and warn him. She grabbed Kevin Tudge, the PE teacher, and pleaded with him to oversee her class while she dashed to the phone box at the end of the street. She dialled Bonnie's number and willed her father to pick it up. The ring seemed to go on endlessly. Perhaps he was with her?

A small, scraggy child dashed past her, the hood of her cheap Day-Glo anorak up, heading for the playground. Catherine recognized Kelly at once.

'Kelly!' Catherine grabbed her by the hood of her anorak, dramatically halting her progress. 'Where're Gary and Tommy?'

Kelly simply sobbed. 'I didn't want to have anything to do with it, miss!'

Catherine took the child's hand and pulled

260

her gently towards the staff car park. 'Right, Kelly, I'm sure you didn't. You're frightened of Gary, I know that. Just show me where they are and I'll sort it out, but we have to do it NOW or it'll be too late for Bonnie.'

She glanced at her watch. It was already ten to nine. Putting out of her mind Brian Wickes's reaction if she missed Assembly, Catherine got into her car with Kelly next to her. She screeched through the streets, jumping a light and seeing out of the corner of her eye a police camera flash. Sod it. And then they were there. It was three minutes to nine and the school gates were deserted apart from a couple of mothers chatting. Some sixth sense guided Catherine to the dense area of ivy where she'd hidden in the bushes months ago. There, sitting on a paving stone, half-hidden, Bonnie sobbed.

'They took my pencil case,' she blurted. 'So I couldn't do the exam.' Bonnie's fat body shook with the pain of having got this far, only to have her hopes dashed.

'What do you need?' demanded Catherine.

'A pencil, rubber and ruler, and fifty pence for a drink.'

Catherine searched her handbag but she had nothing to write with. She was damned if she was going to let those little shits win at this stage. She looked round frantically but the nearest shop was ten minutes away. The school might sell or lend the things Bonnie needed, but it was too late to go looking. Any second now and they would be barred from the exam hall.

It was no good. She could hear the school clock strike nine. Finally they'd beaten her. Catherine almost sat down next to Bonnie and joined her.

'You can have mine if you want,' offered a tentative voice behind them. Catherine had almost forgotten Kelly's presence. 'I've got a pencil and rubber in my pencil case.'

Catherine grabbed them gratefully and shoved them into Bonnie's hand.

'Here's my dinner money,' Kelly shoved three fifty-pence coins into the other child's pocket. 'For your drink.'

There was no time for thanks as Catherine half pulled Bonnie past the astonished secretary, who tried to protest, followed the arrows stuck on the walls, and finally burst into a large hall where a teacher was on the point of telling the children they could now turn over their papers.

Catherine plonked Bonnie down, unpacked Kelly's pencil case and gestured a brief thumbs-up of encouragement before dashing out of the hall again, avoiding the presiding teacher's eye.

It was all down to Bonnie now.

Kelly sat huddled on the same stone previously occupied by Bonnie. Catherine took her hand. 'Thanks, Kelly. That was a kind thing to do.'

Kelly leaped up and grabbed Catherine round the waist. She was so tiny and thin that the top of her ginger head only came up to Catherine's elbows. 'I didn't mean to be so mean to her. It was Gary. He hates Bonnie. I don't know why, but he really hates her.'

Together they walked back to the car, Catherine's arms still round the tearful child, and drove in silence back to school.

It was obvious something was wrong from the ominous silence issuing from Catherine's classroom. Year Six never kept quiet like that. Even when they were occupied with something they enjoyed there would be grunts of concentration, giggles from the girls and protests as one of the less studious boys shoved them around.

Today the whole class sat at the octagonal tables, heads bowed, for all the world like Victorian schoolboys and girls. At the front of the class Brian Wickes stood stony-faced and furious.

12

'Mrs Hope,' Brian congratulated abrasively. 'You've deigned to honour us with your presence at last. Could you spare me five minutes during the lunchbreak, do you think?'

The morning seemed to Catherine to spin out interminably. The class knew something was up and thankfully kept up their cherubic behaviour.

At five past twelve she knocked on the door of Brian Wickes's office, trying not to remember all the comfortable chats she'd had here with Simon as they tried to forge a brilliant school out of the unpromising material that had been handed to them. Stupid thought. Simon had gone, she had fallen out with him in such a way that cosy chats would hardly be on the agenda, and Brian Wickes represented reality whether she liked it or not.

'Perhaps you'd like to tell me, Catherine, exactly where you were this morning when you were supposed to be teaching thirty-four children English language?'

'I was trying to rescue Bonnie Miles from

the bullies who've been making her life a misery. The same bullies I've complained to you about time and time again. They'd tried to sabotage her exam for Wolsey.'

'I thought she'd given up on that scheme.'

'She hadn't.'

Brian stood up, towering over her in an unpleasant way. 'You mean *you* hadn't given up. You've been playing God with that child, and if she's being bullied it's your fault. I warned you, Catherine.'

Catherine felt a molten lava of fury bubble up through her. How dare he blame her for trying to help Bonnie? 'So it's *my* fault you were too feeble to stand up for what's right and let thugs like Gary Webb get away with whatever they want to, is it?'

'Look, Catherine, it's my job to run the school in the way that I see fit.'

Catherine knew she should be diplomatic, that Brian Wickes was as prickly as a sea urchin, but she was just too angry to stop herself. 'Then perhaps it's time you knew how very unhappy the staff is with the changes you are trying to make.'

'If you have any complaints,' Brian's face was pale and taut with fury, 'then I suggest you take them to the governors. After all, if they'd wanted you instead of me, they would have appointed you.' And then he added softly, 'Even sleeping with Simon didn't get you the job, did it, Catherine? No wonder you're bitter.'

Catherine listened in disbelief, his words slicing into her.

'You're pathetic. There's no way I could go on working for you. This school used to be somewhere to be proud of. I'm glad to leave before you ruin every good thing about it.'

She was immensely grateful that it was still playtime and she could clear out her things while her class was still outside and before the full enormity of what she'd done hit her. She couldn't face the tearful goodbyes and the mystified expressions of her class when she said she was going.

She darted into the stock room just as the thunder of returning feet filled the corridor. Gary Webb's boasting bully's voice echoed past the closed door, and she longed to trip him, drag him in here and sit on him until he confessed to making Bonnie's life a misery and promised to leave all the weaker children alone.

Brian Wickes's uncompromising tones rang out behind the children, ordering them to be silent. When the last of them had filed in, Catherine opened the stock-room door.

She was halfway across the playground when Anita rushed up.

'Cath, what on earth are you doing?'

'I've resigned. Brian won't do anything about the bullying. He accused me of trying to play God with children's lives and said I was bitter because not even sleeping with Simon had got me the Head's job.'

'Cath,' Anita was genuinely shocked, 'he didn't really say that. Cath, you can't go! You built the place up. It was nothing before. Now children actually *want* to come here. Besides, you're a brilliant teacher, the best.'

'I'm sorry, 'Nita. I'd love to stay but I can't work for Brian. I can't stand by and watch him shooting down what I've helped build up over eight years. I'd rather do supply teaching in some grotty sink school than watch the life drain out of this one.'

Anita watched helplessly as Catherine took her possessions and left. The truth was she was half-envious, but as a single mother she couldn't afford Catherine's pride. Neither, of course, could Catherine.

Driving home in the middle of the day with no marking and no lesson preparation waiting for her when she got home unnerved Catherine. She tried not to think of how tough her resignation would be for all of them. Her income paid for Rachel's school fees. What would Christopher say? She tried to imagine how she'd feel if he'd just done the same thing. She hoped she would have been understanding, but she might not.

The house was empty and cold. The heating would only click on at four p.m. Catherine looked around for stuff to make a fire. They used to have a real fire every day when she'd been less busy and today it felt like a symbol. Both she and Christopher had been working too hard and there had, literally, been no one to keep the home fires burning. Unfortunately, to even light the home fires you needed firelighters or kindling and Catherine could find neither. She was about to give up, when she discovered some barbecue briquettes and a bottle of meths in the shed. Then she remembered the cherry tree they'd had to chop down before it fell. The chopped wood had been in a lichen-covered pile in the garden for years. Catherine fetched an armful, feeling like something out of Jack London, and watched in great satisfaction as the blaze caught, filling the room with a delicious sweet aroma.

She sat down in front of it, arms round her knees and gazed into the flames. Had she been stupid and selfish walking out like that, throwing away all that she'd worked for over the last eight years? It wasn't as though they had money to chuck around. Just paying Rachel's fees was a huge drain on their finances. On the other hand, it wasn't just the Bonnie business. She hated the way Brian was changing the school. For a second she longed to call up Simon and see what he thought. He would understand her concerns. A hot shiver of guilt shook her whole body at the memory of their disastrous drink. Simon would be the last person to turn to for advice now.

There was one small chink of light in the gloominess. Rachel's mocks were in a few days and at least Catherine would be around to make sure she studied and ate properly. No endless fatty and salty snacks. From now on Catherine would produce proper nutritious meals.

She pulled down a cookbook and began to happily defrost some cubes of beef, humming along to Classic FM. She felt better as she fried the garlic and onions. Naturally, there was no bouquet garni or bay leaves, so she added a pinch of mixed herbs. It might not be exactly River Café but there was nothing wrong with a good wholesome stew. She might even attempt some dumplings if they had any suet.

By mid-afternoon with the fire still glowing and the aroma of slow cooking pervading the kitchen, Catherine felt an answering glow of warmth. She'd stay at home for a month or two, then look for another job. In the meantime she would make a real home for her family. It wasn't such a disaster, after all.

Once the meal was prepared she picked up a magazine. An article on Minimalist Decor, which she would normally be far too busy to read, caught her eye. Here were people who lived in a house like hers, yet with light and bare space! No roller skates or Discman headphones or filthy anoraks or unreturned videos blotted their beige landscape. 'An absence of clutter,' insisted the owners, 'frees the spirit.' No wonder hers was so droopy. Tomorrow she would liberate her soul by binning anything that cluttered her surfaces.

She made an early start by carrying an armload of homeless objects upstairs with her. Most of them belonged in Rachel's bedroom. Out of habit she knocked before going in. It was surprisingly tidy, especially the desk. Rachel's set books were neatly arranged in a row. Catherine picked up a volume of Sylvia Plath's poetry. She'd loved it as a student. Now she was home she and Rachel might even read it together.

So taken was she with the thought of this mother-daughter exchange of ideas that she didn't hear Rachel's boots thunder up the stairs until Rachel exploded into the bedroom like a small herd of elephants, her friend Stephanie in tow.

They looked at Catherine as if she were a house burglar.

'I just came to put these in here,' Catherine indicated the pile of objects on Rachel's duvet defensively.

'You're home early,' Rachel decided to be graciously forgiving. 'What's that smell?'

'Supper. Real food. Boeuf à la Carbonnade with herbed dumplings. That is, if we have any suet.'

'Mu-um,' Rachel managed to encompass a whole world of exasperated disapproval in two short syllables. 'I never eat beef because of Mad Cow Disease, and suet is made of animal fat and it's probably even worse for you. Besides,' she added quickly, 'Steph's invited me for supper.' She kicked her friend.

'Oh,' Catherine tried not to sound too ludicrously disappointed.

'Why *are* you home, anyway?' Rachel persisted. 'You don't usually get home till six tonight.'

'Actually' — there was no point in avoiding the truth — 'I've just resigned.'

'Why on earth did you do that? I thought you loved your job.'

'I *used* to love my job, but not since the new head's started wrecking the school and

271

there's nothing I can do about it.'

'Oh, Mum,' Rachel dropped her briefcase and hugged Catherine tightly. 'Bloody governors, passing you over.'

Catherine closed her eyes. Rachel's hug was lovely but she didn't want her pity; she hated the idea of Rachel seeing her as a failure. 'Don't worry about me,' she said quickly. 'I'm quite glad. It means I'll be around whenever you need me with your exams coming up. In fact,' she hesitated for a moment, 'I thought maybe we could read some Sylvia Plath together. She used to be one of my favourite poets.'

Rachel and Stephanie exchanged a look of silent horror.

'Mum,' Rachel demanded, propelling her mother towards the door. 'Our relationship works because you're *not* around. Don't you think you ought to think twice about giving up your job? I mean,' her face took on a look of concerned seriousness, 'those kids *need* you. Besides,' she shuddered, showing her full horror, 'I don't think I could stand having you full time on my case.'

* * *

'How did the exam go, then?' Bonnie's father had made an unusual effort and bought a

272

packet of Jammie Dodgers and a bottle of Diet Coke, which he had waiting in the shop for her when she got home.

Bonnie didn't dare tempt fate by confessing the truth, which was that she'd loved every minute of it. She could do verbal reasoning standing on her head. Questions like 'Joan and Mary enjoy playing hockey. Karen and Joan enjoy netball. Karen and Mary enjoy swimming. Which girl enjoys both swimming and hockey?' were easy-peasy to Bonnie's way of thinking. Even the harder ones like rotating cubes and seeing patterns in dots or imagining which shapes went with which were fabulous fun to Bonnie. Nor did she breathe a word about Gary Webb and the incident over the pencil case. There was no point imagining her dad would do anything about it. He wasn't the hero type. He might rent out videos of *Batman* or Bruce Willis but her father knew the difference between fantasy and reality.

'It was OK, I s'pose.'

To Bonnie's astonishment, her father produced a bunch of slightly wilting carnations from behind the counter. 'You better give these to your teacher. She seems to have pulled out the stops for you.'

Bonnie grinned and hugged him. She took the flowers away to put them carefully in water. Tomorrow she'd take them in for Mrs Hope.

'Thanks, Dad.' The eyes behind the thick glasses were happier than he'd seen them for months. 'I really appreciate that.'

''Ere, Jon,' demanded a customer looking up from the blurb for *I Was a Massage Parlourmaid*, 'you going soft or something?'

* * *

The mood in the staff room the next day was shocked and subdued.

'Does she mean it, do you think, 'Nita?' demanded Kevin Tudge. 'I mean she hasn't really gone altogether? Surely she'll change her mind?'

'Not if I know Cath.' Anita shrugged. 'She's pretty damn determined once she's made up her mind. I only wish I had her nerve.'

A timid knock at the staff-room door interrupted their conversation. Bonnie, in her winter 'Global Warning' tracksuit and an unaccustomed smile, stood shyly outside holding the bunch of carnations. 'Is Mrs Hope there, please?'

'Don't you know?' Anita was stunned that anyone was still in the dark about Catherine's dramatic decision. 'She resigned yesterday.'

274

'You mean she's left for ever?' Bonnie looked as if someone had flattened her with a steamroller. 'But she can't have. She came to Wolsey yesterday and sorted out my pencil case. She didn't say a thing about leaving.' Suddenly the likely implication of what Catherine had done for her dawned on Bonnie. 'It was something to do with me and my exam, wasn't it?'

Anita gently put an arm around her. 'In a way. But it was much more than that. She just got fed up with the way things are going here and decided she'd had enough. It wasn't your fault, Bonnie.'

Tears welled up behind Bonnie's thick glasses. The one person who'd believed in her and tried to protect her was gone.

She didn't try to go back to the classroom. Instead, without even bothering to collect her anorak, she raced through the grey cold morning until she got back home. Her father was just opening up the shop and emptying the letterbox of all the videos people had dropped back overnight. 'Hang on,' he asked, surprisingly gently, 'what's the matter with you now, Bon? You were bright as a button this morning.'

'It's Mrs Hope. She's had a fight with the head and left and I know it was something to do with my exam. I'm on my own now, Dad.'

275

Jon Miles was the kind of man who liked to let things lie. He had spent a lifetime reckoning that if you stay away from trouble then trouble will stay away from you. But he'd seen the change in Bonnie when Mrs Hope had believed in her, and he was damned if he was going to watch her go back to being a victimish lump of lard. Not if he could help it.

'Right,' he snapped shut the letterbox and pulled himself up to an unimpressive five foot seven. 'I think I've had just about enough of all this. I think it's time we did something about your Mrs Hope, don't you, Bonnie love?'

Bonnie nodded in disbelief, wiping away a tear. Her dad was going to sort it all out, after all.

★　★　★

Brian Wickes was surprised when his secretary buzzed him to tell him that a Mr Miles needed to see him urgently, because he didn't immediately know who Mr Miles was. He'd been at Rosemount for seven years and he'd never met a Mr Miles.

'What exactly,' Brian demanded tetchily, 'does he need to see me *about*?' He'd had a very trying morning reallocating Catherine's teaching load, which he had to admit was more extensive than he'd realized, and dealing with a sullen staff, some of whom were frankly rude. What he didn't need was some irritating parent with a new and trifling problem.

'He's Bonnie Miles's father,' explained his secretary. 'I expect he wants to talk about Bonnie.' Was there even a mutinous tone to his secretary's voice, for God's sake? Anyway what the hell did the man want? As far as Brian could recall, Mr Miles had never set foot inside the school since his wife had left. Parents' evenings, plays, sports days had all passed without the benefit of Bonnie's family. 'Could you try and put him off? I'm up to my eyes at the moment.'

He went back to his work, only to be interrupted by a dumpy, unfit-looking little man in a tired tracksuit bursting into his office.

'Mr Miles? I don't think we've had the pleasure of meeting.' Brian did his best to inject as much abrasive understatement as he could into his tone.

'No.' Mr Miles sat down in the chair opposite Brian uninvited. 'I've always reckoned schools knew best how to deal with pupils without parents sticking their noses in. Until now. Bonnie tells me that her teacher has left and that it's something to do with her exam yesterday.'

'That's correct as far as it goes, but — '

'But nothing. Mrs Hope went after Bonnie because the little thugs who've been making Bonnie's life a misery were still at it. They'd emptied her pencil case so she couldn't sit the exam. Mrs Hope sorted her out.'

'And left thirty-three children unattended in complete derogation of her professional duty,' Brian reminded, sounding more pompous than he'd intended.

'Don't you talk to me about duty.' Jon Miles might be small but he was making up for it in terrier-like ferocity. This was just Brian's bloody luck. 'I've been reading the school's prospectus.' He waved the shiny new booklet all schools had to produce now parental choice meant they actually had to fight for pupils. 'And it says here that Rosemount Primary School has a duty to protect its pupils from bullying. You're the head of Rosemount Primary School — if only for the moment — and it strikes me that *you're* the one who's been falling down on his duty. You know,' Jon Miles was about to tell a lie and was enjoying it, 'I've got a mate on the *Sun* and I think he might be very interested. They really go a bundle on bullying sob stories.'

'Really, Mr Miles, going to the newspapers would hardly help Bonnie.' Brian's palms were beginning to ooze with sweat and he held them firmly in his lap, unwittingly adding to his aura of pomposity.

'But that's not all I'm doing. I've contacted the PTA, haven't I, about holding an emergency meeting. They were very sympathetic. You're not a very popular man, Mr Wickes. Did you know that?'

'I think you'd better leave. Trading insults is hardly helpful.'

'Isn't it? Oh dear.' Jon Miles, who'd never stood up to anyone in his life, was thrilled to find how much he was enjoying himself. 'Because you ain't seen nothing yet.'

After he'd gone Brian closed his eyes. Then, a few seconds later, he pulled himself together. He couldn't take this lying down. No one would back Miles. He was a stupid, uneducated little man who hadn't even bothered to set foot in the school before now. He wouldn't have friends or allies. All the same, Brian reached for his address book and dialled a number.

'Simon? Look, I'm having a little trouble to contend with. It's a rather delicate matter. I wondered if we could have a quick chat.'

Brian felt better. Despite the rumours about their involvement, he had a feeling

Simon resented Catherine Hope nearly as much as he did.

★ ★ ★

Lavinia hesitated between the Colombian high roast and the Kenyan medium. She liked the medium but Alexander favoured the high roast and, she smiled to herself as she tucked the Colombian into her basket, Alexander had been drinking a fair amount of her coffee lately. Next on her list were muffins, some smoked bacon, free-range eggs and, a new addition this, some maple syrup. Alexander was a dab hand at pancakes. You could knock them out on a Primus, he claimed, wherever you happened to be camping.

She wasn't quite sure how it had happened, Alexander slipping so easily into her routine, but it had. She had been neglecting her bridge and her involvement with the church. Instead Alexander had started reading, out loud, E.P. Thompson's *The Making of the English Working Class* in the evenings, which might sound dull, but the way Alexander read it, it was as gripping as a mystery story.

Last week she'd almost missed the village coffee-morning, but Alexander had insisted she go. He'd drawn the line at coming with her, though, and without his company it had been insufferably dull. Everyone seemed to have colds, flu or some major whine about their families or the weather. At least with the Christmas break the road had dropped, temporarily at least, from the top of the agenda.

Lavinia took her basket up to the counter where the ghastly Mrs Benson was deep in conversation with one of the Misses Smith. 'Might I trouble you, Mrs Benson, for a pound of cooked ham?' Ham sandwiches laced with a fearsomely strong English mustard were another favourite of Alexander's.

Mrs Benson tossed her head. 'More than you usually have, Mrs H. Expecting company, are we?' Her tinkling laugh at the ludicrousness of an old lady with a busy social life ricocheted through the shop. God, the woman was ghastly.

'Will there be anything more?'

Alexander had requested some small cigars but she was damned if she was going to give Mrs Benson the pleasure of drawing conclusions from that. Mrs Benson was the kind of person who probably counted sheets on people's washing lines.

'That'll be all, thanks.'

'Nine pounds, eighty-two pence. Just as well you aren't on a state pension,' she trilled, oblivious to Lavinia's stony face. 'Terrible, isn't it, how the government's trying to rob us of our savings. Still,' she handed Lavinia her change, 'at least there's some good news. You've heard that the bypass is definitely going ahead? They're going to start surveying the woods any day now. My son-in-law works for the construction company. I expect it's all thanks to you, Mrs H, getting on the news like that.'

Lavinia picked up her basket and left the shop without answering. Mrs Benson watched her, mystified. Some people didn't know what they wanted. She'd thought the old dear would be over the moon.

Lavinia leaned against the bonnet of the Rover. She'd thought she would be over the moon too, but instead she felt an odd sense of disappointment. And somewhere a tang of apprehension too. Things might start getting dangerous now and the people she loved would be in the thick of it.

★ ★ ★

A few miles away, at their camp in the wood, Zoe watched Marko while pretending to wash out some of her more filthy clothes in the rainwater she'd gathered in their tarpaulin. She tried not to smile. For the first time since she'd known him, Marko was suffering.

Last night they'd been to a meeting of all the protesters in the area and afterwards a band of them had come back here to discuss tactics and drink cider. One of them turned out to be a beautiful dark-haired student, who'd impressed Zoe with her intelligence and passion. And her obvious interest in Marko. But to Zoe's startled amazement, Marko hadn't even noticed.

Marko, Zoe concluded, her wry amusement spiked with jealousy, was in love.

The object of her speculation sat and brooded, oblivious to her contemplation of him, like a sulky satyr. In his hand was a joint made from grass given to him by the girl of last night. He had thought it generous when she'd pressed it upon him, and failed to even consider that she might have ulterior motives.

Zoe's nostrils twitched at the sweet yet acrid smell rising in the evening air. It wasn't just grass but burning hair. 'For God's sake, Marko, you've set light to yourself. I've heard of burning with passion but this is ridiculous.' She took the joint gently out of his hand and stubbed it out. If only he'd felt like this about her, instead of seeing her as part of the facilities, like an alternative room service.

'Cheer up, Marko. Your schoolgirl will be back soon.'

Marko looked sheepish. 'I do miss her.'

Zoe patted his hand. In spite of her jealousy, she liked him better for admitting it.

13

'Mum! Dad!' Rachel rushed into the kitchen like a dervish on Ecstasy. 'Guess what I got in my mocks! Three A stars! Only nerdy Sue Lincoln did better!'

Christopher jumped up and whirled his daughter round the kitchen, narrowly missing the coffee percolating on the worktop. 'Rachel, that's brilliant! I always knew you were a little genius.'

'Well done, darling,' congratulated Catherine.

'So, clever clogs,' Christopher asked, 'what would you like for a reward?'

Without a nanosecond's hesitation, Rachel was ready with her reply. 'To go to Gosse's Wood this weekend! It's incredibly safe there. Dead as a dodo. Marko rang and told me how bored they all are.'

'All right,' he conceded, then catching Catherine's eyes, 'as long as you start work in earnest on Monday. These were only mocks, after all.' Then, feeling unnecessarily Scrooge-like, he added, 'All the same, you're absolutely bloody brilliant!' and slipped a tenner into her hand.

Rachel's eyebrow raised a fraction of an

inch. Christopher added a further ten for inflation.

'Thanks, Dad. I'll go and ring them now. Don't worry, Mum, I won't go chaining myself to any bulldozers. At least not today,' she muttered under her breath as she dashed off to give Marko the good news.

'I can't help wishing,' Catherine sighed, 'that she'd done a little worse. A shock to the system might do her a lot more good at this stage than a pat on the back. Now she'll think she can glide through.'

'For God's sake, Cath,' Christopher snapped, 'Rachel will do fine if you just leave her alone. She's perfectly well motivated. Look,' his voice softened a little, 'maybe you're focusing too much on Rach. Why don't you start looking for a teaching job you'd really enjoy?'

Catherine turned away. Christopher thought she was being an overprotective pain in the arse. And the tough truth was, he was probably right.

Rachel was in such a good mood and so motivated all week, sitting down to essays and revision without a murmur of complaint, that any objections her mother had to her weekend jaunt seemed churlish, even to Catherine herself.

'What's the matter with me?' Catherine

asked herself as she wandered listlessly round the house. She'd thought her children would welcome her involvement in their lives, instead of which even Ricky treated her like an alien in a computer game who needed to be repelled at all costs. The truth was they'd sorted out their own lives without having her around, and they'd done it pretty well. The sum total of achievement she'd come up with since leaving Rosemount was improving their packed lunches. And even there, after a week's smorgasbord of different delicacies, they'd started asking for their old standards of peanut butter sandwiches and cold sausages. The truth was, she missed the Rosemount children's easy affection, their gratitude, she missed Bonnie's eagerness to please, the womb-like fug of the staff room, Anita's barbed cynicism. She hadn't realized how far school had become her support system.

'Then *do* something,' she could hear Anita almost hiss. 'Fight back!'

Catherine sat down with her sixth cup of coffee of the day and thought about her options. If she was going to do anything she'd better do it soon before she died of boredom and caffeine poisoning.

'Do you want me to pick you up from school and drop you at the station?' she asked

Rachel on Friday morning.

'Are you sure?'

'Of course. I'll bring your backpack and you can change in the car.'

Rachel, still shaken by this maternal volte-face, almost added that Marko would probably prefer her in school uniform but stopped herself just in time. There were limits even to this new-found parental tolerance.

'Thanks, Mum,' she grinned as Catherine deposited her later that day at Liverpool Street Station. 'See you on Sunday.'

Once on the train all thoughts of Catherine and home were blotted out by the thought of seeing Marko and the feeling, so strong she could hardly contain it, of setting off on a big adventure. The last time she'd felt this prickle of excitement was going to the Guides' Summer Camp when she was twelve. But she wasn't going to tell either her mother or Marko that.

He was waiting for her on the platform, lounging darkly against the Ladies' Waiting Room, causing a certain amount of fluttering amongst the gaggle of occupants who had retreated inside to avoid the male sex but were prepared to make the odd exception.

Rachel was flattered to see that he had washed his hair. It rippled in black waves around his handsome face. His greatcoat collar was turned up against the icy chill of early February, and in his hand he held a small bunch of snowdrops. He handed them over almost shyly.

'Zoe nearly killed me for picking them,' he announced gruffly. 'You'd think they were children ripped away from their mother the way she was going on. But the wood's covered in them.'

'Thank you,' Rachel clutched them to her as if they were more precious than diamonds. 'How's everything?'

'Boring. Nothing but cold and mud and no sniff of activity. However,' he tapped his nose, 'things are looking up. The cherrypickers, we hear tell, are coming out of hibernation.'

Rachel didn't comment on the irony of road protesting that struck her acute brain. Road protesting was like war. You said you were doing it for the sake of peace, but actually it was exciting only when battle was joined. A battle you were extremely likely to lose. There had to be, Rachel decided, more effective ways of saving the wood than simply camping in its trees. If only she could think of them.

As well as the snowdrops, Marko had actually thrown some vegetables into a pot with couscous and the glutinous result was waiting for them when they arrived at the wood.

'Welcome to our wood,' announced Macduff with a flourish.

Rachel produced two bottles of cider, purchased with her father's reward money.

'Just the thing to accompany couscous à la Marko,' Zoe pointed out, tasting the stew cautiously. She pursed her mouth. 'Mmm. Carrot. Parsnip. Spud. Cabbage. And what's that mystery ingredient that transforms the whole. Ah, I know. It must be love.'

Macduff sniggered.

'By the way,' Zoe continued, 'your gran came round this morning. Brought us some more pallets. Wondered if you might look in this weekend.'

But Rachel wasn't really listening. She was thinking of how, in just a few more moments, she and Marko could retreat to his tent and make up for lost time spent working for her exams.

Marko was clearly thinking the same thing. His hand kept straying to the tiny inch of skin on the back of her neck which was bare to the elements and stroking it, sending little darts of anticipation through her whole body.

'OK, kids,' Zoe commented wryly after they'd eaten, 'time for beddy-byes. Duffo and I will do the clearing up. You two clearly have other things on your mind.'

Washing up consisted of scraping the tin plates into a compost bucket — there were plenty of leftovers tonight, Zoe noted — and a brief scour with a washing-up brush.

'Do you think . . . ?' Macduff asked, gesturing towards Marko's tent, as Zoe clattered away tactfully.

'Yes, Duffo, I do think. Find yourself a nice high-up branch tonight and take some ear plugs. Marko's the technicolor orgasm type. And believe me, I should know.'

* * *

Alexander was the first to see the security guards. They had arrived to do a survey of the wood using video cameras and long lenses, and were dressed in some B-movie producer's idea of camouflage. If the implication of their presence hadn't been so serious, Alexander would have laughed.

He had been intending to go to Lavinia's for a leisurely cup of coffee, but headed off for the small camp instead. The only person up was Macduff. 'Where is everyone, Duffo?'

Macduff, like some human litmus test, went from blue, the legacy of a night in the treetops, to fire-engine red. Zoe appeared from her bender tent and came to his rescue.

291

'What Duffo means is that the lovebirds are still in their little nest, while the rest of us drones face the day. Heigh-ho.'

'Well, you'd all better get up and organized. There are security guards everywhere and unless you want to be captured for posterity on a Securitec video, you'd better avoid them.'

'Why are they here today?'

'The route through the wood has been finally agreed. This is it, Zoe. Unless we stop them the wood will be bulldozed.'

The look of anguish in Zoe's eyes startled even Alexander, a seasoned campaigner.

'I'm sure it won't come to that,' he reassured. 'But we have to get organized now. They need to get the trees down before the bird-nesting season or English Nature will be down on them. That means we have to hold them off for almost three months. It's going to get tough. And nasty.'

'Yes. We'd better start on the tree houses then.' Zoe's nerve came back and she grinned like an alternative Joan of Arc. 'And what about some tunnelling? Macduff's speciality. And maybe I'd better wake up Rachel and Marko. Love can wait. For the moment what we need is work and organization.'

Forgetting all her consideration and tact of last night, Zoe unzipped Marko's tent to reveal a jumble of bodies cloaked by Rachel's long red hair.

'Hey, what's the problem?' groaned Marko.

'There are security guards all over the wood. It's finally starting, Marko.'

By the time Rachel had jumped out of their sleeping bag, considerably faster than Marko, and pulled on her thick leggings plus baggy para trousers secured by a chain — she was particularly proud of finding this in the Army Surplus shop — and natty khaki body to keep warm under her jumper and parka, Alexander had already gone to spread the word to other camps.

'Wow,' marvelled Zoe when Rachel emerged, 'Paratrooper Chic hits Gosse's Wood! Bet you didn't see anything like this when you were on a tour of duty, Duffo.'

Zoe's irony was lost on Macduff. 'No one looked that good either,' he agreed. 'But then they were all blokes.'

'Actually it's entirely practical,' Rachel replied, refusing to let Zoe prickle her. 'What's the plan?'

It was another ten minutes before Marko emerged lazily from the tent, looking like the snake that's just eaten an antelope. He searched around as if coffee and croissants might miraculously materialize, but there wasn't even any hot water on. Food obviously wasn't one of Rachel's preoccupations. Sex, he was glad to say, clearly was. He might have been the first but Rachel was an enthusiastic learner. For the moment Rachel and Zoe were squatted on the floor over an OS map of the wood. Marko came up behind Rachel and kissed the nape of her neck. Rachel shrugged him off.

'Come on, Marko, this is serious. There are security guards everywhere, Zoe says, mapping out the wood.'

'Alexander's gone off to alert the other groups.'

Marko bristled but said nothing.

'So what do you think we should do?' Irritatingly Rachel was addressing her question to Zoe, not him.

'Start building. We need ladders. Rope, nails, hammers. Sheets of industrial polythene. And a chainsaw wouldn't go amiss either. Now, where are we going to find all that?'

'My gran can probably come up with the ladder and hammer and nails. And maybe even a chainsaw. I don't know about the rope and polythene.'

'Alexander can probably fix that,' Zoe said. 'He's an amazing character. Two parts intellectual to one part Del Boy. But, hey, I thought your gran was supposed to be the enemy.'

294

'Yes, there is that. Maybe if I don't tell her what it's for.'

'I think she just might guess,' Marko pointed out. 'Look, *I'll* sort out the rope and polythene if you get the other stuff.'

'No nicking, though, Marko. We can't afford putting the backs of local people up unnecessarily.'

'I wouldn't dream of it.' Then, with a touch of embarrassment, 'Look, Rach, you don't have any money, do you?'

It took Rachel and Zoe a brisk half-hour across the fields to reach Lavinia's cottage, but the sun was glaring above them, bouncing sharp light on the landscape until it seemed to glint and dazzle. It was, even to Rachel's urban eyes, quite immaculately beautiful, almost as if it was determined to prove its ageless grandeur and capacity to fight off any threat.

As they tramped along Zoe pointed out, almost with a naturalist's eye for detail, every species of animal, insect and tree they passed. Towards the edge of the wood they came to a clearing where the trees arched over a central space, letting a shaft of sunlight illuminate the ground in the middle. 'It feels just like a cathedral,' Zoe whispered. 'Only a pagan one, dedicated to nature. To think it's been here thousands of years and a bunch of overweight car owners want to chop it down so they can get to B&Q ten minutes quicker.'

'You really love this place, don't you?' Rachel looked up at the graceful curve of the branches. Zoe was right. It was like a cathedral. 'You see that tree, the huge one at the end,' Rachel pointed.

'The big oak tree, you mean?'

'It reminds me of that Enid Blyton book, *The Magic Faraway Tree*.' Suddenly she felt foolish. Zoe probably despised Enid Blyton for being disgracefully un-PC.

Instead Zoe laughed. 'God, I loved that book. My dad had it when he was a child. He used to read it to me all the time before he buggered off.'

Guilt at how easy and secure her own life had been fought with sympathy for Zoe. She knew so little about this tough, quirky girl.

But Zoe wasn't the kind of person to feel sorry for herself.

They both stared up together at the enormous tree, which stood apart from the others in splendid solitude. It must have been a hundred feet high and its vast gnarled roots twisted outwards over the ground to a height of three or four feet, like the tentacles of a giant octopus. Rachel perched on one of them. 'Do you remember how it was an oak tree like this at the bottom and then it grew plums and cherries as you climbed up it?'

'And the children in the story met Silky the Elf, who lived in it.'

They smiled conspiratorially, embarrassed at still remembering, yet touched they shared this powerful childhood memory.

'There weren't any road schemes in Enid Blyton,' sighed Rachel.

'Maybe we should write one,' Zoe suggested. 'The Famous Five Stop a Motorway.' Suddenly she put her hand on Rachel's shoulder to shut her up. 'Look,' she whispered. 'Are you any good at climbing?' She pointed to the huge tree.

For answer Rachel stripped off her parka and shinned up to the first branch, grinning. 'Are we looking for Silky the Elf? If so, I've got bad news about Enid Blyton stories. They aren't true.'

Zoe shook her head. 'Up a bit. Two more branches. That's it. Now look in the trunk.'

Rachel leaned to peer into the knotty opening just above her head when a grey squirrel darted out. She was so shocked she nearly fell out of the tree.

'You'll have to get used to getting a fright when you're above ground,' Zoe teased. 'Bailiffs are a lot worse than squirrels. They thump you, even when you're fifty feet up.'

Rachel climbed back down, jumping the last six feet.

'So,' Zoe asked when Rachel had steadied herself, 'how did you get on in these famous mocks of yours?'

'Pretty well.' Rachel realized the girl wasn't sneering but genuinely interested. 'Bloody brilliantly actually. That's why I'm allowed to be here this weekend without having to pretend I'm staying with my gran.'

Candid brown eyes raked Rachel's face. 'Marko didn't say anything about the exam results.'

'They were only mocks. Besides, I haven't told him.'

'Oh ho-ho, canny Rachel. You've learned the first lesson of going out with a bloke who's dimmer than you are.'

Rachel chose to ignore that one.

'Look, I don't want to sound patronizing, I really don't, but this is all going to get a lot nastier and rougher than anything you're used to. Enid Blyton it won't be.'

'That's why I want to be here. Look, Zoe, what have I done with my life so far? Taken exams and been a good little girl. I like my parents, even if I do sometimes disagree with them, but I want to find out what *I* think about things. I'm not here because of Marko, or sex, or annoying my family. I just want to see if I'm tough enough to take it, standing up for something. Living in the woods. Not having everything handed to me on a plate.'

'Do you know what,' Zoe admitted, 'you're not so bad for a privileged, privately educated, stunningly good-looking brat.'

'Aren't I?'

'No. That is unless you're all mouth and no trousers.'

'Certainly not. And I'm not like Marko either.'

'And what's that?'

Rachel giggled. 'All trousers and no spine.'

'Poor old Marko. He really is in for a shock this time.'

By the time they got to Lavinia's they were both starving. They ploughed their way through two malt loaves, thickly spread with butter, before they even felt strong enough to put their request.

'Really, Rachel.' The glint of steel in her grandmother's voice made Rachel look up from her malt loaf in surprise. Perhaps she'd misjudged Lavinia's attitude. 'I think it's about time you remembered that I'm in favour of this bypass and that all my friends and neighbours are too. We consider you road protesters a bunch of ne'er-do-wells and layabouts who make a life's work out of protesting because you're too bone idle to get a job.'

Zoe had already reached for her backpack to leave. She was used to this kind of reaction.

'That's why I don't want to hear another single word on the subject of rope or chainsaws or any other instruments of law-breaking.'

As she spoke Lavinia slid the key to her garden shed across the table towards her grand-daughter. 'And don't get me arrested this time.'

Rachel took the key, slipped it into her pocket and winked. 'I suppose it'd be too much for this layabout and ne'er-do-well to bum a quick bath?'

'Only if you promise to use the third-best towels. I don't want my pale pink ones ruined by road protesters' handprints.'

As so often in very old cottages bathrooms were not luxuries that had been built into the original structure but added on later, usually in a freezing extension. Lavinia's had originally been the sty for the cottage pig. The pig would be hard put to recognize his former home, dressed up as it now was with sprigged wallpaper, heated towel rail and an airing cupboard full of beautifully folded warm bath towels. Rachel lay back and let the hot water eddy all around her. She hadn't realized how cold she had been, so cold she'd had to rub each foot before putting it in the water to ward off chilblains, the ailment of tougher times. She washed her hair, marvelling again at how Zoe and the others actually lived like this all the time, with no hot water, no privacy, in sub-zero temperatures. She hoped to God tonight would be warmer than last night.

When she'd finished in the bath she tore through the small sitting room in her towel and made for her grandmother's pretty upstairs bedroom. This, in contrast to the Bohemian colours of the sitting room, had an almost Shaker starkness about it. Rachel loved the bareness of it, with its painted floorboards dotted with rag rugs, the pickled pine dresser, small wardrobe and just one upright chair. On this occasion, though, Rachel almost dropped her towel in surprise.

On the wall opposite Lavinia's bed, where previously a naïve painting of a cow had held court for as long as she could remember, a large oil painting drew her gaze. It was of a cornfield on a summer's day, an image normally conjuring peace and tranquillity and a particularly English calm. But this version was anything but peaceful. A great slash of motorway ripped the field in two like some monstrous gaping wound.

Tucked into one corner was a postcard. She turned it over and read 'The Cornfield by John Constable, 1776–1837, National Gallery.' Her gaze darted back to the picture on the wall. It was the same scene!

Pulling on her clothes, Rachel hopped downstairs. 'Gran! That painting upstairs, that's the field next to Gosse's Wood! Where on earth did it come from?'

Lavinia smiled with a hint of pride in her eyes. 'Alexander painted it. He discovered that the road is scheduled to go through the very field Constable painted; amazing, isn't it, that the authorities don't seem to have realized it?'

'But, Gran, that's amazing! What's Alexander doing about it? It could be the most brilliant propaganda weapon! Far better than just squatting in trees. What's he planning to do with the painting?'

'As a matter of fact,' Lavinia was beginning to see Rachel's point and it was making her distinctly uneasy, 'he gave it to me. And I'm not at all sure I want it used in a publicity campaign. My neighbours and friends all want this road. Maxted is beautiful too, you know, and one of these days someone will be killed in the High Street because of the traffic that needs diverting.'

'OK, Gran, say Maxted does need a bypass, you surely can't want it to go through Constable's cornfield and Gosse's Wood? There has to be a better route that involves less destruction!'

'The council has approved this route because it would be millions of pounds cheaper. All roads involve some disruption.'

'But this would be more than disruption! It would be devastation! I'm sorry, Gran, but I just don't agree. I think Zoe and I had better go. Thanks for the bath.' She handed the key back to Lavinia. 'We'll find the stuff some other way. It isn't fair to involve you when you feel so differently to us.'

Rachel and Zoe grabbed their coats and set off abruptly. The silence in their wake was deafening. Lavinia sat down heavily at her table in front of the window and watched them, wishing Rachel had never come to lunch before Christmas and bumped into that band of protesters from Gosse's Wood. But did that also mean she wished she'd never been to the library and rediscovered Alexander?

'So where are we going to get the stuff we need, O high-principled one?' Zoe demanded as they tramped back down the village street.

Rachel delved into the pocket of her camouflage trousers and retrieved a yellow

Day-Glo wallet attached with chains. 'My running-away fund. I was saving for a week on a Greek island when my mum and dad got too much to bear, but what's a Greek island compared to saving a thousand-year-old wood?'

Two hours later Marko and Macduff came out of the tents at the approach of a shiny new van with Bond & Wilson Builders' Suppliers painted on the sides. Two clean-cut young blokes sat in the cab, accompanied by the two giggling girls.

'Marko,' Zoe shouted, 'you should hear the quality of the CD machine on this thing. It's amazing.'

At the sight of Marko and Macduff the two young men unloaded their supplies in record time and climbed back into their van.

'Thanks for delivering the stuff for us,' shouted Rachel.

'That's OK,' acknowledged one of the young men. 'We enjoyed it. But do us a favour, will you?'

'Whatever you like, within reason,' Zoe answered provocatively.

'Just don't tell anyone you bought the gear from us, right?'

'Nice to be popular, isn't it?' Zoe commented.

In the girls' absence Alexander had already

delivered a ladder and a borrowed chainsaw and they spread their tools out around them. 'Right,' ordered Marko, immediately assuming command, 'Duffo will be stationed up the tree and we'll pass the stuff up to him. Then you can,' he smiled engagingly at Rachel, 'in the time-honoured fashion make us a cup of tea.'

'Sod that,' Rachel replied cheerfully. 'There's no point wasting our time taking anything up trees till we've worked out what we're doing with it. One of my best subjects was DT, so why don't I work out a nice little sketch of exactly what we're going to build.'

Marko looked sulky. 'What the fuck's DT, anyway? Sounds like something you get the morning after.'

'Very funny, Marko,' Zoe said. 'It stands for Design Technology. Making things to you. You're starting to show your age. Or is it just that the posh private school you went to didn't let you get your hands dirty?'

For the next half-hour Rachel experimented with different designs for the tree houses. They had to be simple to build yet strong enough to withstand violent onslaughts.

'For God's sake,' Marko sneered when she showed them her final design. 'We're not building a Barrett home with en suite bathroom and outdoor patio! This design has

305

walls. Tree houses are platforms.'

'These walls are only waist-high. They'd give some protection if a cherrypicker was trying to get you out. And we could put a rail in the middle to tie yourself on to.'

'These designs are bloody brilliant,' Duffo congratulated. 'But how hard will they be to build? It isn't easy when you have to carry everything up forty feet.'

'We build the platform in two halves on the ground with a hole for the trunk and then put wooden brackets underneath to hold it up. For double security we could also secure it to the branches above. What do you think?'

'I think we should get cracking now while there's an hour of light left,' Zoe insisted. 'Right. Where's the measuring tape and the saw? This is going to be the Ritz of tree houses.'

Macduff fetched the wood while Rachel sorted out the hammer, nails and an electric drill one of the young men had lent her, on the strict understanding she returned it by Sunday lunch and had a drink with him when she did so. Rachel intended to tactfully forget the last part but he'd get his drill back all right.

Soon the darkening wood was filled with the sounds of Zoe sawing and Rachel hammering. Macduff's job was to hold the plank steady in the absence of a proper vice. 'Come on, Marko,' he suggested, in a jokey voice so unlike his usual shy one that Zoe and Rachel stopped for a second, 'why don't *you* make that cup of tea you mentioned?'

The sun, when it went down at seven minutes past five, lit the trees with a thin red glow that warned them all what kind of night it was going to be. 'I think I'll keep my clothes on tonight,' Zoe announced, stamping her feet against the bitter cold that had intensified dramatically since the sun disappeared. 'It's such a pissy little sun at the moment you wouldn't think it could make so much difference. How's the fire? For God's sake, Marko, you've let it go out.'

'Right,' announced Macduff a couple of hours later, 'I'm for sleep. Sun's up at seven fifteen. We could start again then. I'll rustle up some breakfast.'

'At seven fifteen?' Marko laughed. 'You must be joking.'

That night, as they got into their sleeping bag, Rachel decided to take Zoe's advice and keep her clothes on. Undeterred, Marko fiddled around until he found the gap between her camouflage trousers and the sweater she had tucked in. Her first thought was to say no, she was too tired, it was too cold, but a fatal stab of sympathy weakened her. 'Come on, then,' she unzipped her trousers and pulled them off, leaving her sweater firmly in place. She wouldn't take that off even if Indiana Jones walked in and demanded it.

Marko didn't wait for her to change her mind.

It was neither a passionate nor a memorable coupling, and it was over so quickly it didn't even warm her up.

During the act itself she was conscious of only one thing: for the first time with Marko she had made love out of sympathy rather than lust.

Duffo was as good as his word. By seven ten, just as the sun was beginning to light up the far edge of the wood, Rachel heard the sizzle of pancakes and groped around for her trousers. Outside the bender tent the ground was still freezing and deeply rimed with white. Rachel thought about sneaking back inside.

'Here,' Duffo offered, 'you can have the first.'

'No lemon, by any chance?'

He shook his head and chucked her a bag of sugar riddled with lumps of brown where someone had dipped in a teaspoon. Even so, it was the best she'd ever tasted. As they sat eating the pancakes the sun lifted slowly above the line of trees, dark pink in a luminous blue sky. 'I love this time of day,' Rachel breathed. 'At this time nearly every day seems as if it will be beautiful. Anything feels possible. Even building a tree house in six hours flat.'

By the time Alexander looked in mid-morning to see how things were going, the first half was already erected and they were close to completing the second. Rachel, hair scraped back severely, hammered away with deadly accuracy.

Alexander watched, amazed. 'I know,' Zoe hissed, 'full of surprises, isn't she? Picked it up in Design Technology, apparently.'

'So education has its uses after all?' Alexander laughed. 'Don't worry, I won't tell your parents that.'

Rachel looked up at him and smiled, loving every moment of the challenge. Alexander's heart leaped. That smile took him back forty years to that other young girl, full of eagerness and laughter. Thank God Rachel lived in a different world. A world where she wouldn't have to bow to the pressures of class and background that her grandmother had had to. But did Lavinia really have to, or had her courage simply failed her at the thought of an uncertain life of poverty and risk with him? The thought depressed him. Her decision had cost them both a lifetime of missed happiness.

'Rachel,' he blurted, hoping she wouldn't think him mad, 'don't ever give in to convention, will you? Always follow your instincts. Only you know what's right for you.' And he hurried back to his ancient Land Rover leaving the others staring after him.

'What on earth was all that about?' Zoe demanded.

'I've no idea,' Rachel shook her head.

'Maybe he's finally losing his marbles,' Marko commented.

'And unlike you he's got plenty to spare,' Zoe snapped, and went back to her saw.

By midday they were ready to erect the second section and build the struts to support it. 'Who's going up first?'

For once Marko remembered himself in time. 'Rachel, of course.'

Rachel shinned up the ladder. When she reached the top she rummaged in her jacket and pulled out a small bottle of Strongbow cider. 'I name this house Liberty!' and she smashed the bottle against the tree trunk, hoping against hope that she didn't have to miss all the fun by going back to do her boring A levels.

14

'Go on, Duffo, you give the nice man back his drill.' They were bang on time but Rachel had lost her nerve, knowing that the youth was hoping for more than his drill back.

Afterwards they went for a walk down by the river and picnicked on damp pitta bread sandwiches and a bottle of cider. The train Rachel had promised to return home on left at four p.m., so after they'd eaten they dropped her at the station.

She looked out of the window at her new friends waving her off from the platform. She knew all her schoolmates' parents would be horrified by them, her own parents too probably, but this weekend had been like none other she could remember. She'd been so cold her hands and feet hurt, she'd been hungry at times, yet the exhilaration of waking up in those beautiful, silent woods had felt, and she knew this sounded a bit Eng. Lit., like being there at the dawn of time. Building the tree house and impressing even Duffo with her practical skills had been terrific. She had felt grown up and autonomous for the first time in her life. She had known she had the wit and skills to survive. There was a sharpness and reality about living in the woods that her London life lacked. Now she had to go home to school and her mother nagging. The sense of loss was almost physically painful.

Her mother was waiting on the platform when the train pulled in. Rachel knew Catherine had come because she loved and missed her and no doubt worried about her, but just at the moment she didn't want to be smothered by her mother's love, no matter how well intentioned.

Catherine's face lit up at the sight of her daughter. Without even being aware of the gesture she reached across and took Rachel's backpack.

'It's OK, Mum, I'll carry it.' She wrested the thing back from her mother, neatly sidestepping the proffered kiss. She felt a shit, but her mother ought to understand.

'So, how was it?'

'Fine.' Rachel hadn't intended giving anything more away, but her excitement was too obvious. 'Actually,' she finally admitted, 'it was absolutely brilliant.'

Catherine felt defeat nipping at her heels. She'd hoped that by giving Rachel a taste of life in the raw, her daughter might realize how lucky she was to have home comforts. It sounded as though the opposite might be true.

If only, Catherine found herself wishing fervently, they hadn't gone to lunch with Lavinia that day and Rachel had never even met Marko and his merry gang.

★ ★ ★

Bonnie's father knew he was at a disadvantage with the Rosemount PTA. There weren't many parents who had, as steadfastly as he had, resisted contact with the school, skipped sports days, ignored parents' evenings, failed to provide gifts for each fête and raffle. As a parent, he was a washout. He could hardly tell them the truth. He had once bothered with all these things, with Bonnie's older brother and sister, who'd long since left the school and home, and had even taken pride in their halting progress. But that had been before his wife had walked out, leaving him with baby Bonnie to bring up alone, and devastated. His daughter's melancholy and depressive side, he suspected, came directly from him. But there was more to Bonnie. She had grit and intelligence. There had been times when she'd shamed him by wanting to better herself with so little encouragement. And she'd told him about the bullying more than once. It had been going on for months. How Terry Webb's thuggish son had hung around waiting for her, stealing her books, trying to make sure she didn't climb up a rung that he was too dumb to even attempt. And he, her own father, had done nothing. He'd hoped it would all go away. But it hadn't.

The chairwoman of the PTA had allowed a brief look of astonishment to cross her face when she opened the door to Bonnie Miles's father. Jon Miles decided honesty was the only policy left to him. The woman, he had to admit, was surprisingly sympathetic when he explained what had been going on. Maybe there were other parents who found Brian Wickes less than the perfect head teacher.

When he left her neat terrace house, the poshest in her road with two plaster lions outside it, Jon was whistling.

A special meeting of the PTA would be called in two weeks' time. And what's more, it wouldn't be held in the school hall, but at the local community centre.

'That should make him think,' the chairwoman said as she accompanied him to the door. 'Mind you,' she added kindly, 'I wouldn't count on everything going your way. A lot of the parents support Brian Wickes's ideas about discipline.'

'So do I,' Jon Miles acknowledged. 'But as far as I can see that's all they are, ideas. When there's genuine abuse right under his nose he does sod all about it.'

'You're ace, Dad,' Bonnie hugged him when he told her the news. 'I mean it's not just for me. There are other kids who get picked on too.'

'Do they now?' Jon Miles was finding that now that he'd stood up to be counted, the experience was rather exhilarating. 'Why don't you write down their names and I might just get in touch with their mums and dads and see what they've got to say about it.'

Bonnie wrote a list of about six names and handed it to him, then she carefully organized her packed lunch. It was a school trip to London Zoo and she'd been looking forward to it for weeks. She even had someone to sit next to on the coach. Things were definitely looking up.

Bonnie and her friend, a new girl, sat and ate their lunch together near the small animals enclosure. They both liked these friendly and unfrightening goats and cows and rabbits better than the tigers and orang-utans. They had just stroked the Chinchilla rabbit's silky ears when a noise behind them made them turn.

Gary Webb was feeding the chocolate-chip

cookies Bonnie had bought with her spending money, and was saving for her and her new friend to share on the journey home, to the long-horned goat. When she tried to stop him he sprayed her with her blackcurrant Capri-Sun.

'You pig, Gary, you bloody great pig!' She was about to shout that this was her best outfit, but Gary would only laugh and torment her for her taste and size. She sat down.

'And tell your dad from mine that he ought to leave being a hero to the people in his crappy videos, or it'll be him and his shop that suffer.'

Bonnie bent down to gather up her things, hiding her sobs as she did so. Now they were trying to frighten her dad just like they frightened her! And she wasn't sure how strong her dad would be in the face of threats like that. Maybe she wouldn't tell him.

★　★　★

'You're not going to believe this, Cath.' Hearing Anita's spiky tones was balm to Catherine's drooping spirits. Anita had turned up on Catherine's doorstep bursting with news. Catherine had hugged her, overwhelmed by a sense of how much she'd missed Anita's company. 'A special PTA meeting's been called for next week and it isn't at school, as usual, but in the community hall. Wickesy's trying to act calm and fatherly but you can see he's got his Y-fronts in a twist. We're all agog. But look, the best thing is, do you know who's behind it all?' Anita was so excited her bangles jingled like a Salvation Army band. 'Jon Miles.'

For a moment Catherine didn't make the connection. She knew the man so little. 'Not Bonnie's father?'

'That's him.' Catherine tried to recall the small, balding, ineffectual little man who had been so unhelpful when she'd appealed to him about the bullying.

'My God. And does he have much support from the other parents?'

'I don't know. Brian Wickes was a popular choice with all his blether about discipline. But Bonnie's dad must have some support to have got this meeting called.' She jumped up and clutched Catherine's hand until it was almost painful. 'Look, Cath, you've got to come. You can't let Brian wriggle out this time. It's our only hope of getting rid of him.'

'I'll never work again if I stand up and attack him in public.'

'You will if he loses. Come on, Cath, come at least. Just having you there will throw him.

317

We'll look after you.'

'When is it, then?'

'Wednesday week. Eight p.m. We can go and get wrecked afterwards. We're missing you.'

Catherine considered the proposition. Polishing her kitchen surfaces and worrying about Rachel had gone on for long enough. It was time she fought back, if not for her own sake, then for the sake of the children and other teachers.

'You're on!' She reached for a bottle of wine from the fridge. 'Now, come on, tell me all the gossip — and don't leave out a single comma. What's been happening in the staff room without me?'

★　★　★

Lavinia could hardly believe that she had run out of extra, extra-strong cheddar, the kind that made Gentlemen's Relish taste like Dairylea. But then, feeding Alexander was rather like feeding The Tiger Who Came to Tea; despite his ascetic build he could eat his way through the larder in days. He made up for it once a week by cooking one of his special curries, which seemed to involve the use of about a hundred different spices. Fortunately, he brought these, sent direct to him from a shipper in Delhi, so deeply suspicious was he of shop-bought versions. Lavinia had to admit the result was magnificent.

Since today was the weekly coffee-morning and she was in a hurry, she took the Rover and parked it, rather precariously, outside the village shop.

The narrow aisles between the doilied shelves were empty and Lavinia was able to manoeuvre her basket through with unusual ease. On her way to the counter she spotted some home-made shortbread and the octagonal extra-thin cheese biscuits that were Alexander's favourite. It was funny how he had somehow eased himself so comfortably into her universe, staking a claim to its centre, without anything even being said between them. Lavinia smiled to herself. His arrival had undoubtedly made her life jollier and more unpredictable.

Quite how unpredictable she hadn't realized until she approached the counter to pay. Mrs Benson, gold bracelets jingling, looked up with a curl of the lips. 'I'm sorry, Mrs Hope,' she pronounced the words loudly and clearly as if she had been practising them in front of a mirror, 'but I'm afraid your custom is no longer welcome in this establishment.'

15

Lavinia reeled. She had shopped here at least twice a week ever since she had moved to Maxted forty years ago. Torn between throwing her purchases in the stupid woman's face and refusing to budge an inch, Lavinia chose to stand her ground. 'And would you do me the honour of explaining why?'

Mrs Benson's smile widened. 'Certainly. Our policy is perfectly consistent. We don't serve road protesters or people who collaborate with road protesters.'

'Mrs Benson,' Lavinia's tone was loud and slow as befitted talking to someone of limited understanding, 'this is not a war.'

'I think you may be about to find out otherwise,' the ghastly woman enunciated smugly.

Lavinia picked up her basket and held it in front of her like a shield. Mrs Benson was a silly incomer and no one would pay any attention to her. Proudly she steered her basket out to the car, grateful for its protection. She was almost tempted to back into the Bensons' ludicrous lead-paned shop window, but resisted the impulse. Calling the police would give Mrs Benson enormous pleasure.

Lavinia glanced at the clock on the dashboard. The coffee-morning had started a quarter of an hour ago. For a split second Lavinia hesitated. What if Mrs Benson wasn't the only person who saw her as a collaborator?

Courage, she told herself as she parked in the village-hall car park. The woman has always been a shallow and self-serving busybody with as much understanding of the countryside as a beautician from Birmingham.

Lavinia climbed out of the Rover, shook out her ancient Barbour and straightened her headscarf. She was sure there was absolutely nothing to worry about.

One of the Misses Smith was circulating with a pot of tea when Lavinia strode proudly into the lion's den. At the sight of Lavinia the old lady's hand wobbled and she poured the boiling liquid all over Colonel Lawley's brogues.

'Good morning, everybody,' Lavinia boomed, heading for a spare seat next to Eunice. The silence was cavernous, apart from a wavering greeting from the older Miss Smith who was as deaf as a post. An elbow in her side made her stop halfway and lapse into confused silence.

Lavinia stopped, rooted. 'Not you lot as well! For God's sake, everyone, what the hell's got into you all? We're friends and neighbours.'

'Not any longer, I'm afraid, Lavinia.' Colonel Lawley, recovered from the tea incident, had appointed himself as spokesman. 'We overlooked the arrest business but we can hardly fail to notice your current liaison. The propriety of such a relationship at your age would be dubious anyway — but with a dangerous radical who opposes the bypass! Have you no shame? We no longer see you as one of us, I'm afraid. People don't feel able to speak freely in front of you.'

Lavinia could feel the silver scone knives of Maxted being aimed at her back. She turned to Eunice. 'Does this include you, Eunice? Are you no longer able to speak freely in front of me?'

Eunice hesitated until a glare from Colonel Lawley bludgeoned her into nodding. 'I'm afraid it does. Sorry, Lavinia.'

After the hurt came a stranger sensation, that of waste. Lavinia had squandered her affection and respect on these people for most of her life. She had thought them dull, perhaps, but solid and right thinking, the backbone of England. To have them exposed in this way meant her life among them had been a sham. She felt momentarily sorry for Eunice. Her friend's life revolved around these people. Hers, thank heavens, did not.

'As a matter of fact,' Lavinia stood up, 'you may be surprised to hear that I have never endorsed Alexander's ideas, nor those of my grand-daughter, in opposing the bypass. I have always believed that Maxted was being choked to death and needed to be saved for its residents. But frankly, I don't think its residents deserve it.' She walked proudly towards the door, helping herself on the way to a ginger biscuit from the serving table. 'By the way, since we're all speaking our minds, the biscuits at this coffee-morning taste like blotting paper.'

★　★　★

Once she was behind her own front door Lavinia fought back the tears she would never have shown the world. How could you live among people for forty years and not really know them at all? To have thought them kind when in fact they were simply self-interested and narrow-minded. Even Eunice! Lavinia had to admit Eunice's rejection had been the deepest cut of all. She didn't give a toss for the Mrs Bensons or the Colonel Lawleys of this world but Eunice was different. She might be silly and easily led, but Eunice had been her friend.

Even though it was only mid-morning, Lavinia reached out to pull her curtains and shut out the world. She stopped mid-gesture. That would simply give them the satisfaction they were looking for, the admission that Lavinia Hope was weak and misguided and couldn't bear to face her neighbours. Instead Lavinia bent down in front of the grate to light a fire, always a comforting thing to do, at once physically warming and spiritually uplifting.

Outside the sun was high in a pale blue sky but Lavinia wasn't cheered by it. She loved this place so much, every corner was filled with memories, but the events of today had soured them, perhaps for ever. How could she go on living here surrounded by people who didn't want to even speak to her?

By the time Alexander arrived in the middle of the afternoon she was sitting, still in her Barbour and head-scarf, by her dwindling fireside.

'Lavinia,' he demanded, shocked, 'what on earth's the matter?'

He switched on all the lights so that the house took on its usual cosy glow, banked up the fire and made tea.

'Right,' he handed her a cup in her favourite eggshell Doulton, 'what's all this about?'

Lavinia took a tentative sip, grateful for Alexander's presence — or she felt she might never have moved again. 'I've been boycotted. Sent to Coventry. They won't serve me at the shop and I'm not welcome at the coffee-morning. Even Eunice turned her back on me. It seems I'm collaborating with the enemy.'

'Oh, my poor Lavinia!' Alexander reached out a hand and gently touched her face. 'I suppose this was inevitable. I should have been more careful instead of foisting myself on you.'

'You didn't.' She almost added that the last few months had been the fullest and most enjoyable of her life, but something stopped her. 'I invited you.'

'But I knew,' he said sadly, his grey eyes clouding with sympathy. 'I've seen it all before, time after time. Neighbours turning on neighbours, communities warring, spitting at each other, filming each other — and all over a wretched road that will lead to more traffic and even more roads to cope with it.' He ran his hand through his thick white hair in a futile attempt to smooth it. 'You should have guessed from the way that pompous Colonel acted at the police station. Poor Lavinia, you haven't learned much about life in forty years.'

His tone, though well intended, touched a raw spot. Even though she might have concluded it herself, she couldn't bear Alexander saying her life had been a waste. How dare he tell her that she hadn't learned anything?

'Perhaps I've learned more than you think,' she flashed, banging down her china cup. 'I've had children, and a marriage, which is more than you have!'

The expression in his eyes appalled her. Behind the determined fighter and the witty intellectual she glimpsed the depth of his loneliness and isolation gaping across the years, empty.

'Alexander, I'm sorry, I . . . '

But it was too late. Alexander was already on his feet. 'You're right, Lavinia, my life has been futile. And who do we have to thank for that?'

As she heard the back door bang behind him, a strong draught lifted the heavy velvet curtain that cloaked it. Lavinia shivered, but not from cold. How could she have said that to Alexander, knowing as she did the truth?

This time she was powerless against the

tears that blurred her eyes and soaked the white lace collar of her blouse as she tried to brush them away. She had just managed to alienate the one friend she had left. Clever old girl, Lavinia.

A few moments later a feeble knock was just audible on the heavy wooden door.

'Come in,' she called, hoping against all rationality that it would be Alexander.

'I'm sorry, Lavinia.' A pale, silly face emerged from behind the velvet curtain. 'I shouldn't have said that to you. We may disagree about the stupid road but that doesn't stop us being friends, does it?'

'Do you know, Eunice,' Lavinia squeezed the out-stretched hand, feeling that a ray of warming, life-saving hope had come into the room with her, 'I've never been gladder to see anyone in my whole life!'

16

Lavinia was right, Alexander told himself bitterly as he drove back to his empty cottage. His life *had* been futile. Somehow he had persuaded himself that this was how he had wanted it. Completely free to come and go as he pleased, accounting to no one. And for most of his life it had worked. He had believed his own propaganda, even taken a certain pride in the simple lines of his existence. But the last few months had changed all that. Ever since meeting Lavinia again he had become agonizingly conscious of what he had missed. The warmth of family life, even its pain. Families connected you to both past and future.

The young Alexander would have dismissed such thoughts as bourgeois and narcissistic. Perhaps it was simply his age and the realization that no part of him would pass on to the next generation, but a new and almost intolerable sadness was threatening to overwhelm him. Alexander, always a man of action despite his intellectual image, found himself at a loss.

You've stopped three roads, he rallied

himself, and helped save whole swathes of this landscape you love; isn't that enough for a man, to make his life worth something?

But somehow it wasn't the consolation he'd hoped for. Alexander Bailey, who had always eschewed suburban comforts of hearth and home, now found himself, in what might be the final stages of his life, consumed with longing for them. Probably it was just another cruel trick of nature. Or was it simply that meeting Lavinia had reminded him too clearly of how life could have been for both of them? And the most painful thing of all was that he had believed Lavinia felt it too.

Alexander unlocked the door of his rented cottage. Until today its simple, monkish quality, the sense that for hundreds of years it had been lived in by a farm worker or gamekeeper, someone associated with toil and rooted strongly in their surroundings, had appealed to the romantic streak in Alexander. Today only its poverty and shabbiness struck him. Instead he longed for the colourful warmth, the bold dramatic touches of Lavinia's home. For a moment he pictured her and Rachel, sitting at either end of her sofa, so different and yet so alike. Both shared that rather British capability. Rachel had designed a tree house that had stayed up and Lavinia had led a sit-in on a zebra crossing. Yet there were differences. Rachel, he suspected, would never, as her grandmother had, bow to convention. She would be the one to take the risks her grandmother had balked at. Partly that was her generation but also some fierce independent streak of her own. And he saw, in that sudden moment of insight, that Lavinia knew this too, and was learning to love her grand-daughter for it with a wild, all-encompassing devotion that even Lavinia herself did not yet fully understand.

★　★　★

'Cath,' Anita's loud and familiar voice boomed down the phone like the wake-up call at a holiday camp, 'stop dusting or whatever useless activity you're up to and listen. Brian Wickes is running scared. He must have decided that this meeting on Monday is a genuine threat. He's wheeled in Simon to back him up.'

'Simon!' Catherine felt her neck redden at the mention of Simon's name. 'But Simon's got nothing to do with the school any more.'

'I know, but obviously the parents all trust him and if he backs Wickesy it'll really help him. I think you should not only come to the meeting but speak. Jon Miles will collapse against those two. He's never even put in an appearance at a school meeting, let alone opened his mouth. Come on, Cath, you've got to come. We need you. *You* need you!'

Christopher's eyes were on her as she put down the phone.

'So, will you go?'

Catherine was startled. 'How did you know about that?'

'Anita doesn't need a phone line. She could just shout. She's got a point, you know. Simon's presence will change things. The parents respect him.'

Catherine had to stop herself from shivering in disgust. The last person she wanted to take on face to face was Simon Marshall. Besides, she had tried to put the school behind her and open a new chapter in her life.

'Look, Catherine,' there was just an edge of impatience in her husband's voice. 'I think you have to make some tough decisions. Like have you been happy since you left Rosemount?'

'I don't know.'

'Perhaps I can assist you then. You love that place. You've been bloody miserable ever since you left. You've got teaching in your bones. Next, do you want your job back?'

'Not under Brian.'

'Right. Then you have to get that meeting to dump Brian.'

'For God's sake, Chris, how am I going to do that?'

'Your daughter's stopping motorways and your mother-in-law's leading sit-ins; if you're prepared to stick your neck out I suspect you'll find a way. Perhaps it's time you played dirty.'

After Christopher had left for work, Catherine fought off the depression that began stealing over her. Was Anita right? Would Jon Miles collapse when faced with Brian and Simon? Then, for the first time, another thought struck her forcibly. What right did Simon have to be there anyway?

She had blamed herself when Simon had made the pass because she had responded to it. But hadn't there also been another feeling? A sense that Simon's sexual interest in her had been in some way connected with her failure to get the headship? If she'd been Acting Head of Rosemount, she suspected, Simon would have thought twice about trying to have an affair. It would have been too politically dangerous.

This was a thought she'd dismissed because she'd liked and admired him and felt embarrassed about the whole thing. But now a vague memory stirred in her. Anita had reminded her about the attractive student teacher, whom everyone had liked and admired, who'd left suddenly and no one had any idea why. It had been the talk of the staff room for days. Had Simon tried something on her too? That would certainly explain the sudden departure.

Beginning to feel scared and excited in equal measure, Catherine tried to remember the girl's name. Something unusual, Anita had said, at least in their rundown corner of London. Serena? No. Georgina. That was it. Georgina Wesley.

I hope to God, Catherine willed, she hasn't given up teaching altogether.

It took a bit of research and persistence and a smattering of fibs to get the information she needed, but by the end of the morning she had it. Georgina Wesley was teaching at a comprehensive in Harrow and lived about a mile from the school. This was going to be a very interesting conversation indeed.

Georgina's home was in a depressing suburb of the kind Stevie Smith wrote about so vividly, where curtain twitching was an art form, and a dog raising its leg on the rubbish bags that dotted the pavements a major event. It was full of terraced redbrick and pebble-dash houses, with the occasional remake in Stoneage 2000 to liven up the symmetry. Replacement windows were obligatory, the uglier the better.

An ancient bike of the sit-up-and-beg variety, with a wicker basket on front, stood propped up in Georgina's front garden.

A young woman answered Catherine's knock, but to her disappointment it wasn't the same woman who had been at Rosemount, Catherine was sure of that.

Georgina Wesley had been highly attractive, with long glossy dark hair and blooming olive skin. This young woman was skeletal and her skin lacked even the lustre of youth.

'You're Mrs Hope, aren't you?' the young woman greeted her. 'You were very kind to me, I remember.'

The shock made Catherine reel. If this was the same young woman then something catastrophic had happened to her.

'It's really kind of you to see me.'

'I didn't want to.' The girl's reluctance was almost tangible as she returned Catherine's handshake. 'In fact, I almost called to cancel. I've put all that stuff behind me. Then I thought,' her face took on something approaching animation for the first time, 'why should I let that man get away with it and go on and ruin someone else's career?'

Catherine's heart began to race. She'd

334

been right! Simon had done something to Georgina Wesley. And in her case it was even more appalling since he'd been in a position of responsibility regarding this vulnerable young woman.

They sat down in the girl's bare sitting room, with its posters of white doves and calm seascapes.

'Do you feel strong enough to tell me about it?'

The animation returned to Georgina's face, and with it some shadow of her former attractiveness. 'The strange thing is, I'm looking forward to it.'

★　★　★

'Hey, Rach,' Rachel's friend Steph shouted across the changing rooms as they got ready for lacrosse, 'have you got any of those Always thingies, you know, with the wings, like they advertise on the telly?'

'Sorry, no.' Rachel could hardly shout out the truth that she preferred Tampax, prompting a spate of low jokes about Prince Charles telling Camilla he wanted to be a tampon if it meant being inside her.

'Actually,' Steph speculated, 'you're looking a bit PMTish yourself.' She plonked herself down next to Rachel. 'Are you coming down with something or just pining for your Man of the Woods?'

Rachel considered this. She was feeling a bit lacking in energy but had ascribed it to an end-of-winter low and the fact that she was here when she'd rather be there. 'I'm all right. Just a bit tired and irritable. Anyway, PMT's a load of old tosh if you ask me.'

'Don't!' squawked Steph. 'I'm relying on it as an excuse for when I fail my A levels. I just thought you had all the classic symptoms.'

Actually, Rachel thought, as she stuffed her uniform into her locker, Steph had a point. It would be absolutely typical if she got her period in the middle of her exams. She pulled her school diary out of her briefcase. She could measure the start of her exams in days now and she'd meant to draw up some kind of chart.

When was the last time she'd had the curse?

A chilling numbness, worse than the coldest nights in the wood, spread slowly through her limbs. She couldn't remember. This was ridiculous. She must have just forgotten in all the excitement. *Think*, she ordered herself sternly, but it was no good. The last time she could actually remember having period pains was before Christmas. She remembered that one quite clearly

336

because it had been the full Nurofen and hot-water bottle variety.

The hideous truth hit her like a cold shower. She hadn't forgotten any others because there hadn't been any others. And Christmas was two months ago.

How could she have been so stupid and careless? It wasn't as if she hadn't had sex education pushed at her from every quarter. She'd known all about condoms since she was ten. It was just that no one told you what to do when you'd run out of the things and you were in a wood four miles from the nearest chemist shop and lust had swooped over you like a wild tornado. It was lust that persuaded you it would be all right just this once.

Except that maybe, just this once, it hadn't been, and clever smarty-pants Rachel, who had been feeling so adult and in control, might end up like any other pathetic pregnant schoolgirl. The irony hit her like a wet sponge in the face. Her parents feared the road protest might sabotage her exams. No one had thought of this.

Oh God, what would she *do*? To have a baby seemed impossible, she hardly felt grown up herself, yet the inconsistency of trying to save a wood while jauntily disposing of a human being wasn't lost on her. She didn't know what the environmentalists' line was on abortion, but she knew the reality struck her as too awful to think about.

'Rach, Rach, are you OK?' Steph had put a hand on her arm. 'You look awful. Why don't you tell them you're not up to lacrosse today.'

'I might do that.' Rachel would be believed because she was keen on sports and rarely tried to make excuses. Steph watched her jealously as she walked slowly back to the school building in the freezing misty afternoon. Lucky bugger.

But Rachel was feeling anything but lucky. She felt as if she'd swallowed a balloon and any moment someone would start pumping it up. 'You silly girl,' everyone would say, 'how did you, clever Rachel with so much ahead of you, make such a stupid mistake?'

She yearned to talk to somebody. Steph was out of the question. Her own parents would be shocked and would quarrel as if it were their fault, not hers, that somehow they had gone terribly wrong in her upbringing. Zoe would be a possibility, or even Alexander, but she was surprised to admit that more than anyone else she really wanted to talk to her grandmother.

The one person she didn't want to tell was Marko. She could imagine his delighted grin at the thought of his genes being replicated in the next generation, and she didn't think she could bear it.

And then one final, cheering idea occurred to her. That maybe the whole damn thing was a false alarm.

★ ★ ★

'Are you all right, Rachel?' The tender concern in her mother's voice when she got home, which so often annoyed her and which she saw as an unfair invasion of her liberty, had an unexpected effect today. Rachel let out a small sob.

'My God, Rachel darling.' Even though she was still excited about her discovery of Georgina, Catherine was alarmed. Her daughter was usually so self-contained. 'What on earth's the matter?' And, with a flash of guilt that perhaps she'd been too hard on her, 'Is it the exams? It is a lot of pressure, I can see that.'

'Yes,' Rachel sniffed, desperate to get up to her bedroom and fling herself on her bed.

'Perhaps you had better go and visit your precious wood this weekend.'

It was a staggering suggestion from her mother, who seemed to hate the mention of the place. 'Actually, Mum, what I'd really like to do is go and stay with Gran.'

Catherine was doubly amazed. This time it couldn't even be a cover. What had Lavinia got in the mothering stakes that Catherine seemed so clearly to lack?

'It's just that Ma's not you,' Christopher comforted his wife later that evening. 'Grandparents are less judgemental. Besides, Ma's just as caught up in the whole thing as Rachel, even if she is on the other side of the fence. Gives them something to talk about.'

Something was up, Catherine knew it, when she took Rachel to the station. Rachel sat curled in the corner like a wounded animal. Had that ghastly young man chucked her? Was that why she wanted to run to Lavinia instead of to their little camp? Catherine could almost feel the weight of her daughter's pain. Being a parent could be so excruciating. Your instincts were to protect your child from this sort of agony and to want to tear the person who'd caused it limb from limb. Yet at the same time you knew your child had to grow up, to suffer, to learn, and that to shield it from reality could be dangerously shortsighted. But that didn't stop you longing to do it all the same.

'Goodbye, darling, take it easy this weekend. Let Gran spoil you, she'll enjoy that.'

At the last minute, just as she ought to be

going on to the platform, Rachel made a sudden dash for the chemist, claiming she needed Clearasil. Catherine, who hated missing trains, was about to snap that surely she could survive a night without spot deterrent, then bit back her words. She must stop trying to run Rachel's life for her.

The train was just starting its engines when they finally made it to the platform. Catherine could feel her heart beating while Rachel seemed infuriatingly dreamy and relaxed. I wonder, thought Catherine with a stab of fear, could she be on drugs? Certainly her mood had swung dramatically. From being wildly keen to see her grandmother yesterday she seemed like a limp lettuce today, as if nothing counted much any more. Really, what *was* the matter with the child?

Catherine knew her too well to try asking.

Rachel flopped into a corner seat and tried to avoid the sight of her mother bouncing up and down waving. If only she *knew*. Tucked into the capacious pocket of Rachel's parka was the answer to her dilemma. She had an hour to herself to find out. By the time she got to Maxted her future would be decided.

Rachel ignored her mother and headed for the toilet. The instructions for the Predictor test were simple, yet she still had to read them three times to get them into her head.

She placed the gear carefully on the side of the basin, then held the sampler into the stream of urine, trying to ignore the unsavoury odour of the place and the quarter inch of water under her feet. Now all she had to do was wait. Outside somebody was knocking on the door. Rachel ignored them. Her need was greater than theirs.

The leaflet claimed it would take only four minutes. To Rachel it felt like the last few minutes on the planet. Although it only took four minutes, it was clearly too long for whoever was waiting outside. They kept banging on the door until Rachel yelled, 'For God's sake leave me alone, will you? I'm doing a pregnancy test!'

That should sort them out, whoever they were.

Rachel went back to counting the seconds. Only one more minute now. She closed her eyes and picked up the vial. For some reason she couldn't have explained, she kissed it. One circle meant she wasn't pregnant, two, that she was. There, right in the centre, were two distinct rings. It was positive all right. She put it away in its packaging and stuffed it into her pocket.

Outside the cubicle the person queuing still waited. It was a nun. She made the sign of the cross as Rachel passed.

The sight of Lavinia leaning on her jaunty red Rover outside Maxted Station cheered Rachel more than she could say.

'Oh, Gran,' she yelped, catapulting herself into her grandmother's astonished embrace.

Lavinia patted Rachel's hair and had the good sense not to pursue the matter further until they got home. Glad that she'd lit a fire and left the hot water on, a rare extravagance for her, she scuppered the idea she'd been toying with of suggesting a pub lunch. Rachel looked as if she needed a cuddle and a calm atmosphere.

'Come on,' Lavinia instructed once they were inside the cottage, 'coat off, slippers on and I'll make us some lunch.'

'Thanks, Gran, but I'm not really hungry.'

'All right then,' Lavinia poured them both a hearty nip of her home-made sloe gin and sat down next to Rachel on the sofa. 'Do you want to tell me what's up? You can say, 'Bugger off, you interfering busybody' if you like.'

For answer Rachel delved into the pocket of her parka and held out the pregnancy test.

17

Lavinia inspected it. 'What a wonderful invention! My God, what a difference these would have made in my day. How long do you have to wait to find out?'

'Four minutes.'

'Four minutes! Heavens, how amazing!' The expression on Rachel's face, like some poor wounded animal limping along unnoticed, stopped Lavinia short. 'Oh, darling, it's positive, is it?'

Rachel nodded. She was staggered that her grandmother had expressed no word of disapproval — and yet, wasn't that why she was telling her, instead of her own mother, because she'd somehow sensed Lavinia might be the person who'd understand.

'And is Marko the father, do you think?'

'He's the only candidate.'

The pain in Rachel's voice made Lavinia want to hold her and tell her everything would be all right. Except that life wasn't that simple, as Lavinia knew to her cost.

'Does he know yet?'

'No. I've only just found out myself. Gran . . . '

'Yes?'

'I don't want him to know. Oh God, Gran, I haven't really faced up to this.'

'The only thing that matters is that you're entirely honest with yourself. What do *you* feel is right? Are you in love with Marko?'

'I don't think so. I don't know. The awful thing is, I think he was just part of the adventure.'

Lavinia said nothing. Rachel's parents would be deeply relieved to hear this.

It was ironic how far the pendulum of disapproval had swung. When Lavinia was faced with the same decision, a baby without marriage was unthinkable, the end of everything. But Christopher and Catherine would probably think that getting married at eighteen was the end of everything, especially getting married to Marko.

'Then whatever you do, don't stay with him just because you're having a baby!' The words, rough and jagged with anguish, seemed prised from some dark place within Lavinia. 'It's the greatest mistake you could ever make to stay with a man you feel nothing for just because your child needs a father. It will make you despise him in the end, believe me, no matter how reliable and kind he is.'

What on earth was her grandmother talking about? Marko was neither reliable nor kind, just sexy and selfish and occasionally rather sweet. Suddenly she understood. 'That's what you did!'

Lavinia turned away, unable to meet her granddaughter's astonished gaze. 'You married Grandfather, yet you didn't love him. It was Alexander you really loved, wasn't it?'

'Your generation didn't invent love. Or sex. Yes, I loved Alexander but I bowed to pressure and gave him up. You're stronger than me, Rachel, it will be different for you. You will follow the course you want to, whether with Marko or not.'

'I don't feel very strong at the moment.' The pain in Rachel's voice brought back an echo of the agony and the indecision Lavinia had suffered herself so many years ago.

The formidable, efficient, sometimes disapproving persona Lavinia had invented for herself began to fall away. She opened her arms to her granddaughter. 'My poor, poor Rachel. I know this will be hard for you to imagine, but I know exactly how you feel. But it won't be the same for you, I promise, because I won't let it.'

The fierce protectiveness in Lavinia's voice moved Rachel. She would never have allowed her mother to adopt this tone, but in her grandmother it was oddly comforting.

When Rachel woke up next morning she felt as if she had been transported back to childhood. The bed she slept in was narrow and pretty and made up with white broderie anglaise sheets, old-fashioned blankets and an eiderdown. Lavinia had never approved of duvets. The walls were lined with stripy wallpaper entwined with bunches of violets and a Delft-blue hyacinth in a pot filled the room with its sweet perfume. Rachel slipped back into sleep, almost convinced that yesterday's revelation might have been a figment of her imagination.

A knock brought her back to reality. Lavinia carried a tray loaded down with tea, toast and orange juice. As her grandmother plumped her pillows and fussed around, Rachel noticed that Lavinia had a frayed and fragile look, like a beloved piece of china that has been worn eggshell-thin. Was it because of her? Rachel wondered guiltily. Perhaps Lavinia, who had always seemed so strong, was getting too old to sustain shocks like this?

'It's because she's not seeing *him*,' whispered Eunice when Rachel was finally dressed and had come downstairs. 'They've fallen out. At this time of all times too, just when she could do with a friend.'

347

'But she knows everyone round here,' Rachel pointed out, mystified.

'They've all cut her dead because she got involved with you lot, didn't she tell you? Sent her to Coventry. That frightful woman at the village shop won't even serve her. Lavinia's lived here all her life and that bouffant bimbo only arrived five minutes ago. Diabolical, I call it, and to think they say the country's friendly. I preferred Beckenham.'

But Rachel was only half listening. She couldn't believe that people round here could be so cruel, and that it was partly her fault. God, what an awful mess.

'I wish to goodness she'd make it up with Alexander. I didn't trust the man at first, but the effect he's had on Lavinia's miraculous. She's been like a girl again. Until now.'

Rachel nodded. She had noticed. She couldn't imagine telling the disapproving grandmother of a few short months ago that she might be pregnant. She just hadn't realized how much of Lavinia's mellowing had been down to Alexander.

She had brought a lot of worry on Lavinia, Rachel could see that. The least she could do would be to try and get Alexander back into Lavinia's life when she needed him most.

She ought to be going back today but the thought of London and school seemed like an impossibility. Rachel wasn't ready yet to face normality and her mother. Instead she rang and announced to Ricky she wasn't feeling great and would probably come back tomorrow. Catherine instantly came on the line. 'Are you all right, darling? I thought you looked a little peaky yesterday.'

'I am a bit shagged out,' conceded Rachel, shuddering slightly at the unconscious truth of her statement. She had expected irritation. Sympathy was a surprise. But then her mother had probably drawn up an exam chart and knew the value of letting the prize cow take it easy to get her fit for the show ring.

'See you tomorrow, probably.'

She put down the phone. Lavinia was upstairs turning out cupboards, always a sign of serious depression. Other people hit the chocolates or snivelled on sofas when life got too much for them. Lavinia reached for the duster.

Rachel put her head round the door to announce that she was going out. Every drawer had been emptied on to the carpet, the bed stripped to its mattress protector, the blankets hung out of the window into the freezing air. Lavinia, at the centre of her planned chaos, wielded the feather duster like a Valkyrie. 'See you later, Gran.' Rachel waved. 'Are you sure you're all right?' The words echoed her own mother's of moments ago. The truth was, neither of them was all right and neither of them knew what to do about it.

Rachel closed the back door and edged her way round the dustbins. Tomorrow was collection day and Lavinia was obviously making the most of it. Six bulging black bags, some with clothes sticking out, were piled up against the wall. Had Rachel been feeling herself she would have leaped on them with glee and tried to retrieve any eccentric gems for her own wardrobe. But not today. She was just easing past two of the bags when a large canvas caught her eye. Rachel's curiosity got the better of her and she tore off the wrapper. It was Alexander's painting of the cornfield. How could her grandmother be throwing it away? It was one of the most powerful paintings she'd ever seen.

Surreptiously she slipped the canvas under her voluminous parka. But where could she put it? She thought about the garden shed, but given her grandmother's dark mood Lavinia might start on emptying that next. If only she had a car. She could take it to the camp, but she didn't feel ready to face Marko yet or Zoe with her spiky perceptiveness.

Next door Eunice was putting out one

small bag of rubbish. She waved. Rachel dashed towards her, looking over her shoulder guiltily to make sure her grandmother wasn't watching from the upstairs window. The curtains were firmly closed. Again, that wasn't a Lavinia thing to do. 'Could you look after this for me?' she whispered.

'My goodness, what an extraordinary picture! I'm not sure I'd like that on my living-room wall. I'd keep expecting a juggernaut to come thundering out of it.'

'I think that's probably the point. Could you keep it somewhere my grandmother can't possibly see it? You see, I think she might change her mind about wanting to throw it away.'

'Of course. How thrilling. I'll put it behind the croquet set. We won't be getting that out for a bit, will we?'

Finding her way to Alexander's cottage wasn't as easy as Rachel had hoped. She'd managed to prise a lift from a farmer on his mini-tractor but for the last mile no traffic passed and she had to trudge through the woods. She still had half a mile to go and she was feeling exhausted. What if she got there and he wasn't in and she had to walk all the way back? She wouldn't let herself think about that and plodded on.

Finally his remote cottage came into view, and, thank God, his ancient Land Rover was in front of it. Rachel cheered up. He might not listen to what she had to say, but at least her freezing walk hadn't been entirely wasted.

She whistled as she speeded up her steps and raised her hand to wave when the front door opened. But the gesture froze as she saw what he was carrying. In one hand was a large and battered suitcase covered in labels, the ancient and classy kind that no amount of money spent on expensive luggage could achieve. In the other hand was a cardboard box of books and a small table lamp. Alexander was clearly moving out.

'Alexander . . . ' She could hear the edge of panic in her own voice, not for her own but for her grandmother's sake. 'You're not leaving, surely?'

'Rachel!' His drawn face softened. 'What a lovely surprise.' He put down the suitcase. 'I am, as you see, going away for a while, yes. The lease is expiring on this place so I decided it was time for a change. Tuscany, I think. I have some friends who have a farm there. It's very pleasant in the early spring. The colours are wonderful for the amateur painter.'

'But what about the road? You said yourself things would be hotting up now.'

'I think I may have had enough of stopping motorways. I'm getting too old. My heart isn't in it like it used to be. It's time I passed the mantle on to you young people.'

Rachel put her hand on his arm, her tone changing. 'Alexander, you can't go! Not now!'

'You mean because the fight is getting rougher? I'm not running away from that, you know. In some ways it's hard to go just when the drama's unfolding. But I'll be leaving things in capable hands. Zoe's. Yours.' He didn't, she noticed, mention Marko's. 'Things will start to move fast now the route has been approved. I have to warn you, Rachel, it could get dangerous.'

'I know. But it isn't because of the road that you've got to stay.'

His grey eyes studied her, waiting, while the wind whipped his white hair around his face. Rachel felt the power emanating from him like some great pylon. He must have been irresistible as a young man amongst all those effete public school boys. 'It's because of Lavinia.'

Alexander looked away. 'Lavinia doesn't need me. She doesn't need anyone except her family. I'm not the self-sufficient one. I might have thought I was, but I've learned otherwise lately.'

'Alexander, that's not true. She's alone. Those awful people in the village have turned against her and it's all because of us. She may not be good at admitting it but you're the one she needs, not us. You've switched her on like a light. She's a different person since you came back into her life. We've all noticed. Please don't abandon her again.'

'Again! What nonsense has Lavinia told you!' He sounded really angry now. He picked up his suitcase.

'Please, Alexander,' the sudden pain and uncertainty in Rachel's voice halted him momentarily, 'there's something else. I'm pretty sure I'm going to have a baby.'

'Oh, Rachel, you poor child, now of all times.'

But Rachel wasn't thinking of herself. Instead she was wondering about another time and another young woman. 'Alexander, if you loved someone very much and even though you were both young and maybe very different and she came and told you she was pregnant, what would you do?'

Alexander studied her in surprise. He hadn't thought this was how Rachel felt about Marko. 'If I loved her that much I would tell her that no matter how hard it might be, having a baby would be the biggest adventure of our lives.' He turned away again, pain clouding his eyes. 'There's just one wrinkle in that declaration of honourable intent. I've never actually had to face the choice.'

Without even being conscious of it, Rachel let out a sob. Should she tell him now what she suspected, or was it too desperately unfair to her grandparents? What if she were wrong after all?

'Alexander, look . . . there's something I think you should know . . .'

As she searched for the words that might rip all their lives into pieces, there was a sudden noise of cracking twigs behind them.

'Rachel!' Marko shouted, flicking back the curtain of his long hair and smiling. 'I don't believe it. I've been trying to reach you in London for days. Why the fuck didn't you tell me you were here?'

18

'Hello, Marko.' Was he imagining it, Alexander wondered, or did Rachel seem less than ecstatically happy at Marko's arrival given what she'd just asked him? She certainly didn't sound like a rapturous young woman who was about to throw in her all for love. Perhaps he just didn't understand young people any more. The rules seemed to have changed so much.

He packed his suitcases into the car and the few possessions he would need in Italy. His easel, a few canvases, his paint-splattered but serviceable radio, some books.

'Can I have a lift to the station?' Rachel asked suddenly. 'Only I promised I'd go back today.'

'Can't you come back to the camp for a bit?' Marko's voice was both intense and yet humble, the latter certainly an unfamiliar emotion for Marko. 'Zoe and Duffo would love to see you. Your tree house has been great.'

The pathos in his voice even struck Alexander. It obviously hit home with Rachel too.

'OK then, just for an hour, and then I really must get back to London. Goodbye, Alexander. Please reconsider.'

'Goodbye, Rachel. And good luck with your A levels.'

Poor Marko, thought Alexander, if he's going to be a father it looks as if he's going to be the last to know. And he felt a sudden temptation to tell him.

Alexander had no more time to ponder on this rash course of action because an impatient BMW driver was trying to pass him on the narrow country lane. In a moment he would be at Lavinia's. It wouldn't take long to say goodbye and he owed Lavinia that much whether they'd quarrelled or not.

The house looked somehow different. The mementoes and knick-knacks that had crowded her shelves and dressers in a way that had always rather appealed to him had been swept away in favour of a pared-down, neater look.

'You've been busy,' he commented.

'Time for a new broom and all that, an early spring clean.'

The sketches he'd given her of the woods had gone too, he noticed. 'And I was part of it, was I, Lavinia?' he couldn't resist adding, even though he hated himself for his weakness.

He hadn't meant to resurrect their quarrel, but the words had slipped out. Even he could hear the bitterness in them.

'Alexander,' her voice was gentler than he'd expected, 'don't.'

He watched her intently for a moment. To his eyes Lavinia seemed like her house, reduced. He couldn't bear to see her without the bossiness and exuberance that had always gone hand in hand. The quintessential Lavinia. He saw that Tuscany might indeed be just what he needed. But not without her.

He took Lavinia's strong but bony hand. 'You need to get away from here, these people and their petty-minded japes. I've friends near Siena. Come with me. The sun will be out, not blazing but warm. The olive groves are blue as grapes and the cafés empty of anyone but locals. I'll teach you to paint. We'll walk and talk and read. It will do you good.'

Lavinia smiled at the tempting picture, as much because it meant he had forgiven her as at the invitation itself.

'It sounds wonderful.' She closed her eyes for a moment and could almost feel the sun on her shoulders.

'You'll come then!' The excitement in his voice was almost boyish now.

'I can't, Alexander. It would be running away.'

'A perfectly commendable response.'

'But not one of mine. I'm pig-headed. You must know that by now and I'm damned if I'll give them the satisfaction of thinking they've driven me out. No, Alexander, I'm staying. But I'll join your side and fight them if you like.'

Alexander sighed, feeling his Tuscan paradise disappear like morning mist. 'But we could be happy there.'

'We could be happy here. I don't care what anyone thinks any more. Sod the lot of them. I'll help you save your wood, by God I will!'

Alexander shook his head. He knew when he was beaten. He just wondered if the other side knew quite what they had handed over. Lavinia Unleashed as a secret weapon. It was quite a thought.

There was a rap at the door and Rachel's pretty elfin face appeared in the lead-paned window. 'Could I have that lift now, do you think?'

She took in the fact that they were both sitting on the sofa and also the small giveaway that her grandmother's hand was in Alexander's.

'Are you going to Italy as well, then?' she demanded, grinning, even though the thought of losing her grandmother for even a few weeks when she was so unsure of life herself was too awful to contemplate.

'No,' announced Alexander in tender exasperation. 'Lavinia seems set on running the gauntlet of village disapproval and moral outrage by joining our campaign.'

'Oh, goody!' Rachel breathed, over-whelmed with selfish relief. 'That'll really make them angry. The cherrypickers are on the warpath, Marko says. They'll be here any day.'

'We should have plenty to keep us busy then, shouldn't we, Alexander?' said Lavinia. 'Come on, Rachel, I'll drop you at the station while Alexander unpacks his suitcase.' She fixed him with a challenging stare. 'You'll find plenty of hangers in the wardrobe.'

'You mean Alexander's actually moving in with you?' demanded Rachel gleefully.

'Why not? His lease is up and the poor man has to live somewhere. Besides, if we're going to make them talk we might as well give them something to talk *about*. So,' Lavinia turned to ask her grand-daughter gently, 'did you break the news about his impending fatherhood to Marko?'

Rachel shook her head. 'I wanted to be surer what *I* want to do first.' Her confidence began to drain away. 'Does that sound dreadfully selfish? I mean it's his baby too.'

'It sounds eminently sensible. After all, it's

very early days. Anything could happen.' She stopped the car in the station car park. 'What about your parents, though? Are you going to tell them? I really think you should.'

Rachel stared out of the window. 'I don't know. In a few weeks, perhaps, when I'm clearer. I need to make up my own mind first, I don't think they're ready for this.'

Lavinia patted her hand. 'Perhaps you'd better not mention about Alexander and me.' She grinned wickedly. 'I'm not sure they're ready for that either.'

Rachel climbed slowly out of the car, feeling pulled between two worlds. 'Oh, Gran, I wish this hadn't happened.' She sounded like a child perched on the brink of adulthood, far too young to take care of a baby of its own.

'I know, but bad things do happen and we survive. Sometimes we even get stronger. Just remember, your parents will always love you, whatever you do, and one of these days you're going to have to tell them.'

* * *

The station platform was crowded for a Monday evening and Rachel almost knocked over an old lady with her backpack as she jumped off the train. At the ticket barrier a few people waited to meet loved ones. Irrationally, since she hadn't even told her family which train she was coming on, Rachel hoped to see her mother standing, arms open, with a welcoming hug, as she so often was. Even Rachel could see the irony of this, because when her mother actually *was* there, she ended up accusing her of overprotection.

The sight of her own house made her feel oddly emotional. It was brightly lit and inviting and she could see Ricky up in his bedroom battling with the Internet. Probably, like most of its devotees, trying to see how much he could find on Sex.

She turned her key, yet again expecting some kind of welcoming committee. There was none, so she called out 'Hello, Mum!' The house was pleasanter and cosier since her mother had given up her job, nicer to come home to really, though she'd never dream of admitting that to her mother. But this time there was no answer.

'Where's Mum, Ricky?' she shouted, interrupting her brother's study of a catalogue of bondage accoutrements.

'Oh hi, Rach. Upstairs on the phone. She's been on the phone all day. Something to do with her job. She's got some big meeting tonight and she's dead nervous.'

Rachel felt a vague sense of outrage that

her mother could possibly have a previous engagement, when she, Rachel, was wandering around pregnant, and might need to choose this moment to tell her.

She slunk up to her own room and threw herself down on to her Forever Friends duvet cover. The truth was, she was on her own. No one could make this decision for her. A message by her bedside asked her to ring Steph, but she ignored it. She couldn't have a normal conversation with Steph and if she told her the truth, Steph would think her barking mad not to go straight down to the doctor and plead that the pressure of her exams made the whole thing impossible. Hardest of all was knowing that the doctor, who had teenagers of his own, would probably sympathize and encourage her into a termination.

She cuddled her pyjama-case dog with the missing ear, the one she'd had since she was six. It seemed suddenly crucial that she talk to her mother right away.

Still holding her dog she went off in search of Catherine.

But her parents' bedroom was empty, the bed covered in pads and pieces of paper as if her mother had been planning a speech. The sitting room was empty too and even the kitchen. Only Ricky tapped away at his keyboard, absorbed in his strange cyber-world.

'Ricky,' Rachel suddenly felt as if she were going to cry, 'do you know where Mum is? Only I absolutely *have* to talk to her.'

'Mum?' Ricky looked at his sister as if she were a slightly backward chimpanzee. 'I told you. Tonight's the night of her big meeting. She must have gone already.'

Rachel's response was to burst into a storm of tears and run back upstairs. Ricky shrugged. Girls. They were so weird. He rather hoped for a world, rather like when he was among his best mates at school, where girls were an unnecessary extravagance which could easily be dispensed with.

★   ★   ★

Catherine turned up the collar of her coat against the night air and breathed deeply to calm her raging nerves. She had dressed carefully, put on more lipstick than usual and higher heels. Nothing tarty, but feminine enough to give her confidence and not feel like a neurotic, middle-aged invisible woman — since this was exactly the kind of picture Brian Wickes would like to draw of her.

The community hall where the meeting was being held was empty, as she'd hoped it would be when she arrived, and she was able to station herself on the stage behind the curtains, so she could witness everything that happened without being seen herself.

The first thing she noticed was how many chairs had been put out. Hundreds. But how many would be filled? What if her own reaction was so out of sync with the parents' that hardly any of them bothered to show up?

But more crucially, and the thing that had kept Catherine awake last night, was whether Georgina Wesley would come. She didn't want to put the girl through a further ordeal, but just her presence here would be warning enough to Simon.

'Is she coming?' pressed Anita, who'd just arrived at the other end of the hall.

'She said she'd think about it,' Catherine responded glumly. 'The trouble is, Simon's powerful in teaching and she's worried about wrecking her career.'

'That's how the bastards get away with it,' Anita spat. 'From Clinton downwards.'

'Then we'll just have to hope Bonnie's father is convincing enough on his own.'

Jon Miles chose his moment to arrive, accompanied by Bonnie. There were still another twenty minutes until the start of the meeting, yet he was sweating profusely. Jon Miles looked like a man who wished he were back in his shop renting videos. Catherine knew how he felt. She wished she were back at home watching one of them. Preferably *Gone with the Wind*.

'Now, Cath, you are going to keep your nerve,' Anita commanded. 'You're not doing this just for you. It's for the rest of us too. Not to mention the kids.'

Bonnie mopped her father's sweating brow with a tissue, looking at him as if he were a hero. Catherine watched them, touched; it was clearly even more of an ordeal for him than it was for her. If he could be brave, so could she.

People were beginning to arrive in twos and threes, the kind of parents who sat at the back, none of the pushy middle-class sort who make straight for row one and maximum eye contact. Catherine stayed out of sight behind the curtain, trying to assess whose side they were on.

The hall continued to fill, the crowd easing forwards like a hesitant wave as another row of seats filled up. Half-full now, which meant that at least there was no need to feel either humiliated or like a madwoman who had simply imagined that the school had any problems.

By five to eight there was still no sign of either Brian or his new ally Simon. They were clearly planning a grand entrance. Neither, as Anita kept feverishly pointing out, was there any sign of their secret weapon, Georgina.

The Chair of Governors bustled in and made a great show of pouring glasses of water for the occupants of the three seats at the table on the dais and checking the microphones. Clearly Jon Miles was expected to speak from the floor without the benefit of a mike.

By a couple of minutes before eight, the trickle of parents had developed into a flood.

There were now so many people that no more seats were available, and Disappearing Dave, the school keeper, had disappeared off to raid the classrooms. It looked to Catherine as if every parent in the school had turned up.

At dead on eight, Brian and Simon arrived.

Simon, ridiculously smart and handsome for a teacher, was ushering Brian in with a discreet hand in his back. There was something about his casual confidence that made her want to spit. He had turned Georgina from a pretty but vulnerable girl into a withdrawn anorexic; he had probably opposed her own appointment because it suited his own purposes; and now he was supporting Brian when bullying was an issue that had always, supposedly, appalled him. Underpinning all Simon's apparent good intentions, male solidarity and personal power had clearly become the real driving forces. And, ever since she'd rejected him, the sting of wounded pride had added a detonator to his already explosive mix of emotions.

'Good evening, ladies and gentlemen.' The Chair of Governors had got to her feet. 'Let's get down to the business of the evening. Our head teacher, Brian Wickes, has been at the helm for two months now and I think we can safely say things have been going well.'

'Hah,' whispered Anita, materializing beside Catherine, 'she should be a fly on the wall in the staff room.'

'But there is one area of concern, which is why we have called this meeting tonight. One of the parents, especially, wished to draw attention to the unpleasant phenomenon of bullying. Mr Miles, perhaps you might like to speak on this point yourself?'

Jon Miles stood up. Even standing up he was almost invisible.

Poor man, Catherine thought dismally, he has the charisma of a balding budgie. If Jon Miles was her Sir Lancelot, God help her.

'My girl, Bonnie,' Jon Miles began, 'has been systematically bullied . . . '

'Can't hear!' shouted a voice from the back.

'My girl,' he began again, 'has been hounded every day of her school life . . . '

'Still can't hear!' came another voice.

Jon Miles looked even more nervous. Neither Simon nor Brian Wickes was giving him any help, Catherine noticed.

'Go on stage, Dad,' Bonnie nudged him, 'they've got microphones up there.'

Her father looked as if she'd suggested joining Indiana Jones in a cryptful of snakes. But Bonnie shoved him forward so that either way he had to make a choice. Unwillingly, wishing the ground would open up under him, he headed for the stage.

Good for you, Catherine breathed.

'My girl, Bonnie,' he began at the third attempt, this time at magnificently impressive volume, 'has been bullied every day of her school life. Sometimes in small ways — taking her books from her school bag, calling her names, laughing at her when she puts her hand up in class. But my Bonnie's learned to live with that. I had it too; we're the kind of people that attract it in our family. Small, fat, the kind bullies see as victims. But Bonnie got fed up of being a victim. My Bonnie got brave.' He was clearly so proud of her, there was a catch in his voice which almost tripped him up. 'So she went to her teacher. You can just imagine how hard that was to do, how scared she was she'd just make it worse, but she did it anyway.'

Anita nudged her. Small, fat, victimish he might be, but Jon Miles had the audience in the palm of his hand.

'And her teacher was great. Said she'd sort it out. Said she'd get the backing of the head teacher. But the bullying went on and the head teacher wasn't interested. Bonnie's own teacher did everything she could; she followed Bonnie, drove her places, took on the bullies herself, but she couldn't do it all on her own. In the end it was too much for her. So Mrs Hope, the best teacher this school had, resigned from her job.' He turned to Brian Wickes. 'But it seems to me it ought to have been the head teacher, not Mrs Hope, who offered their resignation.'

Brian Wickes jumped to his feet before there was time for any reaction. 'That's a terrifying story, Mr Miles, and one we all must feel responsible for,' Brian's tone was humble and penitent.

Catherine loathed him for it.

'All well and good,' shouted a parent, 'but what are you actually *doing*?'

'I was just coming to that. Simon Marshall here, whom you all know as Rosemount's previous head teacher, and I have hammered out a set of radical proposals,' he waved a thick wad of paper, 'which I hope will wipe out bullying from the school for ever.'

Catherine could sense the anger in the hall begin to die down. He'd done it. The self-serving rat. He was getting away with it. 'And with the help of these guidelines I think this isolated incident will not be repeated.'

Seeing the mood begin to swing in Brian's favour, Catherine knew she had to act.

She stepped out from behind the curtains. 'Ah, but it wasn't an isolated case, was it, Mr Wickes?'

Brian Wickes, confronted with Catherine materializing from the wings like the genie in *Aladdin*, was temporarily lost for words.

'Your daughter Kelly was bullied, wasn't she, Mrs Hanlon?' Catherine demanded of a downtrodden-looking woman halfway down the hall. 'But she was bullied in a different sort of way, wasn't she? Made to join a gang and bully others, weren't you, Kelly?'

Kelly, who had come with her mother only in the hope of a bag of chips after, looked dumbstruck. After a moment's hesitation she nodded and burst into tears. 'They made me do it. I never wanted to. But if it weren't Bonnie it'd have been me.'

Simon, sitting next to Brian Wickes, decided it was time he intervened. There was still no real rebellion here. All these parents needed was reassurance and he would give it to them. He stood up.

'Mrs Hope,' Simon asked looking intent and responsible, and full of shit, Catherine thought. 'Isn't it true that the reasons you resigned were a little more complex than that? You had hoped for the headship, hadn't you?'

'Yes, but . . .'

'And you felt you had been passed over?'

'I felt I would have been more active about bullying.'

'But you admit you wanted the headship?'

'I felt I had things to contribute after eight years, yes.'

'Mrs Hope, I feel I should remind you that there are appropriate channels for grievances such as yours.'

Catherine felt her breath tighten. He was actually shifting the blame on to her. Before she could defend herself there was a commotion at the back of the hall.

'And are there appropriate channels for my grievance about the way you treated me, Mr Marshall?'

Georgina Wesley no longer looked like a victim. She looked very angry indeed.

19

Simon's charm and confidence, Catherine noted with glee, had melted like ice in a heatwave.

'I'm sorry, Simon,' Catherine found herself savouring every moment of his panic, 'but what was that you were saying about my being motivated by resentment?'

Simon hastily extricated himself and sat down, his eyes fixed in horror on Georgina.

Jon Miles had clearly discovered a killer instinct. He took advantage of the lull and grabbed the microphone. 'I demand that Mrs Hope be reinstated immediately and put in sole charge of this issue with whatever sanctions she wants. Otherwise I propose a vote of no confidence in Mr Wickes as Acting Head of Rosemount.'

The audience applauded wildly.

'Mr Wickes?' enquired the Chair. 'Would you like to say something?'

But Brian Wickes had had enough. He'd been relying on Simon to charm the audience into supporting him, instead of which Simon was sitting there like a man who'd seen a ghost, and it was Catherine who had somehow emerged as the heroine of the hour. He would apply for early retirement. Even spending all day with his wife would be better than this.

'Well staged, Catherine,' Simon said in a low voice. 'Of course, women have a talent for revenge. The Afghans always hand their torture victims over to the women.'

'And I expect the women greatly enjoy it.'

'Be careful, Catherine. I expect Rosemount will be needing a new head. You may need my backing.'

Catherine glanced at Georgina who was deep in conversation with the Chair of Governors. 'I'm sorry, Simon, but I'm not sure your backing is going to be worth much after this.'

As Simon angrily withdrew, Catherine felt a tug at her shirt.

'I just wanted to tell you, Mrs Hope,' Bonnie announced gleefully, 'that I got offered a place at Wolsey today and it was all thanks to you.'

Catherine hugged her. 'Not thanks to me, Bonnie, thanks to your brain and your guts in going for it in spite of Gary Webb.'

'Do you think your daughter might show me round some time this term?'

The mention of Rachel set off a faint alarm. She thought she'd heard someone coming in before she'd left home, but Rachel hadn't appeared and Catherine had had to rush off.

Oh well, she'd see her soon enough. She gathered up her bag and coat, congratulating a beaming Jon Miles as she did so.

'Yes,' he grinned, 'I'll have to stop seeing myself as Danny DeVito and think a bit more Harrison Ford.'

But Anita wasn't letting Catherine go so easily. 'Come on, Cath, we're off to the pub. I even have a toast. The new head of Rosemount Primary. What do you reckon?'

By the time she left the pub Catherine had been bought so many congratulatory drinks by parents and well-wishers that she just wanted to creep into bed as soon as she got home. The adrenaline surge she'd felt in the meeting had left her exhausted, and her head was beginning to pound. All the same, the joy of defeating that toad Brian Wickes had been delicious. And so, she had to admit, was seeing Simon so utterly humiliated.

★　★　★

The house was silent, everyone must have gone to bed. Relieved to be able to just flop, Catherine nevertheless felt a sliver of disappointment that no one seemed interested enough in how she'd got on to stay up. Perhaps it was her fault. She should have involved Christopher more, but she hadn't even wanted to admit to herself how much it mattered, just in case she'd lost.

She was about to go upstairs when she heard the murmur of the television from the sitting room and swore at Rachel's laziness. She was always watching MTV and forgetting to turn it off.

But it wasn't Rachel. A pair of feet stuck out from under a duvet cover on the sofa. Christopher snored gently, remote control still clutched in his hand. She kissed the top of his head, wondering whether to wake him or leave him, but he made the decision for her. A hand sneaked out from under the duvet and pulled a wine cooler out from behind the armchair. It contained a bottle of sparkling wine. 'The offie didn't run to champagne,' he explained, sitting up. 'Are we celebrating or commiserating?'

'Oh, Chris,' Catherine said, sitting down on the sofa, 'you shouldn't have.'

'Probably not, since it's one o'clock in the morning,' he agreed, 'and you look like you've had a few already, but what the hell? Come on, spill the beans. How was the Harper Valley PTA?'

'Absolutely bloody brilliant! Bonnie's dad turned out to be Superman in a shell suit. Brian didn't have a leg to stand on!'

'What about Simon? You were worried that Simon might get him out of trouble.'

'I don't think we need worry about Simon any more.'

'Why not?' His tone was curiously brittle. Did he suspect something between her and Simon?

Catherine hesitated. There was no real need to confess to Christopher; after all, she and Simon had not had an affair, or anything like it. But the truth was, she'd wanted to have one, however briefly, and maybe that was something that ought not to lie corrosively between them.

'Christopher, about Simon ... ' she hesitated, still unsure of her motives. 'There's something I want to tell you.'

'That Simon fancies you rotten,' interrupted Christopher, 'that he sees you as a soulmate, that he wants to have a torrid affair with you and has done for years?'

Catherine's shock made her hand shake so much she had to put down her drink.

'I know all that, Cath. It's been obvious for years. The man looks at you as if he wants you on toast. You were the only one who didn't see it. I always thought it was rather touching. You never realize how attractive you are. Has something happened between you?'

Christopher's tone was light, but she could hear the ragged note of pain breaking through at the edges and felt indescribably moved by it. Sometimes she feared their emotional life was too calm, but clearly she was wrong.

'He made a pass. Just after Brian was appointed.'

'Sensitive timing. But then I never could see Simon as quite the hero you do.'

'But the thing is, I went along with it for a while. I thought I wanted him to. I was so angry with you about Rachel. I felt you were being too soft and undermining me when I tried to stand up to her. So I almost went to bed with him. Thank God, I stopped in time.'

She saw the look of pain on his face and tried to touch him but he turned away.

'I suppose I realized that wasn't the answer to us not getting on.'

'And did the honourable Simon sympathize with your change of heart?'

Catherine flinched. 'Obviously not. That's why he turned against me. It isn't the first time Simon's tried something like this. He has a record of it, apparently. I just flattered myself our friendship was too strong for him to treat me quite the same way as he did other women. I was wrong.'

Regret flooded through Catherine at the sight of Christopher's stiff and angry back. What if he walked out on her?

'I'm so sorry, Chris,' she offered lamely. For answer he turned and pulled her into his arms, kissing her with a furious strength she'd never seen in him before and that could have been powered equally by love or hate. Whichever it was, Catherine, who had thought she was too exhausted to even climb upstairs to bed, found herself responding with an excitement she hadn't felt for months.

* * *

Rachel sat up in bed and looked at her watch. Almost one a.m. She could hear her parents talking downstairs, for God's sake. Normally they had a struggle to stay awake for the late evening news. She thought about this strange state of affairs for a moment or two and decided it was an omen. She had to tell them some time and at least they were together, alone, and Ricky was out of the way.

She pulled on her slippers and towelling robe with pigs on it and took a deep breath.

Halfway down the stairs she stopped and gasped. The lights in the sitting room were dim, thank heavens, but she was still in no doubt as to what was going on. Her father was kneeling in front of her mother, who was draped along the sofa and he was undoing the buttons of her shirt.

Her parents were about to screw!

Rachel decided one thing at least. She wasn't going to bloody well tell them at all. She would decide what to do on her own and they could find out for themselves later.

* * *

Sharing her home with Alexander had turned out to be terrific, quite unexpected fun. Lavinia's life with Robert had been a careful, ordered, circumspect affair. It had had its modest pleasures but Lavinia's chief joys had been her garden and her children, quite possibly in that order. Alexander actually made her laugh.

He was also surprisingly restful. He could be completely silent for an hour at a time, simply reading a novel in a companionable way. Sometimes he read her out extracts. Zola or Auden or Louis MacNeice. Now and then he would suddenly harangue. But he always stopped and laughed when she said, 'Stop giving me a seminar, Alexander.'

The only anti-social habits she'd discovered so far were dragging her outside to look at the Great Bear and listening to the World Service in the middle of the night. Their one serious quarrel had been over the merits of Earl Grey versus PG Tips.

Everyday intimacy had come naturally to them. The only dark shadow in their sunny new life, apart from the fact that she had outraged the entire village, and not dared break the news to her family, was sex. Here Lavinia felt at a loss. The truth was, she found Alexander extraordinarily attractive but felt inadequate about saying so. It had not escaped her that even young women were drawn to Alexander, his magnetism was not the kind to age. Whatever sexual feelings remained to Lavinia, she had long ago assumed that they had been sublimated into her hostas and her hollyhocks. Until now.

Alexander had moved into her spare room three weeks ago, and the sense of holiday was beginning to fade into habit, in the pleasantest possible way.

All her life Lavinia had said exactly what she thought, as her family would testify. She could hardly stop now.

He was sitting peacefully studying the obituaries when Lavinia removed the paper from his grasp and sat down. 'Alexander, what are we going to do about bed?'

'What are you getting at, Lavinia?' There

381

was a roguish glint in Alexander's eye. 'Am I snoring too loudly? Or is my dislike of wearing pyjamas offending your sensibilities?'

'Neither. If I'd been older, I'd have volunteered as a nurse in the war, remember.'

'Lucky Tommies. Blanket baths from Lavinia.'

'You're changing the subject.'

'And what are *your* thoughts about this prickly, and I'm sorry about the pun, subject?' He was laughing at her again.

Lavinia hesitated, shocked at the depths of her own feelings.

'Everyone thinks we're doing it anyway, so I think we should give it a go.'

Alexander cracked with laughter. 'I can see seduction wasn't your forte. But do you *want* to, Lavinia my love?'

At sixty-three, Lavinia decided the time for false modesty was definitely past. 'Yes, Alexander. I would like to very much indeed.'

'No time like the present then,' Alexander took her hand in a firm and loving grip. 'Let's give them something to really gossip about, shall we?'

★ ★ ★

Lavinia sang softly as she ran a deep bath full of extravagant Crabtree & Evelyn Freesia bath oil. It had been a present from her daughter-in-law the previous Christmas and she had decided it was too expensive to use, so it had remained, unopened, at the back of the bathroom cabinet for nearly a year. Today she was glad. It was a day for luxuries and treats. She might even open the Body Lotion that had come with it. Lavinia had never been one for indulgence. Pond's Cold Cream for her face and a dab of Vaseline Intensive Care on her hands had done her a lifetime of service. She opened up the airing cupboard for a clean towel. A pile stood, neatly folded, staring her in the face. How long had she had them. Twenty years? Thirty years? One or two might just have been wedding presents. Most of them were too small compared with modern bath sheets. Puritans rather than cavaliers of the bath linen world. Lavinia smiled. Today she felt like being a royalist voluptuary. She reached for the soft and enveloping one and made a mental note to throw the rest away. She wouldn't even wait for the July sales to replace them.

A rap on the bathroom window, which, as in many old cottages, was on the ground floor, interrupted her reverie. Lavinia pulled on her candlewick dressing gown and cleared a small viewing hole in the steamy window.

It was Eunice.

'Sorry I came round the back,' Eunice was actually blushing. 'Only your bedroom curtains are drawn and it's after ten a.m. Are you ill?'

Lavinia tried to avoid her friend's eyes. 'Never better actually. Just freshening up.'

'What a lovely perfume.' Eunice sniffed the warm fragrant air. 'What is it?'

'Freesia. Isn't it glorious?' She glanced nervously behind her but Alexander was safely dozing upstairs. 'Was there something you wanted to say, Eunice? You look positively bursting with information.'

'Yes, well, I thought I ought to tell you as soon as possible, I — ' her words stopped as suddenly as if they had been lopped off by a knife.

Behind her, wrapped only in Lavinia's kimono plus a fetching pair of woolly socks, Alexander, book in hand, was in the act of declaiming poetry. ''I wonder, by my troth, what thou, and I / Did, till we loved?' . . . By God, there's no one like Donne to understand sexual passion, is there?'

He took in Eunice's presence without a blink. 'Hello there, Eunice, fancy a cup of tea? None of this Earl Grey nonsense, I've got Lavinia some proper stuff. Do you like John Donne? Or are you more of an earthy D.H. Lawrence sort of lass?'

Eunice, whose knowledge of English poets apart from Walter de la Mare could be written on a postage stamp, stood on one leg like a harassed heron.

'Anyway,' pursued Alexander, suddenly realizing that the woman was ill at ease, 'you were just about to tell Lavinia something.'

Eunice looked as if she'd just been thrown a lifebelt to save her from the swirling waters of illicit sex. 'Yes. I thought you ought to know. The sheriff has given the order to clear Gosse's Wood. Colonel Lawley called us all to give us the news this morning. What he calls The Big Offensive starts two weeks from now.'

'We'd better let Zoe and Marko know as soon as possible,' Alexander announced, his face suddenly grim. 'This is it, Lavinia. War.'

Lavinia shivered and pulled her dressing gown round her more tightly. All this military terminology they bandied about so lightly seemed suddenly to have taken on an edge of sharp reality. There had been previous evictions where young people had been badly hurt, even killed.

And worst of all, once Rachel heard about this new development, she wouldn't be able to resist joining the little camp again. Lavinia knew her well enough to see that.

Damn the road. For the first time, Lavinia

saw it as a sinister force, carving its destructive course through the first real happiness she had known in forty years.

★ ★ ★

'Please let me go, Dad! Just for the weekend. I promise I'll work really hard all week.' Marko had wasted little time before phoning Rachel with the news of the eviction plans. 'You want me to get good grades so I can go to Oxford. So do I. But this is a real, once-in-a-lifetime challenge. *Please*, Dad.'

Catherine, packing her briefcase for her first day back at school, heard the white-hot glow of passion in her daughter's words. She had been about to tell her it was out of the question. Instead she found herself listening to her daughter and hearing, as Christopher had once pointed out, an echo of her own younger self. Hadn't she felt just as passionate about the children at Rosemount, and seen them as a once-in-a-lifetime challenge too?

'All right,' Catherine agreed reluctantly, 'but on one condition. That Dad and I take you down there and see for ourselves what exactly is going on and make our own assessment of how dangerous it is.'

'Oh, Mum, *thank* you!'

Christopher looked on nonplussed, as Rachel dashed off, humming, to get her school bag ready.

'Bit of a volte-face on the protesting front?' he suggested.

'She's only going for the weekend. After all, if we ban her completely she might just decide to run away and join them permanently.'

'Catherine,' her husband raised an eyebrow and said no more. 'Have I told you lately that I love you?'

'Yes,' Catherine grinned. 'Several times. I still have the scars to prove it.'

★ ★ ★

'Alexander, what do you think I should do about Rachel?' Uncertainty was not a familiar state of mind to Lavinia. 'I mean I feel her parents should know about this pregnancy but she's asked me especially not to tell them.'

'Then I think you should respect that. After all, it concerns her more than anyone else. She's an intelligent young girl. She'll come to her own decision.'

'I hope you're right.'

'I have a lot of faith in Rachel. I think she's a quite exceptional young woman.' Lavinia's heart soared with pleasure. 'If you feel the time's right, maybe you should encourage her to tell them herself.'

Lavinia sighed. 'I already have a pretty good idea what they'd say.'

'People aren't always as predictable as you think, Lavinia. Look at us.' He patted her arm. 'Who'd have thought we'd be so happy. The dangerous old radical and the county lady. Even if it did take us a lifetime before we dared to find out.'

'Alexander,' Lavinia chided, 'please do not call me *county*.'

They drove together to the wood. Finally the days were getting longer and lighter. Only the occasional frost whitened the ground and, in the middle of the day, the young and brave even took off their coats.

The small camp had a cheerful, purposeful air about it, as if this was the moment it had waited for all winter. Marko and Macduff were up in the trees constructing more houses, linked by walkways built from planks roped together. Marko swooped down Tarzanlike on a rope to greet them, his long dark hair blowing back from his face, his dark sulky eyes lit by a rare smile.

Heavens, thought Lavinia, hoping her grand-daughter was made of strong resolve, he really is sex on legs. A sudden vision haunted her of Rachel throwing up university to live with Marko in the woods, getting back to nature and having babies. Once Lavinia would have laughed at such an idea, but now she appreciated its powerful draw, especially for an intelligent girl who might find academic life tame after all this excitement.

Deprivation and cold, to some of these young people, seemed to be an attraction rather than a drawback. Living in a society unfamiliar with want, they had created their own deprivations, which would no doubt astonish anyone who was born without the luxury of choice.

'Marko,' Alexander greeted him, 'you all seem busy.'

'Yes. We're building six more houses.'

'But there are only three of you.'

'Reinforcements are on their way. Action at last, eh? About bloody time too.' Then he added, his voice softening, 'Rachel's coming at the weekend.'

Oh dear, Lavinia realized, this boy's in love. That would make things even more complicated. And she wondered if Rachel had told him the news yet.

'Alexander,' Zoe demanded when the last tree house was completed. 'What do you think about a tunnel?'

'Tunnels are extremely hard work,' Alexander looked dubious. 'Where would you put it?'

'Over there by the big oak tree. The one Rach and I call The Magic Faraway Tree,' she grinned in vague embarrassment. 'You know, like in Enid Blyton. Because it's at the edge of the wood it'll be a sitting target for the bulldozers. A tunnel would at least slow them down.'

'I don't know. Could you dig one in time?'

'If we all join in, yeah. Rachel will help.' She grinned again at her own volte-face. 'She's actually quite useful in spite of her background.'

'I'm sure she'd be delighted to hear it,' Lavinia snapped waspishly.

'Really, Alexander,' Lavinia remarked as they drove off to visit the five or six other small camps that had been set up in the wood, 'that girl sounds just like you.'

★　★　★

Rachel was grateful she hadn't let on about her condition when her parents drove her down at the weekend. They were shocked enough at the idea of her sleeping in a tree house.

'Want to come up and see?' Zoe invited,

390

throwing down the rope ladder to Catherine.

'No thanks, I'm not very good at heights.'

'Rachel designed it. She even built most of it, with a little help from Macduff and me.'

Catherine surveyed the tree house in blank amazement. 'Rachel designed *that*?'

'For parents who spend all this money getting me educated, you're very surprised when I can actually *do* something. I don't just sit round reading Shakespeare's sonnets, you know.'

Feeling rightly reprimanded, Catherine reached for the rope ladder. 'I suppose I'd better go up and admire it then.'

'It may not look much,' Zoe held back the tarpaulin that covered the platform, 'but it's the Ritz of tree houses, I can tell you.'

There was just enough room for two people to lie down either side of the platform. Catherine was tempted again to say she couldn't believe this was Rachel's work, but stopped herself in time. 'I feel like the people in that Roald Dahl story who get turned into birds and have to live in a nest,' she said instead. And then, when it struck her, 'How do you go to the loo?'

'Hang your bum over the edge and hope for the best,' Rachel laughed. 'You have to get pretty pragmatic living outside. No time for false modesty.'

Catherine steadied herself. This wasn't the Rachel she knew at home, the one who couldn't tidy her own bedroom or turn on the washing machine. There was a kind of steely self-sufficiency about this Rachel that made her mother feel quite humble. Rachel could actually contemplate, even relish, sleeping rough in the treetops. An unexpected pride flooded through Catherine.

It was getting dark and, even though the days might be warming up, the nights were still bone-chilling. 'Come on,' Rachel teased, 'I'll show you both how to light a fire.'

The embers from the previous night were still glowing dully and the new fire leaped into life in only a matter of minutes. They were all sitting back around the blaze when, behind them, a twig snapped.

Zoe whipped her finger to her mouth to tell them all to be quiet. 'It could be the security guards. They're always spying on us to see what defences we've come up with.'

They waited silently for a yellow-coated security man to blunder out of the trees. Instead it turned out to be Lavinia, clutching a huge Le Creuset pot.

'You've all been busy building and tunnelling,' she announced briskly, 'so I thought the least I could do was provide

392

some catering. Watch it, though, the dish is expensive.'

Zoe and Rachel burst out laughing in unison.

'What's the matter?' asked Lavinia, hurt.

'Nothing, Gran,' Rachel giggled, 'it smells delicious. But how can I be expected to prove myself alone in the wild with Mum worrying about the plumbing and you providing communal casseroles?'

After they'd eaten, Christopher hugged Rachel good-bye. 'I'll take Gran and your mother back to civilization and leave you to rough it a little.'

It was extraordinarily dark in the wood, Catherine noticed as she said good-bye. The darkness had an almost tangible quality like a black screen that you felt you might blunder through at any moment and find yourself in another life. In some ways that was exactly what Rachel seemed to have done.

'She'll be fine,' Christopher murmured.

'I know. It's just that she isn't like our Rachel.'

'I suspect that's the point. She's proving something to herself, not to us. She can only do this on her own.'

'I hope she's not offloading us perma-nently. I quite liked the shopaholic, pop-loving Rachel too.'

'I'm sure she isn't. But we probably have to let go in order to get her back.'

'Even though she's got her A levels coming up?'

'I think we have to trust her, Cath.'

Catherine looked back. Rachel stood in the shadow of the firelight, Marko's arm round her. The truth was, their daughter was having an adventure, like running away to sea. It was a bigger adventure than any Catherine had had in her life, certainly a riskier one.

In that brief snapshot of insight Catherine saw that she envied her daughter.

'I'm middle-aged,' she said softly to Christopher, 'and I've never really taken a risk in my life.'

'All the more reason to let Rachel.'

'I hope you're right.'

There was a touch of vulnerability in Christopher's voice when he answered, 'So do I.'

20

'Hi, Mum. Do you mind if I shove these dirty things in the machine?'

Catherine was so grateful to see Rachel back home, happy and apparently ready to go to school that she would have *bought* her a new set of clothes. The truth was, she'd been half expecting a fuzzy call from a mobile phone, announcing that Rachel was staying at Gosse's Wood. Permanently.

She tried not to convey her joy and relief to Rachel. In the family game of Who's Got the Upper Hand Now? it would, Catherine judged, be unwise. So she contented herself with a quick hug and offered to do her daughter's washing for her.

'Wow,' Rachel marvelled, 'I must scare you about risking my exams more often.'

Catherine threw a plastic container at her. 'Here, you horrible child, put in the fabric conditioner and go away.'

'Bloody hell,' she marvelled to Christopher as they prepared the meal together. 'What's come over Rachel? She's done her own washing and gone up to study without a murmur of protest.'

'She's trying to impress you. She wants to be there when the bailiffs try and clear the wood, so she has to convince you she can handle it as well as her school work. Don't worry, I said you'd never agree.'

Catherine thought about this. Seeing Rachel at the camp this weekend had imprinted itself deeply in her mind. The one thing she'd hoped for in her daughter was that Rachel would be confident and independent. School, for some reason, hadn't given her those things, yet mucking in with these odd types and building homes in the trees had.

'She can go if she wants.'

'Excuse me?' Christopher was staggered. 'Have you thought about how dangerous it could be?'

'Yes. But I think Rachel is sensible enough to avoid it, and presumably Alexander will be around to keep an eye on her.'

'That reminds me. I think you'd better pour me a drink. This has been my second shock of the evening.'

'Oh dear. What was the other one?'

'It's about my mother. Rachel says Alexander has actually moved in with her.'

'As her lodger, surely?'

'Not according to Rachel. Eunice told her she'd caught him reading Donne to Ma in a bath towel.'

'Good God!' said Catherine. 'Come to think of it, Lavinia has mellowed a lot lately. Is it Lasting Passion, do you think, or temporary lust?'

Christopher covered his eyes. 'Don't do this to me, Cath. I can't handle the thought.'

'I have to say, I don't blame her. He is a bit of a charmer and your father wasn't exactly Errol Flynn, was he? Rachel says he's got an amazing mind too. I think it's rather sweet. Anyway, look on the bright side, if you're shocked, think how your brother Martin will feel.'

Christopher grinned wickedly. 'Yes, that is a cheering thought. Do you think I ought to be the one to tell him?'

★ ★ ★

Rachel's eyes might have been on the French play in front of her but her thoughts were not. She was thinking of Gosse's Wood in the moonlight when she'd left it earlier this evening. The moon had already come up, even before the sun had gone down. It had seemed like an omen. Rachel hadn't even known herself how passionately she felt about the place until now, when the threat to it was more than something Zoe and Marko talked about. It was real. The wood had been there,

397

hardly changing, for hundreds, maybe thousands of years, yet bulldozers and chainsaws could wipe it out in a matter of weeks. A white-hot anger burned in Rachel at the thought of anyone being so carelessly destructive. And she knew that Gosse's Wood mattered to her more than anything else.

★　★　★

'Behold the conquering heroine comes!' announced Anita to the rest of the staff room with a flourish as Catherine hung up her coat on her first day back at Rosemount Primary. 'We thought you would like to know that: a) no one has seen Brian Wickes for two days; b) since there is no deputy head, and we assume you will be replacing Brian, you might like to lead Assembly this morning — the theme is What Caterpillars Can Teach Us; and c) the Chair of Governors has been in looking for you twice already this morning and none of us can *think* why . . . '

Catherine felt the blood running from her head, leaving her dizzy. She knew, just as they did, what this must mean.

She sailed through Assembly, giving some garbled nonsense about the regeneration of caterpillars, which brought a puzzled look to the face of the little ones.

The Chair of Governors was waiting, with a representative of the local education authority, in her classroom. 'Mrs Hope, we'd like a word, if we may, in Mr Wickes's office.'

It was a curious feeling, walking into Brian Wickes's empty office, remembering all those idealistic conversations she'd had there with Simon and how betrayed she'd felt since.

'You may have guessed why we've asked you here.' The Chairwoman noticed a small bunch of violets on the desk, next to a card in lopsided six-year-old writing. It said simply 'Congratulashuns'. The woman smiled a wintry smile. 'Everyone else seems to have. Obviously we'd like to offer you the job of head teacher.' Catherine bit her lip. 'It can only be Acting until the proper procedures are followed, but we doubt there will be any problems. Well done.'

'Thank you,' Catherine resisted the temptation to hug the woman.

'One thing, Mrs Hope.' She picked up the eccentrically spelled card on Catherine's new desk. 'Perhaps you could make spelling a priority.'

Outside in the playground they swarmed round her like demented butterflies. 'Is it true, miss?' 'Are you the Head, Miss?' 'Will we still have you for PE when Mr Tudge is ill?'

Catherine smiled and said nothing. Standing in for PE was one penance she would pass on. Perhaps to Anita? That would sort her out for lumbering Catherine with Assemblies about caterpillars at ten seconds' notice.

One child hung back at the side of the playground. Catherine called her over.

'Gary Webb's left too,' Bonnie told her gleefully. 'His dad says he's moving him to Holy Trinity.'

'Oh dear, poor Gary. They're so tough over there *he'll* be the one who gets bullied.'

'At least we can feel safe now, with you as Head and no Gary. There's something else,' she hesitated shyly. 'Kelly says she wants to be my best friend.'

'Bonnie, that's great!' Catherine hugged her. Best friends weren't supposed to be allowed in school, but Catherine had always thought it a stupid rule. Besides, Bonnie had never had one before.

'I couldn't have done it without you, Bonnie. You were the really brave one.'

'And my dad.' The pride in Bonnie's voice brought a lump to Catherine's throat.

'Hey, what's this new top you've got on?' Gone was Bonnie's usual misspelled 'Global Warning' tracksuit, replaced by a navy blue sweatshirt with a white tick on the front.

'It's Nike,' she said proudly. 'My dad got it for me.'

Bonnie had finally joined the peer group.

On the way back to Catherine's classroom Anita leaped out of the stock cupboard, brandishing a bottle. 'Here you are, Esteemed Head Teacher. Just a small bribe to argue the case for my promotion.' She winked outrageously at her friend. 'Or I could always offer to sleep with you instead.'

★ ★ ★

'OK,' Marko pronounced meaningfully the moment Rachel arrived at the camp, 'who's going to stock up the woodpile? How about you, Zo?'

Zoe knew perfectly well that Marko wanted to get rid of her so that he could lure Rachel into bed. 'Actually,' she said, pretending not to get his message, 'I'm really knackered.'

'I'll go,' Rachel offered, jumping to her feet.

'Oh,' Zoe said innocently, 'if there's two of us I'll do it.'

Marko watched helplessly as the two girls strode off. Rachel glanced back at his puzzled face, and wished things hadn't got so complicated.

'You don't really need to come,' Zoe

offered. 'I was just winding Marko up. He's desperate to get you alone.'

'I know.' The uncertainty in Rachel's face surprised her.

'And you don't want to be alone with him? Have you gone off him?'

'It's more complicated than that.'

'It always is,' pronounced Zoe cynically. 'Anyway, I enjoy wooding so, really, don't worry.'

'So do I.' She didn't dare confess to Zoe that being alone with Marko since she'd found out she was pregnant just made her feel uncomfortable, as if she were short-changing him, which perhaps she was.

The best firewood to be found was near the clearing round The Magic Faraway Tree. They walked in companionable silence. In her brief involvement with the campaign, Rachel had become expert on spotting firewood. Oak was only worth having if it was dry, larch and pine burned well but showered you with sparks, willow took too long to catch light, birch burned too fast and cherry filled the air with the scent of flowers. Best of all was ash.

But today Rachel had her mind on more than finding the perfect firewood. She was feeling absolutely miserable and wondering if she dared confide in Zoe. She'd come to trust the slight, spiky blonde and sensed that Zoe was beginning to reciprocate.

'Zoe . . . ' Rachel turned away, frightened she would start crying. 'I know this is a bit rich coming from me, you'll probably think it's just the spoiled little middle-class girl again, but I wondered if you could give me some advice.' The tears started whether Rachel liked it or not. 'The thing is . . . I'm pregnant.'

'And you don't know what to do?'

'I should have decided already but I can't bring myself to.'

Zoe didn't need to ask if Marko was the father. The pain Zoe felt surprised her in its intensity. She hadn't thought she cared so deeply about him still. 'And you're wondering how Marko would react. I think he'd be thrilled. It would give him some security. He's much less Bohemian than he likes to pretend. Have you told your parents?'

'Not yet. I know how *they'll* react.'

'What about you, what do you think?'

Rachel kicked a piece of wood miserably. 'I suppose I feel too young. I haven't made any real decisions about my own life yet, let alone a child's. But, Zoe, it's a life! No matter how stupid and irresponsible I was, have I got the right to just kill it?'

A branch moved behind them and they both swung round guiltily. Macduff's kind and anxious face loomed out of the branches. 'Sorry to startle you. I didn't know whether to interrupt. We were beginning to worry. You've been ages.'

Rachel and Zoe exchanged glances, wondering if Macduff had overheard.

He took Rachel's sack of wood but not, Zoe noticed wryly, her own.

'There's just a few more logs to get over there,' Rachel indicated a fallen tree. 'We won't be long, will we, Zoe?'

Sensing he was intruding on a bastion of female solidarity, Macduff blushed fiercely. 'Oh, all right. I'll see you in a moment then.'

'Why don't you start a fire with the wood we've got?' suggested Zoe.

'Do you think he heard?' Rachel whispered anxiously.

'I don't think so. He is one for lurking in the bushes, but I shouldn't think so. Look, Rach, I don't know whether this helps but although Marko might like the idea of fatherhood, where he's concerned it'd be a fantasy. He couldn't look after you, let alone a child. Marko's charming but he's self-centred and vain. He's always depended on women, from his mother on. You'd have to be the strong one, always. Is that what you want from a man?'

As she said the words, Zoe wondered who she was really talking to, Rachel or herself. 'Now look, we ought to get back or they really will start worrying.'

Back at the camp, activity had broken out. Macduff had decided it was time to start on the tunnel and like a power shovel had already displaced more earth than a team of moles. Marko, characteristically, sat and directed.

'Jeez, I'm knackered,' Macduff announced finally. 'Who wants to take over?'

'I'll have a go,' Rachel offered. She started to dig with all the enthusiasm of a terrier looking for a bone.

'Slow down a bit, you'll wear yourself out, especially since you're ... ' Zoe stopped herself guiltily. Great confidante she'd made. 'Fancy a cup of tea?'

'Great idea,' said Marko, 'it's getting bloody cold now.'

'Not you,' Zoe said more waspishly than usual. 'In fact, you can make it.'

With an injured expression Marko disappeared to put on the kettle. Five minutes later he was back, unable to find the battered old teapot.

Zoe gave Rachel a significant look. Despite herself, Rachel giggled.

Rachel went on digging steadily even though the muscles in her back and neck were killing her and a huge blister was appearing on her palm. Eventually the pile of dirt next to the tunnel kept falling back in. Rachel eased herself out and began shovelling it into some old coal sacks which she then carried to the barricade they were building round the base of The Magic Faraway Tree.

'Hey, Rach, that looks too heavy.' Marko looked up from his copy of the *Fortean Times*, organ of everything Weird and Unexplained. 'Why don't you make two journeys?'

Rachel and Zoe hooted with laughter. Marko, puzzled, couldn't see what was funny.

When Rachel tired, Zoe took over and then some volunteers from a nearby camp.

'How do you stop it caving in?' Rachel asked, staring into the hole and remembering how one famous road protester had stayed underground for days on end.

'Like a mine, with wooden props,' Zoe explained, 'then we line the floor with pallets and the roof with planks to stabilize it. Macduff learned how to do it in the army.'

'Isn't it freezing down there?'

'Yes, but fortunately Duffo doesn't feel the cold, do you, Duff? Maybe we should find you a nice moleskin coat. Only joking,' she added, seeing his horrified expression. 'Do you think your grandmother would have a paraffin heater going begging? And any old carpet she's got hanging around would be great. Plus candles, night lights, anything. Best to plan ahead.'

'How long do you reckon all this will last, then?' Somehow Rachel had seen it as one big clash rather than a long-drawn-out campaign.

'Weeks. Months even. Depends how effective we are at stopping them.'

'We'd better get that tunnel finished then.' Rachel reached for the spade again.

'No, you've done enough,' Zoe stopped her. 'Go and see if you can get that heater. Marko, put down that sodding magazine. The only weird thing round here is why you don't get off your arse and help.'

Looking like a beautiful but wounded god, Marko finally got up and started digging.

'I wish I had a camera,' giggled Zoe, 'to capture this for posterity.'

Rachel tied her parka round her waist as she walked. Spring had woken up the wood and each day the buds on the trees seemed bigger. She felt the warmth of the sun on her back, blissful and invigorating. It felt as if it had been away for a hundred years. A flash of green at the corner of her eye turned out to be a woodpecker. She stopped to absorb it all. She knew, if she was honest, that she was using the threat to the wood to take her mind off her decision about the baby. But it seemed too great, too paralysing and she knew she wasn't ready to make it. She would live for the moment and ignore the stark reality that if she did so long enough that would constitute a decision in itself.

★   ★   ★

'Hello there.' It was Alexander who answered the door like the most genial of hosts. 'Your grandmother's gone shopping. She should be back any minute. Cup of tea?'

Rachel looked round the cottage. It felt subtly different, more masculine. A faint hint of cigar smoke spiced the pot-pourri. There were piles of books everywhere with titles like Trotsky's *History of the Russian Revolution*, *British Post-War Culture*, and an open copy of *Anna Karenina*. Not quite her grandmother's cup of Earl Grey.

Alexander brought the tea in. 'Lavinia's halfway through that one.' He pointed to *Anna Karenina*. 'Got to start her somewhere. For forty years she's read only gardening catalogues. There's nothing she doesn't know about the propagation of perennials but her knowledge of love, life and the death of the soul are a mite rusty.'

Rachel burst out laughing. 'I can see that living with you is going to be an education for her, literally.'

'She's teaching me a thing or two, too, you know. I could do *University Challenge* on Doulton china, scone-making and car maintenance. Did you know Lavinia does her own servicing? Within reason, obviously. Personally, I'm happy never to even open a car bonnet.'

He caught sight of her mud-stained hands. 'Look at you, dirt under your fingernails just like your grandmother. It must be hereditary.'

'Actually I was helping the others dig a tunnel. It's coming along brilliantly. That's why I came. To see if Lavinia had a paraffin heater for it.'

'You're enjoying all this, aren't you?'

Rachel sipped her tea. She didn't feel like another lecture. 'Yes, I am, but if you're about to tell me how dangerous it can be, don't bother. Zoe's told me. Duffo's told me. Gran's told me. My parents have told me.'

'And now I'm telling you, whether you like it or not. It's especially dangerous for you, given the circumstances.' She thought he was going to ask if she'd told her parents yet, but he changed the subject.

Rachel really liked him. He respected her right to be her. Unlike most people of his age, he was still excited by life. On the mantelpiece behind him, she caught sight of a studio portrait of her grandparents on their thirty-fifth wedding anniversary and remembered the rather stuffy party that had marked it. She couldn't imagine spending thirty-five years with anyone, especially her grandfather. Robert Hope had found his grandchildren extremely wearing, so Rachel had never really got to know him, but somehow this didn't seem the loss it should.

The gate clicked outside and they both turned to watch Lavinia humming to herself as she searched for her keys.

Rachel had never seen her look so happy. There was an almost girlish incandescence about her, like a sixteen-year-old diving headlong into first love.

'How's the village taking it?' she asked Alexander. 'You and Gran, I mean.'

'An engaging mixture of disgust, innuendo and back-biting. I don't care for my own sake, I've never wanted to fit in, but it upsets Lavinia even though she pretends it doesn't.' His voice had taken on a tone of gruff protectiveness.

'You really love her, don't you?'

'No, I'm just toying with her emotions. To

get revenge for abandoning me forty years ago.'

'I don't know how she could have done that. You're so obviously made for each other.'

He smiled delightedly. 'Pity it's taken us a lifetime to discover it.'

'Some people never discover it.'

'There is that comfort. You remind me of her, you know. Your hair, that burnished golden colour. Your spirit. Your stubborn obstinacy in the face of sensible advice.'

Rachel laughed out loud. Lavinia, key in the door, stopped and stood still for a moment, listening. Instead of going in she looked in through the small side window. Her hand fluttered up to her neck. Rachel and Alexander sat together on the small sofa, happy and comfortable in each other's company, as if they'd known each other all their lives. The sight gave her more pleasure than either of them would ever be able to imagine.

She opened the front door and shouted inside. 'Could one of you two lazy buggers help me with this, or are you staying there all day gassing like grannies on the bus?'

★ ★ ★

The heater made a huge difference. So did the gas lamp, Primus stove, and bumper pack of two dozen candles Lavinia had provided. 'This is the country,' she said, explaining why she had so many, 'we get power cuts.' But the thing that made most difference was the roll of stair carpet Lavinia fetched down from her loft. 'I knew it would come in handy one day, though lining a tunnel wasn't quite what I had in mind.'

'Fuck me,' Zoe declared when they'd put all the stuff in, 'it's a Five Star tunnel. You don't do room service, do you, by any chance?'

'Well,' stated Duffo in a rare outbreak of conversation, 'we're as ready as we'll ever be. Now all we have to do is wait.'

'The bailiffs aren't due till next Friday,' Marko pointed out, 'so I suggest we wait above ground.'

'I like it here. It's cosy.' Zoe tucked her feet under her. 'I feel like Mr and Mrs Mole.'

Marko sighed. 'It's not Walt bloody Disney, you know.'

'I was thinking more Beatrix Potter actually.'

'All right, so here we are,' Marko said sarcastically. 'Four little moles. What are we going to talk about?'

'I know.' Duffo smiled his good-natured loner's smile. 'We could always try and think of names for the baby.'

21

The silence seemed to reverberate deafeningly in such a contained space.

Zoe could have killed him for his habit of skulking in bushes. He must have overheard them talking after all.

'Is this your bloody weird sense of humour again, Macduff?' Marko demanded.

Macduff looked helplessly at Zoe, realizing too late that he'd jumped in the shit, waist-high.

'No,' Rachel said after what seemed like several decades. 'Duffo's telling the truth.' She reached out a hand towards Marko. 'I'm pregnant. I didn't tell you because I don't know what the hell to do about it. To be frank, I just hoped it might go away.'

'Oh, fabulous!' Marko exploded, trying to jump to his feet but hitting the roof of the tunnel instead, sending two clods of earth falling comically on to his shoulders.

Duffo started to giggle until Zoe kicked him.

'So everyone knows about it except me? That's nice.' His dark eyes sparked in his pale, handsome face. Then, taking them all by

413

surprise, he suddenly knelt at Rachel's feet. 'How're you feeling?' He considered her closed-up face, the anxiety in her eyes. 'Look, I know it must be worrying for you. It isn't what you were expecting, but think about it. It could be good. Lots of protesters have kids, they just travel round in buses instead of tents. A kid could have a real country life, learning all about nature and stuff.'

Rachel stroked his face. The thought of living in a bus with Marko, being some kind of alternative housewife while he smoked dope and sat round a campfire, talking endlessly about world peace, made her see how much she needed goals and structure, the real world.

'I couldn't, Marko. Besides, my exams are in six weeks.'

'You and your sodding exams. You've never been committed like the rest of us. No doubt you'll put your little stint at protesting on your CV, just to show you've got the spirit to rebel a little? Well, good luck to you!'

He scrambled up the ladder and out into the night.

'Rach, it's all my fault!' Duffo was almost in tears, his huge frame rocking backwards and forwards.

Rachel shook her head miserably. 'I should have told him myself. I don't blame him for being furious. It's my fault, not yours.'

She rubbed her mud-stained hand over her eyes. The worst thing was that she had felt a powerful flood of tenderness for Marko. She'd seen the look of love in his eyes, and the puzzlement, as if it had taken him by surprise that he actually cared for someone else more than himself.

'Look,' Zoe took hold of both her shoulders so that Rachel faced her head on, 'remember what I said. I don't think you and Marko are cut out for each other. You've achieved something miraculous. You've made him think about someone else. But you're too different. You're ready to spring while Marko's ready to cling. You wouldn't make him happy, Rach, so don't feel guilty.'

Rachel tried to smile, but tears still blurred her eyes. 'You sound like my mum.'

'Your mum probably wouldn't think of crawling back into Marko's sleeping bag, like I will when you go back to London.'

'Zoe,' Duffo sounded as shocked as a maiden aunt at a hen night, 'you wouldn't. You're always calling him a lazy fucker.'

'Yeah. Well, nobody's perfect. Look, Macduff, I preferred you when you were the strong and silent type. Do you think you could give up on all this conversation?'

Marko had disappeared altogether by the

time they all climbed out of the tunnel. Even his sleeping bag had gone.

'Don't worry, he'll be back,' Zoe predicted. 'He won't miss Friday or I'm a one-legged lesbian.'

Macduff looked at her like a man whose certainties were being rocked to the core. 'But you can't be. You just said you had the hots for Marko.'

'Relax, Duffo, it's just an expression.'

'Time I got the train,' Rachel said reluctantly. 'But I'll be back for Friday too. Nothing could keep me away.'

★ ★ ★

In the event, things that none of them, not even Alexander, veteran of three campaigns, had predicted happened.

Everything was ready to go. Macduff and Zoe had brought in extra food and water in case of a siege. The TV news had been alerted and was sending a crew. Hundreds of supporters and local people had promised to rally round with banners, shout support, and monitor the security guards' activities. A representative of English Nature had prom-ised to watch out for birds' nests that might be damaged. Even Marko had returned — and sat huffily refusing to talk to the others. Everything was set.

Except that the police and security guards arrived two days early.

The first news they got of the surprise attack was via Marko's mobile phone. When it rang at three a.m., Marko was inclined to dismiss it as a wrong number, some fool phoning for a minicab, or a drunken prank. Except that it kept ringing. Marko swore, wishing he'd let the battery run down instead of bothering to charge it up in Alexander's Land Rover.

Eventually he found it, under a pile of dirty clothes and barked a greeting into it.

'Is that Zoe Hastings?' a voice enquired.

'No, it sodding well isn't Zoe Hastings. Unless she's had a sex change. Call her in the morning at a decent hour.'

'You'll be getting an alarm call sooner than that. This is Road Rage. A convoy of police plus security guards is on its way to you.'

Marko sat bolt upright. 'But they're not due till Friday.'

'Then they must want to give you a little surprise. I should get the bacon and eggs on. For about two hundred. They'll be with you in about half an hour.'

'Jesus Christ!' Marko stumbled out of his sleeping bag and hopped across to Zoe's tent in the pitch dark. 'Zoe, the bastards are trying to take us by surprise. Get up!'

Zoe leaped up, instantly alert, and grabbed the phone to ring Alexander.

All around them there was frenzied activity as the new recruits took to the tree houses and walkways, those that had them using safety harnesses, others any rope they could find.

'Right,' Duffo announced, 'I'll go underground. I assume no one's going to fight me for the privilege?'

Zoe thought about the cold, dark tunnel, completely black and silent apart from the candles and nightlights. 'Don't forget the matches.' She kissed him briefly. 'What are you going to do down there?'

'Tell myself jokes. I'm a very good audience. As long as I have time to think about them.'

In the distance they heard the sound of lorries arriving and Macduff ducked down, pulling the makeshift trapdoor behind him. The others piled pallets and logs and any old bits of wood they had been able to find on top. Zoe hoped to God the army had taught him how to build tunnels safely.

Marko swung himself up the last rope ladder into a seventy-foot ash tree. 'Are you coming up?' he shouted to Zoe.

'You go,' Zoe shouted. 'I want to wait for

Alexander. You can throw the ladder down again in a minute.'

But there was no sign of Alexander. Only swarm after swarm of security guards and yellow-coated policemen. In minutes they had formed a human cordon at a distance of twenty feet all around the camp. They left only one small gap opposite the edge of the wood. It was soon obvious why. Two giant cherrypicker cranes, with platforms fifty feet up to drag the protesters on to, lumbered up across the field, their headlights dazzling police and protesters alike.

Zoe looked round frantically. She ought to go up into the trees or she'd get arrested now and the whole thing might fall apart.

'Not wasting much time, are they?' a voice asked softly. She relaxed visibly. It was Alexander. 'You know why this is? They wanted to get here before the TV cameras. Then they don't have to worry how it all looks.'

'That cherrypicker's going to have to come round here to get access to the trees,' Zoe pointed out. 'I think we'd better tell them about the tunnel. Even they know it'd be madness to drive a cherrypicker over unstable ground.'

Alexander walked calmly towards the group of policemen and contractors, calling

419

to the official who appeared to be directing operations, 'Excuse me, officer, but there's a tunnel under that pile of wood, with more protesters occupying it. Drive over it and they could be killed.'

The official looked as if this were a prospect he might personally relish. All the same he halted the cherrypicker and conferred with its driver. 'We might just have to go round the other way then, sir.'

A noise behind them alerted Alexander and Zoe to what the authorities' real plan had been. A second cherrypicker had approached from the other direction. Two men wearing hard hats and safety harnesses were already leaning out from its platform towards the walkway between the tree houses.

'I don't think they'll have too much trouble,' commented the official smugly. 'They're mountain-rescue specialists. This should all be over by nine.'

It wasn't as long.

The mountaineers picked out each protester as if they were ripe apples, ignoring their screams and kicking limbs. As soon as one tree house was empty the security guards moved in to destroy it with axes before it could be reoccupied.

Marko, in an unexpected act of derring-do, tied himself to the trunk of an ash. But without the presence of a TV camera to capture their tactics, three security guards, ignoring Alexander's attempts to stop them, simply kicked him until he could hold on no longer.

'Bloody hell, that's out of order,' said a voice behind them. Alexander turned to find the whippet-owning policeman. 'These security guards are a menace. I hope your friend's all right.'

'So do I,' Alexander replied, tight-lipped.

'Right.' The smug official leading the action was back. 'Where's this tunnel?'

Alexander said nothing.

'I think it's over here, sir.' A young policeman was pulling logs and pieces of wood away from the entrance. 'There's a trapdoor here, sir.'

'Right. Get the dogs.'

Zoe had run up, panting, her face bruised and streaked with dirt. 'You can't do that!'

Macduff, despite his size and toughness, hated dogs.

Two Alsatians and their handlers appeared out of the trees. The dawn was coming and everywhere was suffused with a misleading soft pink glow.

'Come out now or these dogs will be released immediately!' the official shouted down the shaft.

The silence was absolute as they all strained to hear an answer. Zoe could just imagine Macduff's fear.

'All right. Take the dogs down.'

Before they had a chance there was a scrabbling sound of earth falling and Macduff's head appeared.

'I'm sorry, Zo.' Duffo's eyes were wide with fear, and sweat dripped off him despite the cold. 'I didn't mind being in the dark or being underground, but I can't face dogs.'

'Look at the man,' Alexander accused. 'That was completely unacceptable.'

'Was it now?' demanded the official nastily. 'It worked though, didn't it?'

'You bastards,' Marko shouted as they filled the tunnel in systematically until it seemed simply a scar in the earth.

'You ain't seen nothing yet,' smiled a security guard. 'We'll be back with the bulldozers tomorrow.'

The police and guards packed up their gear and disappeared, congratulating the mountaineers on a job well done.

'Sorry,' the whippet-owning cop mumbled. 'It's a lovely spot. I suppose that's progress for you.'

Alexander wanted to yell that no, it wasn't progress, it was the opposite.

'What shall we do now?' Macduff asked, still bewildered.

'We could start rebuilding the tree houses.'

'We haven't got anything to rebuild them with.'

Alexander pointed upwards. 'We are in a wood.'

'That would be cannibalism,' Macduff announced. 'There are spirits in these trees.'

'Look, Duffo,' Marko barked. 'If you're going to turn into a fucking pantheist, can you wait till *after* the protest?'

'Come on,' Alexander insisted. 'We've had a setback and we can't do anything on an empty stomach. I'm sure Lavinia would make us breakfast.'

'Right,' he asked gloomily, when they were all seated round Lavinia's tiny table, wolfing scrambled eggs and sausages. 'Who's brave enough to ring Rachel and let her know she missed it?'

'I am,' decided Lavinia. 'Besides, Alexander, don't be so defeatist. This is only the beginning.'

Lavinia took the decision to wait until Rachel would be back from school. She hoped Catherine and Christopher wouldn't be too furious with her. But even if they were they wouldn't be as angry as Rachel if no one bothered to tell her what had been going on.

'They can't have!' wailed Rachel. 'Not all the tree houses *and* the tunnel! What's everyone doing now?'

'They've gone back to try and rebuild them. Until tomorrow when the bulldozers are moving in. Oh, Rachel darling,' alone, just talking to her grand-daughter, Lavinia allowed her real fears to show, 'I think we may have lost the battle. This could be the end of Gosse's Wood.'

Rachel put down the phone, shaking with anger and helplessness. Here she was, fifty miles away, and everything was happening without her. And the worst thing of all was, they were losing. She could hear it in her grandmother's voice. Lavinia never sounded defeated like that. Gosse's Wood would be lost and they hadn't even managed to tell people about it through the papers or on television.

Rachel sat down for a moment, her hand still on the phone.

Maybe it wasn't too late after all. She dashed upstairs and raided her parents' bedroom. Her mother kept a copy of the *Writers' and Artists' Yearbook* by her bed. Catherine had a fantasy, as yet unfulfilled due to the demands of teaching, that she might write a novel one day. Rachel flicked through it searching for a list of all the major newspapers. She wrote down each address and phone number, then started on the television companies. When she'd finished she rang each in turn to find out when their deadlines were for the following day.

Maybe building tunnels and tree houses wasn't the only way to prove the justice of their case; she'd thought of another way to publicize their case. But first she had to get a train to Maxted and back. It was going to be very tight. So tight she might not be able to pull it off in time to save the wood.

22

'Good heavens, Rachel! How nice to see you. Have you come down for the demonstration tomorrow?' Lavinia's friend Eunice buzzed about like an inebriated bee. 'How rude of me to keep you on the doorstep. Come in. I was just deciding what to wear. I wish I had something Army Surplus now that I'm on the other side. A flak jacket or one of those nice camouflagey things, but I suppose my old Barbour will have to do.'

'Sorry, Eunice, but I'm afraid I'm in a tearing hurry,' Rachel explained, trying not to be rude. 'You've got something of mine and I need it very urgently. I think you said you were going to put it in the garden shed.'

They searched the shed together but there was no sign of what Rachel had come for.

'Come on, Eunice. Try and remember where you put it.' The train back to Liverpool Street left in fifteen minutes and if she missed it all her elaborate plans would collapse.

'I'll tell you what,' Eunice suggested. She seemed to have no concept of speed; all these years in sleepy Maxted had obviously killed it off. 'I'll just ring Mrs Weston, my cleaner.

She's in her eighties but fighting fit. She'll know where it is.'

'Oh my Lord, that thing,' chirped the octogenarian Mrs Weston. 'I tried to give it to some boy scouts for their bazaar but they wouldn't take it. Said no one would want it. So I put it beside the wardrobe in your bedroom, nice and tucked away out of sight.'

Rachel tore upstairs to Eunice's bedroom and pushed aside her wardrobe. Alexander's painting of the cornfield stared up at her, powerful and disturbing.

She'd hoped to get a lift back to the station from her grandmother but there was no sign of the Rover. Her only option was to run.

Zoe, who had needed a quick word of advice from Lavinia, spotted Rachel running off down the street, watched by a group of curious locals. Zoe started to run after her until the Bensons' youngest grandchild shouted, 'Look, there's one of those dirty people from the wood!' and spat at her. 'You're going to get smashed and mashed and bashed tomorrow! My gran says so.'

Zoe stopped, flabbergasted. In her whole life no one had spat at her. This horrible grey-flannelled, posh little prep-school boy was a bigger yob than anyone she'd met.

'You won't be coming to support us, then?' she asked the horrible brat sarcastically.

Mrs Benson swooped out of the shop as if Zoe were a child molester. 'No, we won't be. But we'll be there anyway to see you lot evicted and good riddance.'

Zoe turned calmly away, though she would have liked to slap that vindictive woman's face for her. To her relief Lavinia's familiar red Rover was just pulling up across the road. 'Lavinia, thank God. Can I use your phone? That revolting Mrs Benson says half the village will be turning up tomorrow to cheer the police. We need support troops on our side too.'

'Of course you can use the phone. I'll make a few calls too. Not everyone in this village is behind this, you know.'

Rachel made the train with only seconds to spare. She had to be back at Liverpool Street by five thirty in order to have the painting photographed and prints made. The studio had assured her they could have them ready by seven.

She was just looking longingly at some slices of pizza in a café when it hit her. She'd forgotten the vital link! The Picture Editor on your average national newspaper was probably about as familiar with our great cultural heritage, as embodied in Constable's paintings, as he was with Wagner's Ring Cycle. To achieve any real impact she had to show the original painting alongside Alexander's pastiche.

Rachel looked at her Swatch. It was already five fifty. She had no idea what time the National Gallery closed tonight, but had a shrivelling feeling in her stomach that it had to be no later than six. The rush-hour was in full swing and she had to squeeze herself like a Japanese sardine between the closing doors of a Central Line tube. At Tottenham Court Road she dashed for the Northern Line and down to Leicester Square. Personally, she felt she ought to win the Olympic medal for Creative Tube-Hopping. By the time she finally arrived, flushed and out of breath, outside the National Gallery it was six seventeen.

'Sorry, miss,' the attendant apologized, 'we're closed.'

Rachel thought she might cry. How could she have been so dumb as not to see she'd need the postcard of *The Cornfield*? Desolately, hunger and exhaustion catching up with her as the adrenaline receded, she headed down the alley at the side of the Sainsbury Wing, back towards the tube.

A small knot of coiffed and expensive people stood outside the side entrance.

'What's happening?' she asked the least daunting.

'Friends of the National Gallery shopping evening. Starts in five minutes.'

Rachel nipped around the corner and delved in her backpack for a hairbrush. Her trainers were caked with mud and the assortment of jumpers she wore owed more to Cancer Research than Calvin Klein. Still.

Pulling herself up to an elegant five foot nine, she joined the back of the queue, hiding behind a large Canadian, who might, had he not breathed opulence through every cashmere pore, have passed for her father.

'Are you a Friend?' the doorman quizzed.

'Absolutely. In fact, I'd call myself a Best Friend,' Rachel asserted and she whizzed past him in the direction of the Gallery Shop before he could protest further.

They had twenty postcards of Constable's *The Cornfield* and Rachel bought them all.

By the time she made it back to Liverpool Street the man in the photographic studio was locking up to leave. 'You've certainly taken your time,' he carped.

'I'm really sorry. I'm sure you'd sympathize if I had time to explain.' She smiled her most winning, mad idealist's smile. 'I don't suppose I could borrow, well, have really, a few envelopes to put these in?'

'My wife always says I'm a pushover,' the man confided, handing over the envelopes. As if to prove his point he drove her to deliver her letters to ITN and the BBC.

'I don't suppose you know how I can get to Canary Wharf? Most of the newspapers seem to be there now.'

'Come on, I live out east.'

By the time she reached home she was so tired she could hardly stand up. All the same, she set her alarm for six. She had to get down to the wood. She'd done all she could here in London except pray.

★　★　★

Neither Lavinia nor Alexander slept that night. Instead they got up again and drank endless cups of tea.

'What do you think's going to happen?' Lavinia asked.

For the first time since they had rediscovered each other, Alexander looked his age. His extraordinary energy, the force that drove him, seemed finally to be running out. Lavinia found it hard to bear.

'I don't know,' Alexander confessed wearily. 'The other side's getting better at this, that's the trouble. They've learned from previous road battles. They know the one thing we need is publicity, that's why they moved in early. And the trouble is, it worked.

We know people are broadly sympathetic to us, apart from the few immediate locals. No one really wants England concreted over. Most people have green blood in their veins when the countryside's under threat.'

He stared into the fire, not even noticing that Lavinia had stood up and was staring out of the window. 'And it's my fault, Lavinia. I've been in this game long enough. I should have foreseen that raid. I'm going soft. Being here with you in this cosy cottage was too tempting. Maybe I should have been out there, planning.'

'There are others. Zoe. Marko.' A flash of anger ignited Lavinia. 'It doesn't always have to be you.'

'No, but I'm the strategist and this time my strategy failed.'

She reached out and touched his anxious face. 'Will the TV cameras come tomorrow?'

'I don't know. I faxed all the news people and so did Road Rage but they wouldn't commit themselves. Road schemes are two a penny, apparently, these days. Ours isn't different enough.'

'So this could really be it?'

Lavinia saw that, whether she liked it or not, their own happiness was somehow bound up with the fate of the wood.

'So we just have to wait and see?'

'Would you mind,' he asked gently, 'if I went down there now?'

'Of course not. I'll come too.'

Lavinia went upstairs and put on some warm clothes. It wasn't just to spite her neighbours, no matter how badly they'd behaved towards her, that she wanted Alexander and the others to win. Gosse's Wood mattered to the people she cared about, and in the last few months it had come to matter passionately to her too.

★ ★ ★

The trees were still wrapped in deep velvety darkness, thick as blackout cloth, when they parked Alexander's Land Rover by the edge of the wood. The moon and stars had decided to remain neutral and neither had put in an appearance. An owl screeched and small night creatures rustled underfoot. The camp was still.

Lavinia fanned the embers of the fire into life and put on a saucepan of water, laughing at herself because she came from a generation of Englishwomen who felt every situation could be improved by a cup of tea.

Gradually the huddle of sleeping bags separated into bodies, far more than Lavinia had expected, perhaps twenty or so.

'Road Rage sent them all,' Zoe explained, shaking her tousled blond head and splashing her face with cold water. 'They arrived last night. This time we've built barricades. We're all going to chain ourselves to the trees. By the way, Alexander, did you reach Rachel? I thought she would have come with you.'

'She's probably got better things to do,' Marko said bitterly, emerging from his tent, which he'd somehow salvaged from yesterday's raid. 'Swotting up for her A grades. We were just a phase.'

'Marko's sulking. Rachel turned down his offer of domesticity in a bender tent. Can't think why.'

East of the wood the sun was just beginning to come up, silhouetting the trees blackly against its spreading glow. A faint sound made them all look round.

A figure in a fur jacket, immaculate wellies and a headscarf emerged out of the trees. 'Anyone fancy a croissant? They're still warm.'

'Eunice!' Lavinia couldn't believe her eyes. 'You'd have been there at the tumbrils handing out pain au chocolat!'

'Don't listen to her, Eunice,' Alexander enthused as she passed round a basket with each croissant immaculately wrapped in a kitchen towel. 'You're a bloody heroine!'

'I wanted to get here early in case I missed the action. I must say, Lavinia, I haven't had so much fun since the war.'

They had barely finished their croissants when a horn sounded at the bottom of the adjoining field and two ancient buses, as intricately decorated as New York subway trains, bounced up and disgorged their equally decorated passengers.

'Is this the gig?' asked a dreadlocked youth. 'Then you must be Alexander Bailey. You do a good job, man. There's more arriving. Road Rage put out a call. They'll be coming from all over. What do you want us to do?'

A dog barked behind them and Alexander turned. A man in plus fours and a tweed hat waved a greeting. Behind him a small gaggle of people were negotiating their way past the buses in anoraks and bobble hats. They waved cheerfully as if they were heading off for a ramble.

'There you are, Alexander,' hissed Lavinia, 'you old pessimist. It isn't over yet. Not by a long way.'

★ ★ ★

'Come on, Rach, wake up. You'll be late for school. Ricky's already up and had breakfast.' Rachel hated Catherine shaking her, but today even that didn't seem to work.

Suddenly her daughter's eyes snapped open like the shutter on a camera. 'What time did you say it was?'

'I didn't.' Catherine was stunned at the effect of her words. Rachel threw off the duvet and leaped out of bed. 'But now you ask, it's eight fifteen already and — '

'God! Mum, could you possibly give me a lift to the station?'

'Rachel, what is all this? It's a school day.'

'The police are going to Gosse's Wood today to evict everyone and bulldoze the wood. Unless I've managed to get the TV and newspapers interested enough to stop them. That's what I was doing chasing round last night. I've *got* to go, Mum. This is it. This is what the fight's been all about. You can't make me miss this, you *can't*!'

'Look, Rach, I've seen these evictions on the news. There are hundreds of police. People get hurt.'

'I know, Mum, but I'll be really careful.'

Catherine weighed up the situation. She knew how much Rachel wanted to go, and yet all her instincts as a mother cried out that it was too dangerous.

'I'm sorry, Rachel. I've really tried to be fair to you but this is just too risky. You can't go.'

'But, Mum! That's so unfair! I built the tree houses. My friends are in them. I can't just rat on it all now.'

'I'm sorry, Rachel, but you have to.'

'This is so incredibly unjust!' Rachel blurted. 'No other mother would be as overprotective as you! How can I grow up with you always looking over my shoulder. I hate you!'

Catherine felt her insides churn and plunge as if she were in a small boat adrift in mountainous seas. Why was it so hard for her generation to exercise real authority? And when they finally did, why did they feel so damn guilty about it?

Downstairs, Ricky beamed smugly, enjoying being in the rare position of being ready first. Christopher had left already.

'What's the matter with Rach?' he asked, rather pleased that his big sister wasn't getting her own way for once.

'She's not allowed to go to the wood.'

'Is that all?' Ricky couldn't see what the fuss about the wood was anyway. They were only trees after all. However, one look at his sister's face told him not to outline this position.

And then, to her mother's amazement, Rachel caved in. 'OK, I'll go to school.' She pulled on her school coat and docilely accompanied her mother and Ricky to the car.

'I'm really sorry, Rach love,' Catherine wheedled, hating herself for her weakness, 'only sometimes parents have to draw the line.'

Rachel stamped surlily into the school gates, leaving Catherine, feeling shredded, in the car. Ricky was delighted to see her go. Now he could change tapes to the one he liked.

Through the cloakroom window Rachel watched her mother drive away. She waited five more minutes, but not to compose herself. She wanted to be sure Catherine was safely on her way to school before she bolted in the direction of the station.

Catherine herself was just about to park when the news item about Gosse's Wood filled her car. Rachel had been right. This really was the climax. Rachel would never forgive her. And yet she'd gone to school quietly, if somewhat grudgingly.

The sea-sickness swelled and rose so that Catherine had to put her hand over her mouth as if she really were about to be sick. She'd just worked out why Rachel had been so docile.

She was pretty sure Rachel was going anyway.

The field at the edge of Gosse's Wood was now overflowing with cars and the footpath back to Maxted three-deep with people heading for the protest.

Alexander was flabbergasted. 'Where are they all coming from? Road Rage must be bloody miracle workers to get this lot down here. We haven't even had two men and a dog until now.'

When the first of the police vans was sighted there were so many protesters that it couldn't even get near the wood and the cherrypickers were forced to wait fifty yards away to see if they were needed.

'Come down from the trees today, have you, Tarzan?' one of the security guards asked Marko nastily. He patted Marko's long dark hair. 'Too scared of heights, were you, sweetie?'

Marko looked as if he might take a swing at the man.

'Ignore him, Marko,' Alexander counselled. 'He's just trying to wind you up.'

What amazed Lavinia was the number of ordinary people who'd shown up. These were neither hippy road protesters nor disgruntled locals but your average car-cleaning B&Q customers. A man waved and Lavinia recognized — ironically enough given the cause of the demo — the mechanic from the local garage she resorted to if a job were too challenging for her. She spotted her GP's wife, plus baby in a backpack; goodness, that was brave. There was the girl who manned the checkout at the Spar grocery and Mrs Weston, Eunice's eighty-year-old cleaning lady, plus dozens of others she'd never seen before, some of them carrying home-made banners saying SAVE GOSSE'S WOOD and ANCIENT WOODLAND — HANDS OFF.

On the other side of the clearing she caught sight of Colonel Lawley in a battered fishing hat with a small group of followers. They looked rather pathetic next to the cheery crowd of anti-roaders.

In the middle the security guards, police and people from the contracting firm hired to clear the site were ranged. A man in a suit was pointing out something in a newspaper to the policeman in charge.

Everyone seemed to be waiting.

There was a murmur and some movement from the back of the large crowd. Suddenly it parted like the Red Sea and two television crews, apparently in competition with each other to get to the action, surged through.

'Alexander,' hissed Zoe, 'look, the TV people are here!'

'Right. Once more into the breach, I think.' The glint of battle lit up Alexander's eyes and Lavinia half expected him to emit a war-cry. Instead he bellowed at Zoe, Marko and the rest. 'Grab the chains. One person and a helper to each tree. Now!'

Before the police or security guards had time to stop them, Zoe, Marko, Macduff and the others chained themselves to their trees while the TV cameras burst into action.

'I say, that was dramatic,' Eunice shouted to Lavinia. 'Why not you?'

Lavinia snatched the last chain and made a dash for a giant ash tree. 'Come and do me up then!' she ordered Eunice, like a memsahib addressing her punkah-wallah.

★ ★ ★

On the train to Maxted, Rachel thought she might explode with the tension. She'd only just made it by seconds and hadn't even had time to grab a paper, so she had no idea whether her efforts of last night had worked. But she had to be at the wood today, whether they had or not.

Outside Maxted Station there was a lone taxi with Mrs Benson from the shop clearly haggling with the driver. Rachel ignored her and jumped in the back.

'You don't want to go there,' the taximan informed her when she asked for Gosse's Wood, 'there's just a bunch of revolting hippies and the police walloping them, though I reckon walloping's too good for 'em. I'd seal up their bloody tunnels. Then they'd know what it's like to be a mole.'

Desperate to shut him up, Rachel spotted a newspaper on the floor next to the driving seat. Her heart stopped. 'Could I look at your paper, do you think?'

He passed it over. It was a copy of the *Guardian*, the paper she'd had the highest hopes of running the story.

Rachel scanned it feverishly, and then double-checked. There was nothing there.

'Here you are,' the taxi drew to an abrupt halt. 'I'm not going any nearer than this. They might damage my car.'

Rachel counted out the money and decided he didn't deserve a tip.

The driver watched her. Ungrateful minx. He'd been going to tell her the paper was yesterday's, since she seemed so eager to find something in it. Now he wouldn't bother.

★　★　★

'Isn't there another bloody way?' Catherine demanded of herself in furious frustration.

442

She had been snarled up in traffic for almost three-quarters of an hour and there was still no sign of movement. Thank heavens she'd managed to get Anita to do Assembly for her and reschedule her meetings.

The instant she'd guessed that Rachel had set out for the wood, Catherine had known she had to follow her. But at this rate the whole thing would be over before she even got off the slip road.

She must keep calm. She needed a clear head if she were going to look out for Rachel. Catherine opened her window to breathe in some deep breaths and instead got a spluttering lungful of exhaust fumes. Maybe Rachel had a point in hating cars. Although, Catherine smiled a little at the thought, she didn't seem to have so much objection if it was the only way she could get to a party.

It was another half-hour before the traffic cleared and Catherine saw the first opening ahead. The nausea was, for reasons Catherine didn't quite understand, metamorphosing into blind panic. Forgetting her usual caution, she put her foot flat on the floor. By some sixth sense of instinct and parenthood, she felt frighteningly convinced that Rachel was in dire physical danger.

★ ★ ★

'Right, lads, time we took control of this situation,' the senior policeman commanded. 'Keep calm, now. I want the minimum violence with this bloody great circus here. Now!'

The cordon of yellow-coated police moved steadily forward. Lavinia, watching them, held her breath.

Rachel finally fought her way to the front of the crowd just as the police began to surround each tree with a protester chained to it.

Lavinia recognized one of the policemen from the incident on the zebra crossing. Goodness, that seemed years ago.

'Watch that one,' the policeman advised his colleagues, recognizing Lavinia at the same time. 'She may look like Miss Marple but she fights like Mike Tyson.'

Lavinia allowed herself a moment's pride. At their last meeting he had told her to get back to her bingo. He wouldn't make that mistake today.

At that moment Rachel spotted her grandmother, then, two trees down, Zoe.

Zoe mouthed a greeting. Beyond her Marko, hair fanned out dramatically around his face looking like a latter-day St Sebastian, posed for the cameras.

'He'll probably be offered the cover of

Loaded after this,' Zoe shouted to Rachel.

At that moment a group of police moved in with a wire cutter and began to remove her chains. Zoe did all she could to prevent them. 'Ow, you sodding bully, get off my foot.' She tried to push them off. The wire cutters, aiming for the chain, instead met with the soft flesh between Zoe's thumb and first finger. She screamed as blood spurted over the policeman's yellow waterproof.

'Oh my God, she's hurt!' Rachel sprang forward.

Behind them the official-looking man in pinstripes, who had been clutching a walkie-talkie, whispered in the senior police-man's ear. The policeman looked bewildered, then furious. Finally he reached for his loud-hailer.

'He's calling them off,' Alexander couldn't believe what he was seeing. 'He's actually bloody well calling them off!'

The crowds cheered and waved their banners. As if prompted by its owner, a dog lifted its leg against the nearest bulldozer. At the sight of the police withdrawal Eunice undid Lavinia's padlock. 'But why?' Lavinia demanded. 'What on earth's going on? Has the wood been reprieved?'

'I think,' said Alexander, 'it might have just a slight connection with this.' He brandished

445

the front page of the *Sun*, just handed to him by one of their supporters. It carried the headline COCK-UP OVER CONSTABLE'S CORNFIELD.

Underneath the postcard of the Constable original, half a page was filled with Alexander's pastiche in all its witty but explosive power.

'But how the hell did they get hold of my painting?' Alexander demanded. 'Was it you, Lavinia?'

But Lavinia was one step ahead of them. 'I threw it out. So someone must have rescued it. My absolutely brilliant grand-daughter, I suspect.'

Rachel grinned. 'I did the rounds of the papers last night. I didn't think they'd used it.'

While the others clapped and the TV cameras clamoured to get through to interview them, Lavinia held her grand-daughter in a tight embrace, her heart hammering with pride.

Rachel, it seemed to Lavinia in that moment, had all the courage and nerve that she herself had longed to have as a foolish young girl. 'Don't let your mother hear this,' she whispered wickedly, 'but I couldn't be prouder of you, Rachel darling, no matter how many wretched A levels you got.'

Rachel's smile lit up her pale and pretty face. 'I only did it with the help of my grappling granny. And Alexander, of course.'

'Rachel! Lavinia! Thank God I've found you!' Catherine blundered up and grabbed both their hands, her face white and blotchy with worry. She could hardly form the words she was so out of breath.

'Mum! I thought you were in London!'

'Where you should be, you horrible child.'

'It's all right, Mum, there's no danger. They've called off the bulldozers. We've won! My idea about the painting worked! Isn't it fantastic?'

Catherine saw the thrill of pride and pleasure in her daughter's eyes and her anger and fear began to finally subside. 'So I'm supposed to congratulate you instead of wringing your neck, am I?' Pride and a streak of admiration softened the harshness of her voice.

A loud noise twenty yards away, insistent and whining, drowned out Catherine's words.

Zoe's head whipped round. 'That's a chainsaw. Oh my God, Rach, it's The Magic Faraway Tree! They may have called off the bulldozers but they're trying to chop down The Faraway Tree!'

Zoe tore off through the departing crowds in the direction of the giant oak tree at the far end of the clearing. Rachel followed her.

'Didn't the bastards hear what the policeman said?' demanded Marko. 'It's all over. Our side's won.'

Behind them two lumbering bulldozers, whose moment of glory had never come, angrily tried to squeeze through a gap in the trees and failed. Swearing, the driver of the second one ground into reverse. In his frenzy for some action he narrowly missed Zoe who had run through the clearing and was heading towards the chainsaw operator.

Realizing how near he'd been to disaster, the driver of the huge machine panicked and paused for a split second before moving inexorably backwards in a sudden arc.

Directly in his path, with her back to him so that she had no idea of the imminent danger she was in, stood the unsuspecting Rachel.

Catherine was still at the back of the crowd but Lavinia had followed. She took in the scene in all its nightmarish inevitability.

And she screamed.

The sound, high, animal and terrifying, hung in the air paralysing everyone around, except Lavinia herself. The danger to her grand-daughter propelled her forward without any thought of her own safety.

All Lavinia saw was the wild billowing of

Rachel's hair as it escaped from the hood restraining it, and the look of fear on her grand-daughter's face as she turned and saw the steel teeth of the enormous machine only feet away, waiting to rip her apart.

Behind them both, Alexander shouted a warning. The driver must finally have heard it or seen Alexander's wild gesticulations. But instead of switching the engine off he wrenched the steering wheel round, success-fully avoiding Rachel but reversing head-on into Lavinia.

23

The silence was unearthly, as if the entire world were holding its breath.

There was a dull clunk, like a tyre hitting a bump in the road, and then the screaming started. Rachel didn't even realize it was coming from her own mouth.

Alexander was the first to reach Lavinia. The sight of what had happened tore his heart out. Only Lavinia's battered legs protruded from under the huge machine. She was making no sound at all, not even a groan or whimper.

'For God's sake!' he yelled, beside himself, 'Get someone to call an ambulance.'

A police officer ran towards them, pulling off his yellow plastic raincoat as he came, and covering Lavinia's legs with it. It was the desk sergeant. 'I'm so sorry, sir. The ambulance will be here directly.'

What had happened was so unexpected and terrible that Rachel felt as if she'd been turned to stone, unable to move from the spot. And then her mother was there too, holding her and shielding her eyes from the sight of the accident.

The only sound of crying now came from the driver of the bulldozer. Catherine watched in fury as his huge frame shook with great self-pitying sobs, and she wanted to kill him.

Finally the ambulance arrived, without Lavinia ever regaining consciousness, and they levered her gently on to a stretcher. The visible signs of injury were limited but the extreme stillness of her body chilled them all.

'She's still breathing,' assured the ambulance crew, as they helped Rachel and Catherine in beside her and began their nightmarish journey through the wood towards the local hospital.

Zoe gently took Alexander's arm. 'I'll drive you in the Land Rover.'

Lavinia still hadn't regained consciousness by the time they arrived half an hour later. Catherine and Rachel were led to a small waiting room while Lavinia was wheeled away for examination. Despite the horror and the discomfort and the shock, Rachel, held tightly in her mother's arms, fell deeply asleep and didn't wake at the visits from the various doctors to keep them informed of Lavinia's progress.

'Is she going to be all right?' was the first question on Rachel's lips as she struggled awake. Her voice was ragged and shaky with distress. A wave of guilt washed over her that she could possibly have slept while her beloved grandmother was so ill.

Catherine gripped her daughter's hand, unsure how much of the harsh truth to tell her. The doctors had been guarded. They had dealt as best they could with the external injuries but it was the internal damage, especially to her liver, that concerned them. Lavinia hadn't woken yet and she might, so the senior registrar had just told Catherine as gently as he could, pass straight into a coma. No one had been allowed to see her yet.

All they could do was wait.

'Mum.' Catherine looked up at the sudden sharper note in her daughter's voice. 'I think I need the toilet.' Rachel stood up shakily, one hand to her abdomen. In her exhaustion she had ignored the dull, gnawing pain, but now she couldn't dismiss it any longer.

'I'll come with you. Do you want me to help you?' Catherine asked when they finally made it to the Ladies. It had been years since Catherine had last done this — when Rachel was a small child — but that was how Rachel seemed at this moment, a child again, shaky and white and lost.

Rachel nodded helplessly, able only to hold her blanket round her, as if all other action were beyond her capacity.

Inside the cramped stall Catherine undid the zip of Rachel's army trousers and gently pulled them down. The thick material was stained heavily with blood so bright and red it could have been poster paint. 'My God, Rachel, were you hurt too?'

Catherine had a sudden terrified vision that the bulldozer had somehow run into Rachel and in the confusion she had failed to notice.

Rachel inspected her bloodstained thighs silently, swaying slightly so that Catherine thought she might faint.

Sensing the extremity of her daughter's distress, Catherine held on to her, not speaking, simply patting her rhythmically as she had done when Rachel was a baby. The gesture seemed to comfort them both.

'Oh God, Mum, I think I must have had a miscarriage.'

Catherine's face was blank with horror. 'A miscarriage?' she repeated dully. 'But surely you weren't . . . ' The word seemed too shocking to be spoken.

'Pregnant? Yes, I was. Gran knew. She told me I had to make up my own mind about what I wanted to do, but I just put it off. I didn't want to kill it, so I just hoped it would go away. Now it has.'

She buried her face in her mother's coat and began to sob wildly.

Knowing that whatever she said would matter terribly, Catherine suppressed her own sense of shock and simply went on patting Rachel, praying that no one else chose this moment to interrupt them.

Rachel raised a wild, tear-stained face. 'The terrible thing is, Mum, all I feel is relief.'

'My poor girl, poor, little Rachel.' Her heart went out to her daughter, who seemed almost a child and who was suddenly going through so much. It was impossible to be angry. 'We love you whatever happens. Unconditionally.'

Gradually Rachel's sobs subsided. 'Thanks, Mum,' she murmured into Catherine's shoulder. 'Thanks for not saying it's all for the best.'

Catherine, who had been dangerously close to saying just this, thanked whichever god was responsible for accidental tact and held her daughter more tightly. 'You've had so much growing up to do lately.'

'I don't feel grown up at all.' The lovely face crumpled again. 'Mum, I don't think I could face life without Gran.'

Catherine resisted the temptation of empty reassurance. 'No. I don't think any of us could.' And the extraordinary thing was, she meant it. Her prickly and disapproving mother-in-law, who used to make Catherine feel that her own children were second best to their model cousins, had over the last few months become central to all of them. Rachel's head shot up in alarm. 'Does Dad know about the accident?'

'Yes. I rang him as soon as we got here. He's on his way. Uncle Martin too.'

'You think she's going to die.' It could have been an accusation but the words thudded dully into the gap of silence between them.

For answer Catherine simply said, 'You need clean clothes. The hospital ought to look at you too.'

'But we can't leave Gran!'

'Alexander's there. Zoe brought him. Gran would want you to be properly examined. You must take care of yourself.' Rachel let her mother zip her trousers back up and lead her quietly off to find a nurse.

When she understood what had happened the ward sister summoned an orderly to take Rachel down to Casualty in a wheelchair. There were three patients ahead of them in the queue, one with a bandaged hand, another who seemed to have sprained his ankle and an old man who appeared to be addressing the beleaguered staff at the top of his voice in very angry Glaswegian.

'Started early, did we?' asked the triage nurse, catching a whiff of his breath.

Finally it was their turn. Rachel was asked to lie flat on her back as the doctor carefully removed her trousers. The blood, Catherine saw with horror, was still flowing. It formed a red lake on the paper cover of the hospital bed.

'I'm just going to give you an injection to stop the flow,' advised the doctor, as a nurse placed thick wads of cotton wool between Rachel's legs.

'Please hurry,' Rachel begged, 'my grandmother's upstairs really badly injured. She may die and I've got to be there.'

'Oh, Rach,' Catherine tried not to break down, 'I wish you'd felt you could trust me with this.'

'I didn't tell you because I hadn't made up my mind. It wouldn't have been fair to either of us.

'Can I go back upstairs if I go in a wheelchair and promise to come down later to be checked out?' she demanded of the doctor. 'I couldn't bear it if we were too late.'

'All right then. As long as you promise to come back down and not just go off home. There can be complications.'

'I'll make sure she does,' Catherine said, even before she'd thought about it. There she was, assuming Rachel wasn't old enough to take responsibility for herself again.

To Rachel's distress, when they got back there was no sign of Alexander. 'Oh, Mum. How awful. He's not here and Gran could have needed us!'

The door to Lavinia's room opened and the ward sister emerged, a finger to her lips. 'Are you for Mrs Hope? No change, I'm afraid, but the doctor said you can sit by her bed for a few minutes. I already took her husband in.'

'He's not her . . . ' began Rachel.

Catherine gently stopped her. 'Thank you, Sister. Is there anything we can do?'

'Just hold her hand and talk to her.'

Alexander was already sitting by her bedside, his head bowed against the threadbare white of her bedspread. 'Please come back to me, Lavinia,' he said in a voice shaking with grief. 'Don't leave me. Not just when we've found each other after all these years.'

Before Catherine or Rachel had time to decide if they were intruding, the door opened again and Christopher and his brother Martin appeared.

'My God,' demanded Martin, 'what exactly happened?'

'It was all my fault,' Alexander's eyes had sunk deep into his face like crevices in an ancient rock. The bony angularity of his body, which had always struck Catherine as so appealing and monklike, now seemed simply frail. 'I should never have let her get involved.'

'Too right you shouldn't have!' barked Martin.

'What do the doctors say?' Christopher asked his wife. He had expected to share Martin's anger and outrage, but there was something so totally exposed about Alexander; his pain was so real and obvious that it silenced him.

'They don't know. The rest of her injuries weren't too bad considering what happened, but she hasn't shown any sign of coming round.' Then he noticed Rachel and leaped up. 'Rachel, my God! Are you all right? You didn't say Rachel was hurt too.' He flung at Catherine. 'What happened, for Christ's sake?'

'Don't worry.' She reached out a hand to him. 'She's going to be fine. She'll explain it all when she's on her own with you. The doctor wants another look at her before she leaves.'

Christopher pulled an armchair up to his mother's bed. It was ludicrously low, almost comical, so that his chin was level with the bed.

Alexander seemed finally to remember where he was. 'Here, have mine.' He jumped up and almost forced Christopher to take the chair he'd vacated. 'She's your mother. You must loathe my even being here.'

Christopher could hardly bear to look at the naked pain in Alexander's eyes. How would his own father have reacted at Lavinia's bedside? With polite efficiency, perhaps even a touch of mild irritation at the disruption to his routine? Just like Martin was reacting now, in fact.

'No,' Christopher said, 'I'm glad you're here. She would have wanted it. She's changed in the last few months. We've all noticed and it's largely thanks to you.'

'Oh, for God's sake, Chris!' Martin exploded. 'If it hadn't been for troublemakers like him, Ma would still be playing bridge and gardening.'

'Exactly,' Christopher said softly. 'We'd just like to thank you for making her so happy.'

'Jesus!' Martin banged out of the room just as Zoe burst into it. He eyed her blond dreadlocks with horror. 'It's like a bloody demo in here. Are you sure you don't want to bring any more of your drop-out friends along? Have a party?'

'They've abandoned the road!' Zoe announced, ignoring him. 'It's just been on the news. Between Rachel's coup with *The Cornfield* and Lavinia's accident they say they've decided to find another route. Gosse's Wood's been saved!'

The spirit of joyous celebration bubbled up for a moment, then fizzled back at the thought of what it had cost them all, especially Lavinia.

'Well, that's a relief,' announced a frail voice from what seemed a long way away. 'At least my death won't be entirely in vain.'

There was a beat of disbelieving silence as everyone in the room turned towards the bed. Lavinia, looking drained and pale, but with a familiar glint of steel still in her eye, was smiling weakly at them.

'Gran!' shrieked Rachel, propelling her wheelchair to the bed.

'Ma!' Christopher found there were tears trickling down his face, the first he could remember since he was a boy.

'Lavinia!' The tenderness in Alexander's voice warmed the room. 'Thank God, you're back with us!'

'You don't think I'd croak now, do you,' Lavinia demanded, trying to sit up, 'just when we've sent the enemy packing!'

'Oh, Gran, you're going to be all right. Thank heavens.' Rachel clung to her grandmother's hand as if it were a beacon of hope in a blackened landscape.

'Darling, what happened? You weren't hurt too?'

'Oh, Gran. The most awful thing: I lost the baby.'

Christopher shot a look of horrified amazement at his wife, who simply shook her head to stop him saying anything. There would be plenty of time for explanations later.

'Is that so awful?' Lavinia asked her grand-daughter gently. Catherine marvelled that Lavinia could put the question she had dared not ask, and it seemed to be simply sensible. Possibly because it was asked out of sympathy rather than self-interest. 'You were so unsure about it. Perhaps it wasn't the right time for you. You're very young to have to make such hard decisions.'

'Like you had to, you mean?' Rachel asked, stunned at her own daring.

Lavinia's face registered shock, but only for a moment. 'Like I had to,' she echoed, taking her grand-daughter's pretty face in her hands. 'Exactly.'

Behind them Christopher and Catherine exchanged glances of puzzlement. What was Rachel talking about?

But before Christopher could ask for enlightenment the ward sister reappeared to remind them that although Lavinia had

461

regained consciousness she was still very ill.

'Please don't tire Mrs Hope out. She must be extremely weak. I think it's time you said goodbye for the moment so that she can get some rest.' She took hold of the back of Rachel's wheelchair. 'The doctor's been asking after you, young lady.'

'I'll take her down,' insisted Catherine.

Smiling at each other as if it were Christmas now that Lavinia had finally come round, they all got up to leave.

But Lavinia had one more shock in store for them.

'There's something Rachel reminded me of, something I want to tell you. Just in case I have a relapse.' She looked searchingly at her son, praying he would understand and that she would be strong enough to cope if he didn't. 'I should have told you years ago, Christopher, but I always backed out. There's nothing like staring death in the face to make you feel braver.'

Rachel held her breath. She was almost sure she knew what was coming. She just hoped to God it was the right thing to do.

'I watched you over the years trying to get your father to love you and how hopeless it was.' She put a gentle hand on her son's arm. 'I also saw what that did to you, how guilty you felt, and how rejected. And I longed to tell you the truth.'

'The truth about what, Ma?' Christopher felt totally confused. He had just heard that his eighteen-year-old daughter had been pregnant and lost a baby, now his mother was telling him there was something else he ought to know, God alone knew what.

'The reason I left Oxford so suddenly and never even told you I'd been there.'

Christopher listened, still at a loss as to why she should have kept this from him all these years.

'I left Oxford because — just like Rachel — I found I was going to have a baby. You.'

'My God.' He could hardly see his strait-laced and unimaginative father getting Lavinia pregnant outside of marriage, especially in those days.

Rachel held her breath, her eyes darting to Alexander who stood, his body rigid, clutching the foot of Lavinia's hospital bed.

'But the problem was, Robert wasn't the father of my baby.'

Christopher could hardly believe what he was hearing. His mother appeared to be telling him that his father wasn't his father after all. 'Then who the hell was?'

'The man standing next to you. The man I loved more than life itself.'

Christopher and Alexander's eyes locked in

sudden understanding. 'You mean . . . '
Christopher began, not quite daring to voice
the truth.

'I mean that Robert wasn't your father.
Alexander is.'

464

24

Christopher found he couldn't move. All his life he had felt guilty for not loving his difficult and undemonstrative father, and believed that the problem was his own. A spurt of anger scorched through him at his mother for hiding the truth from him for so long. 'Ma, if what you're saying is true, why the hell didn't you tell me?'

'I was too much of a coward. I felt it would cause too much damage. If I had done it at the start, perhaps. But as the years passed I knew it would hurt all of you, perhaps break up the family.'

'And not knowing didn't hurt us? I always felt that somehow Dad didn't like me, I might be the oldest, but Martin was the special son.'

Catherine heard the anguish in her husband's voice and wanted to reach out to him. Lavinia's revelation explained so much. Why loving and wanting to understand his own children instead of disciplining them mattered so dearly to him, the fact that he and Martin seemed to come from different planets.

'I thought what I'd done was honourable.

But then Alexander came back into my life and I felt I'd wronged him as much as your father and you.' Lavinia looked suddenly old and frail, as if the strength and certainty that had fuelled her for so long were leaking away.

Christopher saw that whatever answers there were, he couldn't ask for them today. 'I'm sorry, Ma, I'm sure you did it for the best.' Christopher, to his wife's eternal gratitude, had the good sense to let his anger go. 'And, after all, I've gained a father.' He turned to Alexander, who for the first time since Lavinia had ever known him seemed lost and paralysed. Maybe he would never forgive her either for a lifetime of deceit.

Christopher reached out his hand tentatively to the man he had discovered was not just an interesting stranger but his own father. 'I meant it when I said you'd changed my mother, and perhaps my daughter too. In a way you've already become part of the family.' He stopped, not knowing how to continue, afraid of being overcome with emotion. 'I'm not sure what I should call you.'

The older man looked as uncertain as he did. He stood silently, reminding Lavinia of a stranded seabird. 'Alexander would be fine.'

Ever since he could remember, Christopher had resented the man he thought was his father for his polite containment, his incapacity to feel or express emotion, and he was damned if he was going to behave the same way. Without warning, he enveloped Alexander in a hug so sudden and unexpected that they almost toppled over on top of Lavinia.

Catherine, watching them, found her eyes begin to fog up with tears. 'Welcome to our family, Alexander.'

Rachel leaned towards her grandmother's ear. 'I knew it was Alexander you were really talking about when you told me not to settle down with someone I didn't love just because my baby needed a father,' she whispered loudly. 'I almost said something, but you can be quite fierce, Gran.'

'Fierce? Me?' Lavinia smiled. 'I'm just a little old lady.'

Rachel laughed. 'And I'd just like to say I can't think of anyone I'd like better as an unexpected grandfather.'

'Thank you, Rachel.' Alexander, loosened from Christopher's grip, turned away, brushing something from his eye. 'It's extraordinary, you know. I'd been facing the rather bleak knowledge that I had no family and now, by this miracle, I seem to have a son and a grand-daughter.'

'And a grandson,' added Catherine. 'I

don't suppose you enjoy PlayStation. Ricky's an addict.'

Alexander looked bemused. 'Never heard of it. I'm a dab hand at Meccano.'

Catherine didn't tell him that Ricky outgrew that five years ago.

'The best thing is,' Rachel chipped in finally, 'that now Alexander's my grandfather he can pull a few strings to get me on to a course in environmental studies.'

'I thought you were doing English,' protested Christopher, not sure he could deal with another shock.

'Not any more. One thing fighting for the wood has shown me is that I want to do something worth while.'

'And stopping a motorway while you're still eighteen isn't enough for you?'

Rachel grinned. 'That's just the beginning!'

'What about Marko?' Lavinia asked gently. 'Is he going to help you?'

'Don't worry about Marko,' Zoe had been so discreet everyone had forgotten she was there. 'He's got a new role. Media darling. He's been giving interviews to all and sundry about his heroic stand. I think the hacks were more enchanted by his looks than his passionate commitment, but the *Daily Post*'s taken him off anyway. They're planning a makeover and putting him in an Armani suit.

The eco-warrior tamed. I wouldn't be surprised if he gets a slot on daytime television.'

The ward sister clucked at them that it really was time to go. Lavinia looked suddenly stricken. 'Don't leave, Alexander.'

Alexander sat down again at her bedside. 'I wasn't intending to. You ought to get some rest though. The sister says so.'

'Goodbye, Gran, we'll be back to see you tomorrow.' Rachel kissed her grandmother, feeling light-headed with relief that Lavinia clearly wasn't going to die after all in spite of what she'd been through.

★ ★ ★

The Casualty doctor examined Rachel and agreed to her going home provided she checked in with her GP the next day. Catherine, about to say that she would make sure Rachel did so, closed her mouth.

Outside the hospital, Catherine was almost surprised to find everything so normal. They'd been through so much that she almost expected the world to be somehow different. 'Do you want to go back to the wood one last time?' she asked Rachel.

'No thanks, Mum, I've got my A levels coming up, remember? One thing, though.

Could Zoe come and stay for a while? She's at a bit of a loose end now Marko's off getting famous. Just for a couple of weeks?'

Catherine glanced at Zoe in her filthy camouflage gear, her short hair standing up aggressively now with dreadlocks at the back, her variety of studded body parts. Would she put Rachel off her work?

Catherine laughed at herself bitterly. Would she *never* learn? Rachel was grown up enough to plan her own life. Six months ago she was an immature schoolgirl. Now she was coolly confident enough to take on anything. Any university would be mad to turn her down.

Zoe seemed to read her thoughts. 'Marko was right. In these trendy times it will look good on her CV to say she stopped a motorway.'

Zoe and Rachel giggled together, suddenly like kids again.

Christopher watched his daughter, still stunned at what he'd found out. He turned to Catherine. 'Did *you* know anything about this pregnancy?'

'Of course not. I was as amazed as you were. But then there were a lot of things we didn't know. Are you really coping with the news about Alexander?'

'Do you know, I think I am. I've got to rather like him, which is more than can be said for my other father. And it certainly explains my rebellious streak. Rachel's too. And I can't wait to see Jennifer's face when she finds out.'

'Will Martin be OK, do you think?'

'Eventually, I suspect. Though I don't know whether he'll ever forgive Ma for her indiscretion.'

'The one then or the one now?'

Christopher laughed and squeezed her hand, high on relief that they'd got through all this, things he wouldn't have imagined, and survived as a family.

'It's been an extraordinary time, hasn't it?' Catherine asked, glad that he looked happier than she'd seen him for years.

'Maybe, if this hadn't happened, I would have ended up wanting my pipe and slippers by the fire like Martin, and you would have run off with a sexy young supply teacher. This way there'll still be plenty of surprises ahead.'

'Don't you ever envy Martin and Jennifer their safe suburban existence?'

'When I can have a daughter who's a road rebel and a new father who's a Marxist? How could I? Let's just hope Ricky doesn't decide to be a rock star or a heroin addict.'

Catherine laughed. 'He's a bit young yet. I love you, you know.'

'That's a relief. I don't think I could take

any more dramatic revelations.'

'You know,' Catherine watched her daughter walking ahead of them with Zoe, her chestnut hair flowing out behind her, 'I used to think she looked like me, but suddenly it's Lavinia she reminds me of.'

'Then God help us all,' answered Christopher.

* * *

'Alexander, it's breaking my heart that for all these years I deprived you of your own son, of a family of your own. You must hate me for that.'

'I never saw myself as a family man, Lavinia. It's only through knowing yours that I see what I've been missing.'

'Then it's not too late? Will you come and live with me again once they let me go home?'

'We'll find a cosy cottage, miles from anywhere, and you can grow roses and I'll reminisce about my fiery past and bore all our visitors into leaving us alone together.'

'We've already got a cosy cottage.'

'Lavinia! Surely you don't want to stay on in Maxted after all this?'

'Of course I do. Do you think I'm going to give up my chance of gloating now that

472

they've nearly killed me? In fact I've got a brilliant idea. Maybe you and I should run the village shop. That frightful woman's gone back to Purley, so there must be an opening. You could sell Trotskyist tracts along with the cooked ham and the gobstoppers.'

A look of horror crossed Alexander's face.

'Only joking. I can't see you as a shopkeeper.'

'Why do I suspect my life is going to be very different from now on?'

'Maybe because it is. I've got another idea. Just in case I do peg out, I think it's time you made an honest woman of me.'

'And scandalize your neighbours even further?'

'I think you'd be surprised. There's more goodwill around than you think. And Eunice could catch the bride's bouquet. No point waiting until the children are dead.'

'No, indeed.'

'Now come over here and lie down.'

When the senior registrar looked through the glass panel of Lavinia's door five minutes later he was greeted with the sight of his patient locked in a tender embrace. He thought about advising her against such rash behaviour, but what the hell. If she died now at least she would die happy.

Had he known Lavinia Hope better, he

would have known that she had no intention of dying. Not now, and not in the foreseeable future. In fact, she fully intended staying alive for another thirty years and becoming, if luck smiled on her, a very disreputable old lady indeed.

THE END

We do hope that you have enjoyed reading this large print book.

Did you know that all of our titles are available for purchase?

We publish a wide range of high quality large print books including:
Romances, Mysteries, Classics
General Fiction
Non Fiction and Westerns

Special interest titles available in large print are:
The Little Oxford Dictionary
Music Book
Song Book
Hymn Book
Service Book

Also available from us courtesy of Oxford University Press:
Young Readers' Dictionary
(large print edition)
Young Readers' Thesaurus
(large print edition)

For further information or a free brochure, please contact us at:
Ulverscroft Large Print Books Ltd.,
The Green, Bradgate Road, Anstey,
Leicester, LE7 7FU, England.
Tel: (00 44) 0116 236 4325
Fax: (00 44) 0116 234 0205

Other titles in the
Ulverscroft Large Print Series:

STRANGER IN THE PLACE

Anne Doughty

Elizabeth Stewart, a Belfast student and only daughter of hardline Protestant parents, sets out on a study visit to the remote west coast of Ireland. Delighted as she is by the beauty of her new surroundings and the small community which welcomes her, she soon discovers she has more to learn than the details of the old country way of life. She comes to reappraise so much that is slighted and dismissed by her family — not least in regard to herself. But it is her relationship with a much older, Catholic man, Patrick Delargy, which compels her to decide what kind of life she really wants.

BLACKBERRY SUMMER

Phyllis Hastings

Debbie converted a wing of the old farmhouse into an Academy for Young Ladies. She hoped this would enable her to make provision for her children's future careers. But she could not foresee the disastrous fire or the regret and guilt she would feel for giving her youngest son to be reared by her twin sister Dolly. Next to the farm, Dolly's wealthy husband Christopher built an imposing mansion in the Gothic style, and planned to run a racing stable, but his schemes were doomed to end in tragedy.

HOT POPPIES

Reggie Nadelson

A murder in New York's diamond district. A dead Chinese girl with a photograph in her pocket. A plastic bag of irradiated heroin in an empty apartment. A fire in a Chinatown sweatshop. The worst blizzard in New York's history. These events conspire to bring ex-cop Artie Cohen out of retirement and back into the obsessive world of murder and politics that nearly killed him. The terrifying plot uncoils first in New York — in Artie's own back yard — then in Hong Kong, where everything — and everyone — is for sale.